The Boy Who Would Live Forever

Books by Frederik Pohl

*A Tor book

The Boy Who Would Live Forever

Frederik Pohl

A TOM DOHERTY ASSOCIATES BOOK
New York

THE BOY WHO WOULD LIVE FOREVER

Copyright © 2004 by Frederik Pohl

Portions of this novel have been previously published in different form.
"From Istanbul to the Stars" and "In the Steps of Heroes" were published as "The Boy Who
Would Live Forever" in *Far Horizons*, edited by Robert Silverberg. Copyright © 1999 by Frederik
Pohl.
"A Home for the Old Ones" was published in *30ᵗʰ Anniversary DAW Science Fiction*, edited by
Elizabeth R. Wollheim and Sheila E. Gilbert. Copyright © 2002 by Frederik Pohl.
"Hatching the Phoenix" appeared as a two-part serial in *Amazing Stories*, Fall 1999 and Winter
2000. Copyright © 1999, 2000 by Wizards of the Coast, Inc.

Edited by James Frenkel

Book Design by Mary A. Wirth

A Tor Book
Published by Tom Doherty Associates, LLC
175 Fifth Avenue
New York, NY 10010

www.tor.com

Tor® is a registered trademark of Tom Doherty Associates, LLC.

Library of Congress Cataloging-in-Publication Data

Pohl, Frederik.
    The boy who would live forever : a novel of Gateway / Frederik Pohl.—1st ed.
        p. cm.
    "A Tom Doherty Associates book."
    ISBN 0-765-31049-X
    EAN 978-0765-31049-1
    1. Human-alien encounters—Fiction. 2. Space colonies—Fiction. I. Title.

PS3566.O36B69 2004
813'.6—dc22   2004049579

First Edition: October 2004

Printed in the United States of America

0 9 8 7 6 5 4 3 2 1

To Ian Ballantine

Contents

The Boy Who Would Live Forever

1

From Istanbul to the Stars

I

On Stan's seventeenth birthday the Wrath of God came again, as it had been doing every six weeks or so. At the time Stan was alone in the apartment, cutting up vegetables for his birthday dinner. When he felt that familiar, sudden, overwhelming, disorienting, *horny* rush of vertigo he knew that it was what everybody he knew called "the Wrath of God" and nobody understood at all. Screams and sirens from outside the building told him that everybody else in that part of Istanbul was feeling it, too. Stan managed to drop the paring knife to the floor so he wouldn't cut himself. Then he staggered to a kitchen chair to wait it out.

People said the Wrath was a terrible thing. Well, that was true enough. Whatever the Wrath of God really was, it struck everyone in the world at once—and not just the people still living on Earth, either. Ships in space, the colonies on Mars and Venus, as long as human beings were still within the confines of the Solar System, they all were caught up in its madness at the same moment, and the Wrath's costs in accidents and disasters were enormous. Personally, Stan didn't mind it all that much. What it felt like to him was like suddenly being overwhelmed by a vast, lonely, erotic nightmare. Like, Stan thought, probably what it would be like to get good and drunk. The erotic part was not very different from some of the yearnings Stan himself felt often enough.

It didn't last very long. When it passed, Stan shook himself, picked up the things he had knocked to the floor and turned on the local TV news to see how it had gone this time.

It had gone badly enough. Fires, car smashes—Istanbul's aggressive drivers relied on their split-second reflexes to avert disaster, and when the Wrath took away their skill the crashes came fast. The single worst thing that happened this time was an oil tanker that had been coming into the Golden Horn. With everyone on both the tanker's tugs and its own bridge suddenly incapacitated, the vessel had plowed, dead slow and irresistible, into one of the cruise-ship docks on the Old City side, and there it had exploded into flame.

That was a really bad accident. Like any teenager, however, Stan had a high tolerance for other people's misfortunes. He yawned and got back to his chores, hoping only that the commotion wouldn't make his father too late in getting back home with the saffron and mussels for the birthday stew. When Stan finished with the vegetables he put them in a pot of cold water, and put a couple of his precious old disks on to play. This time it was Dizzy Gillespie, Jack Teagarden and the Firehouse Five Plus Three. Then he sat down to wait as he listened, thumbing through some of his comics and wondering if, this time, his father would have stayed sober long enough to get him some kind of a present for his birthday.

That was the moment at which the polis came to the door.

There were two of them, male and female, and they looked around the shabby apartment suspiciously. "Is this where the American citizen Walter Avery lived?" the woman demanded, and the past tense of the verb told Stan the whole story.

It didn't take the polis long to tell Stan just how it was that the Wrath had made a statistic of his father. Walter Avery had fallen down while crossing the street and a spellbound taksi driver ran right over him. There was no hope of holding the driver responsible, the woman said at once; the Wrath, you know. Anyway, the driver had long since disappeared. And, besides, witnesses said that Stan's father had been drunk at the time. Of course.

The male polis took pity on Stan's wretched stare. "At least he didn't suffer," he said gruffly. "He died right away. There was no pain."

The woman was impatient. "Yes, I suppose that is possible," she said, and then: "So you've been notified. You have to come to the morgue to collect the body before midnight, otherwise there'll be a charge for holding it an extra day. Good-bye."

And they left.

II

Since there would be neither mussels nor saffron for his birthday meal, Stan found a few scraps of leftover ham and tossed them into the pot with the vegetables. While they were simmering he sat down with his head in his hands, to think about what it meant to be an American—well, half American—orphan, alone in the city of Istanbul.

Two facts presented themselves. First, that long dreamed-of day when his father would sober up, take him back to America and there make a new life for the two of them—that day, always unlikely, was now definitely never going to come. From that fact it followed that, second, there was never going to be the money to pay for his college, much less to indulge his dream of flying to the Gateway asteroid and its wondrous adventure. He wasn't ever going to become one of those colorful and heroic Gateway prospectors who flew to strange parts of the Galaxy. He wasn't going to discover a hoard of priceless artifacts left by the vanished old race of Heechee. And he wasn't going to become both famous and rich.

Neither of these new facts was a total surprise to Stan. His faith in either had been steadily eroding since skepticism and the first dawn of puberty arrived simultaneously, when he was thirteen. Still, they had seemed at least theoretically *possible*. Now, nothing seemed possible at all.

That was when Stan at last allowed himself to cry.

While Stan was drearily cleaning up the kitchen after his flavorless birthday meal, Mr. Ozden knocked on the door.

Mr. Ozden was probably around seventy years old. To Stan he looked more like a hundred—a shriveled, ugly old man, hairless on the top of his head, but with his mustache still bristly black. He was the richest man Stan had ever met. He owned the ramshackle tenement where Stan lived, and the two others that flanked it, as well as the brothel that took up two floors of one of them. Mr. Ozden was a deeply religious man, so devout in his observances that he did not allow alcohol on his premises anywhere except in the brothel, and there only for the use of non-Islamic tourists. "My deepest sympathies to you on your loss, young Stanley," he boomed in his surprisingly loud voice, automatically scanning everything in sight for traces of a forbidden bottle of whiskey. (He never found any; Stan's father had been clever about that.) "It is a terrible tragedy, but we may not question the ways of God. What are your plans, may I ask?"

Stan was already serving him tea, as his father always did. "I don't exactly know yet, Mr. Ozden. I guess I'll have to get a job."

"Yes, that is so," Mr. Ozden agreed. He nibbled at a crumb of the macaroon Stan had put on a saucer for him, eyeing the boy. "Perhaps working at the consulate of the Americans, like your father?"

"Perhaps." Stan knew that wasn't going to happen, though. It had already been discussed. The Americans weren't going to hire any translator under the age of twenty-one.

"That would be excellent," Mr. Ozden announced. "Especially if it were to happen quickly. As you know, the rent is due tomorrow, in addition to last week's, which has not been paid, as well as the week's before. Would they pay you well at the consulate, do you think?"

"As God wills," Stan said, as piously as though he meant it. The old man nodded, studying Stan in a way that made the boy uneasy.

"Or," he said, with a smile that revealed his expensive teeth, "I could speak to my cousin for you, if you like."

Stan sat up straight; Mr. Ozden's cousin was also his brothel keeper. "You mean to work for him? Doing what?"

"Doing what pays well," Mr. Ozden said severely. "You are young, and I believe in good health? You could have the luck to earn a considerable sum, I think."

Something was churning, not pleasantly, in Stan's belly and groin. From time to time he had seen the whores in Mr. Ozden's cousin's employ as they sunned themselves on the rooftop when business was slow, often with one or two boys among them. The boys were generally even younger than himself, mostly Kurds or hill-country Anatolians, when they weren't from Algeria or Morocco. The boys didn't last long. Stan and his friend Tan had enjoyed calling insults at them from a distance. None of them had seemed very lucky.

Before Stan could speak, Mr. Ozden was going on. "My cousin's clients are not only men, you know. Often women come to him, sometimes wealthy widows, tourists from Europe or the East, who are very grateful to a young man who can give them the pleasures their husbands can no longer supply. There are frequently large tips, of which my cousin allows his people to keep nearly half—in addition to providing his people with Term Medical as long as they are in his employ, as well as quite fine accommodations and meals, at reasonable rates. Quite often the women clients are not unattractive, also. Of course," he added, his voice speeding up and diminishing in volume, "naturally there would be men as well." He stood up, most of his tea and macaroon untouched. "But perhaps the consulate will make you a better offer. You should telephone them at once in any case, to let them know of your father's sad accident. It may even be that he has some uncollected salary still to his account which you can apply to the rent. I will come again in the morning."

When Stan called the consulate, Mr. Goodpastor wasn't in, but his elderly secretary was touched by the news. "Oh, Stanley! This terrible Wrath thing! How awful for you! Your father was a, uh, a very nice man." That part was only conditionally true, Stan knew. His father had been a sweet-natured, generous, unreliable drunk, and the only reason the consulate had given him any work at all was that he was an American who would work for the wages of a Turk. And when Stan asked diffidently if there was any chance of uncollected salary she was all tact. "I'm afraid not, Stanley. I handle all the vouchers for Mr. Goodpastor, you know. I'm sure there's nothing there. Actually," she added, sounding embarrassed, "I'm afraid it's more likely to be a little bit the other way. You see, your father had received several salary advances lately, so his account is somewhat overdrawn. But don't worry about that, dear. I'm sure no one will press a claim."

The news was nothing Stan hadn't expected. All the same, it sharpened his problem. The Americans might not demand money from him, but Mr. Ozden certainly would. Already had. And would soon be doing his very best to collect. The last time someone had been evicted from one of his tenements Stan had been watching from the roof and had seen Mr. Ozden seizing every stick of their possessions to sell for the rent owed.

Which made Stan look appraisingly around their tiny flat. The major furnishings didn't matter, since they belonged to Mr. Ozden in the first place. Even the bed linens and the kitchenware were Ozden's. His father's skimpy wardrobe would certainly be taken. Stan's decrepit music player and his stacks of ancient American jazz recordings; his collection of space adventures, both anime and morphed; his school books; the small amount of food on the shelves—put them all together and they would barely cover the rent. The only other things of measurable value were the musical instruments, his battered trumpet and the drums. Of course Mr. Ozden had no proper claim to the drums, since they weren't Stan's. They'd been brought there and left by his friend Tan Kusmeroglu, when Tan's parents wouldn't let them do any more music making in their house.

That Stan could do something about. When he phoned Tan's home it was Tan's mother who answered, and she began weeping as soon as she heard the news. It was a while before Mrs. Kusmeroglu could manage to tell Stan that Oltan wasn't home. He was at work, but she would get the sad message to him at once, and if there was anything they could do. . . .

When he got off the phone with Mrs. Kusmeroglu, Stan looked at the clock. He had plenty of time before he had to get to the morgue, so he opened up the couch he slept on—he wasn't quite ready to move into his father's bed—and lay down in case he needed to cry some more.

He didn't, though. He fell asleep instantly, which was even better for him. What woke him, hours later, was Tan Kusmeroglu standing over him. Stan could hear the braying of the muezzin, calling the faithful to prayer from the little mosque around the corner, almost drowned out by Tan's excited voice as he shook Stan awake. "Come on, Stan, wake up! The old fart's at prayer now and I borrowed my boss's van. You'll never have a better time to get your stuff out!"

That meant they had ten minutes at most. Stan didn't argue. It took less than that to load the drums, the trumpet, the precious music disks and player and a handful of other things into the van. They were already driving away before Stan remembered. "I have to go to the morgue," he said.

Tan took his eyes from the tour bus that was weaving from side to side before them and the delivery truck that was trying to cut in from the side long enough to glance at Stan. His expression was peculiar—almost un-Tanly sympathetic, a little bit flushed in the way he always looked when about to propose some new escapade. "I have been thinking about that," he announced. "You don't want to go there."

"But they want me to identify my father's body. I have to."

"No, you don't. What's going to happen if you do? They're going to want you to pay for a funeral, and how are you going to do that? No. You stay out of sight."

Stan asked simply, "Where?"

"With us, stupid! You can share my room. Or," he added, grinning, "you can share my sister's if you'd rather, only you would have to marry her first."

III

Everybody in the Kusmeroglu family worked. Mr. Kusmeroglu was a junior accountant in a factory that made Korean-brand cars for export. Tan delivered household appliances for a hardware store. His sixteen-year-old sister, Naslan, worked in the patisserie of one of the big hotels along the Bosphorus. Even Mrs. Kusmeroglu worked at home, assembling beads into bracelets that spelled out verses from the Koran, for the tourist trade—when she wasn't cleaning or cooking or mending the family's clothes. Even so, Stan knew without being told, they were barely making ends meet, with only the sketchiest of Basic Medical and a constant fear of the future. Going back to complete his schooling was now as hopelessly out of the question for Stan as it had been for Tan. So was sponging off the Kusmeroglus for any length of time.

He had to find a way to make money.

That wasn't easy. Stan couldn't get a regular job, even if there was one to be got, because under Turkish law he was now an unregistered nonperson. He wasn't the only one of that sort, of course. There were millions like him in poverty-stricken Istanbul. It wasn't likely the authorities would bother trying to track him down—unless he turned up on some official record.

The good part was that the season was nearly summer. The city's normal population of 25 million, largely destitute, was being enriched each week by two or three million tourists, sometimes even more. These people, by definition, had money and nothing better to spend it on than Istanbul's sights, meals, curios and inhabitants. "You can become a guide," Mr. Kusmeroglu pronounced at dinner. "You speak both Turkish and English without flaw, Stanley. You will do well."

"A guide," Stan repeated, looking, out of courtesy to his host, as though he thought it a good idea, but very far from convinced.

"Of course a guide," Tan said reprovingly. "My father is right. You have learned all you need to know about Istanbul already—you remember all those dull history classes when we were at school together. Simply subtract the Ottoman period and concentrate on those crazy empresses in the Byzantine, which is what tourists want to hear about anyway. Also we can get guide books from the library for you to study."

Stan went right to the heart of the matter. "But I can't get a guide's license! The polis—"

"Will not bother you," Tan's mother said firmly. "You simply linger around Topkapi, perhaps, or the Grand Bazaar. When you see some Americans who are not with a tour group you merely offer information to them in a friendly way. Tell them you are an American student here—that is almost true, isn't it? And if any polis should ask you any questions, speak to them only in English, tell them you are looking for your parents who have your papers. Fair-haired, with those blue eyes, you will not be doubted."

"He doesn't have any American clothes, though," Naslan put in.

Her mother pursed her lips for a moment, then smiled. "That can be dealt with. You and I will make him some, Naslan. It is time you learned more about sewing anyway."

———

The endless resources of the Lost & Found at Naslan's hotel provided the raw material, the Kusmeroglu women made it all fit. Stan became a model American college student on tour: flared slacks that looked like designer pants, but weren't, spring-soled running shoes, a Dallas Dodgers baseball cap and a T-shirt that said, "Gateway or Bust," on the front, and on the back, "I busted." The crowds of tourists were as milkable as imagined. No, more so. The Americans on whom he concentrated all seemed to have more money than they knew what to do with. Like the elderly couple from Riverdale, New York, so confused by the hyperinflated Turkish currency that they pressed a billion New Lira banknote on Stan as a tip for helping them find clean toilets when a million or two would have been generous. And then, when he pointed out the error, insisted that he keep the billion as a reward for his honesty. So in his first week Stan brought back more than Tan earned at his job and almost as much as Naslan. He tried to give it all to Mrs. Kusmeroglu, but she would take only half. "Save for the future, Stanley," she instructed him kindly. "A little capital is a good thing for a young man to have."

And her daughter added, "After all, some day soon you may want to get married."

Of course, Stan had no such plans, although Naslan certainly was pretty enough in the perky pillbox hat and miniskirt that was her uniform in the patisserie. She smelled good, too. That was by courtesy of the nearly empty leftover bits of perfume and cosmetics the women guests of the hotel discarded in the ladies' room, which it was part of her duties to keep spotless. It had its effect on Stan. Sometimes, when she sat close to him as the family watched TV together in the evenings, he hoped no one was noticing the embarrassing swelling in his groin. He was, after all, male, and seventeen.

But he was also thoroughly taken up by his new status as an earner of significant income. He memorized whole pages from the guidebooks, and supplemented them by lurking about to listen in on the professional guides as they lectured to their tour groups. The best places for that were in sights like the Grand Mosque or Hagia Sofia. There all the little clusters of a dozen or a score tourists were crowded together, with their six or eight competing guides all talking at once, in half a dozen languages. The guide gossip was usually more interesting than anything in the books, and always a lot more scurrilous.

Eavesdropping on them carried a risk, though. In the narrow alleyway outside the great kitchens that had once served Topkapi Palace he saw a couple of the licensed guides looking at him in a way he didn't like as they waited for their tour groups to trickle out of the displays. When both of them began talking on their carry phones, still looking at him, he quickly left the scene.

Actually, he was less afraid of the guides, or of the polis, than he was of Mr. Ozden finding him. What the old man could do if that happened Stan didn't know. In a pinch, he supposed he could actually pay off the overdue rent out of the wads of lira that were accumulating under his side of the mattress he shared with Tan. But who knew what law he had broken by his furtive departure? Mr. Ozden would, all right, and so Stan stayed far away from his old tenement.

It wasn't all work for Stan. If he got home in time he helped Mrs. Kusmeroglu with the dinner—she affected to be amazed by his cooking skills, which were actually pretty rudimentary. Then usually they would all watch the family's old thousand-channel TV together. Mrs. Kusmeroglu liked the weighty talk shows, pundits discussing the meaning of such bizarre events as that inexplicable Wrath of God that visited them from time to time, or what to do about the Cyprus question. Mr. Kusmeroglu preferred music—not the kind the boys played, though. Both Tan and Stan voted for programs about space or sports. But then it seldom came to a vote, because what Naslan liked was American sitcoms—on the English-language channels, so she could practice her English—happy groups of wealthy, handsome people enjoying life in Las Vegas or Malibu or the Tappan Sea, and Naslan talked faster than anyone else. It didn't matter. They shared things as a real family. And that was in some ways the best part of all for Stan, who had only the sketchiest memories of what living in a family was like.

Although the Kusmeroglus were all unfailingly kind to Stan, their tolerance did not extend to allowing the boys to get out the drums and trumpet in the house. So once or twice Stan and Tan lugged their instruments to the school gym, where the nighttime guard was a cousin and nobody cared how much noise you made when school was out.

It wasn't the same, of course. When they were twelve-year-olds in school, they had had a plan. With the Kurdish boy on the bass fiddle and the plain little girl from the form below theirs on keyboard, they were going to be a group. The four of them argued for days, and finally picked out a winner of a name: "Stan, Tan and the Gang." The plan was to start small, with birthday parties and maybe weddings. Go on to the clubs as soon as they were old enough. Get a recording contract. Make it big. . . . But then the Kurdish boy got expelled because his father was found to be contributing money to the underground Kurdistani movement, and the little girl's mother didn't want her spending so much time with boys anyway.

It wasn't too much of a blow. By then Stan and Tan had a larger dream to work on. *Space.* The endless frontier. Where the sky was no limit to a young man's ambitions.

If they could only somehow get their hands on enough money to do it, they were determined to go to Gateway, or maybe to one of the planetary outposts. Tan liked Mars, where the colonists were making an almost Earthlike habitat under their plastic domes. Stan preferred the idea of roaming the ancient Heechee catacombs on Venus, where—who knew?— there might still be some old artifacts to discover that might make them almost as rich as a Gateway prospector.

The insuperable problem was the money to get to any of those places. Still, maybe you didn't need money, because there were other chances. The famed old explorer Robinette Broadhead, for instance, was rich beyond avarice with his Gateway earnings, and he was always funding space missions. Like the one that even now was gradually climbing its years-long way toward the Oort cloud, where some fabulous Heechee object was known to exist but no one had found a way to get to it other than on a slow, human rocket ship. Broadhead had paid the way for volunteers to make that dreary quest. He might pay for others, when Tan and Stan were old enough. If by then everything hadn't already been explored.

Of course, those were childish dreams. Stan no longer hoped they could actually become real. But he still dreamed them.

Meanwhile there was his work as a guide and his life with the Kusmeroglu family, and those weren't bad, either. In his first month he had accumulated more money than he had ever seen before. He made the mistake of letting Naslan catch him counting it, and she immediately said, "Why, you're loaded, Stanley! Don't you think it's about time you spent some of it?"

He gave her a guarded look. "On what?"

"On some decent clothes, for God's sake! Look, Friday's my day off. Dad won't let me skip morning prayers, but afterward how about if I take you shopping?"

So the first thing that Friday morning Stan and Naslan were on a bus to the big supersouks and Stan was accumulating his first grown-up wardrobe. Everything seemed to cost far more than Stan wanted to pay, but Naslan was good at sniffing out bargains. Of course, she made him try on six different versions of everything before letting him buy any. Then, when they had all the bundles they could carry and half his bankroll was gone, they were waiting for a bus when a car pulled up in front of them. "Hey, you!" a man's voice called.

It was a consulate car, with the logo of the United States of America in gold on its immaculate black door, and the driver was leaning out, gesturing urgently to Stan. "Aren't you Stan Avery, Walter Avery's son? Sure you are. Listen, Mr. Goodpastor's been looking all over hell and gone for you. Where've you been hiding yourself, for God's sake?"

Stan gave Naslan a trapped look. "I, uh, I've been staying with friends."

Behind the stopped car half a dozen others were stuck, and they were all blowing their horns. The driver flipped them an obscene gesture, then barked at Stan: "I can't stay here. Look, Mr. Goodpastor's got something for you. Have you at least got an address?"

While Stan was trying to think of an answer, Naslan cut in smoothly. "But you're not sure of what your address will be, are you, Stan? He's getting ready to move into his own place," she informed the driver. "Why don't you send whatever it is to where he works? That's the Eklek Linen Supply Company. It's in Zincirlikuyu, Kaya Aldero Sok, Number 34/18. Here, I'll write it down for you." And when the consulate driver at last unplugged the street and was gone, she said sweetly, "Who knows what it might be, Stan? Maybe they want money for something or other, maybe your father's funeral? Anyway, there's a foreman at the linen supply who likes me. He'll see that I get whatever it is, and he won't tell anybody where it went."

But when Naslan brought the envelope home, thick with consular seals, it wasn't a bill. There was a testy note from Mr. Goodpastor:

> Dear Stanley:
>   When we checked the files it turned out your father still held a life-insurance policy, with you as beneficiary. The face amount is indexed, so it amounts to quite a sum. I hope it will help you make a proper life for yourself.

• Stan held the note in one hand, the envelope it was attached to in the other, looking perplexedly at Mr. Kusmeroglu. "What does 'indexed' mean?"

"It means the face value of the policy is tied to the cost of living, so the amount goes up with inflation. Open it, Stanley. It might be quite a lot of money."

But when Stan plucked the green U.S. government voucher out of its envelope the numbers were a cruel disappointment. "Well," he said, trying to smile as he displayed it to the family, "what shall we do with it? Buy a pizza all around?"

But Naslan's eyes were sharper than his. She snatched it from his hand. "You stupid boy," she scolded, half laughing, "don't you see? It isn't lira, it is in American *dollars!* You're rich now, Stan! You can do what you like. Buy yourself Full Medical. Marry. Start a business. Even go to a whole new life in America!"

"Or," Tan put in, "you can pay your way to the Gateway asteroid, Stan."

Stan blinked at him, then again, more carefully, at the voucher. What Naslan had said was true. There was plenty of money there—easily enough for the fare to Gateway, indeed much more than even that would cost.

Stan didn't stop to think it over. His voice trembled as he said, "Actually, there's enough for two. Shall we do it, Tan? Shall we go to Gateway?"

2

In the Steps of Heroes

I

The first thing that struck Stan about the Gateway asteroid was that, since he weighed next to nothing at all there, the place had no real *up*. His body had only one way of dealing with that. It became violently ill. This sudden *mal d'espace* took Stan completely by surprise. He had never had any experience of being seasick or airsick—well, couldn't have, since he had never been on either a ship or a plane at all before the trip to the asteroid. He was wiped out by the sudden dizzying vertigo as much as by the quick and copious fountaining that followed. The guards at Reception weren't surprised. "New meat," one sighed to another, who quickly produced a paper sack for Stan to finish puking into.

Mercifully, Stan wasn't the only one affected. Both of the other two strange men in his group were hurling as violently as he. The one woman, sallow, frail and young—and with something very wrong about the way her face was put together, so that the left side seemed shorter than the right—was in obvious distress, too, but she waved the sick bag away. Tan was spared. So he was the one who collected their belongings—drums, trumpet, music and not much else—and got himself and Stan registered. Then he managed to haul Stan, baggage and all, through the labyrinthine drops and corridors of Gateway to their assigned cubicle. Stan succeeded in hitching himself into his sleeping sack, miserably closed his eyes and was gone.

When he woke, Tan was looming over him, one hand on a holdfast, the other carrying a rubbery pouch of coffee. "Don't spill," he cautioned. "It is weak, but it is coffee. Do you think you can keep it down?"

Stan could. In fact, he was suddenly hungry. Nor was the twisting, falling feeling as bad as it had been, though there were enough remnant discomforts to make him uneasy.

Tan remained immune. "While you slept I have been busy, old Stan," he announced affectionately. "I have found where we eat, and where we can go for pleasure. There do not seem to be any people from Istanbul on Gateway, but I have met another Moslem here. Tarsheesh. He is a Shiite from Iran, but seems a good enough fellow. He checked and told me that we have funds enough to stay for eighteen days, while we select a mission. Unfortunately there are not very many missions scheduled for some reason, but we'll find something. We have to. If our funds run out before that they will simply deport us." Then he grinned. "I also spoke with the young woman who came up with us. One could get used to the way her face looks, I think. With luck, soon I will know her quite well."

"Congratulations," Stan said. Experimentally he released himself from the sleep sack, grabbing a holdfast. Weightlessness was not permanently unbearable, he discovered, but there was another problem. "Have you also discovered where I can pee?" he asked.

"Of course. I'll show you. Then we can start studying the list of missions. There is no sense hanging around here when we could be making our fortunes."

Time was, Stan knew, when any brave or desperate volunteer who got to Gateway could have his choice of a score of the cryptic Heechee ships. You got into the one you had picked. You set the funny-looking control wheels any which way you liked, because nobody had a clue which ways were "right." You squeezed the go-teat. And then—traveling faster than light, though no one knew how that was done—you were on your way to adventure and fortune. Or to disappointment and frustration, when the chance-set destination held nothing worthwhile. Or, frequently enough, to a horrible death . . . but that was the risk you had to take for such great rewards.

That was then. It was different now. Over the years, nearly two hundred of the ships that had bravely set off had never come back. Another few dozen of those that remained on the asteroid—particularly the larger ships, the Fives and a few Threes—were now employed in transport duty, ferrying their trickle of colonists to such livable worlds as Valhalla or Peggys Planet, or to exploit the other cache of usable ships that had been found on Gateway Two. When the boys checked the listings they were disappointed. Three or four missions were open, but every one of them was in a One—that is, in a ship that would hold any one person—no use at all to two young men who were determined to ship out together.

They didn't stop at watching the postings on the screen. They went to see the dispatcher himself, a fat and surly Brazilian named Hector Montefiore. To get to Montefiore's office you had to go all the way to Gateway's outermost shell, where the ships nestled in their pods as they waited for a mission. Some of the pods were empty, the outer port closed against the vacuum of space; their ships were actually Out. The boys looked their fill, then shook the curtain of Montefiore's office and went in.

The dispatcher was idly watching an entertainment screen, eating something that had not come out of the Gateway mess hall. He listened to them for a bare moment, then shook his head. "Fuck off, you guys," he advised. "I can't help you. I don't assign the missions. The big domes do that. When they decide on a flight, the computer puts it up on the board and I just take the names of the volunteers. Next big one? How the hell do I know?"

Stan was disposed to argue. Tan pulled him away. In the corridor outside Stan snarled at his friend. "He's bound to know *something*, isn't he?"

"Maybe so, but he isn't going to tell us, is he? We could try bribing him—"

Stan laughed sourly. "With what?"

"Exactly, Stan. So let's get out of here."

They retired to the common space in Gateway's central spindle, the place they called the Blue Hell, to consider their options over cups of Gateway's expensive and watery coffee. Coffee was not all you could buy in the Blue Hell. You didn't have to pay for your basic meals on Gateway; their cost, like the price of the water they drank, the cubicle they lived in and the air they breathed, was covered by their daily rent. If you wanted more than that, you had to go to the Blue Hell. There was fine food, if you could pay the price, and liquor of all sorts, and the gambling that gave the place its name. The boys jealously smelled the great steaks they saw more fortunate others devouring, and watched the magnetized roulette ball spin around. Then Stan took a deep breath.

He poked Tan in the shoulder. "Hey, man! We're on *Gateway!* Let's at least do a little wandering around the joint!"

———

They did, almost forgetting that their money was going and the mission they had come for had not appeared. They went to a place called Central Park, where fruit trees and berry bushes grew—but were not to be picked unless you paid their price. They looked at Gateway's great water reservoir, curling up with the shape of the asteroid's shell but, to them, mostly reminiscent of the big underground reservoir lakes of Istanbul. And they went, reverently, to Gateway's museum.

Everything they saw there was halfway familiar to Stan, from the Gateway stories he had devoured in his youth. Being in the museum itself was different. It was filled with Heechee artifacts, brought back from one mission or another: prayer fans, fire pearls, gadgets of all kinds. There were holos of planets that had been visited; the boys admired Peggys Planet, with its broad, cultivated fields and handsome woods; they shivered at Valhalla—habitable, the Gateway authorities claimed, but more like Siberia than Paradise. Even worse were the holos of the murdered planets, the mysterious ones that had once held civilizations of which nothing was left but ruins. How? Why? No one knew. The boys looked at the holos in silence, and turned away.

Most interesting, in a practical way, were the holos of the various models of Heechee ships, the Ones, the Threes and the Fives. (Well, that was what the human beings on Gateway called them, according to the size of the crew they held. What the Heechee themselves called them was more than anyone could say.)

Some of the ships had fittings that didn't seem to do anything, particularly the few that contained a Heechee-metal dome that, after a few disasters, no one had dared try to open. Many were armored, particularly the Threes and Fives. Nearly all had human-installed external sensors and cameras, as well as racks of food, tanks of oxygen, rebreathers, all the things that made it possible for a prospector to stay alive while he flew; if the Heechee themselves had had anything of the sort it was long gone.

While they were puzzling over these questions they heard a cough from behind. When they turned it was the girl with the lopsided face who had come up from Earth with them, whose name was Estrella Pancorbo. She seemed a lot less pale. Surprised, Stan said, "You're looking, uh, well." Meaning, apart from the fact that your face looks as though someone sat on it.

She gave him a searching look, but bobbed her head to acknowledge the compliment. "Better every day, thank you. I fooled them," she added cryptically, but didn't say who the "them" was. She didn't want to continue the conversation, either; had studying to do, she said, and immediately began running through the ship holos and taking notes.

The boys lingered for a while, but then they left because it was clear she preferred to be alone—but not without having had her effect on Stan, who had not been near a girl of anything like his own age since Naslan.

On the way out Tan mused, "I wonder how the folks are getting along back home."

Stan nodded. He recognized homesickness when he saw it. He even felt a little of it himself, though he hadn't had much experience of having a real home. "We could write them a letter," he offered.

Tan shook himself, and gave Stan a grin. "And pay transmission costs? Not me, Stan. I'm not much for writing letters anyway, and besides, what would we have to say? Let's get some more of that piss-poor coffee."

II

That day passed. So did another day. A couple of Ones appeared on the mission screen, but nothing better, and even those were snapped up at once by less picky prospectors. The boys spent more and more of their time hanging around the Blue Hell, wondering, but not willing to ask each other, what they were going to do when their money ran out.

They did not lack for advice. Old Gateway hands, many of them wearing the wrist bracelets that showed that they had been Out, were often willing to share their lore. The friendliest was a spry, middle-aged Englishwoman with a drawn face and unshakable views on what missions to take. "Do you know what the Heechee control wheels look like? What you want are settings that show two bands in the red on the first wheel and none in the yellow on the second," she lectured.

"Why?" Tan asked, hanging on every word.

"Because they are safe settings! No mission with those settings has ever been lost. Trust me on this, I know." And when she had finished the coffee she had cadged from them and left, Tan pursed his lips.

"She may have something there," he said.

"She has *nothing* there," Stan scoffed. "Did you count her bangles? Nine of them! She has been Out nine times and hasn't earned the price of a cup of coffee. No, Tan. We want something that might be less safe, but would be more profitable."

Tan shrugged, conceding the point. "In any case," he said philosophically, "it is true that if any of them did know what to do they would be doing it instead of telling us about it. So let us go eat."

"All right," Stan said, and then shook his head, struck with a thought. "The hell with that. I'm not hungry. Besides, I've got a better idea. We lugged those instruments with us, why not jam a little?"

Tan blinked at him. "Here? They'd throw us out."

"So we can go somewhere where nobody would be bothered by our practicing. Maybe Central Park?"

Stan was right, there was nobody there. They picked a corner with plenty of holdfasts, and set up to play.

Stan had no problem with his trumpet, once he was securely hooked to a wall bracket. Tan's drums were another matter. He had to lash them to each other and to a pair of holdfasts, and then he complained that the sticks wouldn't bounce properly without solid gravity. All the same they managed "When the Saints Come Marching in," after a fashion, and did better on "A String of Pearls." Stan was riffing on "St. James Infirmary Blues" when Tan stopped drumming and caught his arm. "Look there!"

Tarsheesh was hurtling toward them around the rim of the lake. As soon as he came close, Tan called, "Are we making too much noise?"

Tarsheesh grabbed a bracket and stopped himself, panting in excitement. "Noise? No! It is the news that just came! You haven't heard? The Herter-Hall party has reached the object in the Oort cloud, and it is big, and it is Heechee, and it is *still working!*"

There hadn't been that much excitement in Gateway in years. The Herter-Hall mission—the Broadhead-financed human-built rocket ship that had been chugging its way up to the Oort cloud for as long as Stan could remember—had indeed found something that made it all worthwhile. Hanging out there was nothing less than a whole working Heechee orbiter, the size of an ocean liner, of a kind never seen before! The thing was not simply dead in its orbit there, it actually manufactured *food!* CHON-food, they called it, made mostly out of the basic elements that were in the comets of the Oort cloud, C(arbon), H(ydrogen), O(xygen), N(itrogen). And that antique Heechee creation was still doing it, after all those hundreds of thousands of years. And if they could bring it to a near-Earth orbit, as the Herter-Hall people were trying to do, and if they could feed it with comets and things as they entered the lower solar system, why, hunger for the human race might one day be over!

They speculated enviously on what that could be worth to the Herter-

Hall family and to Robinette Broadhead himself, as backer of the expedition. "Billions," Stan said profoundly, and Tan gave him a look of scorn.

"Only billions? For a thing like that?"

"Billions of American dollars, you cow. Many billions for all of them,
so Robinette Broadhead can add more billions to the billions he already
owns. So you see, old Tan, what one lucky find can do?"

Tan did see. So did everybody else. When they checked the listings
every one of the few missions offered had been snapped up. "Not even a
One left! Nothing at all," Tan complained. "And yet they take money out
of our balance every day, even when there is nothing for us to sign up for."

So they did. And kept on doing it, one day, and then another day, and
then another. The boys followed the mission listings obsessively, but without much luck. A One showed up, then two more—both of them also
Ones, and taken as soon as they appeared. Tan groaned when he saw the
notice that the third ship was filled, because the name on the roster was
his friend Tarsheesh. "I was hoping the three of us could ship together," he
said, angry. "He wouldn't wait!"

Stan couldn't blame him. He even toyed with the thought of taking a
One himself, leaving Tan behind. But then no more Ones showed up, either, so he didn't have to deal with that strain on his conscience.

There was a little traffic in the other direction. Two or three ships
straggled back from their missions. All Ones, and mostly duds of one kind
or another. And then a lordly Five made it back, and this one had had success. Well, *some* success. Not the dazzling kind, but not bad. They had
reached an airless moon of a gas-giant planet they couldn't identify. It had
Heechee artifacts, all right. They could see a domed Heechee-metal
structure, and things nearby that looked sort of like they had been trac-
tored vehicles, but they could only look. They couldn't touch. Their ship
had no equipment to let them get out and move around in vacuum. The
pictures they did come back with earned them enough of a bonus to retire
to, respectively, Cincinnati, Johannesburg, Madrid, Nice and Mexico
City, and their Five was thus open for anyone who cared to take it.

Not right away, of course. The elderly Englishwoman with the nine Out
bangles caught Tan and Stan as they were leaving the mess hall, giddy with
excitement. "There's your best bet, ducks! They'll clean it up and put in fresh
stores, and then they'll send it right back to make the finds—this time with
space suits and handling equipment aboard. Oh, it'll take a while. A fortnight
or so, I imagine, but wait for it! Good color, too—but we don't want everyone
to know, so, remember, softly-softly-catchee-monkey!" And hurried happily
off to tell her secret to anyone else with the price of a cup of coffee.

Of course, the secret wasn't worth much more than that, especially to two young men who didn't have a fortnight or so to spare.

. Then, without warning, a Five did appear on the list. It didn't do Stan and Tan any good, though. The listing appeared while they were asleep, and by the time they saw it the crew roster was long since filled.

What made it worse was that every day, *every* day of those few remaining days, there were fresh bulletins from the people who were making it réally big, the Herter-Hall party on the Food Factory in the Oort. The Herter-Halls were strapping ion rockets onto the object to nudge it out of orbit and back toward Earth. Then further news: the object wouldn't be nudged. Somehow it counteracted the force applied, they couldn't say how. Then they found indications that there was someone else aboard. Then—oh, miraculous event!—they met that someone. And he was a human boy, with the human name of Wan! And he seemed to have a Heechee ship of his own that he used to commute between the Food Factory and some even larger, more complex Heechee vessel. A vast one, stuffed with Heechee machines of all kinds, and still working!

Tan was surly with envy, Stan little better. Snapping at each other, they parked themselves in front of the mission screen, taking turns to pee, refusing sleep. "The very next one," Tan vowed. "Three or Five, we will be on it!"

Stan concurred. "Damn right we will! We may not make trillions, like these people, or even billions, but we'll make something out of it, and we won't let anything get us away from this screen—"

But then something did.

Stan stopped in the middle of his vow, suddenly stricken. His eyes burned. His throat was suddenly agonizingly raw. His head pounded, and he could hardly breathe.

It was the Wrath of God again. Not exactly the same as before. Worse. Stan felt his whole body burning with fever. He was *sick*. Tan was in equal distress. Sobbing, his hands to his temples and curled up like a baby in the womb, he was floating away, the holdfast forgotten. It wasn't just sickness, either. Under the malaise was the familiar desperate sexual yearning, the loneliness, the unfocused, bitter anger. . . .

And it went on, and on. . . .

And then, without warning, it was over.

Stan reached out to catch Tan's flailing arm and dragged him back to a holdfast. "*Jesus*," he said, and Tan agreed.

"That was a pisser." And then, urgently, "Stan! Look!"

He was staring at the mission monitor. Gateway's computers, unaffected by whatever it was that drove every human momentarily mad, had been carrying out theirs programmed routine. Something new was posted on the screen:

MISSION 2402
ARMORED THREE, IMMEDIATE DEPARTURE

"Let's take it!" Tan yelled.

"Of course," Stan said, already logging in. In a moment their names appeared on the roster:

MISSION 2402
ARMORED THREE, IMMEDIATE DEPARTURE
STANLEY AVERY
OLTAN KUSMEROGLU

Rapturously the two boys pounded each other's arms and backs. "We made it!" Tan shouted.

"And just in time," Stan said, pointing. "Look at that!" Only seconds later another name had appeared:

MISSION 2402
ARMORED THREE, IMMEDIATE DEPARTURE
STANLEY AVERY
OLTAN KUSMEROGLU
ESTRELLA PANCORBO
roster complete

III

The dream had come true. Stanley Avery was actually in an actual Heechee ship, actually following in the footsteps of those immortal Gateway heroes who braved the perils of star travel and came back to wealth unimaginable and fame that would go down through the ages. . . .

"Or," Tan growled, when Stan ventured to say as much to him, "to some very unpleasant death. I do not care for this shit-struck little ship. Why is it armored?"

Across the cabin, Estrella Pancorbo looked up from her task of stowing her possessions. "If this trip is to be bearable at all," she said, "it would be better if you spoke only English when I am present."

Tan's lips compressed. "And, in this closet we are to live in, when will you not be?" he demanded, but Stan spoke quickly.

"She is right," he told Tan. And, to the woman, "We'll try to remember. He was only wondering why our ship is so heavily armored."

"Because it accepts some destinations which would damage a ship that wasn't, of course. Don't be afraid. Such destinations are rare; this particular Three has been Out four times, but not to any such dangerous place. Didn't you familiarize yourself with its specifications? All the data for every working ship was on file," she said.

The reproof didn't improve Tan's mood. "I'm not *afraid*, Estrella," he snapped, wounded, and cast about for something hurtful to say in return. He found it. "Why does your face look like that?" he demanded.

She gave him a long stare. Her left eyelid, Stan noticed, hung lower than the other. "Because a bull stepped on it," she said at last, and added, "I think this is going to be a very long cruise."

How long the trip was going to take was a question always in their minds. Estrella's researches had given them some information. "This Three has never gone more than eighteen days in each direction," she informed them. "We have supplies for more than sixty. It shouldn't be more than that. We'll know at the halfway point."

They would. Stan knew that much, as everybody did. Gateway prospectors always kept their eye on that funny-looking drive coil every waking minute, because it held the secret of life or death. When it changed color they were at the halfway point; the gentle micro-G that tugged them toward the stern of the craft would change so that then they would drift gently toward the bow. That was the time for doing arithmetic. If they had by then used up no more than a quarter of their air, water and stores, that meant they had enough to last them for the remainder of their outbound leg and for the return. If they hadn't, they didn't.

The three of them lived, ate and slept in the same tiny space, no bigger than Stan's very small bathroom in Mr. Ozden's tenement. Being so intimately close with a girl of more or less his own age—well, not so much more, anyway, however old she actually was—was a disturbing experience for Stan. They were very intimate. They couldn't help it. When Tan was in the toilet Stan averted his eyes from Estrella's, because the sound of Tan's urination was loud and clear. All three of them had to get used to each other's smells, too, of which there were many. There were not many opportunities for exercise in a Three, and so the diet the Gateway authorities provided for them was high in fiber. Stan tried to break wind inconspicuously; Tan didn't, grinning every time he farted. Estrella paid no attention.

The funny thing was that the more time Stan spent with Estrella's damaged face seldom out of his sight, the less damaged it looked. Tan was affected, too. Once or twice, when Estrella was momentarily more or less out of earshot—in the crapper, or asleep—he muttered something dark and lecherous in Stan's ear. In Turkish, of course. There wasn't any place in the Three that was really out of hearing range except for the lander, tucked in its bay in the bottom of the vessel and not comfortable enough for anyone to stay in it for very long.

Estrella spent most of her time reading from a little pocket screen, but after the third day she allowed herself to be persuaded into a card game with the boys. When Tan had lost his third big pot to her he gave her a suspicious look. "I thought you said you didn't know how to play poker," he growled.

"I didn't. It's a very simple game," she said carelessly, and then realized she had hurt his feelings. She tried to be complimentary. "I meant to tell you that I was surprised at your command of English, Tan. You speak it very well."

He shrugged. "Why should I not? I went to the English-language school from the age of six until I had to leave to go to work, at fourteen." But he was somewhat mollified. More cheerfully, he went on. "It is where I met Stan. We became friends quickly, because we were interested in the same things. Even as small boys, in recess we would run out to the teeter-totter and climb on, bouncing each other up and down and pretending we were on a Gateway ship."

"And no one more surprised than I that we are finally here," Stan added, grinning. "What was your life like, Estrella?"

She picked up the cards and shuffled for a moment without answering. Then she said briefly, "I was a butcher. Whose deal is it now?"

By the seventh day the three of them were having trouble keeping their eyes off the coil. It didn't change. "Well," Estrella said brightly, "it's possible that this Three may be about to set a new record for itself. Still, we have a good margin in supplies, and anyway it will probably change tomorrow."

It didn't, though, not on the eighth day and not on the ninth. On the eleventh day Tan sighed, pushed the cards away and said, "Now we must face the facts. We may go on forever in this flying rathole."

Estrella patted his arm. "You give up too easily, Tan."

He glowered at her. "What do you know? Such things have happened before! Haven't you heard the story of, I forget his name, the old prospector who only got home because he ate his shipmates?"

"Don't quarrel," Stan begged.

But Estrella's temper was up. "Why did I sign on with two teenage Turkish boys—well, a Turkish boy and a half—who are willing to be cannibals? I suppose you have already decided which of us you will eat first, Tan. Me? Because you are both strong and I am the smallest? Well, let me tell you—"

Her voice trailed off. Her damaged face looked startled, then seraphic. Stan felt it, too, as *down* in the little ship slipped gently to *up* and the coil brightened.

It was the halfway point at last. So they were not going to die, after all, or at least not in that particular way.

Since they were to live, the atmosphere became more relaxed. Tan gave Estrella a great smile, and to Stan he muttered, in Turkish, "Perhaps we will eat this one after all, but in a more friendly way."

Estrella heard, and even in the rapture of the moment her expression froze. "Tan," she said, "I do not understand Turkish, but I understand fully the way you look when you speak it. You have pricks sticking out of your eyes, Tan. Save them for someone else. I am a virgin. I have remained so when it was more difficult than it is here, and will go on as a virgin until I marry."

"Hell and devils," Tan groaned. "I thought it was only Muslim girls who kept their knees locked so, not free-spirited Americans."

She chose to be friendly. "So you have learned something new about American women. Now shall we play cards again, or get some sleep?"

IV

For most of a day Tan was glumly quiet, but his good nature came back. After all, they were on their way to a great adventure together. Stan could see him revising his attitude toward Estrella. All right, she was not going to be a lover. A sort of a sister, then, and Tan had long practice at living with a sister.

The thing at which Tan had had no practice at all was being confined in a tiny space with nothing to do. "I wish we had at least brought our damn instruments," he growled to Stan, who shrugged.

"No room," he said.

Estrella looked up from her plate. "We could play a few hands of poker," she offered. Tan, his lips pressed tightly together, shook his head.

"Or," she added, "we could just talk. There is so much I don't know about you guys. Oltan? What was your life like in Istanbul?"

He declined to be cheered up. "I drove a van for a living," he said sourly. "I lived with my mother and father and my kid sister, Naslan, and I had five, actually five, regular girlfriends, who were very fond of me and extremely obliging. What else is there to tell?"

She nodded as though that were a pleasing answer and turned to Stan. "How about you?"

Stan did his best to cooperate. "My father was a code clerk at the American consulate, a very well-paid job, when he met my mother. She was Turkish, but Christian—a Methodist, like him. I was born in the hospital at the embassy in Ankara, which was American soil so I would be born as an American, like you."

That made her smile. "Not much like me."

"You mean the well-paid part? That was only when I was little. My mother died when I was seven, and after that—" He shrugged without finishing the sentence, not willing to tell her about his father's steady decline to drunkeness.

Tan, listening without patience, straightened up and pushed himself away. "I have to pee," he said.

Stan looked after him, then back to Estrella. "And you?" he said, over the plashing sounds from the crapper. "You said you were a butcher?"

She reached up to stroke her left, off-center cheekbone. "Until the accident, yes. In Montana. I'm a mixture, too, Stan. My father was Basque, mostly. My mother was Navajo, with a little Hopi, but a big woman, and strong. There was no work around the Four Corners so they managed to get up to Montana to work in the corrals. You know the bison ranches in America?"

"Oh, yes. Well, sort of. I read stories when I was little. Before I thought of Gateway I thought it would be great to be a cowboy, sitting around the campfire at night, herding the bison across the prairies."

That time she laughed out loud. "You don't herd bison, Stan. They won't let you. You let them run free, because the prairie grasses are all they need to eat anyway. Then, when they're old enough for slaughter, you lay a trail of something they like to eat even better than the prairie grasses. That takes them right into the corrals, that have a three-meter steel-plate fence all around them, because the bison can jump right over anything smaller. They can run fast, too, a hundred kilometers an hour. And then, one by one, handlers like my parents let them into the chutes to the slaughterhouse. And then the pistoliers shoot them in the head with a big gun that has a kind of a piston, goes right into the brain and comes out again, ready for the next one. When they're dead the belt carries them to me, to slit their throats. Then I clamp on the irons from the overhead tracks and they're picked up so the blood can drain, and taken to the coolers before they're cut into steaks and roasts. Each bison has nearly fifty liters of blood, which goes into the tank below—what doesn't go onto me."

Tan had come out of the head, fastening his clothes as he listened. "Yes, Estrella," he said argumentatively, "but you said a bull stepped on you and broke your head. How does a dead bison step on you?"

"It wasn't a dead one," she said shortly.

"But if the pistolier shot it in the head—"

"This time he shot it only in the shoulder. It was very alive when it came to me, and very angry."

"It sounds like a nasty accident," Stan offered.

"No. It wasn't an accident. He did it on purpose. He was a man with pricks in his eyes, too, Tan, and when I would not go to bed with him he taught me a lesson."

Twentieth day. Twenty-first day. They didn't play cards much anymore, because they couldn't concentrate. They didn't even talk much. They had already said everything they could say to each other about their hopes, and none of them wanted to speak their fears out loud. Their nerves were taut with the itch of a gambler with a ticket on a long-shot that is coming up fast in the stretch, but maybe not quite fast enough. Finally Estrella said firmly, "There is no use fidgeting around. We should sleep as much as we can."

Stan knew that was wise. They would need all their strength and alertness to do whatever there was to be done when they were—there. Wherever "there" turned out to be.

The wise advice was hard to follow, though. Hard as it was for Stan to make himself fall asleep, it was even harder for him to make himself stay that way. He woke frequently, counting the time by minutes as the twenty-first day passed and the twenty-second began.

Then none of them could sleep at all. Looking at the time every few seconds. Arguing fiercely about at what hour and what minute turnaround had come, and thus at what minute and hour they would arrive. . . .

And then they did arrive. They knew it when the coil winked out.

And, at once, every instrument on the ship went wild.

The readings were preposterous. They said their Three was immersed in a tenuous plasma, hotter than the Sun, drenched with death-dealing radiation of all kinds, and then Stan understood why their Three was armored.

This was no planet to make them rich with its abandoned trove of Heechee treasures. There wasn't even a star close enough to matter. "Get us the hell out of here!" Tan was bellowing, and Estrella shrilled:

"No, take readings first! Pictures! Make observations!"

But there was nothing to observe beyond what the instruments had told them already. When Stan closed his hand on the go-teat Estrella didn't object anymore, but only wept.

The flight back was no longer than the flight out, but it seemed interminable. They could not wait for it to be over, and then, when it was, the bad news began.

The ancient Oriental woman who climbed aboard their Three as soon as it docked listened to their story with half an ear. It was the instrument readings that interested her, but she absently answered a few questions. "Yes," she said, nodding, "you entered a supernova remnant. The Heechee were very interested in stars that were about to explode; many courses led to where they could observe one. But in the time since, of course, some of those stars have actually exploded. Like yours. And all that is left is a nebula of superheated gases. It is a good thing for you that your Three was armored."

Estrella was biting her lower lip. "Do you think there will be a science bonus, at least?"

The old woman considered. "Perhaps. You would have to ask Hector Montefiore. Nothing very big, though. There is already a large body of data about such objects."

The three looked at each other in silence. Then Stan managed a grin. "Well, guys," he said, "it's like my father used to say. When you fall off your horse, the best thing to do is get right back on again."

The woman peered at them. "What is this talk of horses?"

"He means," Estrella explained, "we will all ship out on another mission the first chance we get."

"Oh," the old woman said, looking surprised, "you were Out when it happened, weren't you? You didn't hear. They've solved the guidance problem. There are no more missions. The Gateway exploration program has been terminated."

V

Terminated! Gateway terminated? No more missions? No more of those scared, valiant Gateway prospectors daring everything to fly out on magic mystery flights to pick over the tantalizing scraps the long-ago Heechee had left behind when they went away—whenever they went, and wherever it was they went to?

It was all Robinette Broadhead's doing again. While Estrella and the boys were Out, things had gone crazy at the Food Factory his people had discovered, and at some other fabulous Heechee ship that was nearby. Broadhead had flown there solo to straighten it out, and had succeeded. And in the process had not only elevated the value of his already sky-high fortune to incalculable heights with this fabulous new cache of Heechee wonders, but in the process had learned the secret of controlling Heechee spacecraft.

The other thing he had done was to turn Gateway itself into a backwater. There would be no more random flying to God knew where. There would be no more flying to anywhere at all until the big brains who planned Gateway missions decided how to use all this new data. Meanwhile, there was nothing at all. Everything was on hold. The scores of would-be explorers had nothing to do but grit their teeth and practice patience.

In the mess hall Tan nibbled at his meal, glowering. "So what's our plan supposed to be now?" he demanded.

Stan swallowed his mouthful of vegetarian lasagna. "We wait. What else can we do? This can't last forever. The ships are still there! Sooner or later they'll start up again, and then maybe we'll have a chance at going on a different kind of mission. Better! Knowing where we're going before we start! Maybe even knowing that we'll live to come back!"

Tan gazed around the mess hall, where a couple of dozen other would-be adventurers were as subdued as themselves. "Maybe," he said.

"At least we're not using up capital," Stan pointed out. The Gateway Corporation had elected to show that it had a heart. No per diems would be charged until further notice, so at least their clocks were not running out.

"The bastards can afford it," Tan grumbled.

Of course the bastards could afford it. The bastards were the Gateway Corporation, and they owned a piece of every discovered piece of Heechee treasure. The Corporation was owned—on paper—by a consortium of the world's governments, but it was just about as true to say that the world's governments were owned by Gateway Corp. After due deliberation, the Corporation decided it could even afford to donate a little something for their efforts to Tan, Stan and Estrella.

They found out about it when, for lack of anything better to do, Tan and Stan were nursing their weak, but more or less drinkable, coffees in the Blue Hell, watching the other prospectors gamble away their no longer needed per diems. Estrella was perched beside them, as always studying something or other from her pocket plate. This time, Stan saw wonderingly, she was studying music, and she fingered the air as she read. "Do you play?" he asked, surprised.

She flushed. "A little. On the flute," she said.

"Well, why didn't you say so? Maybe the three of us can play together sometime. What do you think, Tan?"

Tan wasn't listening. He nudged Stan. "Here come the big shots," he said as Hector Montefiore sailed in, along with two or three others of the permanent party. They were obviously looking for action, and Stan was not pleased to see that Montefiore was coming in their direction. He did not care for Hector Montefiore. He liked him even less when the man slapped his shoulder and patted Estrella on the rump. "Congratulations," he boomed. "Getting ready to celebrate, are you?"

"Celebrate what?" Tan demanded.

The fat man gave him a look of surprise. "Your science bonus, of course. Didn't you know? Well, check it out, for Christ's sake! Who knows, then you might loosen up and buy me a drink!"

He didn't wait for it, though; he went off, chuckling, while the three of them bent over Estrella's plate as she switched to the status reports.

And, yes, their names were there. "Not bad," Tan said, when he saw the amount.

Estrella shook her head. "Divided among the three of us, not all that good, either," she said practically. "Are you willing to settle for a *little* money?"

"A little money would be enough for me to go home and buy my own van, so I could go into business for myself," Tan said stiffly.

"If that is what you wish. It isn't, for me. I didn't come all this way to spend the rest of my life struggling to stay alive in a one-room condo with Basic Medical and no future. Anyway, Hector says there will surely be more missions soon. Missions of a different kind, where we will know where we will be going."

Stan gave her a thoughtful look. "How do you know what Hector says?" he asked, surprising himself by the tone of his own voice. He almost sounded *jealous*.

Estrella shrugged. "He likes me," she said, as though that explained everything.

"He likes everybody," Tan sneered. "Boys, girls, sheep, he doesn't care, as long as it has a hole in it."

Estrella gazed at him for a moment in silence. "He has not got into any of mine," she said finally. "Let's talk sensibly. What do you want to do? Take your share and go home? Or wait for something worthwhile?"

They waited. While they waited they watched the unfolding story of what Robinette Broadhead had discovered on the news.

And what had he not! Strange, semi-human creatures that at first everyone thought, heart-stoppingly, might actually be Heechee, but were not. (They were, it seemed, relatives of primitive pre-humans called australopithecines, captured by the Heechee on Earth millennia ago and transported to one of their space outposts for study.) There were a clutch of surviving—well, sort of surviving—lost Gateway prospectors, too, their ships taken to this place by the luck of the draw and unable to leave. Now the marooned prospectors were more or less dead, but also more or less still alive, preserved in some bizarre sort of Heechee machinery. There was the half-wild living human boy named Wan, descendant of other Gateway castaways and now, somehow, through some Heechee wizardry that broadcast his yearnings and hatreds to the entire solar system, the source of the Wrath of God. (A boy's wet dreams, costing so many lives!) And—the final secret Broadhead had learned—now he even knew where the Heechee had fled to! They had holed up inside an immense black hole in the Galaxy's Core, and they were still there, all of them!

It was one wonder after another. Everyone was talking about it—well, everyone but Estrella, it seemed to Stan. For whatever reason, she was spending more and more time with the permanent party and less with her old shipmates. Stan didn't approve. "She shouldn't do that," he told Tan seriously. "They mean her no good."

Tan laughed coarsely. "Depends on what you think 'good' is. Montefiore has his own ideas. But don't worry about Estrella," he advised. "That one'll take good care of her maidenhead."

Stan did worry, though. He told himself that what Estrella did was none of his business, but he thought about her a lot as the days passed.

The nine-bangle Englishwoman came back safe and sound in her One, having earned not only a tenth bangle but, at last, a stake. She had roamed a tunnel on a world not much kindlier than Mercury, wearing a space suit that kept her in air but didn't keep out the blazing heat that radiated from the tunnel walls. Pushed to the limit she had scoured the empty corridors until she found—something; no one was sure what. Possibly it was a game, something like a 3-D version of Go. Or it might have been some sort of computing machine, like an abacus, or even a musical instrument. At any rate her bonus was enough to pay her way back to a decent retirement in the little village in Sussex she had come from. She even bought coffees for the boys before she left, listening to them tell her about all the amazing things that had happened while she was gone. "Heigh-ho," she said, grinning the grin of someone who no longer had to worry about such things, "sounds like fun and games, doesn't it? Well, good luck to you! Don't give up. You never know, you might hit a good one yet."

Tan looked sourly after her as she made the payback rounds, buying drinks for everyone who had bought them for her. "I doubt it," he said, half under his breath.

"You've been doubting it ever since we got here," Stan said in irritation, though the fact was that he was beginning to doubt it, too. It might have turned into a really serious argument, but that was when Estrella appeared in the entrance, looking around for them.

Estrella didn't hesitate. As soon as she saw the two of them she launched herself in their direction with a great, accurate kick against the door frame. Tan caught her as she came in range, but she grabbed a holdfast and freed herself. Her twisted face looked grim, but the news she brought was great. She looked around, then whispered: "There's a mission coming up. A big one."

Stan's heart leaped, but Tan was unresponsive. "One of these guaranteed new ones, where the Corporation will keep most of the profits?"

"Yes," she said, "and no. They know the destination, but that's all they know. They don't know how long it will take, so it will be in an armored Five, one of the ones with the special fittings no one understands—but Broadhead has said that they're essential for this trip. They will load this Five with supplies and material, enough for a very long flight, so it will be able to carry only two people. I'm going to be one of them. There's room for one other."

She was looking from one to the other of them, but mostly at Stan. Tan spoke up. "Not me," he declared. "I don't want any more mystery bus rides."

Stan ignored him. "You said they knew the destination?"

Estrella took a deep breath. "It will go to where the Heechee have gone. Where they have been hiding all this time, in the Core of the Galaxy."

Stan swallowed convulsively. You came to Gateway hoping for a big score—but *this* big? Not nibbling at bits and pieces the Heechee had left behind, but going straight to those vanished super-creatures themselves?

And what sort of reward might there be for *that*?

He didn't think. He heard himself saying, "I'll go!" almost before he realized he had made the decision. Then he turned to Tan. "Look. There's only room for two, so you take my share of our bonus, too. Go home and have a good life. Buy Naslan the prettiest wedding dress she can find." And then he added, "But tell her not to wait for me to come back."

VI

A Heechee Five was supposed to be much bigger than a Three. Not this one, though. Certainly not any roomier. One whole corner of its space was taken up with the peculiar, unexplained device that—Broadhead had said—was necessary for them to enter the Core. Another couple of cubic meters were filled with the goods they were told to deliver to the Heechee—records of Gateway explorations and Heechee finds, background material on the human race, all sorts of odds and ends along with a recorded Message to the Heechee that was meant to explain just who human beings were. Add in their year's worth of supplies for themselves, and there wasn't much room for Stan and Estrella to get around.

As far as Estrella was concerned, not much room was needed. She didn't move around much. She didn't talk much to Stan, either. She went directly to her sleep sack as soon as they took off and stayed there, coming out only to eat or excrete, and uninterested in conversation in either case. When Stan asked her if something was wrong, she said only, "Yes." When he asked her if there was anything he could do, she shook her head and said, "I have to work through this myself." When he asked her what "this" was, all she would say was, "I have to find a way to like myself again." Then she went back to her sleep shelf again, and stayed there. For three whole days, while Stan wondered and stewed.

Then, on the fourth day, Stan woke up and found Estrella studying him. She was perched on the uncomfortable forked Heechee pilots' seat, and she seemed to have been there for a long time. Experimentally he said, "Hello?" with a question mark at the end.

She gazed at him thoughtfully for a moment longer, then sighed. "Excuse me," she said, and disappeared into the head again.

She was in there for quite a while. When she came out it appeared that she had spent the time fixing herself up. She had washed her hair and brushed it still damp, and she was wearing fresh shorts and top. She gave him another of those long, unexplained looks.

Then she said, "Stan. I have something to say to you. We will be together for a long time, I think, and it would be better if there were no tensions between us. Do you want to make love to me?"

Startled, Stan said the first thing that came into his head. Which was, "I've never made love to a virgin before."

She laughed, not joyously. "That is not a problem, Stan. I'm not a virgin anymore. How do you think I got us on this mission?"

Stan's only previous coupling, when he had painfully saved up enough to afford one of Mr. Ozden's cousin's less expensive girls, had not taught him much about the arts of love. Estrella didn't know much more than he did, but inexperience wasn't their only problem. A Heechee Five wasn't designed for fucking. They tended to float away from the hold-ons the first time he tried to enter her.

But experimenting was enjoyable enough on its own, and they finally found that what worked best was for him to come to her from behind, with Estrella curling her ankles over his while he gripped her waist with both hands. Then it was simple enough.

Then, finished and still naked, they turned around to face each other and hung so, their arms wrapped around each other, without speaking. Stan found the position very comfortable. His cheek was pressed against her ear, his nose in her still damp and sweet-smelling hair. After a bit, without moving away, she asked, "Are we going to be friends, Stan?"

"Oh, yes," he said. And they were.

Now that they were friends, especially friends who fucked, their Five didn't seem so crowded anymore. They touched often, and in all kinds of ways—affectionate pats, casual rubs in passing, quick kisses, sweet strokings that, often enough, turned into more fucking. Estrella seemed to like it well enough; Stan very much.

They talked, too. About what the Core might be like. About the race of Heechee who might (or might not) still be there. About what it would be like when they came back and collected the unquestionably enormous bonus that would be due them. "It'll be *billions*!" Stan gloated. "Enough to have a waterfront estate like Robinette Broadhead's, with servants, and a good life—and we'll have plenty of time to enjoy it all, too, because we'll have Full Medical."

"Full Medical," Estrella whispered, sharing his dream.

"Absolutely! We won't be old at forty and dead at fifty-five. We'll live a long, long time, and—" he swallowed, aware that he was getting into a commitment—"and we'll live it together, Estrella." Which naturally led to more tender kissing, and to not so tender sex.

They had much to talk about, including the chapters in their earlier lives that had been omitted in their previous telegraphic summaries. When Stan talked about his mother's death and what it had done to his father, Estrella took his hand in hers and kissed it. When he told her about life in Istanbul she was interested, and more so when he talked about the city itself—about its centuries as the mighty Christian city of Constantinople, about the Crusaders, also Christian but eager for some loot of any kind so they elected to loot it anyway, about the Emperor Justinian and his Theodora and the—well—the Byzantine, really Byzantine, court of Byzantium. All that fascinated her. She had known nothing of the Holy Roman Empire, little enough of Rome itself, its Caesars, its conquests, its centuries of world rule. To her it was all exciting myths and legends, all the better because they were true. Or as true, anyway, as Stan's memory allowed.

While Stan, of course, knew even less of the America that had belonged to the Native Americans, before their subjugation by the white man and since. It was not the American history he had learned in school or heard about in his father's stories. Her people, Estrella told him—the ones on her mother's side—had a history of their own. Sometimes they had even built great cities like Machu Picchu and the immense Mayan structures in the south, and the mysterious works of the Anasazi nearer to her family's home. But that, she said, sounding both wistful and proud, had lasted only until the Europeans arrived and took their lands away, and often enough their lives as well, and pushed them into harsher lives in reservations, and endless, retreating battles, and finally defeat. "There wasn't much left for us, Stan," she said. "The only good thing—well, it isn't really good, is it?—is that now most of the Yankees are as poor as we."

Which reminded Stan of an unsolved puzzle. "But you weren't all that poor, were you? I mean, personally. Like when you had your, uh, accident. If that had happened to Tan, or almost anybody else I knew, there wouldn't have been any big payoff to finance your going to Gateway. Did you have Full Medical or something?"

She laughed, surprised. "We had no medical at all. What I had was my brother." Who, she said, let it be known that he was going to kill the pistolier. Whose sister's husband was a clerk in the slaughterhouse's accounts department. Who had juggled the books to pay them off, just to save his brother-in-law's worthless life. "It was supposed to be a death benefit, but I double-crossed them. I lived. Then, when I was well enough to travel, I took the rest of the money and used it to come to Gateway."

She looked so sad when she was telling about it that Stan couldn't help kissing her, which before long led to more of that pleasurable love-making. And why not? After all, they were really on a sort of honeymoon cruise, weren't they?

The days passed, ten, twelve, twenty. They slept holding each other tight, and never seemed to tire of it. It was a little cramped, to be sure. But the one-size-fits-all sleep sacks were constructed to be long enough for a stringbean Maasai or a corpulent Bengali, and skinny Stan and slim Estrella could fit inside together well enough for lovers. Sometimes they played music together, weird combinations of Stan's trumpet and the flute Estrella produced from her bags. Sometimes they talked. Sometimes they played cards or read or just sat companionably together in silence. And sometimes Stan pulled out the recorded Message to the Heechee—the reason they were on this trip in the first place—and they played it for themselves and wondered what the Heechee (if any) would make of it.

This Message had been cobbled together in a hurry by God knew who—some of the big brains in the Gateway Corp, no doubt, and no doubt with Robinette Broadhead leaning over their shoulder. It didn't have any narration; the Heechee were not likely to understand any human language. Its only sound was music, first Tschaikowsky's somber "Pathetique" in its entirety, then, to show that humans had more than one musical mood, Prokoviev's jokey, perky *Classical Symphony*.

But mostly the Message was pictures: the empty Heechee tunnels on Venus; the nearly equally empty corridors on Gateway, when human beings first got there; a crew of prospectors warily climbing into an early Five; another crew, travel-stained, coming out of a Three bearing prayer fans and other Heechee gadgets; a picture of the pinwheel of the Galaxy, seen from above, with an arrow showing Earth's position in the Orion Arm; a slowly spinning globe of the Earth itself; quick flashes of human cities—New York, Tokyo, Sao Paolo, Rome; shots of people doing things—painting landscapes, running a tractor, peering through a telescope, masked around a hospital birthing bed where a new baby was coming into the world; then things that neither Estrella nor Stan had ever seen before. There was a series of pictures of an enormous floating object, then of a huge spindle-shaped chamber, blue Heechee metal walls and a strange, huge machine squatting on tractor treads in the middle of it. "The Food

Factory and that other thing Broadhead discovered," Estrella guessed. Then the object's internal passageways, their walls Heechee metal that glowed in several colors, and a couple of—they both caught their breaths— queer, hairy creatures that looked almost human, and had to be the prim- itives Broadhead had discovered there. And, at the last, the shot of the Galaxy again, with a tiny image of a Heechee Five that was probably meant to be their own craft, slowly moving from the Orion arm to the Core.

When the showing was over—for the fourth or fifth time—Stan was thoughtfully rubbing the place where his wispy mustache had been until Estrella had teased him into shaving it off. They had been watching with their arms around each other. He yawned, which made her yawn, too, be- cause they had both been getting sleepy. She moved slightly for a better fit, but not away, as she saw that he was staring at their stacked piles of supplies.

"What is it, Stan?" she asked.

He said pensively, "This is, what, the thirty-fifth day we've been out?"

She counted on her fingers. "Yes, something like that. Maybe the thirty-fourth. What about it?"

He sighed. "It's just that it looks like a long flight. I don't know if any- body's gone this far before."

She tried to reassure him. "Sometimes short flights take a long time, and the other way around, too. With Heechee ships you never can tell."

"I guess," he said, turning his head to kiss her ear in the way she liked. She wriggled companionably and put up her lips, and that was better than reassurance.

For Stan was happy with Estrella, who not only shared his sleeping pod but never, ever reminded him he was only a teenaged boy. He thought about it drowsily. He had never been happier in his life than he was this minute. So why worry about how long the trip would take? He didn't want it to end at all, would have been content if it had lasted a very long time indeed. . . .

But it didn't.

It ended that day, almost at that very moment, when kissing had turned to caressing but before they began to take each other's clothes off, and it ended in a startling way.

The great drive coil gave them no warning. It was that other thing, the squat, domed gadget whose purpose had never been explained to them in any terms that made sense. It opened up. It extruded a crystalline corkscrew thing that began to mutter and glow, then growl, then begin to scream on a rising pitch until they could hear it no more, as the glow brightened, Fat, silent sparks showered all over them, making them wince—in surprise, not pain, because the sparks could not be felt. Then at last the drive coil got into the act, beginning to glow and brightening to an eye-hurting incandescent white, with revolving barber-pole stripes of hot red and chrome yellow. It began to shudder. Or the ship did; Stan couldn't tell which because he was shaking too, in a way that was frighteningly unlike anything he had felt before. He wasn't sleepy anymore as they clung to each other. . . .

Then, without warning, everything stopped.

Estrella pulled herself free and turned on the outside eyes. Behind them was a scary spread of mottled pale blue. Before them, a sky of unbelievable stars, so many of them, so bright. And, very near, a large metallic dodecahedron, twelve symmetrical sides, each with a little dimple in its center. Their ship plunged at breakneck speed into one of the dimples and nestled there. Before Stan or Estrella could move, the port was opened from outside.

Something that looked like a furry, animated skeleton was glaring in at them. "I think it must be a Heechee," Estrella whispered numbly.

And, of course, it was. And that was the beginning of the longest, the unbelievably longest, day in Stan's life.

VII

Nothing in Stan's previous seventeen years of life had taught him how to greet an alien creature from another planet. He fell back on memories of the comic magazines of his childhood. He raised his hands above his head and declaimed: "We come in peace!"

In the comics that had seemed to work pretty well. In this real world it didn't. The Heechee fell back in obvious panic. A low, hooting moan came from its queerly shaped mouth as it turned and ran away. "Shit," Stan said dismally, staring after it.

Estrella clutched his arm. "We frightened it," she said.

"I certainly hope so. It frightened the hell out of me!"

"Yes, but we have to show it we're friendly. Maybe we should start playing the Message for them?"

That sounded like a good idea. At least Stan didn't have a better one, but while they were trying to start the playback the Heechee came running back, and this time he brought all his friends with him. There were half a dozen of the creatures, dressed in smocks with curious pod-shaped objects hanging between their skinny legs—king-sized jockstraps? Heavy-duty condoms? Stan couldn't guess. The creatures were jabbering agitatedly among themselves as they hurried in. The tallest of them came barely up to Stan's chin. The short ones hardly reached his navel, and they wasted no time. One of them slapped Estrella's hand away from the playback machine while a couple of the others grabbed Stan. They were surprisingly strong. They were armed, too. More or less armed, or at least several of them were; they carried an assortment of knives, bright blue metal or gold, some curved like a scalpel, all of them looking dangerous. Especially when one of the Heechee held a knife with its extremely sharp point almost touching Stan's right eyeball and tugged him toward the exit. "Don't fight them!" Estrella cried, herself captive in the same way.

He didn't. He let himself be dragged unresisting into a larger chamber—red-veined blue metal walls, with unidentifiable machines and furnishings scattered around. The ceilings were very close. As they crossed the threshold Stan bumped his head on the doorway and stumbled, taken unaware by the sudden return of weight. They were in gravity again, not as strong as Earth's, maybe, but enough to make him totter against his captor. He jerked his head back from the blade just in time to avoid losing an eye. The Heechee with the knife screeched a warning, but Stan wasn't trying to give him any trouble. Not even when he and Estrella were dragged against a wall and chained, spread-eagled, to what might have been coat racks—or statuary—or anything at all, but were solid enough to hold them.

Things were coming to a boil. More Heechee were arriving on the run, all of them chattering agitatedly at the tops of their voices. As one batch of them disappeared into the Five, others began to use their assorted knives to cut away the captives' clothing. "What the hell do you think you're doing?" Stan squawked, but as far as he could tell the Heechee weren't even trying to understand what he was saying. They didn't stop doing what they were doing, either. As each scrap of garment was cut away, underwear and all, all the way down to bare skin, it was searched and sniffed and carried away somewhere for further study.

Halfway through the process Estrella yelped in sudden shock as one of those knives nicked her thigh. The Heechee wielding it jumped back, startled. "Be careful with her!" Stan shouted, but they didn't even look at him. The one with the knife screeched an order; another produced a little metal cup and caught a drop of the blood that was oozing from Estrella's cut. "Are you all right?" Stan called, suddenly more angry and solicitous than afraid.

"It's only a scratch," she said, and then added uncomfortably, "but I have to pee."

There didn't seem to be any way to communicate that urgency to their captors—assuming the Heechee would have cared if there had been. They didn't seem at all interested in any needs or desires of their prisoners. More and more of the Heechee were crowding into the room, yammering to each other without stop. When a Heechee appeared who wore a fancier tunic than the rest, gold-streaked and silky, there was a momentary hush, then they all began talking to him at once. The newcomer had a sort of frazzled look, the way a man might appear if he had just been wakened from sleep with very unwelcome news. He listened for just a moment before waving for silence. He snapped what sounded like a command, then raised one skeletal hand to his narrow lips and began to speak into what looked like a large finger ring.

Heechee were beginning to come out of the Five carrying things—spare clothes, packets of food and, very gingerly, Stan's trumpet. There was a babble over that as they presented it to the one with the ring microphone. He considered for a moment, then issued more orders. Another Heechee bustled forward with what looked like a stethoscope and touched it to the trumpet, here, there, all over, listening worriedly and reporting to the leader.

A moment later there was a sudden squawking from inside the Five, and Stan heard the familiar blare of the opening bars of Tschaikowsky's Sixth Symphony. "Listen, Stan, they've turned on the Message!" Estrella cried gladly. "Maybe it'll be all right now!"

It wasn't. It didn't get any better at all. If the Heechee made any sense of the Message, which did not seem likely, it did not seem to make them friendlier.

How long the two of them hung there, poked and palped and examined, Stan could not know. It seemed to be a very long time. The good thought, the *only* good thought, that Stan was able to summon up was that back on Gateway people would be beginning to worry about them. Might even be thinking about sending out a rescue party. If not that, at least they would definitely be having Stan Avery and Estrella Pancorbo in their minds.

For whatever good that might do them.

Stan worried about himself, but worried more about Estrella. Now and then he called empty reassurances to her. She spoke bravely back. "It'll work out, Stan," she said, and then, in a different tone, "Oh, *damn* it."

Stan saw the problem. Though she had been squeezing her knees together as hard as she could, her bladder would not be denied. Urine was running down her legs. Among the Heechee that produced a new flurry of excitement, as one of them ran for another cup to catch a few drops for study.

What Stan felt was shame—for his lover's embarrassment—and a sudden hot flash of rage at these coarse and uncaring Heechee who had caused it; and that was the end of the first hour of Stan's long, long day.

Then, for no reason that Stan could see, things did improve. Once begun they improved very rapidly.

The Heechee in the gold-embroidered robe had gone off to do whatever Heechee bosses had to do. Now he returned, puffing importantly as he issued orders in all directions. When he marched up close to Estrella, Stan strained against his chains, expecting some new deviltry. That didn't happen. The Heechee reached up with one wide, splay-fingered hand, stretching to do it, and patted her cheek.

Was that meant as reassurance? It evidently was, Stan saw, because other Heechee were hurrying toward them to remove their chains, the boss Heechee chattering at them all the while. Stan didn't listen. Staggering slightly—the chains had cut off circulation, and he weighed less than he had expected here—he reached out for Estrella. Naked as they were, they hugged each other while the Heechee stared at them in benign fascination.

"Now what?" Stan asked the air. He didn't expect an answer, and got none, unless there was an answer in what happened next. A couple of Heechee hustled toward them, one bearing a few scraps of their ruined clothes, as though to apologize or explain, the other with a couple of Heechee smocks as replacements, gesturing that they might put them on.

The garments didn't fit them all that well. Human beings were a lot thicker front to back than the squashed frames of the Heechee; what for a Heechee had been a loose smock for Stan was more like a corset. All the same, having their nakedness covered before these weird beings did make Stan feel a little less helpless.

What it didn't do for Stan was allow him to figure out just what was going on. The Heechee were doing their best to explain. They were chirping, gesturing, trying with all their hearts to make something understood. But in the absence of any language in common they weren't getting very far.

"At least we're not trussed up like Christmas pigs anymore," Estrella offered hopefully, holding tightly to Stan's hand. They weren't. They were allowed to roam freely around the chamber, the busy Heechee dodging apologetically around them on their errands.

"I wonder if they'll let us go back in the ship," Stan said, peering inside. A couple of Heechee were playing the Message again, holding what might have been a camera to record what it showed. Another patted Stan's shoulder encouragingly as he stood at the entrance.

He took it for permission. "Let's try it," he said, leading the way. No one interfered, but Estrella gasped when she saw what had been done to their Five. Most of the movables had been taken away, and two Heechee were puzzling over the fixtures in the toilet.

Estrella asserted herself. "Get out!" she ordered, flapping her arms to show what she meant. The Heechee jabbered at each other for a moment, then hesitantly complied.

That made a difference. The toilet had been partly disassembled, but it still worked. So did the washstand. A little cleaner, a lot more comfortable, Stan and Estrella took care of their next needs: they were hungry. It was impossible to use the food-preparation equipment, because that was already in fragments, but among the odds and ends that had been hauled out of the Five they found a packet of biscuits that could be eaten as they were, and a couple of bulbs of water. Every move they made was watched by the Heechee with interest and approval.

Then the boss Heechee came back, trailing half a dozen excited assistants who trundled what looked like a portable video screen. One of the Heechee touched something, and a picture appeared in the screen.

They were looking at a Heechee male who was talking to them excitedly—and, of course, incomprehensibly. Behind him was what seemed to be the interior of a Heechee ship, but not any ship Stan had ever seen before. It was much larger than even a Five, and the only recognizable item in it was one of those queer, dome-shaped machineries that had got them into the Core.

Then the Heechee who had been talking from the screen gestured. The scene widened, and then they saw something else that was familiar.

"Mother of God," Estrella whispered. "Isn't that Robinette Broadhead?"

Indeed it was Broadhead. He was grinning widely, and he was touching the Heechee in the screen, offering a handshake, which the Heechee clumsily accepted.

Beside Stan, the boss Heechee was patting his shoulder enthusiastically with his splayed hand. It seemed to be a gesture of apology, and hesitantly Stan returned it. The Heechee's shoulder was warm but bony, and his flat, bony face bore an expression that could have been intended as something like a smile.

"Well," Estrella said wonderingly. "It looks like we're all friends together now." And that was the end of the second hour in this longest of days.

It was good to be friends with these people, better to have had the chance to eat and drink and relieve themselves, best of all to be *free*. Stan appreciated all those things, though what he really wanted was some sleep. There didn't seem much chance of that. All of the Heechee, singly and in groups, kept trying to tell them things with their jabbering and their crude sign language. Stan and Estrella kept not comprehending. When the boss Heechee approached, inquiringly carrying Stan's horn, Stan got that message right away. "It's a trumpet," he told them. He repeated the name a couple of times, touching the instrument, then gave up. "Here, let me show you." And he blew a scale, and then a couple of the opening bars of the Cab Calloway version of the "St. Louis Blues." All the Heechee jumped back, then made gestures urging him to play more.

That was as far as Stan was prepared to go. He shook his head. "We're *tired*," he said, demonstrating by closing his eyes and resting his check on his folded hands. "*Sleep. We need rest.*"

Estrella took a hand. Beckoning to the nearest Heechee, she led him to the entrance to the Five, pointing to their sleep shelves, now bare. After more jabbering, the Heechee seemed to get the idea. A couple of them raced away, and the boss Heechee gestured to them to follow. They left behind that single big chamber that, until now, had been their entire experience of the no doubt multitudinous and various worlds of the Heechee, and followed the leader down a short corridor. Its walls, Stan saw, seemed to be Heechee metal still, but, like some of those on the huge vessel Robinette Broadhead had found, with a veined rose-pink instead of the familiar blue. They paused at a chamber. A waiting Heechee showed them the ruins of their own sleep sacks, then pointed hopefully inside. There were two side-by-side heaps of something on the floor. Beds? Anyway the Heechee closed the door on them, and Estrella immediately stretched out on one of the pods. When Stan followed her example, it felt more like burrowing into a pile of dried leaves than any bed he had ever had. But it wasn't uncomfortable, and best of all it was both flat and horizontal, and no one was yelling at him.

Thankfully he stretched out and closed his eyes. . . . But only for what seemed like no more than a moment.

He was awakened as the door opened again. It was the boss Heechee, jabbering in excitement but beckoning insistently.

"Oh, hell," Stan muttered. Things happened pretty fast in this place; but the two humans got up and followed. Farther, this time, along the rose-pink corridor and then one where the veining was bright gold. They stopped in a chamber like the one they had first entered, where half a dozen Heechee were chattering and pointing at the airlock.

"I think they're trying to tell us that another ship's coming in," Estrella said.

"Fine," Stan grumbled. "They could've let us sleep a little bit, though."

They didn't have long to wait. There was a faint sound of metal against metal from outside the door. One of the Heechee, watching a display of color from something beside the door, waited just a moment, then opened it. A pair of Heechee came in, talking excitedly to the equally excited ones meeting them, and then they were followed by a pair of human beings.

Human beings!

Stan's mouth dropped open, and beside him he heard Estrella's gasp. The human beings were talking, too, but the people they were talking to were the Heechee. In their own Heechee language. And then one of the human arrivals caught sight of Stan and Estrella. His eyes went wide. "Jesus," he said unbelievingly. "Who the hell are you?"

Who the hell the man himself was was somebody named Lon Alvarez, one of Robinette Broadhead's personal assistants, and as soon as Stan told him their names Alvarez snapped his fingers. "Oh, God, yes! The kids who took off from Gateway right after the discovery! Sure, I remember hearing about you. I guess everybody thought you were dead."

"Well, we're not," Estrella said, "just dead tired."

But Stan had a sudden sense of guilt. Everybody thought they were dead? And so they'd be telling Tan that that was so, and Naslan. "Is there some way you can communicate with Gateway? Because if there is I'd better get a message off to them right away."

Puzzlingly, Lon Alvarez gave Stan a doubtful look. "A message to who?"

"To the Gateway authorities, of course," Stan snapped. "They'll be waiting to hear from us."

Alvarez glanced at the Heechee, then back at Stan. "I don't think they're exactly waiting, Mr. Avery. You know you're in a black hole, don't you?"

"A black *hole?*" Stan blinked at the man, and heard Estrella make a little moan beside him.

The man nodded. "That's right. That's what the Core is, you know. It's a big black hole, where the Heechee went to hide long ago, and inside a black hole there's time dilation." He looked at Stan to see if he was following this, but Stan's muddled stare wasn't reassuring. Alvarez sighed. "That means things go slower inside a black hole. In this one, the dilation comes to about forty thousand to one, you see, so a lot of time has passed Outside while you were here. How much? Well, when we left it would have been about, let's see, about eleven years."

VIII

When Stan and Estrella could take no more, they staggered back to those queer Heechee beds. They didn't talk; there was too frighteningly much that needed to be talked about, and no good place for them to begin.

Estrella dropped off at once, but not Stan. His head was too full of arithmetic, and all the sums were scary. The man had said forty thousand to one! Why, that meant that every minute that passed here in the Heechee's Core was more than a *month* in the outside world! An hour was five *years!* A day would be over a century, a week would be—

But then fatigue would no longer be denied. He fell into an uneasy sleep, but it didn't last. There was too much haunting his dreams. But when he woke enough to reach out for Estrella her bunk was empty, and she was gone.

Stan staggered to his feet and went in search of her. It was urgent that he find her. Even more urgently there was only one thing that he really wanted, and that was for the two of them to get right back in their Five, if it would still work after everything the Heechee had done to it, and head for home . . . before everyone they knew was irrevocably dead and gone.

Estrella wasn't in the hallway, though there were voices coming from somewhere, lots of them. She wasn't in the room they had entered in, either, though there were plenty of Heechee there who were looking very busy, at what Stan could not say. One of the Heechee took pity on him. He led Stan, chattering cheerfully, with plenty of those reassuring shoulder pats, to still another entrance chamber. It was the biggest yet, and the most crowded, with a constant stream of Heechee going in and out of the port to a docked ship. The guide led Stan to the door and gently nudged him inside.

The ship was the biggest he'd ever seen, and it was full of people, both human and Heechee. When one of the humans looked up he saw that it was Estrella, and she was talking—yes, apparently talking—to a couple of Heechee. She beckoned Stan over, holding up a flask of something brown. "It's coffee, Stan," she said with pleasure. "They've got a great kitchen on the immigrant ship. Want some?"

"Sure," he said absently, staring at the Heechee. Incongruously, the creature was wearing a Texas sombrero, a sweatshirt that bore the legend *Welcome to Houston* and what looked like red and gold leather cowboy boots. He stuck out an affable hand to Stan.

"Great seeing you again, Mr. Avery," he said—in English! "I've been introducing your good wife to our exploration pilot, Achiever. He's about to go Outside on a very important mission, and we've been briefing him on conditions." When Stan stared dumbly, the Heechee said apologetically, "Oh, sure, you don't remember me, do you? My name is Gradient. I was the Doorwatcher in charge of the entry lock when you and Ms. Pancorbo arrived." And added proudly, "I went with the first party of ours to go Outside, as soon as we saw what was happening."

"Nice to see you again," Stan said faintly. "You, ah, speak English very well."

The Doorwatcher made a deprecating gesture with those skeletal hands. "I spent four years on your planet, so I had plenty of time to learn. Then when this ship was leaving to bring some of your people to the Core I came home." Someone was chattering urgently to him in the Heechee language. He replied briefly, then sighed. "I'd better get back to work. Achiever's about to leave and I've got to finish the briefing. And I'm anxious to see my significant persons, too. It's been a long time for me . . . though they don't even know I was gone!"

IX

Later on when Stan tried to remember that very long day, that forty-thousand-days-in-a-day day, its events and discoveries flew wildly around in his mind like infuriated bees when the hive is attacked. The surprises were too many and too great. The humans on that ship weren't captives or invaders. They were *immigrants*. They had come to the Core to visit the Heechee for a few days or weeks (which was to say, centuries!). Then that same ship was going to go right back to Earth for more. The Door—the floating dock they had come to—was already aswarm with other humans from previous ships, waiting for still other ships which would take them to one of the Heechee planets, where they would go on display for the fascinated Heechee people. Some of these arrivals were dignitaries from Gateway Corp or from one of the nations of Earth, now in the Core to open embassies from the human race to the Heechee. Some of them were simply people who hadn't liked the lives they had on Earth, and jumped at the chance to start new ones in the Core. "Like us, Stan," Estrella told him as he blearily tried to take it all in. "Like everybody who came to Gateway, and the wonderful thing is that they're going to get what they want here. The Heechee are wild to meet us, Stan. Every human being who gets here is going to live like a king." And then she added worriedly, "Drink your coffee, hon. I think they put something in it to wake us up. You'll need it."

They had. It did. When Stan had swallowed his second flask of the stuff, fatigue was banished, and his mind was racing. "What do you mean, live like a king?" he demanded.

"What I said, Stan," she said patiently—or not all that patiently; she was on overdrive, too, her eyes sparkling in a way Stan had never seen before. "They're *welcoming* us, Stan. They want to hear *everything* about the human race. They're fascinated by the idea that we have different nations and cultures and all. When I told the Doorwatcher about herding bison, he begged me to come to his own planet and talk about it—seems he'd missed that when he was on Earth. He says they'll give us our own home, and a *wonderful* home, too, and . . . and I don't think they know anything about Istanbul, either, or human history, and they'll want to hear it all from you—"

But Stan was shaking his head. "We won't have time," he announced.

Estrella stopped short, peering at him from under her dragging eyelid. "Why won't we?" she asked, suddenly shot down from her enthusiasm.

"Because we've got to be on that ship when it goes back, Estrella. We have to get there while we're still news, the first people to come back from the Core. Can you imagine what that will be worth? Not just the bonus— I bet that'll be *huge*—but we'll be famous! And rich, Full Medical and all!" He ran out of steam then, peering at Estrella's face, trying to read her expression. "Don't you see what we're missing, Estrella?"

She said contemplatively, "Full Medical. Long, rich lives. On Earth."

He nodded with vigor. "Exactly! And time is passing us by. We have to go back!"

Estrella took his hand and pressed it to her cheek. She asked simply, "Why?"

He blinked at her. "What do you mean, why?"

"Well, Stan," she said reasonably, "there's no real hurry, is there? What have we got to go back to that we won't have right here?"

"Our friends—" he began, but she shook her head. She kissed his hand before she released it and spoke.

"Have you looked at the time, dear? Our friends are getting old. They might even have died by now. You wanted to live a long, long time. Now we're doing it." She took pity on the look on his face and hugged him tightly. "Besides," she said persuasively, "we've come all this way. As long as we're here, we might as well see what the place looks like."

Stan found words at last. "How long?"

"Not long, if that's what you want. A week or two—"

"Estrella! That'll be—what? A thousand years or more on Earth!"

She nodded. "And by then maybe it'll be worth going back to."

3

Hunting the Hunters

I

Before Estrella and Stan ever got to the Core—indeed, when you factor that enormous 40,000-to-1 time difference into your calculations, long before they had even been born—a Heechee space pilot named Achiever was there already. That was because he lived there. He had lived in the Core all his life and had no desire ever to leave it. Achiever knew that there were a lot of highly interesting things Outside. However, he also knew how dangerous those interesting things might be, and so he had no more desire to see them for himself than did any other Heechee. (Not that Achiever thought of himself as a "Heechee." That was a human word. Achiever at that point had never heard it, and was not going to like it when he did.)

The flight for which Achiever was preparing certainly was not intended to take him Outside—though, curiously, his ship happened to be one of the few in the Heechee fleet that could actually have made the journey. It was also one of the larger Heechee ships, and so it would have flabbergasted any of those early Gateway prospectors if they had ever seen it. Any one of the Ones and Threes and Fives those early adventurers flew could have fit easily into one of its cargo holds.

Cargo was what Achiever's mission was all about. He was preparing to ferry essential supplies from the factories of the planet he was orbiting to the free-floating space station called Door. It was a run that he had made more than thirty times already, without a single accident of any kind and with no serious delays. For this reason Achiever had just been promoted. His new title might be translated as "Pilot Who Is Sufficiently Capable and Cautious to Be Both Permitted and Required to Instruct Others," and the physical evidence of his new status was standing there before him. Her name was Breeze. She was the very first student pilot he had had assigned to him for training.

Although Achiever had never had a trainee before, he knew what was expected of him. "Tell me, Breeze," he addressed her, his voice kindly but in the tone of one who had the right to ask, "what would you do if you were approaching an object such as Door and your lookplate flipped from nearspace to a panoramic view?"

She didn't hesitate. "First I would check the bias on the lookplate and correct it if needed. If that didn't work I would activate the standby plate. If that too was inoperative, I would abort the docking, enter a holding orbit and disassemble the lookplate for repair. Do you want me to tell you how I would go about troubleshooting the system?"

He flapped his wrists, the equivalent of a shake of a human head. "Not just yet. First I want to know why you didn't simply allow the automatic systems to land you."

"That is of course what I would do for a planet landing, provided we had already passed the planet's radiation shield, Achiever, but you specified a destination like Door. Even a small excess of velocity at docking might breach Door's hull integrity, with loss of interior pressure. I would not take that risk. Now would you like me to describe the troubleshooting?"

Indeed he would. He listened attentively to her reply, and to her answers to the other technical problems he posed for her. They were all satisfactory. He could have complimented her. He didn't. He simply said, "Let's finish getting the cargo on board, shall we?"

By that time the human female Estrella had been born on her parents' New Mexican ranch, a very long distance away. As Breeze activated the handlers and the cargo began to move out of the landers into the ship itself, the male human, Stan, also was born in the American embassy hospital in Ankara, and a youth named Robinette Broadhead was dismally wondering if there was any possible way for him to escape a lifetime of drudgery in the Wyoming food mines.

These particular persons were all human beings. Of course Achiever had never heard of any of them, yet.

By the time loading was complete, Achiever had decided that he liked Breeze—liked her not in any sexual way but simply because she was smart and diligent and willing.

This might have been thought curious by any young human male in the presence of a good-looking young female. To Achiever there was nothing curious about it. He was hardly even aware that Breeze was pleasingly broad in the shoulders and slim in the waist, with her soft, gray neck fuzz decorously brushed flat. All those things were true enough, but what was also true was that Breeze's female genital organs were not in their mating configuration. That being so, her attractive features hardly mattered.

It is a known fact that the Heechee were reasonably like humans in that, now and then, some of them liked sorts of sexual practices that others might conceivably describe as "kinky." Not that kinky, though. Very few Heechee males were perverted enough to desire intercourse with a female who wasn't in estrus.

Achiever waved Breeze to the seat beside his own. "You may perch here," he informed her in the language of Do, but then, less formally, he added in the language of Feel, "At this point I think I should begin the voyage, but probably at some later time I will allow you to run the controls."

"Thank you, Achiever," she said gratefully, stowing her pod in the space between the leaves of the perch and watching attentively—although, in truth, she had experienced the setting of a course many times in her previous training. As he perfectly well knew.

Achiever put his splayed fingers on the knurled control wheel. That produced an immediate display of colored light that would have baffled any human—that had indeed baffled thousands of humans in the ancient Gateway days when every new prospector had to confront the fact that those incomprehensible settings could make the difference between life and death for him.

With quick competency Achiever set the course, paused and asked, "What about temperature, humidity, trace gases, all those parameters? I usually let the settings go to default, but if you have any special preferences?"

"Default is acceptable," she assured him. "I generally do that, too. I wonder sometimes why we bother with those settings."

Achiever made a woofling sort of sound, partly of sympathy, partly of good-humored reproach. "Yes. One might wonder so. But if someday you have a passenger with a medical problem, or a cargo that can be damaged if the settings are wrong, then you will know why."

Abashed, Breeze watched in silence as he squeezed the start control. All the subsidiary wheels crawled to their default settings, and they were off.

Unlike the largest vessels in the Heechee fleet, Achiever's craft did not require a hand on the controls after launch. He sat back and regarded his charge. "I could not help but notice," he said mildly, "that you have shown interest in this craft's special feature." He gestured toward the twisted crystal rod that rose in the center of the control chamber.

"I paid close attention to your teaching, Achiever!"

"Of course you did," he said, "but you could hardly fail to notice it, could you? You may have thought it was a penetrator, to let us through planetary radiation screens?"

"It does not look like one, Achiever."

"No," he agreed. "It does not. You've probably never seen one before. It is an order disruptor."

He expected a reaction to that. It took a moment, but then it came. "Oh," she said, and then, "Oh!"

"Yes," he said, with the shoulder shrug that was the Heechee equivalent of a human nod of sympathy. "It is the instrument that the generation of our parents used to transit into aligned systems." (Which is to say, in human terms, black holes. The Heechee didn't see them as holes, though. To be fair, even a human would have had to admit that, with all the radiation from infalling material, they were hardly ever black, either.) "You need not be alarmed," he added. "Naturally we are not going to be using it for that purpose. It is an interesting fact, however, that it is fully functional."

She was looking at it now with full attention. "There was nothing like that on any of the spacecraft I learned on," she said, sounding almost apprehensive.

"Of course there wasn't. There is no need for such things here, because there are no aligned systems here in the Core—other, of course, than the Core itself. None were brought in from the external galaxy at the time of the Withdrawal. For that reason, none of our newer spacecraft have anything of this sort, except for the very few scoutcraft that patrol the outside galaxy from time to time. This particular spacecraft is quite old, you know. It is in excellent condition, certainly, or else it would not have been given the important task of supplying Door, but it happens to have been built before our ancestors migrated here. There is much history in this spacecraft, Breeze. It is likely that when it was new this order disrupter you see before you penetrated many a Schwarzschild"—he didn't use the word "Schwarzschild," of course, but what he was talking about was the light-trapping shell around a black hole that humans called by that term—"penetrated many a Schwarzschild barrier in the days before the Withdrawal. The system was left intact, as you see it there, simply because there was no reason to remove it. In any case," he went on, "I'm glad our ship still has it installed. Every student pilot should learn how this model of the order disrupter works—in case, you know, a time when it might be of value should ever come."

He watched her expression approvingly. There was no further sign of nervousness, though the mere thought of breaking through the perimeters of the enormous black hole they lived in was still scary for any Heechee. Then, practically, "Now let us recheck the stowage of our cargo."

She shrugged assent and touched the viewer controls. The first icons that appeared represented tanks of liquid atmospheric gases—replenishments for Door's air supply; the station was nearly gas-tight but there was always some leakage. Other icons represented personal effects for Door's permanent party, still others water and fuel. Breeze reported: "They are all secure, Achiever. Do you want anything else checked?"

Achiever touched his fingertips to his thin lips—it was the equivalent of a yawn. "I think not, not right now. However, since there are two of us, I suggest that one of us should remain in the control chamber at all times."

Breeze looked perplexed. "Is that necessary, Achiever?"

"Necessary? Perhaps not, but it is what I wish." He was pleased to see that that settled the matter for her; she would be a credit to him as his first student. He went on, "I will take the first shift, Breeze. You may wish to sleep, or to make yourself a meal—our food manufactury is quite good. Or perhaps you would like to avail yourself of the ship's library. I have chosen the library's fans personally, and I think you will find enjoyable reading there. Which would you prefer?"

Breeze considered for a moment, then said, "I would like best, Achiever, simply to stay here and watch you for a time. How else am I to learn?"

She could not have chosen a better response. Achiever was once again well pleased with his trainee, and remained so throughout his shift. There was little enough for her to watch, of course. The ship flew itself. But while Achiever himself was reading, or eating, or chatting with his student, he always kept one eye on the screen, just in case, and Breeze was suitably impressed.

Later on, when it was Achiever's resting time, he crawled into his bundle of sleeping grasses—they weren't real grasses, of course, because real vegetation might release pollens that would pollute the spacecraft's air, but they were manufactured to look and feel as much like grass as anything the primitive forebears of the Heechee race had plucked and wrapped around themselves when they found a moment to rest. Achiever didn't let the grasses cover his face, though. He kept his eyes on Breeze. She was doing well, he thought with satisfaction.

And continued to think so through the next shift, and the next.

It wasn't until they were almost at their destination that anything happened to worry him. He was in his sleeping bundle, this time really asleep, when the urgent-message bell rang.

Well, it wasn't a bell and it didn't ring, it growled. But no matter. Its sound meant that something somewhere was very amiss. It had never sounded before in Achiever's experience, and he was fighting his way out of his sleep bundle almost before it stopped. Even so, Breeze was before him. The communicator had begun to flicker, rapidly and frighteningly, in the bright green that announced an urgent message, as did every other communicator in the Core at the same moment.

Breeze was scanning the message screen with an expression somewhere between stupefaction and horror. "What is it?" Achiever demanded, and she looked at him in bewilderment.

"There have been visitors," she said, every muscle writhing under her skin at once. "They are on Door now, but they are not Heechee. They are visitors who have come from Outside, and they are of another species, not our own."

II

Achiever didn't go back to sleep. Neither did Breeze. Nor did any other Heechee on the night-time sides of any of the hundreds of inhabited planets of the Core's thousands of captive suns. *Visitors?* From *Outside?* No, there wasn't much sleep for any Heechee after that news had spread. What there was instead was something close to terror. When the view screens displayed the actual images of these actual intruders the terror was mixed with gut-wrenching revulsion. The alien creatures were sickening to look upon. They were horrible travesties of the Heechee form, bloated, hairy, altogether hideous.

The rest of Breeze and Achiever's flight was brief. When their ship docked at Door, they discovered that the situation had become even worse. The people of Door's permanent party were running about in confusion, and alarming fresh news was arriving, it seemed, every minute. Another ship had come in from outside! No, now there were two of the alien ships—no, three! And one of those ships had not only brought more of these "humans," as they called themselves, but even a couple of Heechee who had been Outside on a scout patrol ship.

The resulting wild confusion was un-Heecheeishly total. There were no handlers at the landing dock to arrange the unloading of Achiever's cargo. Worse, there weren't any instructions from the dispatch officer about their return flight, either. So Achiever left Breeze with the ship and went looking for the dispatcher, but when he reached the dispatcher's quarters the man wasn't there—wasn't where anyone could say, because who knew where anybody was in this madhouse? A madhouse it was. The orderly calm that usually marked the activities of the outpost—indeed, that had always marked almost all of the transactions of the Heechee race, from the beginning of time to this moment—had vanished, destroyed by the news that had taken the whole Heechee race unaware. News of any kind from Outside was rare. But this news was *terrifying*!

On the other hand, Achiever told himself as he fought his way through the disorderly throng, perhaps they should have been less surprised. After all, you always knew that someday someone might suddenly appear from Outside. You knew it in the same way that you knew that someday you would die and join the Massed Minds, or that, someday, that ill-chosen F-type star the Heechee had brought with them into the Core might grow unstable, and if it did do that, then great damage could be done for a considerable volume of space around it. But you certainly didn't expect such a thing to happen now. Never now!

The good part, of course, was that the news could have been much, much worse. These hideous and unexpected creatures from Outside were quite horrible, with their bloated bodies and flabby faces. But they definitely were not, indeed were not anything like, the ones who were called "the Assassins" or "the Foe," those disembodied energy creatures who had decimated the living population of the galaxy before the Withdrawal. The appearance of these new aliens was revolting, yes, but they were not destroying anything.

Achiever did the best he could to reassure himself. He had one never-failing resource for such problems. It was time for him to consult it.

He found a corner to huddle in and called for help from the Stored Mind in the pod that hung between his wide-set, skinny thighs. "Ancestral Mind," he said, trying to keep the turmoil out of his voice, "awaken and help me, please. What are these creatures?"

The Stored Mind took a moment to answer, and then it—it was actually a she—sounded grumpy. "One moment, Achiever," she said.

Achiever expected no more from that particular ancestor. She had been stored for a long time, and, Achiever thought, was beginning to show it. It took a perceptible couple of seconds before there was a response. The ancestor's tired voice said, "Forgive me, Achiever. I have been resting. I am now querying other Stored Minds about the nature of your question—" Then, with a sort of hiccough, the voice abruptly changed tone. "Achiever!" she said more strongly. "They are indeed from Outside! There is much confusion among the Stored Minds on this question! I am attempting to find a consensus." The voice sounded startled, even worried—though Stored Minds never sounded startled, and especially not worried, since they no longer had anything to worry about.

When she spoke again the voice was less worried, but no less confused. "This is quite puzzling, Achiever," she said. "These new aliens appear to be the remote descendants of some kind of presentient being from the time before the retreat—perhaps, it is said, descendants of the race of hairy bipeds one of our survey ships had turned up on one not very interesting planet before the Withdrawal."

"They aren't all that hairy," Achiever objected.

"It has been a long time for them, Outside. They have evolved. Now they appear to be civilized, at least to a degree." Then the tone changed again. "Achiever, should you not be helping to deal with this matter instead of spending your time in idle curiosity?"

Achiever accepted the rebuke and terminated the linkup. He could not, however, stop thinking about the aliens, even as he continued on his quest for the dispatcher. Civilized? Yes, they could be called civilized, he thought. In fact, they seemed to be even technologically sophisticated enough to have mastered interstellar flight on their own. . . .

Well, no, not exactly that, he corrected himself. They hadn't done it on their own. The word was that their first ships were clearly Heechee-made, undoubtedly some of the handful of ships that the Heechee themselves had left behind long ago.

That made Achiever wonder. Had it been a mistake? Would it not have been better to let the primitives do their own inventing?

Achiever didn't want to think such thoughts. That was coming close to accusing the ancestral Stored Minds of committing an error. That was not only unfair, but, by every lesson he had ever been taught, quite impossible. The Massed Minds were never wrong.

Achiever was glad when the dispatcher at last appeared, emerging from a knot of supplicants with three of his subordinates hanging on his arm and demanding answers to urgent questions. He shook them all off when he saw Achiever. "You," he said. "Your ship is in the third amber-gold dock. It is being offloaded to prepare it for your expedition."

Expedition? Achiever opened his mouth to ask what expedition the dispatcher was talking about, but he was hurrying on. "See that the off-loading is finished, and that your own stores are put on board as quickly as possible. You have a copilot to relieve you when necessary, do you not? Good. Once your ship is ready, you are to wait for a passenger, who will have additional equipment to be stowed. Then you are to launch at once."

"Yes, certainly," Achiever said, his abdominal muscles twisting in eager assent. "But where am I to launch to?"

The dispatcher gave him an incredulous stare, then shook his head. "Where do you think we are sending you? Outside, of course. Why else would we have chosen your ship?"

Quickly they went, straight up and out, out through the shell that enclosed the Core, the ship shuddering wildly, throwing them against their restraints, and the twisted crystal rod firing off its showers of sparks that didn't burn, didn't last, didn't seem to do anything at all except mark the fact that they were *going Outside.* It was like nothing Achiever had ever experienced before. A faint sound from Breeze, almost a whimper, told him that she was hit as hard as himself. Her face was dark with—not with fright, no, but at least with a severe case of worry. And when the fat sparks sputtered and died away, and the jolting stopped, and they all three were staring at the lookplate, Breeze was the first to speak. "How very . . . many stars there are," she said.

Indeed there were countless stars out there, so many that they seemed to coalesce into one vast milky mist of starshine. Even their passenger was held to the plate. "I did not expect to see this spectacle again in my life," he said softly, more to himself than to the pilots.

Achiever turned away from the lookplate to gaze at him. The passenger, whose name was Burnish, was old, older than almost anyone Achiever had ever met, his scalp fuzz no longer gray but turned a muddy white. But he was a long way from frail. He returned Achiever's stare, then flapped his hands. "Perhaps you would like to see for yourself," he offered. "One moment and I will show you."

He gestured Achiever away from his pilot's perch and took his place. Carefully he set the control wheels to a new position. On the lookplate a colorful overlay sprang into existence, first a line of tiny orange course-marking bubbles, with the fishhooks and arrowheads that marked navigational features. Burnish pointed with one bony hand.

"We will proceed on this course that I have set until we are farther from the Core," he said. "Then, you will see, the stars will be much more sparse and it will be easy to observe them optically. Do you have any other questions?"

He was looking at Breeze, but it was Achiever who answered. "One question, yes," he said. "We are Outside now. Isn't there more you should tell us?"

The old one looked him over carefully, his mouth widening with thought. Then he reached a decision. "Of course," he said. "It is your right to know. The reason we have come into the Outside galaxy is that we are conducting a search which is of great importance to all our race—indeed to all intelligent living things everywhere. What we are searching for is the present location of the Foe."

III

When they grew hungry, they ate. When they grew tired, they slept—both pilots at the same time, although in their separate nests, and neither mentioned Achiever's preference for having someone always at the controls. And Burnish did not reappear.

Which left them plenty of time to consider the meaning of what he had said, and to contemplate its consequences.

If the thought of pursuing those creatures called the Assassins, or sometimes simply the Foe, terrified Achiever, it was no discredit to him. He was as brave as any other Heechee in the Core—which is to say, not very, except in such exceedingly rare times when bravery was absolutely necessary.

This seemed to be one of those times. If it was true that they were going to track down the Foe, that faceless, formless embodiment of evil that had haunted every Heechee's nightmares, then Achiever was going to have to use up quite a lot of bravery. He would also have to have more information about the nature of this horror they were trying to track down. Since he couldn't ask Burnish, he sought other sources, pulling down from the shelves of the ship's library one after another of the crystalline fans that were the Heechee equivalent of books. As he fed them, one by one, into the reading machines, the first thing he was looking for was the record of those intelligent galactic races that had been found by Heechee explorers to have gone suddenly and violently extinct, thus leading to the discovery of the source of those extinctions and thus, very soon afterward, to the Heechee's Withdrawal to the Core.

But after Achiever had scanned every document on the subject he still had not found answers for all the questions in his mind, so he turned to the Stored Mind in the pod that hung between his wide-set, skinny thighs. As he tapped the pod's medallion, "Ancestral Mind," he said to the air, but knowing the mind would hear, "is there no additional information on this race?"

The Stored Mind took a moment to answer, and then she still sounded annoyed at being disturbed. "One moment, Achiever," she said. And then: "The file you were just accessing dealt with the race of amphibious lizard-like creatures who had managed to send person-carrying rockets into their nearby space before their whole population was wiped out overnight. Is it additional material on them that you seek?"

"Exactly," Achiever said.

"There isn't any," said the Stored Mind, and went silent.

Gloomily Achiever checked the time. It was the period when it would be appropriate to sleep again, and still no sign of Burnish. As he burrowed into his nest he thought sourly that he probably would have insomnia, and if he did get to sleep his dreams would be unpleasant.

They weren't, though. He dropped off at once, and if he had any dreams at all he was not aware of them.

When Achiever awoke, he did what any Heechee did upon arising: he removed the pod that held his Ancient Ancestor in order to void his wastes; he replaced it when through and brushed himself clean; he put on a fresh tunic and tossed the old one into the laundering machine; he snipped off a few shoots of the vine that grew over the door and chewed them for a moment before discarding them, his teeth now satisfactorily oiled; he ordered a morning-menu selection from the food machine and consumed it. Its textures and flavors were of the sorts he was on record as preferring, and he ate it with as much pleasure as on any normal day. In fact, nothing in his actions suggested this day was anything out of the way at all.

Achiever had not suddenly stopped being afraid. He had simply reached a state of acceptance. Since he could not rid himself of the fear, he had done the next best thing; he had made up his mind to live with it, and get on with his life.

When he entered the control chamber, Breeze was perched on the pilot's rest, a couple of reading fans in her hands, gazing glumly at the lookplate. He greeted her in the language of Feel, and added: "You have been reading up on the Foe, haven't you?"

She looked at him almost angrily. "I have done that, of course," she told him, "but there wasn't much to learn, was there? They killed off sentient races; our ancestors thought they would kill us if they found us; so we ran into the Core to hide. Is there anything else?"

"Not much," Achiever admitted.

"That's what I thought. So then I decided to do something more useful, so I checked out the course Burnish laid for us, so at least I would have some idea of where we were going."

Achiever could feel the dense fur at the back of his head bristle in the startlement reflex. Why, of course! Clearly that was the most sensible thing to do, and why had he not thought of it himself? "And what did you find?" he asked.

She shrugged her belly muscles irritably and touched the control console. A 3-D plot of the galaxy sprang up at once. "There," she said. "But it means nothing to me."

Achiever studied it. It was a model to scale, which meant it could show almost no detail. What there was was a bright string of orange course-marking bubbles, like the beads on a child's toy necklace that began among the thick wash of starlight at the Galaxy's center. The first quarter or so of it was unremarkable, arrowing straight out of the dense galactic center. Then it looped around three or four of the dozen snakey galactic arms and the relatively barren spaces between them, until it ended partway out one of the arms.

"If that line is our course," Achiever said slowly, "we seem to be getting to our destination in a pretty roundabout way." And from behind him another voice said:

"So it is, Achiever. Would you care to try to guess why?"

Both the pilots turned to see Burnish entering the control chamber. He seemed rested and at ease. "Well, Achiever?" he said. "Or you, Breeze?"

"We're looking for something that will lead us to the Foe," she said, a beat before Achiever was about to make the same guess.

"I hope it will not actually lead to a confrontation," Burnish said wryly, "but, yes, that is the general plan. However, before we can even begin we must go out some distance from the Core. That is where the living things are. It is only out where the stars are farther apart that life can evolve, Breeze. Here in the center of the galaxy nothing organic exists. The radiation is far too intense for organic life to survive."

Breeze looked puzzled. "I didn't think the Foe were organic life, exactly."

"No, they are not. But their prey is."

He glanced at Achiever, who had just straightened up with a baffled expression on his leathery face. "Do you have a problem?" Burnish asked.

"No. That is, yes. I mean I just remembered, didn't the explorers find that the Foe had holed up in a sort of aligned system that was actually outside the galaxy?"

"They did. We did, that is, since I was one of those explorers. The Foe were found to be in a cluster of such systems just outside the galactic halo."

"Then what are we looking for?" Achiever demanded.

"We are looking to make sure that they are still there," Burnish said somberly. He looked thoughtful for a moment, then his belly muscles rippled in the equivalent of a shrug. "Come into my chamber, both of you. Let me show you what I have been doing."

The small chunks of unidentifiable instrumentation that Burnish had brought aboard had now been assembled into larger masses of unidentifiable instrumentation. A pile of blue-glowing boxes were stacked against one wall, the one at the top displaying a lookplate like the lookplate over the piloting module, but blank. Against another wall was a lustrous silvery cage, and within it a jagged diamond. Burnish touched a knurled wheel and the wall lookplate lit up, displaying a pebbly gray field. "It might be better if I had some help here," he said, "so perhaps I had best teach you two how to do this. Watch." As he adjusted the wheel the gray dissolved, and they were looking at the same exterior scene of the central galaxy. No, Achiever corrected himself, not quite the same. This lookplate narrowed the field and increased the magnification; now individual stars were visible, and many showed actual disks.

"You know," Burnish said professorially, "that each voyage of a highspeed ship like ours leaves a sort of ripple in space behind it?"

"I have been taught this, yes," Achiever said, and Breeze nodded.

"Then let me show you what these ripples look like." He made other adjustments. The magnification increased again, while the stars themselves faded slightly. Breeze gasped, and then Achiever saw it too. Images like bundles of pinkly luminous straws showed among the stars. What they resembled most of all was what human scientists would have called Feynman diagrams. As no one in the ship had ever heard of Richard Feynman nor his graphic displays of the summation of probabilities, they only called them "representations of potential loci."

"Those are signatures of such faster-than-light travel," Burnish went on. "As it happens, our ships leave a particular identifiable signature, like those you are looking at; those are the ripples left by the transit of known ships, all of them our own. The tracks of the Assassins' ships are quite different. If," he corrected himself, "the Assassins have ships of any kind at all; it is not clear what means they employed to travel through space. Those artifactual signatures, however, do exist. Or at least they did, because they were observed and identified at the time of the Withdrawal. Some of them I observed myself. Such artifacts may take thousands of years to dissipate, and it is for those that I seek."

"I see," Achiever said, and then it was his turn to correct himself. "That is, there is one point that is unclear to me. You spoke of some thousands of years, but we were inside the Core for much longer than that. Is it not likely that they will all have dissipated by now?"

"Oh, I hope not," Burnish said gloomily. "Because if the traces are gone we will have to start looking in places I do not wish to visit."

IV

As the days passed the lookplate displays thinned out. What had been an undistinguishable fog of white now became a sprinkle of countless single stars—white ones or golden, bright-hot blue or darkly smoldering red. It became possible to isolate individual stars among them and even to see which ones had planets, though none of the orbiting worlds Achiever detected seemed likely to have borne life. "Planets are common enough," Burnish assured his crew, "but life is not." Which, Achiever thought, made those ancient crimes of the Foe even worse; if life was rare, how much more horrid was its violent extinction?

At the beginning of each watch he made sure to display the plot of their ship's course in order to keep track of their progress; on the display the portion of their course they had already traveled was pale pink, the part yet to come in that shocking orange. But how slowly the pink line lengthened, and how depressingly long the orange remained!

When, in the old days, Achiever had found himself thinking about what might be Outside of the Core—which was not all that often, because he had had more than enough to think about in his everyday life on Three-Moon Largely Wet Planet, and in his regular job of flying back and forth to the other planets of other stars that were his usual destinations—

when, that is to say, Achiever had thought about the matter at all, perhaps stimulated by those lessons that he had thought would never be put to use, on running the order disrupter—when, anyway, he had thought about what it would be like to really be Outside, the single thing that had seemed oddest to him was the incredibly rapid pace of events as they went on Outside the Core.

Now, however, he actually was Outside, and it did not seem that way at all. His fellow passengers did not flit rapidly about. They moved, as Heechee generally moved, sedately and not really very fast by any standard. Neither did those planets their instruments detected as they passed by spin dizzyingly around their primaries. Nor did the stars themselves wink when they were variables, nor visibly bloat and decay when they were supergiants.

But the difference in the rate of time was real enough on the personal level, and it made Achiever glum. Sometimes, as he burrowed into his sleep nest at the end of a shift, it occurred to him that he would sleep and wake and work and sleep again a dozen times in a time that, back on his own planet, would be measured by a single beat in either of his hearts.

Not only was time not passing faster than was normal. Sometimes it seemed to have stagnated entirely. Those were the times when Achiever woke to a work day that was different in no respect from the day that had gone before it. And when at last something did happen that hadn't happened a dozen times before, it was a development of an unanticipated kind.

Breeze had just brought him a meal. She reported that Burnish had once again refused his own food. "He is quite obsessed," she told Achiever as they shared their own spicy protein and sweet carbohydrates in the pretty pastel colors Breeze herself had chosen. "I think he wishes he could find that the Assassins are still roaming the galaxy somewhere. If it were me, I would have no such feelings. I would hope they had never stirred from their hideaway."

Achiever considered that, then gave the belly-writhing that was the Heechee equivalent of a shrug. "I suppose he knows what he is doing."

"I suppose," she agreed. "He seemed pretty worried, though." She chewed for a moment, then said reflectively, "Do I imagine this or is this food unusually tasty?"

"How surprising!" Achiever exclaimed. "I was on the point of making the same observation to you." And what was most surprising about that, to both of them, was that taste in CHON-food was not a variable. Unless the specifications were changed, which Breeze denied, the flavor of any particular form of CHON-food remained identically the same year in and year out. Amused at the thought, Achiever widened his mouth in the Heechee equivalent of a smile. He noticed that Breeze was smiling back at him. Charmingly. Almost enticingly. . . .

Enticingly?

The muscles under Achiever's cheek skin suddenly stilled. Realization came; of course! The food wasn't unusually tasty, Breeze's smile no different from any other time. What colored everything for him—for both of them—was simply pheromones.

As soon as that thought crossed his mind he saw what he had not noticed before. The color of Breeze's skin had perceptibly darkened. In some places—the hollow of her throat, the eyelids—it had become almost purplish.

She was, without warning, coming into sexual season.

The mating customs of the Heechee were thoroughly civilized. When an available male and a sexually receptive female were proximate, they did not at once spring into copulation. The process took time. From the first signs of approaching receptivity to the culminating act seldom took less than a full day, sometimes—particularly when the female was young—as much as ten days, or even more. And Breeze was still quite young. So at this early stage nothing sexual passed between Achiever and Breeze. Well, nothing overt. Covert, however, you bet. When Breeze had finished eating the pale blue and crunchy part of the meal it was Achiever who unwrapped and handed her the sweet, gummy next course. When Breeze accepted it she allowed her skinny forefinger to rest for a moment on the back of his wrist.

Things might have progressed farther—a little—but that was the moment when Burnish chose to join them. He wore an expression Achiever could not read—sorrowful? Yes, probably that was one description, but also he looked even more worn and worried than usual. The muscles of his cheek working agitatedly, but he brought up short in the doorway, sniffing curiously.

Although jealousy is not a very marked Heechee trait, it would be untrue to suggest that Achiever failed to take note of Burnish's actions. But Burnish's evident worry was considerable—not to mention, Achiever thought to himself, that old Burnish must have been nearly past the maximally sexual phase of life. His worries overrode Breeze's pheromones. "I have made a decision," he said sternly. "We must accept the fact that there are no recent traces of the Assassins."

Achiever was not wholly distracted from his new concerns, but he gave Burnish a puzzled look. "But surely," he said, "that is welcome news?"

The old one paused, seeming to weigh the question in his mind, and, Achiever thought, taking a lot longer to do it than seemed reasonable. At length he exhaled through his nose. "It is better news, perhaps, than if we had found evidence they had come out," he said meditatively, "but it means that you and I must do certain things that I would have preferred to avoid. Two of us must inspect the place where the Foe have hidden themselves, and make sure that they are still there."

He crossed the room to the lookplate and touched its knurled knob. At once it displayed the assorted blobs that marked the Foe's hiding place. "There is the Kugelblitz," he said—well, of course "Kugelblitz" is not the word he used; it was simply the word that humans would come to use once they had learned that such things existed. But Burnish's explanation was very much how a human physicist would have described it: "The Assassins are creatures of energy, not matter. Energy, however, also has mass. Consequently the nature of the locus into which they have withdrawn is an aligned system"—a "black hole," we would say—"of their own, one in which the density of the energy it contains has created it."

Breeze seemed more exhilarated than frightened by the news, even after Burnish added, "Our visit will not be a simple look-and-depart. No," he said somberly, "the two of us who do this must remain for a significant period of time, perhaps a year, perhaps more, so that we can make as sure as we can that the Foe are staying inside their hole. Achiever, you have a question?"

"You said two of us. What about the third?"

Burnish looked away. "As you may know," he said, "at the time of the Withdrawal we left a number of small ships in various places around the galaxy. One particular cache of them was discovered, and those ships have been used, by that other species which has just visited us. Each ship, of course, records all its flights. Each of those records must be checked to see if they have any data regarding the Assassins. So one of us will need to go there and access all available records, while the other two go to observe the place of the Foe." He glanced at Achiever, who knew before the words were spoken what they were going to be. "That one person remaining there, Achiever," he said, "will be you."

4

Three Days on Door

I

Here is what Stan and Estrella discovered: it was one thing to be the very first visitors from Outside ever to have crashed in on the flabbergasted Heechee. It was quite another thing just to be two out of dozens of them . . . then out of scores . . . then to be merely a tiny fraction of a flood of more visitors than either Stan or Estrella could count. Especially when most of the other visitors had a lot more interesting things to say than either Estrella or Stan.

They weren't neglected, exactly. Now and then some particularly kindly Heechee might pause in its dash from one part of Door to another long enough to inquire if they needed additional food or drink, or a place to relieve their bladders. But if the answer was no, that was the end of it, and that particular Heechee was gone, never to be seen again. "Or," Stan said moodily, "maybe it's the same one every time, because how do you tell them apart?"

Estrella didn't give him an answer to that, because she didn't have one. Some of the Heechee were considerate enough to wear something unusual about their costume—an unexpected color of the tunic, a gewgaw around their thin necks, an unusual pattern on the eight-sided medallion they wore on their undignified between-the-legs pouches—unusual enough that Estrella could keep it in her mind for a time, but not usually for a very long time.

This place they called "Door" was really getting crowded. Ship traffic seemed to be heavy both ways, plenty of Heechee ships heading Out into the great external galaxy, even more ships coming in. Sometimes these latter were returning Heechee back from hastily surveying the outside worlds, but by the second day, more and more often they were ships with human crews. And those were just the ships that had slipped through the Schwarzschild barrier in one direction or the other. Local traffic was heavier still. Ships were coming to Door from all over the Core, either because they were needed for some Heechee purpose Estrella could not imagine, or simply because Door was where the excitement was. The *extreme* excitement. In fact just about the only real excitement the Heechee race had known for that whole generation that had passed since they had hidden themselves in the Core.

It was no wonder that half the Heechee race seemed to want to come and share in it.

After spending so many dull and lonely days in the cramped space of their souped-up old Five, Stan and Estrella weren't averse to a little company. Not necessarily this company, though, with their skull-bare heads and squeezed-flat bodies. The press of alien bodies cramped their style.

As their second day in this bizarre new place became their third, the problem began to be acute. During the many days they had been locked up in their spartan Five Stan had rarely suffered boredom because, when all else failed, there had always remained one always delightful, never-failing source of entertainment for the two of them.

But that was then. This was now. *Now* Estrella demurred whenever Stan put a friendly hand on her, because there was always the chance, often a very good chance, that some Heechee would burst in to catch them at some private moment.

Then the bad situation got worse.

As the crowding increased, the two humans could no longer be spared a chamber of their own. Their room now had to be shared with two, three, even more fellow tenants, Heechee tenants, who might look as though they were sound asleep in their bundles of fake vegetation, but were as likely as not to be peering out at the strangers.

At least Estrella thought they might, and that was just as bad. She didn't even seem to want to cuddle, either, not with those skeletal snorers in the same room. Even more perplexing to Stan was that Estrella, who on the trip had given as much attention to lovemaking as Stan himself, now didn't seem to regret its absence. The novelty of the place excited her. She was trying to learn a few words of the Heechee language, without success. Fortunately there were humans arriving who spoke Heechee and, wonderfully, even a few Heechee who spoke English. It seemed that Estrella had met one or two of them.

In fact, she made a friend.

Stan found this out while he was standing in the hallway, looking up and down to see where Estrella had gotten herself this time. A Heechee approached purposefully. This Heechee was taller and heavier than most but was, Stan was pretty sure, female. "Are you the Stan person?" she asked—blessedly, in English! "By my name I am called Salt, and I have an inviting for you. That is inviting to come to my home in valley below Shining Mica Mountains, on Forested Planet of Warm Old Star Twenty-Four. Climate will have been to your liking. Diurnal cycle, same. And there many persons of my species are extremely eager to meet persons of your species. To live there with us. For, if this is your wish, all of your life."

"Not a chance," Stan said at once, thinking that was a pretty hateful proposition—live the rest of his life as a spectacle for a planet of nosy scarecrows!—and almost immediately changing his mind because it did seem a lot better than anything they had going for them here on Door. "I mean, uh—well, I'll have to ask Estrella about that before I can say one way or another. She's gone off somewhere, I don't know who with—"

"Was with I," said Salt. "Has agreed pending confirmation. Now up to you."

II

Salt had spent some eighteen months Outside, mostly on Peggys Planet, Estrella told him when she came back. "That's where she learned English. Notice anything different about me?"

She pirouetted before him, waiting for a response. He didn't have one, so he tried the standard male cop-out: "You look prettier than ever, hon."

Estrella seemed resigned. "Not *me*, I mean. My *dress*. Salt helped me let it out, out of human-being clothes she brought home from Peggys Planet. Do you like it?"

"Of course I do," Stan said, doing his best to be reasonable, "but is that what we want to talk about right now?"

"Not if you don't want to. I was just thinking that, you know, you've never seen me in a real dress before. Salt has lots of them, too. You can see them on the ship."

Stan didn't have to say, *What do you mean, on the ship? What ship?*

The expression on his face said it for him, and Estrella answered just as though he had asked it out loud. "The ship to Forested Planet of Warm Old Star Twenty-Four, of course. I'm sure we'll like it." She paused, then remembered the other thing she wanted to tell him. "Oh, yes. Salt says it's a big ship. Big enough so that you and I will have a room of our own."

The ship was big indeed. Stan was sure of that, although all he could see of the spacecraft's outside was the metal snout that protruded into its docking bay, like the lander on a Gateway ship. This one didn't seem to be a lander, though. When they got into it they found themselves in a spindle-shaped chamber with Heechee resting-props scattered about, three separate control carrels with knurled boards and viewscreens and two two-meter tall pillars stuffed with racks of, of all things, those rolled-up crystalline things the Gateway people called prayer fans. A young male Heechee was perched before one of the control boards. He looked up as Salt led them in, and spoke briskly to her. She replied in more placating tones, but without apparent success. She turned to Stan and Estrella. "He, whose name is called by Dark Smoke, wants that you two go away," she said.

"Why?" asked Stan, but Estrella took his hand.

"Come on," she whispered softly. "We don't want to make trouble." Sulkily he let her lead him back toward the outer bay, but the Heechee female, who had turned back to the male, caught sight of what they were doing.

"Stop at once," she said. "Where do you wish to go?" And then, when Estrella tried to explain that they were leaving the ship, as ordered, "No, do not do that. It is not the needed thing at this time. Dark Smoke has no adequate authority of this sort to deny you passage. You will wait while I discuss."

Discuss the two Heechee did, for rather longer than seemed reasonable to Stan. A third Heechee appeared from the entrance and immediately joined in the debate. They weren't shouting at each other, as Stan would have expected from humans trying to settle a controversial point, but all three of them sounded quite insistent as they gestured toward each other, toward the human pair and toward one of the doors at the end of the chamber.

Then the argument stopped, as though cut off by some invisible stage director, and Salt came back to the humans. "I will direct you to place of privacy chamber now," she said. "You will follow."

Estrella tarried. "What was the problem, Salt?"

"No problem. No problem now," the Heechee corrected herself. "You go to chamber. We start spacecraft. You come out later, if you so want. One thing only. If during trip to Forested Planet of Warm Old Star Twenty-Four you see male dressed in peculiar clothing who also is passenger you do not speak to him. He extremely tired of your kind."

5

A Home for the Old Ones

I

Let me tell you what really happened with this annoying young guy. He came into the reservation while we were busy, bold as brass. He didn't belong there, and as soon as I had a moment I was going to tell him so. But just then we were too busy to pay him much attention. We were aversion-training a leopard cub.

That always takes all the attention we have. This particular cub was a healthy little male, no more than a week old. That's a little bit young to begin the aversion training, but we'd been tracking the mother, looking for a good opportunity, since she began showing the signs that she was about to give birth. When we spotted the mother this day she had dropped off to sleep in a convenient place, at the edge of a patch of brush that wasn't large enough to conceal any other leopards. So we jumped the gun a little. We doped the mother with an airgun and borrowed her cub while she slept.

That is a job that takes all three of us. Shelly was the one who picked up the baby. Shelly was completely covered, and sweating, in a gas-proof isolation suit so the cub wouldn't get any memories of a friendly human smell. Brudy kept an eye on the mother so we wouldn't have any unpleasant surprises from her—the mother had had her own aversion training long before, but if she had awakened and seen us messing with her cub she might have broken through it.

I was the head ranger. That was because I had the best "resume" when they were hiring. In fact I had a D.V.M. Although the Old Ones weren't exactly animals, they weren't exactly people either, so a veterinarian seemed like the right person for the job. As boss, I was the one who manipulated the aversion-training images. These were 3-D simulations of an Old One, a human and a Heechee, one after another, along with a cocktail of smells of each that was released as we displayed the images. There was also a sharp little electric shock each time that made the kit yowl and struggle feebly in Shelly's arms.

Aversion training isn't actually a hard job. We do it four or five times for each cub, just to make sure, but long before we're through with the training the animals'll do their best to run away as fast as they can from any one of the images or smells, whether they're simulations or the real thing. Which is what they're supposed to do.

I don't mind handling leopard cubs. They're pretty clean, because the mother licks them all day long. So are cheetahs. The ones that really stink are the baby hyenas; that's when whoever holds the animal is glad that the gas-proof suit works in both directions. As far as other predators are concerned, lions and wild dogs are long extinct in this part of the Rift Valley, so the leopards, hyenas and cheetahs are the only carnivores the Old Ones have to worry about on their reservation. Well, and snakes. But the Old Ones are smart enough to stay away from snakes, which aren't likely to chase them, anyway, since the Old Ones are a lot too big for them to eat. Oh, and I should mention the crocs, too. But we can't train crocodiles very reliably, not so you could count on their running the other way if an Old One wandered near. So what we do is train the Old Ones themselves to stay away.

What helps us there is that the Old Ones are sort of genetically scared of open water, never having experienced any until they were taken out of the big old spacecraft where the Heechee had left them and brought here. The only reason the Old Ones would ever go near water would be that they were tormented by thirst and just had to get a drink. We never let it come to that. We've taken care of that problem by digging boreholes and setting up little solar-powered drinking fountains all over their reservation. The fountains don't produce a huge gush of water, but there's a steady flow from each fountain, a deciliter a second year in and year out, and anyway the Old Ones don't need much water. They're not very interested in bathing, for instance. You catch a really gamy Old One, which we sometimes have to do when one of them is seriously sick or injured, and you might wish you could trade it for a hyena cub.

The first indication we got that we had a visitor was when we'd given the baby leopard four or five aversion shocks, and he suddenly began to struggle frantically in Shelly's arms, nipping at her gas-proof clothing, even when he wasn't being shocked. That wasn't normal. "Let him go," I ordered. When a cub gets really antsy we don't have any choice but to call it off for the day. It isn't that they'll hurt whoever's holding them, because the gas-proof coveralls are pretty nearly bite-proof as well. But it's bad for the cubs themselves. Wild animals can have heart attacks, too.

We backed away, keeping an eye on the mom as her baby, whining, scooted over to creep under her belly and begin to suckle. What I didn't know was what had set the cub off. Then I heard it: motor and fan noises from afar, and a moment later a hovercar appeared around a copse of acacias. Leopard cubs had better hearing than people, was all. The vehicle charged right up to us and skidded to a halt, the driver digging its braking skids into the ground for a quick stop and never mind how much dust it raised or how much damage it did to the roadway.

The man who got out when the bubble top popped open was skinny, tall, dark-complected and quite young looking—for what that's worth, since young looking is pretty much what everybody is these days. He was quite peculiar looking, too, because he was wearing full city clothing, long pants and long sleeves, with little ruffs of some kind of fur at the cuffs and colar. (A fur collar! In equatorial Africa!) He gave Brudy a quick, dismissive glance, looked Shelly and me over more thoroughly and ordered, "Take me to the Old Ones."

That was pure arrogance. When I sneaked a look at my indicator, it did not show a pass for his vehicle, so he had no right to be on the reservation in the first place, whoever he was. Brudy moved toward him warningly, and the newcomer stepped back a pace. The expression on Brudy's face wasn't particularly threatening, but he is a big man. We're all pretty tall, being mostly Maasai; Brudy is special. He boxes for fun whenever he can get anybody to go six rounds with him, and he looks it. "How did you get in?" Brudy demanded, his voice the gravelly baritone of a leopard's growl. What made me think of that was that just about then the mother leopard herself did give a ragged, unfocused little coming-awake growl.

"She's waking up," Shelly warned.

Brudy has a lot of confidence in our aversion training. He didn't even look around at the animals. "I asked you a question," he said.

The man from the hover craned his neck to see where the leopard was. He sounded a lot less self-assured when he said, "How I got in is

none of your business. I want to be taken to the Old Ones as soon as possible." Then he squinted at the leopard, now trying, but failing, to get to
her feet. "Is that animal dangerous?"

"You bet she is. She could tear you to shreds in a minute," I told
him—not lying, either, because she certainly theoretically could, if she
hadn't had her own aversion training. "You'd better get out of here, mister."

"Especially since you don't have a pass in the first place," Shelly
added.

That made him look confused. "What's a 'pass'?" he asked.

"It's a radio tag for your hover. You get them at the headquarters in
Nairobi. If you don't have one, you're not allowed on the reservation."

"'Allowed,'" he sneered. "Who are you to 'allow' me anything?"

Brudy cleared his throat. "We're the rangers for this reservation, and
what we say goes. You want to give me an argument?"

Brudy can be really convincing when he wants to be. The stranger decided to be law-abiding. "Oh, all right," he said, turning back to his hover;
he'd left the air-conditioning going and I could hear it whine as it valiantly
tried to cool off the whole veldt. "This petty bureaucracy crap stinks, but
I'll go back to Nairobi and get the damn pass."

"Maybe you will and maybe you won't," Shelly said. "We don't want
the Old Ones disturbed any more than we can help, so you'll need to give
them a pretty good reason."

He was already climbing into the vehicle, but he paused long enough
to give her a contemptuous look. "Reason? To visit the Old Ones? What
reason do I need, since I own them?"

II

The next morning all us rangers had to pitch in, because the food truck
had arrived. Brudy and Carlo were unloading little packets of rations from
the Food Factory in the Mombasa delta while the rest of us kept the Old
Ones in order.

I don't know why the Old Ones needed to be kept orderly in the first
place. For most people that Food Factory stuff is the meal of last resort—
that is, it is unless it's been doctored up, when you can hardly tell it from
the real thing. The Old Ones chomp the untreated stuff right down,
though. That's natural. CHON-food is what they grew up on, back when
they were floating around out in the Oort cloud. The Old Ones had come
running in from all over the reservation when they heard the truck's food
bell. Now they were all pressing close to the vehicle, all fifty-four of them,

chattering "Gimme, gimme!" at the top of their voices as they competed for the choicest bits.

When I came to work at the reservation I had only seen the Old Ones in pictures. I knew they all had beards, males and females alike. I hadn't known then that even the babies did, or did as soon as they were old enough to grow any hair at all, and I hadn't known about the way they smelled.

The ancient female we called "Spot" was pretty nearly the smelliest of the lot, but she was also about the smartest, and about as close as they had to a leader. And, well, she was kind of a friend. When she saw me she gave me an imploring look. I knew what she wanted. I helped her scoop up half a dozen of the pink and white packets she liked best, then escorted her out of the crowd. I waited until she had scarfed down the first couple of packets, then tapped her on the shoulder and said, "I want you to come with me, please."

Well, I didn't say it like that, of course. All of the Old Ones have picked up a few words of English, but even Spot was a little shaky on things like grammar. What I said was, "You," pointing at her, "come," beckoning her toward me, "me," tapping my own chest.

She went on chewing, crumbs of greasy-looking pale stuff spilling out of the corners of her mouth, looking suspicious. Then she said, "Is for?"

I said, "Is because today's the day for your crocodile-aversion refresher." I said it just like that, too. I knew that she wasn't going to understand every word but headquarters wanted us to talk to them in complete sentences as much as we could, in the hope they might learn. To reinforce the process I took her by one skinny wrist and tugged her away.

She had definitely understood the word "crocodile," because she whimpered and tried to get free. That did her no good. I had twenty kilos and fifteen centimeters on her. I let her dally long enough to pick up a couple of extra food packets. Then I put her in our Old Ones van, the one that never stops smelling of the Old Ones, so we never use it for anything else. I picked five more Old Ones pretty much at random and waved them in. They got in, all right. That is, they followed Spot, because she was the leader. They didn't like it, though, and all of them were cackling at once in their own hopelessly incomprehensible language as I drove the van to the river.

It was a pretty day. Hot, of course, and without a cloud in the sky. When I turned off the motor it was dead silent, too, not a sound except the occasional *craaack* of a pod coming in from Low Earth Orbit to be caught in the distant Nairobi Lofstrom Loop. I took a deep breath. Even the air smelled pretty, a dry scent of spiky grass and acacias. Times like that are when I'm glad I decided to take my park-ranger job instead of lawyering or doctoring, the way my parents wanted me to go.

The place in the river where the hippos hang out is what we call the Big Bend. The stream makes pretty nearly a right-angle turn there, with a beach on the far side that gets scoured out every rainy season. There are almost always fifteen or twenty hippos doing whatever they feel like doing in the slack water at the bend—basically just swimming around, sometimes underwater, sometimes surfacing to breathe. And there's almost always a croc or two squatting patiently on the beach, waiting for one of the babies to stray far enough away from the big hippos to become lunch.

This time there were three crocs, motionless in the hot African sun. They lay there with those long, toothy jaws wide open, showing the yellowish inside of their mouths—I guess that's how they keep from being overheated, like a pet dog in hot weather. What it looks like is that they're just waiting for something edible to come within range. Which I guess is also true, and why I can't help getting sort of shivery inside whenever I see one. So did the Old Ones. They were whimpering inside the van, and I nearly had to kick them out of it. Then they all huddled together, as far from the river bank as I would let them get, shaking and muttering fearfully to each other.

Fortunately they didn't have long to wait, because Geoffrey was right behind us in the truck with the goat projector.

That was Geoffrey's own invention. Before I came, he used to use live goats, but I put a stop to that. We raise the goats for food and I'm not sentimental about slaughtering them, but I made sure the ones we used for aversion training were dead already.

While he was setting up I gave myself a minute to enjoy the hippos. They're always fun, big ones the size of our van and little ones no bigger than a pig. They look to me like they're enjoying themselves, and how often do you see a really happy extended family? I'm sure the big ones were aware of our presence, and undoubtedly even more aware of the crocs on the bank, but they seemed carefree. They aren't particularly violent, either, unless you get in their way. Given a chance, I would have liked to swim with them someday—except for the crocs.

"Okay, Grace," Geoffrey called, hand already on the trigger of the launcher.

"You may fire when ready," I said to him, and to the Old Ones, "Watch!" They did, scared but fascinated, as the goat carcass soared out of the launcher and into the water, well downstream from the hippo families so there wouldn't be any accidents.

You wouldn't think a crocodile could run very fast, with those sprawly little legs and huge tail. You'd be wrong. Before the goat hit the water all three of the crocs were doing their high-speed waddle down to the river's edge. When they hit the water they disappeared; a moment later all around the floating goat there were half a dozen little whirlpools of water, with an occasional lashing tail to show what was going on under the reddening surface. The show didn't last long. In a minute that goat was history.

I glanced at the hippos. They hadn't seemed to pay any attention, but I noticed that now all the big ones were on the downstream side of the herd and the babies were on the other side, away from the crocs.

"Show's over," I told the Old Ones. "Back in the van!"—pointing to make sure they understood what I said. They didn't delay. They were all shivering as they lined up to climb back in, one by one. I was just about to follow them in when I heard Geoffrey calling my name. I turned around, half in the van, and called, "What's the problem?"

He pointed to his communicator. "Shelly just called. You know that guy who claims he owns the Old Ones? He's back!"

All the way back I had one hand on the wheel and my other hand on my own communicator, checking with Shelly—yes, the son of a bitch did have a pass this time—and then with Nairobi to see why they'd allowed it. The headquarters guy who answered the call was Bertie ap Dora. He's my boss and he sounded really embarrassed. "Sure, Grace," he said, "we gave him a pass. We didn't have any choice, did we? He's Wan."

It took me a moment. Then, "Oh, my God," I said. "Really? Wan?" And when Bertie confirmed that Wan was who the mysterious stranger was, identity checked and correct, it all fell into place.

Since he was Wan, he had been telling the truth, almost. He wasn't really the owner of the Old Ones, but you could make an argument that he was something pretty close, because legally he was the man who had discovered them.

Well, that argument didn't actually make much sense in my book. If you stopped to think about it, Wan himself had been discovered by that Herter-Hall party as much as the Old Ones had. However, it didn't have to make sense. That was the way Gateway Corp had ruled—had given him a finder's share of property rights in the place where the Old Ones had been discovered and everything on it—and nobody argued with the findings of Gateway Corp.

The thing about the Old Ones was that they had been found on a far-out, Sun-orbiting Heechee artifact, and it was the Heechee themselves

THE BOY WHO WOULD LIVE FOREVER fix

who had put them there, all those hundreds of thousands of years ago when the Heechee had come to check out Earth's solar system.

The Heechee were looking for intelligent races to be friends with. What they discovered was the ancestors of the Old Ones, the dumb, hairy little hominids called australopithecines. They weren't much, but they were the closest the Earth had to the intelligent race the Heechee were looking for at the time, so the Heechee had taken away some australopithecine breeding stock to study. And then, a little later, when the Heechee got so scared that they ran off and hid in the Core, all the billions of them, they left the australopithecines behind. They weren't exactly abandoned. The Heechee had left them the Food Factory they inhabited, so they never went hungry. And so they stayed there, generation after generation, for hundreds of thousands of years, until human beings finally got to Gateway and its abandoned Heechee spacecraft. And, the story went, one of those human beings on that huge old artifact, and the only one of them who had survived long enough to be rescued, was the kid named Wan.

As soon as I got to the compound I saw him. He wasn't a kid anymore, but he wasn't hard to recognize, either. His size picked him out. He wasn't all that much taller than some of the Old Ones, a dozen or so of whom had gathered around to regard him with tepid interest. He was dressed better than the Old Ones, though. In fact, he was dressed better than we were. He'd deep-sixed the fur collars, sensibly enough, and the outfit he was wearing now was one of those safari-jacket things with all the pockets, that tourists are so crazy about. His, however, was made of pure natural silk. And he was carrying a riding crop, although there wasn't a horse within five hundred kilometers of us. (Zebras don't count.)

As soon as he saw me he bustled over, hand outstretched and a big told-you-so grin on his face. "I'm Wan," he said. "I don't hold that thing yesterday against you."

I didn't feel any blame, but I let it go. I shook his hand. "Grace Nkroma," I said. "Head ranger. What do you want?"

The grin got bigger. "I guess you'd call it nostalgia. Is that the right word? I'm kind of sentimental about my Old Ones, since they sort of took care of me while I was growing up. I've been meaning to visit them ever since they were relocated here, but I've been so busy—" He gave a winsome little shrug, to show how busy he'd been.

Then he gazed benevolently around at the Old Ones. "Yes," he said, nodding, "I recognize several of them, I think. Do you see how happy they are to see me?" Well, maybe they were. The one we called Beautiful was jabbing a muddy thorn into the arm of her son, Gadget, to make one of

their ugly tattoos. The rest of them were a fifty-fifty split, half looking at
Beautiful, the other half at Wan. He didn't seem to mind. He told me,
"I've brought them some wonderful gifts." He jerked a thumb at his vehicle. "You people better unload them. They've been in the car a while, and
you need to get them into the ground as soon as possible." And then he
linked arms with a couple of the Old Ones, seemingly unaware of how
they smelled, and strolled off, leaving us to do his bidding.

III

There were about forty of the "gifts" that Wan had brought for his former
family, and what they turned out to be were little green seedlings in
pressed-soil pots. Carlo looked at them, and then at me. "What the hell
are we supposed to do with those things?" he wanted to know.

"I'll ask," I said, and got on the line with Bertie ap Dora again.

"They're berry bushes," he told me, sounding defensive. "They're
some kind of fruit the Old Ones had growing wild when they were out
there. They're supposed to love the berries. Actually, it's quite a thoughtful gift, wouldn't you say?"

I wouldn't. I didn't. I said, "It would be a lot more thoughtful if he
planted the damn things himself. What's with this guy, anyway? Is he always like that?"

It was pretty much a rhetorical question, but Bertie chose to answer
it. He took a moment to think first. Then he said delicately, "Wan has
done quite a few—ah—*impulsive* things, now and then. Some of them
caused some trouble. Police trouble, even."

"You mean he's a criminal?"

"Oh, well," Bertie said dismissively, "never with any kind of real jail
time. There wouldn't be, would there? With the kind of lawyers his kind
of money can buy?" Then he changed the subject. "One thing I should tell
you about. Those berry bushes are supposed to need quite a lot of water,
so make sure you plant them near the runoff from the drinking fountains,
all right? And, listen, see if you can keep the giraffes from eating the
seedlings before they grow out."

"How are we supposed to do that?" I asked, but Bertie had already cut
the connection. Naturally. He's a boss. You know the story about the second lieutenant and the sergeant and the flagpole? There's this eight-meter
flagpole and the lieutenant only has six meters of rope. Big problem. How
does the lieutenant get the flagpole up?

Simple. The lieutenant says, "Sergeant, put that flagpole up," and
goes off to have a beer at the officers' club.

As far as Bertie is concerned, I'm his sergeant. I don't have to be, though. Bertie keeps asking me to come in and take a job as a sector chief at the Nairobi office. There'd be more money, too, but then I'd have to live in the big city. Besides, that would mean I wouldn't be in direct contact with the Old Ones anymore.

Everything considered, you might think that wouldn't sound so bad, but—oh, hell, I admit it—I knew I'd miss every smelly, dumb-ass one of them. They weren't very bright and they weren't very clean, and most of the time, although I liked them, I wasn't a bit sure that they liked me back. But they needed me.

By the time Wan had been with us for three days, we had got kind of used to having him around. We didn't actually see a lot of him. Most of the daylight time he was off in his hover with a couple of the Old Ones for company, feeding them ice-cream pops and lemonade out of his freezer—things that really weren't good for them but, I had to admit, wouldn't do them much harm once or twice in a lifetime. When it got dark he was always back in the housing compound, but he didn't mingle with us rangers even then. He stayed in his vehicle, watching soaps and cartoons again with a couple of Old Ones for company. He slept in it, too.

When I finally asked Wan just how long he intended to be with us, he just gave me that grin again and said, "Can't say, Gracie. I'm having fun."

"Don't call me Gracie," I said. But he had already turned his back on me to collect another handful of Old Ones for a joyride.

Having fun seemed to be what Wan's life was all about. He'd already been all over the galaxy before he came back to see us, flying around in his own private ship. (Did you get that? His own private ship!) He could afford it. Those royalties on the Heechee stuff that came out of the Food Factory made him, he told us, the eighth richest person in the galaxy, and what Wan could afford was pretty nearly anything he could think up. He made sure he let us all know it, too, which didn't endear him to most of the staff, especially Carlo. "He gets on my nerves with his goddamn bragging all the time," Carlo complained to me. "Can't I run the son of a bitch off?"

"As long as he doesn't make trouble," I said, "no. How are you coming with the planting?"

Actually that was going pretty well. All the guys had to do was scoop out a little hole in the ground, a couple of meters away from a fountain, and set one of the pressed-earth pots in it. That was the whole drill. Since there were a couple of patrols going out all over the reservation every day anyway, checking for signs of elephant incursions or unauthorized human trespassers, it only took them a couple of extra minutes at each stop.

Then, without warning, Wan left us.

I thought I heard the sound of his hover's fans, just as I was going to sleep. I considered getting up to see what was going on, but—damn it!—the pillow seemed more interesting than Wan just then and I rolled over and forgot it.

Or almost forgot it. I guess it was my subconscious, smarter than the rest of me, that made my sleep uneasy. And about the fourth or fifth time I half woke, I heard the voices of Old Ones softly, worriedly, murmuring at each other just outside my window.

That woke me all the way up. Old Ones don't like the dark, never having had any back home. I pulled on a pair of shorts and stumbled outside. Spot was sitting there on her haunches, along with Brute and Blackeye, all three of them turning to stare at me. "What's the matter?" I demanded.

She was munching on a chunk of CHON-food. "Grathe," she said politely, acknowledging my existence. "He. Gone." She made sweeping-away gestures with her hands to make sure I understood her.

"Well, hell," I said. "Gone where?"

She made the same gesture again. "Away."

"Yes, I know *away*," I snarled. "Did he say when he was coming back?"

She swallowed and spat out of a piece of wrapper. "No back," she said.

I guess I was still pretty sleepy, because I didn't take it in right away. "What do you mean, 'no back?'"

"Gone," she told me placidly. "Also Beautiful. Pony. Gadget. They too."

IV

I woke Shelly and Carlo and sent them up in the ultralight to check out the whole reservation, but I didn't wait for their report. I was calling headquarters even before they were airborne. Bertie wasn't in his office, of course—it was the middle of the night, and the headquarters people kept city hours—but I got him out of bed at home. He didn't sound like he believed me. "Why the hell would anyone kidnap a couple of Old Ones?" he wanted to know.

"Ask the bastard yourself," I snarled at him. "Only find him first. That's three of the Old Ones that he's kidnaped—Beauty and her two-year-old, Gadget. And Pony. Pony is the kid's father, probably."

He made a sound of irritation. "All right. First thing, I'll need descriptions—no, sorry," he said, catching himself; how would you describe three Old Ones? And why would you need to? "Forget that part. I'll take it from here. I guarantee he won't get off the planet. I'll have cops at the Loop in ten minutes, and a general alarm everywhere. I'll—"

But I cut him off there. "No, Bertie. Not so much *you* will. More like *we* will. I'll meet you at the Loop and, I don't care how rich the son of a bitch is, when we catch him I'm going to punch him out. And then he's going to see what the inside of a jail looks like."

But that wasn't the way the hand played out.

I took our two-man hover, which is almost as fast as the ultra-light. The way I was goosing it along, maybe a little faster. By the time I got within sight of the Lofstrom Loop, with Nairobi's glowing bubble a few kilometers to the north, I was already aware of police planes crisscrossing across the sky—once or twice dropping down to get a good look at me before they were satisfied and zoomed away.

At night the Loop is picked out with lights, so that it looks like a kind of roller-coaster ride, kilometers long. I could hear the whine of its rotating magnetic cables long before I got to the terminal. There weren't many pods either coming or going—maybe because it was nighttime in this part of the world—so, I figured, there wouldn't be so many passengers that Wan and his captives might not be noticed. (As though anybody wouldn't notice three Old Ones.)

Actually at that time of night there were hardly any passengers waiting around in the terminal. Bertie was there already, with half a dozen Nairobi city cops, but they didn't have much to do. Neither did I, except to fret and swear to myself for letting him get away.

Then the cop manning the communicator listened to something, snarled something back and came toward us, looking shamefaced. "He won't be coming here," he told Bertie. "He didn't use the Loop coming down. He used his own lander, and it looks like he used it to get off, too, because it's gone."

And so he had.

By the time Bertie, fuming, was able to get in touch with any of the authorities in orbit, Wan had had plenty of time to dock with his spaceship and be on his way, wherever it was he was going, at FTL speeds. And I never saw him, or any of the three missing Old Ones, again.

Heard about him, though. You bet I heard about him. Everybody did, because everybody likes to read about nasty, spoiled rich kids, and this Wan sure filled the bill.

The whole thing made you wonder, though. They brought the Old Ones to Africa to make them safe, and that certainly hadn't worked out. So what were they going to do with them next?

6

The One Who Hated Humans

I

The private place that had been provided for Estrella and Stan on the ship was about the size of an elevator cage. Apparently it had been intended for occupancy by only one person. Only one Heechee person, that was to say, because it obviously was not meant for habitation by any number of humans at all. The furnishings made that clear. There was one of those bifurcated perches that the Heechee used to sit on, one sack of the weedy things they used for sleeping in and one shelf, like a child's desk built into the wall, with one of the flowerpot-shaped things Stan had seen before, for which he could see no use at all. There was also, conspicuously out in the open, one of those shining Heechee slit-trench receptacles for the disposal of bodily wastes. That was about it, not counting the collection of fifteen or twenty of the crystalline things the first Gateway prospectors called "prayer fans," which, Estrella then told him, fitted into the flowerpot. "They're like books," she said. "I saw Salt doing it. You put them in the reader." She pointed to the flowerpot-shaped thing. "That's the reader."

"Huh," he said, turning one of the fans over in his hand. He was less interested in it than in the passing time. He was wishing he had a watch so he could see how long they were being kept waiting; wishing the Heechee female would come and tell them that they could go out of this room; and wishing even more that someone would feed them pretty soon, because it was getting to be a long time between meals.

He tried sitting down at the desk, but didn't remain sitting there for long; unlike the ones in their old Five, this Heechee-designed perch had not been modified to the contours of the human butt. Finally he turned to Estrella, where she was sitting on the bundle of sleep-rushes. "Can I borrow those for a moment?" he said, and lugged the bundle over to the desk. When he jammed it between the prongs of the Heechee perch it made a seat that wasn't comfortable, no, but at least didn't feel like he was sliding, rump first, into some lethal vise.

When he went back to fiddling with the prayer fan and its holder, Estrella, now standing beside him and watching with interest, said, "Don't break it, Stan dear. I don't know how valuable those things are—" And then, in a quite different tone, "Oh."

That made Stan look around and discover they were no longer alone. A male Heechee stood in the opened doorway, watching them with clinical interest. "That is most excellently good advice," he said—in fair, if accented, English!—"You two had better not be messing around with things not understood."

To Stan, the Heechee in the doorway was undistinguishable from any other male Heechee in terms of color of pelt, shape of face or body silhouette, but there was one thing about him even Stan could not mistake. That was the clothes he had on. This visitor was wearing bright green sports shoes—human sports shoes—over his splayed Heechee feet, along with a kilt that covered him from waist to ankles—perhaps, Stan thought, to conceal that universal Heechee between-the-thighs pod. And on his Heechee head he wore a human sports cap, pulled down low over his eyes.

Stan had no doubt that this must be the male Heechee Salt had warned them against talking to, the one in "peculiar clothing." But the decision to stay away from him wasn't in their hands anymore, because he was already present and speaking to them. "Hello," he said. "Give to me that for a minute." He advanced on Stan and took the prayer fan out of Stan's hand without waiting for permission. "Two of you, now listen to that which you will hear!" he commanded.

He juggled the fan expertly and then pulled the thing open by one protruding edge. When he released it it made a thin, metallic, almost tuneful whispering sound as it slithered back into its ice-cream-cone shape. "What is that sound sounding like?" he asked.

Stan looked up at him, open-mouthed, then turned in puzzlement to Estrella. It was she who answered. "Some kind of machine?" she hazarded.

The stranger emitted what might have been a human chuckle, or an attempt to copy one. "Yes, a machine, I agree to that," he said. "It sounds like a machine because that is what it is. Agreed? Right? Now listen to this other sound." He fiddled with the base of the fan, then pulled out a pearly little globe which he held up. "This is called fuel button, what you of human extraction designate 'fire pearl.' Again listen." He rubbed it with his skinny thumb, producing a faint, sibilant whisper. "You have now heard. Therefore tell this to me. Do either of them sound like this human-speaking word 'Heechee'?"

Both shook their heads. The stranger said morosely, "Must have sounded so to some of your people, because it is that which they called us. Heechee. After what they considered those sounds sounded like. Do you know, I have even heard some of own people use that same to represent ourselves?"

Stan took another quick look at Estrella, then answered for both of them. "I'm sorry if that offends you. We aren't the ones who did it, though. We weren't even there."

"No," the male said. "Is correct you were not even there, you two." He looked them both up and down with an expression Stan couldn't read. Then he turned to leave. At the door he paused. "Is very interesting to me that of your people none accept to be responsible for that which others of your people have done." Another pause, and then he contemptuously blew air out through his nostrils and said, "You two are considered to be some kind of heroes on Gateway. Of course, do not have too many persons which actually be proud of, correct?"

II

Alone again, Stan and Estrella took sitting-down turns. First Stan sat on the bundle of reeds, now detached again from the Heechee perch, and Estrella did her best to be at ease in the forks of the perch. Then the other way around. Then one standing while the other was something approaching comfortable lying on the reeds. Then both of them standing, or, more accurately, roaming around, because they were getting hungrier, and more tired of being in this room, and considerably more irritable, not just at their Heechee hosts but at each other for asking, over and over, questions that they had no way to answer: Who had that weirdo in the funny clothes been? When was the ship going to take off? What did the weirdo Heechee mean about them being heroes on Gateway, and what the hell did he know about Gateway in the first place? Why didn't Salt come through that door and let them out of this place? Wasn't it, for God's sake, about time they got something to *eat*?

Stan also had to go to the bathroom. Despite the long intimacy that had existed between them on their Five, he was reluctant to make use of the bodily-waste receptacle while she was right there watching him. When the pressure in his bladder matched, without canceling out, the yearning void in his belly he gave up. "The hell with it," he said, and marched to the door, determined to find a way to get it open, no matter what weird Heechee locks held it shut, or at least to hammer on it until someone came to let them out.

That problem solved itself. The moment he touched the door it quietly slid open. He found himself looking out at the passage they had come in, terminating in that big spindle-shaped chamber. Estrella was close behind.

That faint Heechee odor of ammonia told him what he was going to see before he saw it. There were quite a few Heechee in the chamber now, a couple of them talking quietly to each other at one of the control carrels, another absorbedly selecting among the fan-shaped books to put into one of the reading machines. The rest of them, half a dozen at least, were eating and drinking around a couple of tables that had produced themselves from nowhere. None of these Heechee appeared to be the male who had visited them in their cabin, and, whatever they were doing, they all stopped it to look at Stan and Estrella.

After a moment's hesitation the female named Salt got up from the table and came toward them. "You persons wish to join us now for the eating?" she asked. "Are almost through here, us others. Did not know what to do when the eating began, since did not wish to disturb privacy."

"Oh, yes, we'd love to eat," Estrella said eagerly, and Stan chimed in: "Me too. Absolutely. But give me a minute to, ah, freshen up first."

When the Heechee saw Stan and Estrella trying to fit themselves into the Heechee perches some of them made a series of sneezing sounds, perhaps the equivalent of a laugh. When Estrella told Salt what they had done about the problem in their own room, there was a quick discussion in the Heechee language. Then additional reed-clusters were quickly brought in to fill the space between the prongs.

Then they were served a meal.

It was Heechee food again, and there was no way to avoid eating it because the ship they were on had nothing else. Reluctantly Stan gave it a try, several varieties of it. The stuff was odd of texture, bizarre of color, indescribable of taste—Stan was sure of that last part, because he tried to describe it to himself as he ate, and failed. Was this pink, stringy stuff supposed to be mint-flavored? Something aromatic, certainly, but more like catnip than any Christmas candy cane. And the dark brown pebbles that shattered crisply in the teeth had no taste at all that he could detect. Nevertheless, he resolutely told himself, they were food, and indeed they did seem to fill that interior void.

They had missed their ship's takeoff, Salt told them. "Did not feel what-you-call lurch of passage? Small shaking up? But have been en route for quite lengthy time. Hope had nice sleep."

"Oh, we didn't sleep," Estrella said. "We had a visitor, you know."

That made Salt pause in her desultory nibbling, done, Estrella was sure, mostly to keep them company. "Understanding minimal," she said. "Why say this? No person of ours intruded, I am of this sure."

"One did, though," Stan corrected her, his mouth full of something bitter in flavor but with the sticky texture of marshmallows. "He had funny clothes and a funny hat, and he spoke very good English."

The effect of those words on Salt was remarkable. The fur on the sides of her head bristled, her face muscles writhed like snakes under the skin, her mouth hung open. She seemed to be having trouble taking it in. "Person entered privacy of your private room?" she asked incredulously.

"Sure did," Stan said, nodding.

"But that is—" she began, then cut herself off. She flopped her wrists in obvious distress, then turned to speak to the other Heechee in the chamber. What she was saying neither Stan nor Estrella had any hope of understanding, because it was in Salt's own language, but it produced its effect. Suddenly all the Heechee seemed to be talking at once, flapping their skeletal arms, shaking their skull-like heads, pointing bony fingers at Estrella and Stan, and the faint ammoniacal smell grew more intense with emotion.

Stan swallowed the last of the fibrous wad in his mouth and turned to Estrella. "Are we in trouble?" he asked.

She shrugged worriedly. "Salt did tell us not to speak to him," she said. "I don't know how we could have avoided it, though. He's the one who came and talked to us."

And then, wonderfully, when every Heechee in the room had had his say, most of them several times, what Salt said to the two humans was much the same. "You have not offended," she told them. "The person visited and addressed to you. You did not visit or address to him. So there is no fault for you. Also should be no repetition of same, because person is now in own compartment with responsible senior companion name of Slightly Bitter. Who," she added glumly, "should not have allowed such visit in first place." She was silent for a moment, and then went on: "But is quite surprising to us he should do this thing of seeking out you company. You see, he hate you very much."

III

Estrella wanted to know why they were hated. ("Why should he hate us? He never even met us!") Stan wanted to be told what this person was likely to do to them if he hated them so. After half a dozen unsuccessful attempts to answer the questions individually Salt flopped her wrists in resignation and began from the beginning.

Their visitor (whose name, she said, was the word in the Heechee language for something like "One Who Accomplishes Much") had been part of the crew of an exploring party. There were three of them in this crew, and their mission had been to look for a race of spacefaring sentients known as "the Assassins."

When Estrella wanted to know why they were called that, Salt looked puzzled. "Because is what they were, assassins," she explained. "In days of old before Withdrawal these Assassins killed off every person they found, totally. Unanimously. What else may they be called? Although," she corrected herself, "we do sometimes also call them by the term the 'Foe,' since is what they are to us."

"I get it. This guy thought we were the Assassins?" Stan hazarded.

Salt made the choking Heechee laughter sound, then politely stopped herself. "Not at all is that the case. Please allow me to complete elucidation."

Resignedly Stan told her to elucidate away, and so she did. Those three Heechee explorers had traveled around the galaxy looking for signs of these Assassins without success. Stan couldn't quite figure out what "signs" Salt was talking about; as near as he could understand her their ship was sniffing various corners of the galaxy hoping to pick up some scent of the Assassins on the loose in inhabited portions of the galaxy. Literally she had used the word "scent." Stan objected, "But you can't smell anything in space," and then shook his head. "Never mind. Go on the way you want to."

The explorers didn't find their quarry, but they tried another tack. They took the ship to a place where, before the Withdrawal, the Heechee had left a number of their ships on an asteroid in orbit around a rather small yellowish star—

"Jesus!" Stan cried, and Estrella whispered:

"Gateway. You're talking about Gateway."

Salt waggled her jaw in agreement. "So he spoke of the place, yes. Was there for four years." And then she had trouble explaining just what the person had been doing for four years. It had something to do with the Gateway ships. One by one he had analyzed the mission plans each ship had stored, in case one of them could have tracked the Assassins in that last frantic period before the whole of the Heechee race ran into the Core to hide. And he went on doing this for four years.

"In which time," Salt said earnestly, "this person was alone. With many hundreds, even thousands, human persons, yes, but completely otherwise alone."

"Now wait a minute," Stan said. "Surely some other Heechee came there now and then."

"Not much now. Not that much even then. A few visited only. Even such few not for long."

Estrella cut in. "But he still wasn't *alone*, was he? There were three of them."

"Oh, did I not say? Not the case. This person, Achiever, he check records of spacecraft all time. Other two are gone for other purpose, while he stay on asteroid continuing checking records. And for that reason—" She hesitated, as though reluctant to say the next thing. Then she plunged ahead. "Only him, you see? And many, many of you. Toward end he could not stand sight of one more human person. Had no choice. Had to go on standing it. Must now receive relaxing and repairing on Shining Mica Mountains on Forested Planet of Warm Old Star Twenty-Four—this, you understand, is identical place to which I invited you."

Stan and Estrella thought that over for a moment. It was Estrella who asked, "What kind of relaxing and repairing?"

"Is hard to explain. Is resting. Is associating—" She flapped her wrists in chagrin. "Have no proper words of your speaking. Perhaps proper words for same not existing." She looked glum. "Actually, most sad thing is, we do not exactly know what is to be done. What is wished is to rid him of total hatred of your kind. Among you this is called—?"

She stopped there. Stan filled in for her. "You mean craziness?"

"I think perhaps so, yes," Salt said reluctantly. "That is, deficiency of intellect leading to unusual and harmful actions. Except among us is no such thing, ever. Therefore we do not know how to treat."

"No such thing ever?" Estrella said skeptically.

"Not ever never," Salt said with emphasis. "Not a trait of our persons, this deficiency."

Estrella was still doubtful, but she asked, "So what will you do with him?"

The muscles under the skin of Salt's face writhed worriedly. "Will house him in certain place on Forested Planet of Warm Old Star Twenty-Four. Place is for purpose of remediating deficiencies. For example, in this place are old ones nearing death. You know, no longer controlling appropriate functions of body and so forth." But the more she tried to explain the purpose of this sanitarium, or whatever it was, the harder it got. "Is for—" she would begin, and then pause for a while, sometimes quite a while, before venturing, "To make some persons Stored Ancestors, this place is. Not for this person, though." Another long pause. "Or like, supposing some person is to wear tunic not one's own? Without permission? So is there to make needed repairs to person so not to do again, you see?" But Stan and Estrella didn't see. Finally she flapped her wrists at them in surrender. "Place is not exactly right for this person, no," she conceded. "But is all we have."

7

Hatching the Phoenix

I

My name is Gelle-Klara Moynlin, and I probably don't need any additional introduction. If I do, you just haven't been paying attention, because I'm in the newscasts often enough.

When we crossed the wavefront from the Crab supernova we were about half a day out from Earth. The crossing didn't set off any alarms or anything. I wouldn't even have noticed it, but my shipmind, Hypatia, is programmed to notice things that I don't, if she thinks they might interest me. So she asked me if I wanted to take a look at it, and I did.

Of course I'd already seen that doomed old star blow up two or three times already in simulations, but as a flesh and blood human being I like reality better than simulations—most of the time, anyway. Hypatia had already turned the Heechee screen on, but it showed nothing but the pebbly gray blur that's the Heechee idea of a good default. Hypatia can read that stuff, but I can't, so she changed the phase for me.

Then I saw a field of stars, looking exactly like any other field of stars. I had to ask her, "Which one is it?"

She said, "You can't see it yet. We don't have that much magnification, but keep your eyes open. Wait a moment. Another moment. Now, there it is."

She didn't have to say that. I could see it for myself. Suddenly a point of light emerged and got brighter, and brighter still, until it outshone everything else on the screen. It actually made me squint. "It happens pretty fast," I said.

"Well, not really *that* fast, Klara. Our vector velocity, relative to the star, is quite a lot faster than light, so we're speeding things up. Also we're catching up with the wavefront, so we're seeing it all in reverse. It'll be gone soon."

And a moment later it was. Just as the star had become brightest of all, it unexploded itself. It became a simple star again, so unremarkable that I couldn't even pick it out. The planets that they told me it had were unscorched again, their populations, if any, not yet whiffed into plasma. "All right," I said, somewhat impressed but not enough to want Hypatia to know it, "turn the screen off and let's get back to work."

Hypatia sniffed—she has built herself a whole repertory of human behaviors that are all her own idea, because I had never had them programmed into her. She said darkly, "We'd better, if we want to be able to pay all the bills for this thing. Do you have any idea what this is *costing*?"

Of course, she wasn't serious about that. I have problems, but I'm Gelle-Klara Moynlin, and being able to pay my bills isn't one of them.

I wasn't always this solvent. When I was a kid on that chunk of burned-out hell they call the planet Venus, driving an airbody around its baked, bleak surface for the tourists all day and trying not to spend any of my pay all night, the thing I wanted most was to have money. I wasn't hoping for a whole lot of money. I just wanted enough money so that I could afford Full Medical and a place to live that didn't stink of rancid seafood. I wasn't dreaming on any vast scale.

It didn't work out that way, though. I never did have exactly that much money. First I had none at all and no real hopes of ever getting any. Then I had much, much more than that, and I found out something about having a lot of money. When you have the kind of money that's spelled M*O*N*E*Y, it's like having a kitten in the house. The money wants you to play with it. You can try to leave it alone, but if you do it'll be crawling into your lap and nibbling at your chin for attention. You don't have to give in to what the money wants. You can just push it away and go about your business, but then God knows what mischief it'll get into if you do, and anyway then where's the fun of having it?

So most of the way out to the PhoenixCorp site Hypatia and I played with my money. That is, I played with it while Hypatia kept score. She remembers what I own better than I do—that's what she was designed to do—and she's always full of suggestions about what investments I should dump or hold or what new ventures I should get into.

The key word there is "suggestions." I don't have to do what Hypatia says. Sometimes I don't. As a general rule I follow Hypatia's suggestions about four times out of five. The fifth time I do something different, just to let her know that I'm the one that makes the decisions here. I know that's not smart, and it generally costs me money when I do, but that's all right. I have plenty of money to spare.

There's a limit to how long I'm willing to go on tickling the money's tummy, though. When I had just about reached that point Hypatia put down her pointer and waved the graphics displays away. She had made herself optically visible to humor me, because I like to see the person I'm talking to, wearing her fifth-century robes and coronet of rough-cut rubies and all, and she gave me an inquiring look. "Ready to take a little break, Klara?" she asked. "Do you want something to eat?"

Well, I was, and I did. She knew that perfectly well. She's continually monitoring my body, because that's one of the other things she's designed to do, but I like to keep my free will going there, too. "Actually," I said, "I'd rather have a drink. How are we doing for time?"

"Right on schedule, Klara. We'll be there in ten hours or so." She didn't move—that is, her simulation didn't move—but I could hear the clink of ice going into a glass in the galley. "I've been accessing the PhoenixCorp shipmind, if you want to see what's going on?"

"Do it," I said, but she was already doing it. She waved again—pure theater, of course, but Hypatia's full of that—and at once we got a new set of graphics. As the little serving cart rolled in and stopped just by my right hand we were looking through PhoenixCorp's own visuals, at a dish-shaped metal spiderweb. Little things were crawling across it.

I could form no real picture of its size, because there was nothing in the space around it to compare it with. I didn't have to compare. I knew it was big.

"Have one for yourself," I said, lifting my glass.

She gave me that patient, exasperated look and let it pass. Sometimes she does simulate having a simulated drink with me while I have a real one, but this time she was in her schoolteacher mode. "As you can see, Klara," she informed me, "the shipment of optical mirror pieces has arrived and the drones are putting them in place on the parabolic dish. They'll be getting first light from the planet in an hour or so, but I don't think you'll care about seeing it. The resolution will be poor until they get everything put together; that should take about eighteen hours. Then we should have optimal resolution to observe the planet."

"For four days," I said, taking a pull at my glass.

She gave me a different look—still the schoolteacher, but now a schoolteacher putting up with a particularly annoying student. "Hey, Klara. You knew there wouldn't be much observing time. It wasn't my idea to come all the way out here, anyway. We could have watched the whole thing from your island."

I swallowed the rest of my nightcap and stood up. "That's not how I wanted to do it," I told her. "The trouble with you simulations is that you don't appreciate what reality is like. Wake me up an hour before we get there."

And I headed for my stateroom, with my big round under-occupied bed. I didn't want to chat with Hypatia just then. The main reason I had kept her busy giving me financial advice so long was that it prevented her from giving me advice on other things, like the thing she was always trying to talk me into. Or that one other big thing that I really needed to make up my mind about, and couldn't.

The cart with my black coffee and fresh-squeezed orange juice—make that quote fresh-squeezed unquote orange juice, but Hypatia was too good at her job for me to be able to tell the difference—was right by my bed when she woke me up. "Ninety minutes to linkup," she said cheerily, "and a very good morning to you. Shall I start your shower?"

I said, "Um." Ninety minutes is not a second too long for me to sit and swallow coffee, staring into space, before I have to do anything as energetic as getting into a shower. But then I looked into the wall mirror by the bed, didn't like what I saw, and decided I'd better spruce myself up a little bit.

I was never what you'd call a pretty woman. My eyebrows were a lot too heavy, for one thing. Once or twice over the years I'd had the damn things thinned down to fashion-model proportions, just to see if it would help any. It didn't. I'd even messed around with my bone structure, more cheekbones, less jaw, to try to look a little less masculine. It just made me look weak-faced. For a couple of years I'd gone blonde, tried redhead once but checked it out and made them change it back before I left the beauty parlor. They were all mistakes. They didn't work. Whenever I looked at myself, whatever the cosmetologists and the medical fixer-uppers had done, I could still see the old Gelle-Klara Moynlin hiding there behind all the trim. So screw it. For the last little while I'd gone natural.

Well, pretty natural, anyway. I didn't want to look *old*.

I didn't, of course. By the time I was bathed and hair fixed and wearing a simple dress that showed off my actually pretty decent legs, I looked as good as I ever had. "Almost there," Hypatia called. "You better hang onto something. I have to match velocities and it's a tricky job." She sounded annoyed, as she usually does when I give her something hard to do. She does it, of course, but she complains a lot. "Faster than light I can do, slower than light I can do, but when you tell me to match velocity with somebody who's doing exactly *c* you're into some pretty weird effects, so—oh, sorry."

"You should be," I told her, because that last lurch had nearly made me spill my third cup of coffee. "Hypatia? What do you think, the pearls or the cameo?"

She did that fake two or three second pause, as though she really needed any time at all to make a decision, before she gave me the verdict. "I'd wear the cameo. Only whores wear pearls in the daytime."

So of course I decided to wear the pearls. She sighed but didn't comment. "All right," she said, opening the port. "We're docked. Mind the step, and I'll keep in touch."

I nodded and stepped over the seals into the PhoenixCorp mother ship.

There wasn't any real "step." But there was a sharp transition from the comfortable one gee I kept in my own ship to the gravityless environment of PhoenixCorp. My stomach did a quick little flip-flop of protest, but I grabbed a hold-on bar and looked around.

I don't know what I'd expected to find, maybe something like the old Gateway asteroid. PhoenixCorp had done itself a lot more lavishly than that, and I began to wonder if I hadn't maybe been a touch too open-handed with the financing. The place certainly didn't smell like Gateway. Instead of Gateway's sour, ancient fugg it had the wetly sweet smell of a greenhouse. That was because there were vines and ferns and flowers growing in pots all around the room—spreading out in all directions, because of that zero-gee environment, and if I'd thought about that ahead of time I wouldn't have worn a skirt. The only human being in sight was a tall, nearly naked black man who was hanging by one toe from a wall bracket, exercising his muscles with one of those metal-spring gadgets. ("Humphrey Mason-Manley," Hypatia whispered in my ear. "He's the archeologist-anthropologist guy from the British Museum.") Without breaking his rhythm Humphrey gave me a look of annoyance.

"What are you doing here, miss? No visitors are permitted. This is private property, and—"

Then he got a better look at me and his expression changed. Not to welcoming exactly, but to what I'd call sort of unwillingly impressed. "Oh, crikey," he said. "You're Gelle-Klara *Moynlin*, are you not? That's a bit different. Welcome aboard, I guess."

II

It wasn't the most affable greeting I'd ever had. However, when Humphrey Mason-Manley woke up the head engineer for me, she turned out to be a lot more courteous. She didn't have to be, either. Although I had put up the seed money to get the project started, PhoenixCorp was set up as a nonprofit quango, owned by nobody but itself. I wasn't even on the board.

The boss engineer's name, Hypatia whispered to me, was June Thaddeus Terple—*Doctor* Terple. I didn't really need the reminder. Terple and I had met before, though only by screen. In person she was taller than I'd thought. She looked to be about the age I looked to be myself, which is to say, charitably, thirtyish. She was wearing a kind of string bikini, plus a workman's belt of little pouches around her waist so she could keep things in it. She took me into her office, which was a sort of wedge-shaped chamber with nothing much visible in it but hand-holds on the walls and a lot more of those flowering plants. "Sorry I wasn't there to meet you, Dr. Moynlin," she said.

"The only kind of doctor I am is honorary, and Klara's good enough."

She bobbed her head. "Anyway, of course you're welcome here any time. I guess you wanted to see for yourself how we're coming along."

"Well, I did want that, yes. I also wanted to set something up, if you don't mind." That was me returning courtesy for courtesy, however unnecessary it was in either direction. "Do you know who Wilhelm Tartch is?"

She thought for a moment. "No."

So much for his galaxy-wide fame. I explained. "Bill's a kind of a roving reporter. He has a program that goes out all over, even to the Heechee in the Core. It's kind of a travelogue. He visits exciting and colorful places and reports on them for the stay-at-homes." He was also my present main lover, but there wasn't any reason to mention that to Terple; she would figure it out for herself fast enough.

"And he wants to do Phoenix?"

"If you don't mind," I said again. "I did clear it with the board."

She grinned at me. "So you did, but I sort of lost track of it. We've been deploying the mirror-builder drones, so it's been kind of busy." She shook herself. "Anyway, Hans tells me your shipmind displayed the actual supernova explosion to you on the way out—"

"That's right, she did." In my ear Hypatia was whispering that Hans was the name of their shipmind, as though I couldn't figure that out for myself.

"And I suppose you know what it looks like from Earth now?"

"Well, sort of."

I could see her assessing how much "sort of" amounted to, and deciding to be diplomatic to the money person. "It wouldn't hurt to take another look. Hans! Telescopic view from Earth, please."

She was looking toward one end of her office. It disappeared, and in its place we were looking out at a blotchy patch of light. "That's it. It's called the Crab Nebula. Of course, they named it that before they really knew what it was, but you can see where they got the name." I agreed that it did look a little like some sort of deformed crab, and Terple went on. "The nebula itself is just the gases and stuff that the supernova threw off, a thousand years or so later. I don't know if you can make it out, but there's a little spot in the middle of it that's the Crab pulsar. That's all that's left of the star. Now let's look at the way it was before it went super. Real-time. From here."

Hans wiped the nebula away and we were looking into the same deep, black space Hypatia had shown me already. There were the same zillion stars hanging there, but as the shipmind zoomed the picture closer, one extraordinarily bright one appeared. "Bright" didn't do it justice. It was a blazing golden yellow, curiously fuzzy. It wasn't really hot. It couldn't be; the simulation was only optical. But I could almost feel its heat on my face.

"I don't see any planet," I offered.

"Oh, you will, once we get all the optical segments in place." Then she interrupted herself. "I forgot to ask. Would you like a cup of tea or something?"

"Thanks, no. Nothing right this minute." I was peering at the star. "I thought it would be brighter," I said, a little disappointed.

"Oh, it will be, Klara. That's what we're building that 500-kilometer mirror for. Right now we're just getting the gravitational lensing from the black hole we're using—there's a little camera in the mirror. I don't know if you know much about black holes, but—oh, shit," she interrupted herself, suddenly stricken. "You do know, don't you? I mean, after you were stuck in one for thirty or forty years. . . ."

She looked as though she had inadvertently caused me great pain. She hadn't. I was used to that sort of reaction. People rarely brought up the subject of black holes in my presence, on the general principle that you don't talk about rope when there's been a hanging in the house. But the time when I had been trapped in one of the things was far back in the past. It had gone like a flash for me in the black hole's time dilation, however many years it was on the outside, and I wasn't sensitive about it.

On the other hand, I wasn't interested in discussing it one more damn time, either. I just said, "My black hole didn't look like that. It was a creepy kind of pale blue."

Terple recovered quickly. She gave me a wise nod of the head. "That would have been Cérenkov radiation. Yours must have been what they call a naked singularity. This one's different. It's wrapped up in its own ergosphere and you can't see a thing. Most black holes produce a lot of radiation—not from themselves, from the gases and stuff they're swallowing—but this one has already swallowed everything around it. Anyway." She paused to recollect her train of thought. Then she nodded. "I was telling you about the gravitational lensing. Hans?"

She didn't say what she wanted from Hans, but evidently he could figure it out for himself. The stars disappeared and a sort of wall of misty white appeared in front of us. Terpel poked at it here and there with a finger, drawing a little picture for me:

"That little dot on the left, that's the Crabber planet we want to study. The circle's the black hole. The arc on the right is our mirror, which is right at the point of convergence—where the gravitational lensing from the black hole gives us the sharpest image. And the little dot next to it is us, at the Cassegrain focus of the mirror. I didn't show the Crabber sun— actually we have to avoid aiming the camera at it, because it could burn out our optics. Am I making sense so far?"

"So far," I agreed.

She gave me another of those assessing looks, then said, "We'll actually be doing our observing by looking toward the mirror. There too we'll have to block out the star itself, or we won't see the Crab planet at all, but that's just another of the things we'll be adjusting. We'll actually be looking diametrically away from the planet in order to observe it."

I hadn't been able to resist the temptation with Hypatia, and I couldn't now with June Terple. "For four or five days," I said in my friendliest voice.

I guess the tone wasn't friendly enough. She looked nettled. "Listen, we didn't put the damn black hole where it is. It took us two years of searching to find one in the right position. There's a neutron star that we could've used. Orbitwise it was a better deal because it would have given us nearly eighty years to observe, but it's just a damn neutron star. It wouldn't have given us anywhere the same magnification, because a neutron star just doesn't have anywhere near as much mass as a black hole, so the gravitational lensing would've been a lot less powerful. We'll get a lot more detail with our black hole. Anyway," she added, "once we've observed from here we'll move this whole lashup to the neutron star for whatever additional data we can get—I mean, uh, if that seems advisable we will."

What she meant by that was if I was willing to pay for it. Well, I probably was. The capital costs were paid already. It would only mean meeting their payroll for another eighty years or so, and none of them were getting big bucks. Hypatia had seen to that.

But I wasn't ready to make that commitment. To take her mind off it, I said, "I thought we were supposed to have almost thirty days of observing right here."

She looked glum. "*Radio* observing. That's why we built the mesh dish. But it turns out there's no artifactual radio coming from the Crabber planet, so we had to get mirror plates so we could convert it to optical. Took us over three weeks, which is why we lost so much observing time."

"I see," I said. "No radio signals. So there might not be any civilization there to observe, anyway."

She bit her lip. "We know definitely that there's *life* there. Or was, anyway. It's one of the planets the Heechee surveyed long ago, and there were advanced living organisms there at the time—pretty primitive, sure, but they certainly looked as though they had the potential to evolve."

"The *potential* to evolve, right. But whether they did or not we just don't know."

She didn't answer that. She just sighed. Then she said, "As long as you're here, would you like a look around?"

"If I won't be in the way," I said.

Of course I was in the way. June Terple didn't let it show, but some of the others barely gave me the courtesy of looking up when we were introduced. There were eight of them altogether, with names like Julia Ibarruru and Mark Rohrbeck and Humphrey Mason-Manley and Oleg Kekuskian and—well, I didn't have to try to retain them all; Hypatia would clue me as needed. Julia was floating in a harness surrounded by fifteen or twenty 3-D icons that she was busy poking at and glowering at and poking at again, and she gave me no more than a quick and noncommital nod. If my name meant anything to her, or to most of the others, they didn't show any signs of being impressed. Especially Rohrbeck and Kekuskian didn't, because they were sound asleep in their harnesses when we peeked in on them, and Terple had a finger to her lips. "Third shift," she whispered when we'd closed the flaps on their cubicles and moved away. "They'll be waking up for dinner in a little while, but we should let them get their sleep. And there's only one other. Let's go find her."

On the way to that one other member of the crew Hypatia was whispering bits of biography in my ear. Kekuskian was the quite elderly bisexual astrophysicist; Rohrbeck the quite young and deeply depressed program designer, whose marriage had just come painfully apart. And the one remaining person was—

Was a Heechee.

I didn't have to be told that. Once you've seen any one Heechee you know what they all look like, skeletally thin front-to-back, squarish, skulllike face, a data pod hanging between its legs where, if it were male, his balls should be, and if female (as this one turned out to be) there shouldn't be anything much at all. Her name, Terple said, was Starminder, and as we entered her chamber she was working at a set of icons of her own. But as soon as she heard my name, she wiped them and barreled over to me to shake my hand. "You are very famous among persons in the Core, Gelle-Klara Moynlin," she informed me, hanging on to my hand for support. "Because of your Moynlin Citizen Ambassadors, you see. When your Rebecca Shapiro person came to the Core I met her. She was quite informative about human beings; indeed, it was because of her that I volunteered at once to come out. Do you know her?"

I tried to remember Rebecca Shapiro. I had put up grant money for a good many batches of recruits since I funded the program, and she would have had to be one of the earliest of them. Starminder saw my uncertainty and tried to be helpful. "Young woman. Very sad. She sang music composed by your now-dead Wolfgang Amadeus Mozart for our people, which I almost came to enjoy."

"Oh, right, *that* Rebecca," I said, not very honestly. By then I'd paid the fare to the Core for—what?—at least two or three hundred Rebeccas or Carlos or Janes who volunteered to be Citizen Ambassadors to the Heechee in the Core because they had lives that were in shambles. That was a given. If their lives hadn't been, why would they want to leave the people and places they couldn't ever come back to?

Because, of course, the Core was time-dilated, like any black hole.

I knew what that meant. When you were time-dilated in the Core, where a couple of centuries of Outside time went by every day, the problems you had left behind got really old really fast. Time dilation was better than suicide—though, when you came to think of it, it was actually pretty much a kind of reverse suicide. You didn't die yourself, but every troublesome person you'd ever known did while you were gone.

I wish all those Citizen Ambassadors of mine well. I hope it all works out for them . . . but being in a black hole hadn't done a thing for me.

Once I'd met all the people on PhoenixCorp, there wasn't much else to see. I had misjudged my budget-watcher. Terple hadn't been particularly spendthrift after all. If you didn't count the opulent plantings—and they were there primarily to keep the air good—PhoenixCorp actually was a pretty bare-bones kind of spacecraft. There were the sleeping quarters for the help, and some common rooms—the big one I'd come into when I first entered, plus a sort of dining room with beverage dispensers and netting next to the hold-ons to keep the meals from flying away, a couple of little rooms for music or virtuals when the people wanted some recreation. The rest of it was storage and, of course, all the machinery and instrumentation PhoenixCorp needed to do its job. Terple didn't show me any of the hardware. I didn't expect her to. That's the shipmind's business, and that sort of thing stays sealed away where no harm can come to it. So, unless somebody had been foolish enough to open up a lot of compartments that were meant to stay closed, there wouldn't have been anything to see.

When we were finished she finally insisted on that cup of tea—really that capsule of tea, that is—and while we were drinking it, holding with one hand to the hold-ons, she said, "That's about it, Klara. Oh, wait a minute. I haven't actually introduced you to our shipmind, have I? Hans? Say hello to Ms. Moynlin."

A deep, pleasant male voice said, "Hello, Ms. Moynlin. Welcome aboard. We've been hoping you'd visit us."

I said hello back to him and left it at that. I don't particularly like chatting with machine intelligences, except my own. I finished my tea, slid the empty capsule into its slot and said, "Well, I'll get out of your way. I want to get back to my own ship for a bit anyway."

Terple nodded, without asking why. "We're going to have dinner in about an hour. Would you like to join us? Hans is a pretty good cook."

That sounded like as good an idea as any, so, "That would be fine," I told her.

Then, as she was escorting me to the docking port, she gave me a sidewise look. "Listen," she said, "I'm sorry we bombed out on the radio search. It doesn't necessarily mean that the Crabbers never got civilized. After all, if somebody had scanned Earth any time before the twentieth century they wouldn't have heard any radio signals there, either, but the human race was fully evolved by then."

"I know that, June."

"Yes." She cleared her throat. "Do you mind if I ask you a question?"

I said, "Of course not," meaning that she could ask anything she wanted to, but whether or what I might I choose to answer was another matter entirely.

"Well, you put a lot of money into getting Phoenix started, just on the chance that there might have been an intelligent race there that got fried when their sun went super. What I'm wondering is why."

The answer to that was simple enough. I mean, what's the point of being about the richest woman in the universe if you don't have a little fun with your money now and then? But I didn't say that to her. I just said, "What else do I have to do?"

III

Well, I did have things to do. Lots of them, though most of them weren't very important.

The only one that was really important—to me—was overseeing what was going on on the little island off Tahiti that I live on when I'm home. It's a nice place, the way I've fixed it up. Most of my more-or-less family is there and when I'm away I really miss them.

Then there are other important things, like spending some time with Bill Tartch, who was a fairly sweet man, not to mention all the others like Bill Tartch who have come along over the years. Or such things as all the things I can buy with my money, plus figuring out what to do with the power that that kind of money gives. Put them all together, I had *plenty* to do with my life. And I had plenty of life to look forward to, too, especially if I let Hypatia talk me into immortality.

So why wasn't I looking forward to it?

That's the trouble with questions I can't answer. I keep trying to find answers for them.

When I came back into my ship, Hypatia was waiting for me—optically visible, in full 3-D simulation, lounging draped Roman-style on the loveseat in my main cabin and fully dressed in her fifth-century robes.

"So how did you like your investment?" she asked sociably.

"Tell you in a minute," I said, heading for the head and closing the door behind me. Of course, a closed door makes no real difference with

Hypatia. She can see me wherever I am on the ship, and no doubt does, but as long as a machine intelligence acts and looks human I want it to pretend to observe human courtesies.

I wasn't long, but that was the main reason I'd come back to my ship just then. I don't like peeing in free fall, in those awful toilets they have. Hypatia keeps ours at a suitable gravity for my comfort, like the rest of the ship. Besides, it makes her nervous if I use any other toilets, because she likes to rummage through my excretions to see if I'm staying healthy.

Which she had been doing while I was in the head. When I came out she didn't seem to have moved, but she said, "Are you really going to eat their food?"

"Sure. Why not?"

"You've been running a little high on polyglycerides. Better you let me cook for you."

Teasing her, I said, "June Terple says Hans is a better cook."

"She said he's a *good* cook," she corrected me, "but so am I. I've been accessing him, by the way, so if there's anything you'd like to know about the crew. . . ."

"Not about the crew, but Starminder said something about a Rebecca Shapiro. Who was she?"

"That data is not in the Phoenix shipmind's stores, Klara," she said, reproving me. "However. . . ."

She whited out a corner of my lounge and displayed a face on it while she gave me a capsule biography of Rebecca Shapiro. She had been the dramatic soprano with a brilliant operatic future ahead of her until she got her larynx crushed in a plane crash. They'd repaired it well enough for most purposes, but she was never going to be able to sing "The Queen of the Night" again. So, with her life on Earth ruined, Rebecca had signed up for my program. "Any other questions?" Hypatia finished.

"Not about Rebecca, but I've been wondering why they call their shipmind Hans?"

"Oh, that was Mark Rohrbeck's idea; he wanted to name him after some old computer pioneer. The name doesn't matter, though, does it? I mean, why did you decide to call me Hypatia?"

I had an answer for that. "Because Hypatia of Alexandria was a smart, snotty bitch," I told her. "Like you."

"Humph," she said.

"As well as being the first great woman scientist," I added, because Hypatia always likes to talk about herself.

She did. "The first *known* one," she corrected. "Who knows how many of them there were whose accomplishments didn't manage to survive? Women didn't get much of a break in 'your ancient meat world—or, for that matter, now."

"You were supposed to be beautiful, too," I reminded her. "And you died a virgin anyway."

"By choice, Klara. Even that old Hypatia didn't care much for all that messy meat stuff. And I didn't just die. I was brutally murdered. It was a cold wet spring in the year AD 450, and a gang of those damn Nitrian monks tore me to shreds because I wasn't a Christian. Anyway," she finished, "you're the one who picked my identity. If you wanted me to be someone else you could have given me a different one."

She had me grinning by then. "I still can," I reminded her. "Maybe something like Joan of Arc?"

She shuddered fastidiously at the idea of being a Christian instead of a gods-fearing Roman pagan, and changed the subject. "Would you like me to put a call through to Mr. Tartch now?"

Well, I would and I wouldn't. I wasn't quite ready to talk to him. I shook my head. "I've been wondering about these extinct people we're trying to resurrect. Have you got any Heechee records of the planet that I haven't seen yet?"

"You bet. More than you'll ever want to watch."

"So show me some."

"Sure thing, boss," she said, and disappeared, and all at once I was standing on an outcropping of rock, looking down on a bright, green valley where some funny-looking animals were moving around.

The difference between PhoenixCorp's major simulations and mine was that mine cost more. Theirs were good enough for working purposes, because they showed you pretty much anything you wanted to see, but mine put you right in the middle of it. Mine were full sensory systems, too, so I could smell and feel as well as I could see and hear. As I stood there a warm breeze was riffling my hair, and there was a distinct reek of smoke. "Hey, Hypatia," I said, a little surprised. "Have these people discovered fire?"

"Not to use, no," she murmured in my ear. "There must've been a lightning strike up in the hills from the storm."

"What storm?"

"The one that just passed. Don't you see everything's wet?"

Not on my rock, it wasn't. The sun overhead was big and bright and very hot. It had already baked the rock dry, but I could see that the jumble of dark-green vines at the base of my rock were still dripping, and when I turned around I could see a splotch of burning vegetation on the distant hill.

The valley was more interesting. Copses of trees, or something like trees; a herd of big, shaggy things, Kodiak bear–sized but obviously vegetarians because they were industriously pushing some of the trees over to eat their leaves; a pair of rivers, a narrow, fast-moving one with little waterfalls that came down from the hills to my left and flowed to join a broader, more sluggish one on the right to make a bigger stream; a few other shaggy creatures, these quite a lot bigger still, feeding by themselves on whatever was growing in the plain—well, it was an interesting sight; maybe a little like the Great American Prairie must have looked before our forebears killed off all the wild meat animals.

The most interesting part of it was a pack of a dozen or so predators in the middle distance, circling furtively around a group of three or four creatures I couldn't easily make out. I pointed. "Are those the ones?" I asked Hypatia. And when she said they were I told her to get me up closer.

At close range I could see the hunted ones were something that looked like pigs—well, they looked like pigs, that is, if pigs happened to have long, skinny legs and long squirrely tails. There was a mommy pig baring her teeth and trying to snap at the predators in all directions at once, and three little ones doing their best to huddle under the mother's belly. It was the predators I was paying attention to. They looked vaguely primate. That is, they had apelike faces and short tails. But they didn't look like any primate that ever lived on Earth, because they had six limbs: four that they ran on, and two more like arms, and in their sort-of hands they held sharp-edged rocks. As they got into position they began hurling the rocks at the prey.

The mother pig didn't have a chance. In a couple of minutes two of her babies were down and she was racing away with that long tail flicking from side to side like a metronome, and the surviving piglet right behind her, its tail-flicks keeping time with its mother's, and the six-limbed predators had what they had come for.

It was not a pretty scene.

I know perfectly well that animals live by eating, and I'm not sentimental about the matter—hell, I eat steak! (Not always out of a Food Factory, either.) All the same, I didn't like watching what was happening on this half-million-year-old alien veldt, because one of the piglets was still alive when the wolf-apes began eating it, and its pitiful shrieking got to me.

So I wasn't a bit sorry when Hypatia interrupted me to say that Mr. Tartch hadn't waited for me to call him and was already on the line.

———

Nearly all of my conversations with Bill Tartch get into some kind of intimate areas. He likes sexy talk. I don't particularly, so I tried to keep the call short. He looked as good as ever—not very tall, not exactly handsome but solidly built and with a great, challenging I-know-what-fun-is-all-about grin—and he was just two days out. That's not a lot of hard data to get out of what was more than a quarter of an hour of talk capsuled back and forth over all those light-years, I guess, but the rest is private; and when I was finished it was about time to get dressed for dinner with the PhoenixCorp people.

Hypatia was way ahead of me, as usual. She had gone through my wardrobe and used her effectuators to pull out a dressy pants suit for me, so I wouldn't have a skirt to keep flying up, along with a gold neckband that wouldn't be flopping around my face as the pearls had. They were good choices; I didn't argue. And while I was getting into them she asked chattily, "So did Mr. Tartch say thank you?"

I know Hypatia's tones by now. This one made my hackles rise. "For what?"

"Why, for keeping his career going," she said, sounding surprised. "He was pretty much washed up until you came along, wasn't he? So it's only appropriate that he should, you know, display his gratitude."

"You're pushing your luck," I told her, as I slipped into a pair of jeweled footstockings. Sometimes I think Hypatia gets a little too personal, and this time it just wasn't justified. I didn't have to do favors to get a man. Christ, the problem was to fend them off! It's just that when it's over I like to leave them a little better off than I found them; and for Bill, true enough, a little help now and then had been useful.

But I didn't want to discuss it with her. "Talk about something else or shut up," I ordered.

"Sure, hon. Let's see. How did you like the Crabbers?"

I told her the truth. "Not much. Their table manners are pretty lousy."

Hypatia giggled. "Getting a weak stomach, Klara? Do you really think they're much worse than your own remote predecessors? Because I don't think *Australopithecus robustus* worried about whether its dinners were enjoying the meal."

We were getting into a familiar argument. "That was a long time ago, Hypatia."

"So is what you were looking at with the Crabbers, hon. Animals are animals. Now, if you really want to take yourself out of that nasty kill-and-eat business—"

"Not yet," I told her, as I had told her many times before. And maybe not ever.

What Hypatia wanted to do was to vasten me. That is, take me out of my meat body, with all its aches and annoyances, and make me into a pure, machine-stored intelligence. Like other people I knew had done. Like Hypatia herself, though in her case she was no more than a simulated approximation of someone who had once been living meat.

It was a scary idea, to be sure, but not altogether unattractive. I wasn't getting as much pleasure as I would have liked out of living, but I certainly didn't want to *die*. And if I did what Hypatia wanted, I would never have to.

But I wasn't prepared to take that step yet. There were one or two things a meat person could do that a machine person couldn't—well, one big one—and I wasn't prepared to abandon the flesh until I had done what the female flesh was best at. For which I needed a man . . . and I wasn't at all sure that Bill Tartch was the particular man I needed.

When I got back for dinner in the PhoenixCorp vessel, everybody was looking conspiratorial and expectant. "We've got about twenty percent of the optical foils in place," Terple informed me, thrilled with excitement. "Would you like to see?" She didn't wait for an answer, but commanded: "Hans! Display the planet."

The lights went dark, and there before us floated a blue and white globe the size of my head, looking as though it were maybe ten meters away. It was half in darkness and half in sunlight, from a sun that was out of sight off to my right. There was a half-moon, too, just popping into sight from behind the planet. It looked smaller than Luna, and if it had markings of craters and seas I couldn't see them. On the planet itself I could make out a large ocean and a kind of squared-off continent on the illuminated side. Terple did something that made the lights in the room go off, and then I could see that there had to be even more land on the dark side, because spots of light—artificial lights, cities' lights—blossomed all over parts of the nighttime area.

"You see, Klara?" she crowed. "Cities! Civilization!"

IV

Their shipmind really was a good cook. A fritto misto, with a decent risotto and figs in cream for dessert, all perfectly prepared. Or maybe it just seemed so, because everybody was visibly relaxing now that it had turned out we really would have something to observe.

However, there wasn't any wine to go with the meal. "We're not doing anything alcoholic until we've completed the obs," June Terple volunteered, half apologetic, half challenging. "Still, I think Hans could get you something. . . ."

I shook my head, wondering if Hypatia had said anything to Hans about how I liked a drink now and then. Probably she had. Shipminds do gossip, and it was evident that the crew did know something about me. The conversation was lively and far-ranging, but it never, never touched on the subject of black holes.

It was a nice meal of it. The only interruptions were when one crew member after another briefly excused himself to double-check how the spider robots were doing as they clambered all over that 500-kilometer dish, seamlessly stitching the optical reflection foils into their perfect parabola. None of the organic crew really had to bother. Hans was permanently vigilant, about that and everything else, but Terple obviously ran a tight ship. A lot of the back-and-forth chat was in-jokes, but that wasn't a problem because Hypatia explained them, whispering in my ear. When somebody mentioned homesickness and Oleg Kekuskian said jestingly— *pointedly* jestingly—that some of us weren't homesick at all, that was aimed at Humphrey Mason-Manley: "He's pronging Terple, Klara, and Kekuskian's jealous." Julia—that was *Hoolia*—Ibarruru, the fat and elderly Peruvian-Inca former schoolteacher, was wistfully telling Starminder how much she wished she could visit the Core before she died, and was indignant when she found out that I'd never been to Machu Picchu. "And you've been all over the Galaxy? And never took the time to see one of the greatest wonders of your own planet?" The only subdued one was Mark Rohrbeck. Between the figs and the coffee he excused himself and didn't come back for nearly half an hour. "Calling home," Mason-Manley said wisely, and Hypatia, who was the Galaxy's greatest eavesdropper when I let her be, filled me in. "He's trying to talk his wife out of the divorce. She isn't buying it."

When the coffee was about half gone, Terple whispered something to the air. Evidently Hans was listening, and in a moment the end of the room went dark. The planet appeared, noticeably bigger than it had been before. She whispered again, and the image expanded until it filled the room, and I had the sudden vertiginous sense that I was falling into it.

"We're getting about two- or three-kilometer resolution now," Terple announced proudly.

That didn't give us much beyond mountains, shorelines and clouds, and the planet was still half in sun and half dark. (Well, it had to be, didn't it? The planet was rotating under us, but, in just the few days we were going to be observing it, its position relative to its sun wasn't going to change.) When I studied it, something looked odd about the landmass at the bottom of the image. I pointed. "Is that ocean, there, down on the left side? I mean the dark part. Because I didn't see any lights there."

"No, it's land, all right. It's probably just that that part is too cold to be inhabited. We're not getting a square look at the planet, you know. We're about twenty degrees south of its equator, so we're seeing more of its South Pole and nothing north of, let's say, what would be Scotland or southern Alaska on Earth. Have you seen the globe Hans put together for us? No? Hans, display."

Immediately a sphere appeared in the middle of the room, rotating slowly. It would have looked exactly like the kind my grandfather kept in his bedroom, latitude and longitude lines and all, except that the land masses were wholly wrong. "This is derived from old Heechee data that Starminder provided for us," Hans's voice informed me. "However, we've named the continents ourselves. You see the one that's made up of two fairly circular masses, connected by an isthmus, that looks like a dumbbell? Dr. Terple calls it 'Dumbbell.' It's divided into Dumbbell East and Dumbbell West. Fryingpan is the sort of roundish one with the long, thin peninsula projecting to the southwest. The one just coming into view now is Peanut, because—"

"I can see why," I told him. Hans was a perceptive enough program to recognize, probably from the tone of my voice, that I found this geography lesson a little boring. Terple wasn't.

"Go on, Hans," she said sharply when he hesitated. So he did.

Out of guest-politeness I sat still while he named every dot on the map for me, but when he came to the end I did too. "That's very nice," I said, unhooking myself from my dining place. "Thanks for the dinner, June, but I think I'd better let you get your work done. Anyway, we'll be seeing a lot of each other over the next five days."

Every face I saw wore a suddenly bland expression, and Terple coughed. "Well, not quite five days," she said uncomfortably. "I don't know whether anyone told you this, but we'll leave before the star blows."

I stopped cold, one hand stuffing my napkin into its tied-down ring, the other holding onto the wall support. "There wasn't anything about leaving early in your prospectus. Why wasn't I told this?"

She said doggedly, "When the star begins its collapse, I'm getting out of here. It's too dangerous."

I don't like being surprised by the people who work for me. I gave her a look. "How can it be dangerous when we're six thousand light-years away?"

She got obstinate. "Remember I'm responsible for the safety of this installation and its crew. I don't think you have any idea of what a supernova is like, Klara. It's *huge*. Back in 1054 the Chinese astrologers could see it in *daylight* for almost the whole month of July, and they didn't have our lensing to make it brighter."

"So we'll put on sunglasses."

She said firmly, "We'll *leave*. I'm not just talking about visible light. Even now, after six thousand years of cooling down after it popped, that thing's still radiating all across the electromagnetic spectrum, from microwave to X-rays. We're not going to want to be where all that radiation comes to a focus when it peaks."

As I was brushing my teeth Hypatia spoke from behind me. "What Terple said makes sense, you know. Anything in the focus is going to get fried when the star goes supernova."

I didn't answer, so she tried another tack. "Mark Rohrbeck is a good-looking man, isn't he? He's very confused right now, with the divorce and all, but I think he likes you."

I looked at her in the mirror. She was in full simulation, leaning against the bathroom doorway with a little smile on her face. "He's also half my age," I pointed out.

"Oh, no, Klara," she corrected me. "Not even a third of your age, actually. Still, what difference does that make? Hans displayed his file for me. Genetically he's very clean, as organic human beings go. Would you like to see it?"

"No." I finished with the bathroom and turned to leave. Hypatia got gracefully out of my way just as though I couldn't have walked right through her.

"Well, then," she said. "Would you like something to eat? A nightcap?"

"What I would like is to go to sleep. Right now."

She sighed. "Such a waste of time. Sooner or later you know you're going to give up the meat, don't you? Why wait? In machine simulation you can do anything you can do now, only better, and—"

"Enough," I ordered. "What I'm going to do now is go to bed and dream about my lover. Go away."

The simulation disappeared, and her "Good night, then," came from empty air. Hypatia doesn't really go away when I tell her to, but she pretends she does. Part of the pretense is that she never acts as though she knows what I do in the privacy of my room, though of course she does.

It wasn't exactly true that I intended to dream about Bill Tartch. Maybe I thought about him, a little bit, especially when I tucked myself into that huge circular bed and automatically reached out for someone to touch, and nobody was there. I truly enjoy having a warm male body to spoon up against to drift off to sleep. But, if I didn't have that, I also didn't have anybody snoring in my ear, or thrashing about, or talking to me when I first woke up and all I wanted was to huddle over a cup of coffee and a piece of grapefruit in peace.

Those were fairly consoling thoughts, but as soon as I put my head down I was wide awake again.

Insomnia was one more of those meat-person flaws that disgusted Hypatia so. I didn't have to suffer from it. Hypatia keeps my bathroom medicine chest stocked with everything she imagines I might want in the middle of the night, including half a dozen different kinds of anti-insomnia pills, but I had a better idea than that. I popped the lid off my bedside stand, where I keep the manual controls I use when I don't want Hypatia to do something for me, and I accessed the synoptic I wanted to see.

I visited my island.

Its name is Raiwea—that's rah-ee-WAY-uh, with the accent on the third syllable, the way the Polynesians say it—and it's the only place in the universe I ever miss when I'm away from it. It's not very big. It only amounts to a couple thousand hectares of dry land altogether, but it's got palm trees and breadfruit trees and a pretty lagoon that's too shallow for the sharks ever to invade from the deep water outside the reef. And now, because I paid to put them there, it's got lots of clusters of pretty little bungalows with pretty, if imitation, thatched roofs, as well as plumbing and air-conditioning and everything else that would make a person comfortable. And it's got playgrounds and game fields that are laid out for baseball or soccer or whatever a bunch of kids might need to work off excess animal energy. And it's got its own Food Factory nestled inside the reef that's constantly churning out every variety of healthful food anyone wants to eat; and it's mine. All of it is mine. Every square centimeter. I paid for it, and I've populated it with orphans and single women with babies from all over the world. When I go there, I'm Grandma Klara to about a hundred and fifty kids from newborns to teens, and when I'm somewhere else I make it a point, every day or so, to access the surveillance systems and make sure the schools are functioning and the medical services are keeping everybody healthy, because I—all right, damn it!—because I love those kids. Every last one of them, and I swear they love me back.

Hypatia says they're my substitute for having a baby of my own.

Maybe they are. All the same, I do have a couple of my own ova stored in the Raiwea clinic's deep freeze. They've been there for a good many years now, but the doctors promise they're still 100% viable. The ova are there just in case I ever decide I really want to do that other disgustingly meat-person thing and give birth to my own genetically personal child. . . .

But I don't seem to meet the man I want to be its father. Bill Tartch? Well, maybe. I had thought he might be for a while, anyway, but then I wasn't really so sure.

The thing is, I thought I had met that man once. It might even have worked out, only then I got stuck in that damn black hole for a couple of decades, and by the time I got rescued, why, somewhere along those years, old Rob Broadhead had got himself hooked up with some other woman.

Too bad, right?

But what's the use of worrying about what can't be fixed?

When I was up and about the next morning Hypatia greeted me with a fresh display of the Crabber planet. The image was too big now to fit in my salon, but she had zeroed in on one particular coastline. In the center of the image there was a blur that might have been manmade—personmade, I mean. "They're down to half-kilometer resolution now," she informed me. "That's pretty definitely a small city."

I inspected it. It pretty definitely was, but it was very definitely small. "Isn't there anything bigger?"

"I'm afraid not, Klara. Hans says the planet seems to be rather remarkably underpopulated, though it's not clear why. Will you be going over to PhoenixCorp now?"

I shook my head. "Let them work in peace. We might as well do some work ourselves. What've you got for me?"

What she had for me was another sampling of some of the ventures I'd put money into at one time or another. There were the purely commercial ones like the helium-3 mines on the Moon, and the chain of food factories in the Bay of Bengal, and the desert-revivification project in the Sahara and forty or fifty others; they weren't particularly interesting to me, but they were some of the things that, no matter how much I spent, just kept making me richer and richer every day.

Along about then Hypatia cleared her throat in the manner that means there's something she wants to talk about. I guessed she wanted to discuss my island, so I played the game. "Oh, by the way," I said, "I accessed Raiwea last night after I went to bed."

"Really?" she said, just as though she hadn't known it all along. "How are things?"

I went through the motions of telling her which kids were about ready to leave, and how there were eighteen new ones who had been located by the various agencies I did business with, ready to be brought to the island next time I was in the neighborhood. As she always did, whether she meant it or not, she clucked approvingly. Her simulation was looking faintly amused, though. I took it as a challenge. "So you see there's one thing us animals can do that you can't," I told her. "We can have babies."

"Or, as in your own case at least so far, not," she said agreeably. "That wasn't what I was going to tell you, though."

"Oh?"

"I just wanted to mention that Mr. Tartch's ship is going to dock in about an hour. He isn't coming alone."

Sometimes Hypatia is almost too idiosyncratically human, and more than once I've thought about getting her programs changed. The tone of her voice warned me that she had something more to tell. I said tentatively, "That's not surprising. Sometimes he needs to bring a crew with him."

"Of course he does, Klara," she said cheerfully. "There's only one of them this time, though. And she's very pretty."

V

The very pretty assistant was very pretty, all right, and she looked to be about sixteen years old. No, that's not exactly true. She looked a lot *better* than sixteen years old. I don't believe I had skin like that even when I was a newborn baby. She wore no makeup, and needed none. She had on a decorous one-piece jump suit that covered her from thigh to neck and left no doubt of what was inside. Her name was Denys. When I got there—I had taken my time, because I didn't want Bill to think I was eager—all three of PhoenixCorp's males were hanging around, watching her like vultures sniffing carrion.

Bill didn't seem to notice. He had already set up for his opening teaser and Denys was playing his quaint old auto-cameras for him. As they panned around the entrance chamber and settled on his face, wearing its friendliest and most intelligent expression, he began to speak to the masses:

"Wilhelm Tartch here again, where PhoenixCorp is getting ready to bring a lost race of intelligent beings back to life, and here to help me—" one of the cameras swung around as Denys cued it toward me—"once again I have the good luck to have my beautiful fiancée, Gelle-Klara Moynlin, with me."

I gave him a look, because, whatever I was to Wilhelm Tartch, I definitely wasn't someone who was planning to marry him. He tipped me a cheeky wink and went right on:

"As you all remember, before the Heechee ran away to hide in the Core, they surveyed most of the Galaxy, looking for other intelligent races. They didn't find any. When they visited Earth they found the australopithecines, but they were a long way from being modern humans. They hadn't even developed language yet. And here, on this planet—" That view of the Crabber planet, pre-supernova, appeared behind him. "—they found another primitive race that they thought, someday, might become both intelligent and civilized. Well, perhaps these Crabbers, as the PhoenixCorp people call them, did. But the Heechee weren't around to see it, and neither are we, because they had some bad luck.

"There were two stars in their planet's system, a red dwarf and a bright type-A giant. Over the millennia, as these lost people were struggling toward civilization, the big star was losing mass, sucked into the smaller one. Then, without warning, the small one reached critical mass. It exploded. And the Crabber people, along with their planet and all their works, were instantly obliterated in the supernova blast."

He stopped there, gazing toward Denys until she called, "Got it." Then he kicked himself toward me, arms outstretched for a hug, big grin on his facé; and when we connected he buried his face in my neck, whispering things like, "Oh, Klaretta, we've been away from each other too long!"

Bill Tartch is a good hugger. His arms felt fine around me, and his big, male body felt good against mine . . . as I looked over his shoulder at Denys. Who was regarding us with an affectionate and wholly unjealous smile.

So, I thought, that part might not be much of a problem. I decided not to worry about it. Anyway the resolution of the Crabber planet was getting better and better, and that was what we were here for, after all.

What the Crabber planet had a lot of was water. As it turned on its axis the continental shore had disappeared into the nighttime side of the world, and what we were looking at was mostly ocean.

Bill Tartch wasn't pleased. "Is that all we're going to see?" he demanded of the room at large. "I thought there was at least some kind of a city."

Terple answered. "A small city—probably. Anyway, that's what it looked like before the planet turned and we lost it. I can show you that much if you like. Hans? Go back to when that object was still in sight."

The maybe-city didn't look any more exciting the second time I saw it, and it didn't impress Bill. He made a little tongue-click of annoyance. "You, shipmind! Can't you enhance the image for me?"

"It is enhanced, Mr. Tartch," Hans told him pleasantly. "However, we have somewhat better resolution now, and I've been tracking it in the infrared. There's a little more detail—" the continental margin appeared for us, hazily delineated because of the differences in temperature between water and land—"but, as you see, there are hot spots that I have not yet identified."

There were. *Big* ones, and very bright. What was encouraging, considering what we were looking for, was that some of them seemed to be fairly geometrical in shape, triangles and rectangles. But what were they?

"Christmas decorations?" Bill guessed. "You know, I mean not really Christmas, but with the houses all lit up for some holiday or other?"

"I don't think so, Mr. Tartch," Hans said judiciously. "There's not much optical light; what you're seeing is heat."

"Keeping themselves warm in the winter?"

"I don't know if it's their winter, Mr. Tartch, and that isn't probable in any case. Those sources read out at up to around three hundred degrees Celsius. That's almost forest-fire temperature."

Bill looked puzzled. "Slash-and-burn agriculture? Or maybe some kind of industry?"

"We can't say yet, Mr. Tartch. If it were anything like that there should be more visible light; there's very little. We'll simply have to wait for better data. Meanwhile, however, there's something else you might like to see." The scene we were viewing skittered across the face of the planet—huge cloud banks, a couple of islands, more cloud—and came to rest on a patch of ocean. In its center was a tiny blur of something that looked grayish when it looked like anything at all; it seemed to flicker in and out of sight, at the very limit of visibility.

"Clouds?" Bill guessed.

"No, Mr. Tartch. I believe it is a group of objects of some kind, and they are in motion—vectoring approximately seventy-one degrees, or, as you would say, a little north of east. They must be quite large or we would not pick up anything at all. They may be ships, although their rate of motion is too high for anything but a hydrofoil or ground-effect craft. If they are still in sight when the mirror is more nearly complete we should be able to resolve them easily enough."

"Which will be when?"

Hans gave us that phony couple-of-seconds pause before he answered. "There is a small new problem about that, Mr. Tartch," he said apologetically. "Some of the installed mirror plates have been subjected to thermal shock and they are no longer an exact fit. Most of the installation machines have had to be diverted to adjust them, and so it will be some time before we can go on with completing the mirror. A few hours only, I estimate."

Bill looked at me and I looked at him. "Well, hell," he said. "What else is going to go wrong?"

What had gone wrong that time wasn't June Terple's fault. She said it was, though. She said that she was the person in charge of the whole operation, so everything that happened was her responsibility, and she shouldn't have allowed Ibarruru to override Hans's controls. And Julia Ibarruru was tearfully repentant. "Starminder told me the Heechee had identified eleven other planets in the Crabber system; I was just checking to see if there were any signs of life on any of them, and I'm afraid that for a minute I let the system's focus get too close to the star."

It could have been worse. I told them not to worry about it, and invited all three of them to my ship for a drink, Starminder included. That made my soi-disant fiancé's eyebrows rise, because he had certainly been expecting that the first person I welcomed aboard would be him. He was philosophical about it, though. "I'll see you later," he said. Then he led Denys off to interview some of the other people.

Hypatia had set out tea things on one table, and dry sherry on another, but before we sat down to either I had to give all three of the women the usual guided tour. The sudden return to normal gravity was a burden for them, but they limped admiringly through the guest bedroom, exclaimed at the kitchen—never used by me, but installed just in case I ever wanted to do any of that stuff myself—and were blown away by my personal bathroom. Whirlbath, bidet, big onyx tub, mirror walls—Bill Tartch always said it looked like a whore's dream of heaven, and he hadn't been the first guest to make that observation. I don't suppose the Phoenix-Corp women had ever seen anything like it. I let them look. I even let them peek into the cabinets of perfumes and toiletries. "Oh, musk oil!" Terple cried. "But it's real! That's so expensive."

"I don't wear it anymore. Take it, if you like," I said, and, for the grand finale, opened the door to my bedroom.

When at last we got to the tea, sherry and conversation, Ibarruru's first remark was, "Mr. Tartch seemed like a very interesting man." She didn't spell out the connection, but I knew it was that huge bed that was in her mind. So we chatted about Mr. Tartch and his glamorous p-vision career, and how Terple had grown up with the stories of the Gateway prospectors on every day's news, and how Ibarruru had dreamed of an opportunity like this—"Astronomy's really almost a lost art on Earth, you know," she told me. "Now we have all the Heechee data, so there's no point anymore in wasting time with telescopes and probes."

"So what does an astronomer do when there's no astronomy to be done?" I asked, being polite.

She said ruefully, "I was teaching an undergraduate course in astronomy in a community college in Maryland. For students who aren't ever going to do any real astronomy, because if there's anything somebody really wants to see, why, they just get in a ship and go out and look at it."

"As I did, Ms. Moynlin," said Starminder, with the Heechee equivalent of a smile.

That was what I was waiting for. If there was a place in the universe I still wanted to see, it was her home in the Core. "You must miss the Core," I told her. "All those nearby stars, so bright—what we have here must look pretty skimpy to you."

"Oh, no," she said, being polite, "this is quite nice. For a change. What I really miss is my children."

It had never occurred to me that she had children, but, yes, she had left two young offspring behind when she came out. It was a difficult decision, but she couldn't resist the adventure. Miss them? Of course she missed them! Miss her? She looked surprised at that. "Why, no, Ms. Moynlin, they won't be missing me. They're asleep for the night. I'll be back long before they wake up. Time dilation, you see. I'm only going to stay out here for a year or two."

Ibarruru said nervously, "That's the part that worries me about going to the Core, Starminder. I'm not young anymore, and I know that if I went for even a few days nearly everyone I know would be gone when I got back. No, not just 'nearly' everyone," she corrected herself. "What is it, forty thousand to one? So a week there would be nearly a thousand years back home." Then she turned to the Heechee female. "But even if we can't go ourselves, you can tell us about it, Starminder. Would you like to tell Dr. Moynlin what it's like in the Core?"

It was what I wanted to hear, too. I'd heard it often enough before, but I listened as long as Starminder was willing to talk. Which was a lot, because she was definitely homesick.

Would it really matter if I spent a week in the Core? Or a month, or a year, for that matter? I'd miss my kids on the island, of course, but they'd be taken care of, and so would everything else that mattered to me. And there wasn't any other human being in the universe that I cared enough about to miss for more than a day.

I was surprised when Hypatia spoke up out of the air. "Ms. Moynlin"— formal because of the company— "there's a call for you." And she displayed Bill Tartch's face.

I could see by the background that he was in his own ship, and he looked all bright and fresh and grinning at me. "Permission to come aboard, hon?" he asked.

That produced a quick reaction among my guests.

"Oh," said Ibarruru, collecting herself. "Well, it's time we got back to work anyway, isn't it, June?" She was sounding arch. Terple wasn't; she simply got up, and Starminder followed her example.

"You needn't leave," I said.

"But of course we must," said Terple. "Julia's right. Thank you for the tea and, uh, things."

And they were gone, leaving me to be alone with my lover.

VI

"He's been primping for the last hour," Hypatia reported in my ear. "Showered, shaved, dressed up. And he put on that musk cologne that he thinks you like."

"I do like it," I said. "On him. Let me see you when I'm talking to you."

She appeared obediently, reclining on the couch Ibarruru had just left. "I'd say the man's looking to get laid," she observed. "Again."

I didn't choose to pick up on the "again," which could have meant any of a couple of things. That's one of Hypatia's more annoying traits, of which she has just not quite enough to make me have her reprogrammed. When I chose Hypatia of Alexandria as a personality for my shipmind, it seemed to be a good idea at the time, but my own Hypatia took it seriously. That's what happens when you get yourself a really powerful shipmind; they throw themselves into the part. The first thing she did was look up her template and model herself as close to the original as she thought I would stand—including such details as the fact that the original Hypatia really hated men.

"So do you want me out of the way?" she asked sociably.

"No," I said. "You stay."

"That's my girl. You ask me, sexual intercourse is greatly overrated anyway."

"That's because you never had any," I told her. "By which I mean neither you, my pet program, nor the semi-mythical human woman I modeled you after, who died a virgin and is said to have shoved her used menstrual cloths in the face of one persistent suitor to turn him off."

"Malicious myth," she said comfortably. "Spread by those Christian monks of St. Cyril's, after they dragged her off and hacked her to death. Anyway, here he comes."

I would have been willing to bet that the first words out of Bill Tartch's mouth would be *Alone at last!*, along with a big grin and a lunge for me. I would have half won. He didn't say anything at all, just spread his arms and lurched toward me, grin and all.

Then he saw Hypatia, sprawled on the couch. "Oh," he said, stumbling as he came to a stop—there evidently wasn't any gravity in his rental ship, either. "I thought we'd be alone."

"Not right now, sweetie," I said. "But it's nice to see you."

"Me, too." He thought for a moment, and I could see him changing gears: All right, the lady doesn't want what I want right now, so what else can we do? That's one of those good-and-bad things about Bill Tartch. He does what I want, with none of this sweeping-her-off-her-feet stuff. Viewing it as good, it means he's considerate and sweet. Viewing it the other way—the way Hypatia chooses to view it—he's a spineless wretch, sucking up to somebody who can do him favors.

While I was considering which way to view it, Bill snapped his fingers. "I know," he said, brightening. "I've been wanting to do a real interview with you anyway. That all right? Hypatia, you can record it for me, can't you?"

Hypatia didn't answer, just looked sulkily at me.

"Do what he says," I ordered. But Bill was having second thoughts.

"Maybe not," he said, cheerfully resigned to the fact that she wouldn't take orders from him. "She'd probably screw it up on purpose for me, anyway, so I guess we'd better get Denys in here."

It didn't take Denys much more than a minute to arrive, those quaint little cameras and all. I did my best to be gracious and comradely. "Oh, yes, clip them on anywhere," I said—in my ship's gravity the cameras wouldn't float. "On the backs of the chairs? Sure. If they mess the fabric a little Hypatia will fix it right up." I didn't look at Hypatia, just gestured to her to get herself out of sight. She did without protest.

Bill had planted himself next to me and was holding my hand. I didn't pull it away. It took Denys a little while to get all the cameras in place, Bill gazing tolerantly at the way she was doing it and not offering to help. When she announced she was ready the interview began.

It was a typical Wilhelm Tartch interview, meaning that he did most of the talking. He rehearsed our entire history for the cameras in one uninterrupted monologue; my part was to smile attentively as it was going on. Then he got to Phoenix.

"We're here to see the results of this giant explosion that took place more than a thousand years ago—What's the matter, Klara?"

He was watching my face, and I knew what he was seeing. "Turn off your cameras, Bill. You need to get your facts straight. It happened a lot longer than a thousand years ago."

He shook his head at me tolerantly. "That's close enough for the audience," he explained. "I'm not giving an astronomy lesson here. The star blew up in AD 1054, right?"

"It was in 1054 that the Chinese astronomers *saw* it blow up. That's the year when the light from the supernova got as far as our neighborhood, but it took about five thousand years to get there. Didn't you do your homework?"

"We must've missed that little bit, hon," he said, giving me his best ruefully apologetic smile. "All right, Denys. Take it from the last little bit. We'll put in some shots of the supernova to cover the transition. Ready? Then go. This giant explosion that took place many thousands of years ago, totally destroying a civilization that might in some ways almost have become the equal of our own. What were they like, these people the Phoenix investigators call 'Crabbers'? No one has ever known. Now, through the generosity of Gelle-Klara Moynlin, who is here with me, we are at last going to see for ourselves what these tragically doomed people achieved before their star exploded without warning, cutting them off— oh, come on, Klara. What is it this time?"

"We don't know if they had any warning or not, do we? That's one of the things we're trying to find out."

Denys cleared her throat. She said diffidently, "Bill, maybe you should let me do a little more background research before you finish this interview."

My lover gave her a petulant little grimace. "Oh, all right. I suppose you might as well."

I heard the invisible little cough that meant Hypatia had something to say to me, so I said to the air, "Yes?"

She spoke right up. "The PhoenixCorp shipmind tells me they're back at work on the dish, and they're getting somewhat better magnification now. There are some new views you may want to see. Shall I display here?"

Bill looked slightly mollified. He looked at me. "What do you think, Klara?"

It was the wrong question to ask me. I didn't want to tell him what I was thinking.

For that matter, I didn't want to be thinking it at all. All right, he and this little Denys lollipop hadn't done any of their backgrounding on the way out to Phoenix. So what, exactly, had they been doing with their time?

I said, "No, I think I'd rather see it on PhoenixCorp. You two go ahead. I'll follow in a minute." And as soon as they were out of sight I turned around, and Hypatia was sitting in the chair Denys had just left, looking smug.

"Can I do something for you, Klara?" she asked solicitously.

There was, but I wasn't ready to ask her for it. I asked her for something else instead. "Can you show me the interior of Bill's ship?"

"Of course, Klara." And there it was, displayed for me, Hypatia guiding my point of view all through it.

It wasn't much. The net obviously wasn't spending any more than it had to on Bill's creature comforts. It was so old that it had all that Heechee drive stuff out in the open; when I designed my own I made sure all that ugliness was tucked away out of sight, like the heating system in a condo. The important fact was that it had two sleeping compartments, one clearly Denys's, the other definitely Bill's. Both had unmade beds. Evidently the rental's shipmind wasn't up to much housekeeping, and neither was Denys. There was no indication that they might have been visiting back and forth.

I gave up. "You've been dying to tell me about them ever since they got here," I said to Hypatia. "So tell me."

She gave me that wondering look. "Tell you what exactly, Klara?"

I snarled at her, "Tell me! *Did they?*"

She made an expression of distaste. "Oh, yes, hon, they certainly did. All the way out here. Like dogs in rut."

I looked around the room at the wineglasses and cups and the cushions that had been disturbed by someone sitting on them. "I'm going to the ship. Clean up this mess while I'm gone," I ordered, and checked my face in the mirror.

It looked just as it always looked, as though nothing were different.

Well, nothing was, really, was it? What did it matter if Bill chose to bed this Denys, or any number of Denyses, when I wasn't around? It wasn't as though I had been planning to *marry* the guy.

VII

None of the crew were in the entrance lock when I came to the Phoenix-Corp ship, but I could hear their voices. They were all gathered in the dining hall, laughing and chattering excitedly. When I got there I saw that the room had been darkened. They were looking at virtuals of one scene or another as Hans displayed them, and no one noticed me come in.

I hooked myself inconspicuously to a belt and looked around. I saw Bill and his sperm receptacle of the moment hooked chastely apart, Denys chirping at Mason-Manley, Bill talking into his recorders. Mason-Manley was squeezing Denys's shoulder excitedly, presumably because of the euphoria of the moment, but she seemed to be enjoying it. If Bill noticed, he didn't appear to mind. But then Bill was not a jealous type.

Until recently I hadn't thought that I was, either.

Well, it wasn't a question of jealousy. It was a question of—oh, call it good manners. If Bill chose to bed a bimbo now and then that was his business, but it did not excuse his hauling the little tart all the way from Earth to shove her in my face.

A meter or so away from me Mark Rohrbeck was watching the pictures, looking a lot less gloomy than usual. When he saw me at last he waved and pointed. "Look, Ms. Moynlin!" he cried. "Blimps!"

So I finally got around to looking at the display. In the sector he was indicating we were looking down on one of the Crabber planet's oceans. There were a lot of clouds, but some areas had only scattered puffs. And there among them were eight fat little silver sausages, in a Vee formation, that surely were far too hard-edged and uniform in shape to be clouds.

"These are the objects we were viewing before, Ms. Moynlin," Hans's voice informed me. "Now we can discriminate the individual elements, and they are certainly artifacts."

"Sure, but why do you think they're airborne? How do you know they aren't ships of some kind?" I asked, and then said at once, "No, cancel that." I had figured it out for myself. If they had been surface vessels they would have produced some sort of wake in the water. They were aircraft, all right, so I changed the question to, "Where are they going, do you think?"

"Wait a minute," June Terple said. "Hans, display the projection for Ms. Moynlin."

That sheet of ocean disappeared, and in its place there was a globe of the Crabber planet, its seas in blue, land masses in gray. Eight little oval figures, greatly out of proportion, were over the ocean. From them a silvery line extended itself to the northeast, with another line, this one golden, going back past the day-night terminator toward the southwest. Terple said, "It looks like the blimps came from around that group of islands at the end of the gold course-line, and they're heading toward the dumbbell continents up on the right. Unfortunately, those are pretty far north. We can't get a good picture of them from here, but Hans has enhanced some of the data on the island the blimps came from. Hans?"

The globe disappeared. We were looking down on one of those greenish infrared scenes: shoreline, bay—and something burning around the bay. Once again the outlines of the burning areas were geometrically unnatural. "As we speculated, it is almost certainly a community, Ms. Moynlin," Hans informed me. "However, it seems to have suffered some catastrophe, similar to what we observed on the continent which is now out of sight."

"What kind of catastrophe?" I demanded.

Hans was all apologetic. "We simply don't have the data as yet, Ms. Moynlin. A great fire, one might conjecture. I'm sure it will all make sense when we have better resolution—in a few hours, perhaps. I'll keep you posted."

"Please do," I said. And then, without planning it, I found myself saying, "I think I'll go back to my ship and lie down for a while."

Bill looked suddenly happy and began to unhook himself from his perch. I gave him a little shake of the head.

"I'm sorry. I just want to rest," I said. "It's been an exhausting few days."

That wasn't particularly true, of course. I didn't want to rest. I just wanted to be by myself, or at any rate with no company but Hypatia, which comes to pretty much the same thing.

As I came into my ship she greeted me in motherly mode. "Too many people, hon?" she asked. "Shall I make you a drink?"

I shook my head to the drink, but she was right about the rest of it.

"Funny thing," I said, sprawling on the couch. "The more people I meet, the fewer I am comfortable around."

"Meat people are generally boring," she agreed. "How about a cup of tea?"

I shrugged, and immediately heard the activity begin in the kitchen. Hypatia had her faults, but she was a pretty good mom when I needed her to be. I lay back on the couch and gazed at the ceiling. "You know what?" I said. "I'm beginning to think I ought to settle down on the island."

"You could do that, yes," she said diplomatically. Then, because she was Hypatia, she added, "Let's see, the last time you were there you stayed exactly eleven days, wasn't it? About six months ago?"

She had made me feel defensive—again. I said, "I had things to do."

"Of course you did. Then the time before that wasn't quite that long, was it? Just six days—and that was over a year ago."

"You've made your point, Hypatia. Talk about something else."

"Sure thing, boss." So she did. Mostly what she chose to talk about was what my various holdings had been doing in the few hours since I'd checked them last. I wasn't listening. After a few minutes of it I drank the tea she'd made for me and stood up. "I'm going to soak in the tub for a while."

"I'll run it for you, hon. Hon? They've got some new pictures from the Crabber planet if you want to see them while you soak."

"Why not?" And by the time I'd shucked my clothes the big onyx tub was full, the temperature perfect as always. I closed my eyes and lay back to let the sweet-smelling foamy waters make me feel whole and content again. As I had done many thousands of times, sometimes with success.

This was one of the successes. The hot tub did its work. I felt myself drifting off to a relaxed and welcome sleep. . . .

And then, suddenly, a vagrant thought crossed my mind and I wasn't relaxed anymore.

I got out of the tub and climbed into the shower stall, turning it on full; I let cold water hammer at me for a while, then changed it to hot. When I got out I pulled on a robe.

As I was drying my hair, the door opened and Hypatia appeared, looking at me with concern. "I'm afraid what I told you about Tartch upset you, hon," she said, oozing with compassion. "You don't really care what he does, though, do you?"

I said, "Of course not," wondering if it were true.

"That's my girl," she said approvingly. "There are some new scenes from the planet, too."

"Not now," I said. "I want to ask you something."

She didn't move, but the scene disappeared. "What's that, Klara?"

"While I was dozing in the tub I thought for a moment I might fall asleep, and slip down into the water, and drown. Then I thought you surely wouldn't let that happen, because you'd be watching, wouldn't you?"

"I'm always aware of any problems that confront you, yes, Klara."

"And then it occurred to me that you might be tempted to let me go ahead and drown, just so you could get me into that machine storage you're always trying to sell me. So I got out of the tub and into the shower."

I pulled my hair back and fastened it with a barrette, watching her. She didn't speak, just stood there with her usual benign and thoughtful expression. "So would you?" I demanded.

She looked surprised. "You mean would I deliberately let you drown? Oh, I don't think I could do that, Klara. As a general rule I'm not programmed to go against your wishes, not even if it were for your own good. That would be for your good, you know. Machine storage would mean eternal life for you, Klara, or as close as makes no difference. And no more of the sordid little concerns of the meat that cause you so much distress."

I turned my back on her and went into my bedroom to dress. She followed, in her excellent simulation of walking. What I wanted to know was how general her general rule was, and what she would have deemed a permissible exception. But as I opened my mouth to ask her, she spoke up.

"Oh, Klara," she said. "They've found something of interest on the planet. Let me show you." She didn't wait for a response; at once the end of the room lit up.

We were looking again at that first little fleet of blimps. They were nearly at the coast, but they weren't in their tidy Vee formation anymore. They were scattered over the sky, and two of them were falling to the sea, blazing with great gouts of flame. Small things I couldn't quite make out were buzzing around and between them.

"My God," I said. "Something's shooting them down!"

Hypatia nodded. "So it would appear, Klara. It looks as though the Crabbers' blimps are filled with hydrogen, to burn the way they do. That suggests a rather low level of technological achievement, but give them credit. They aren't primitives, anyway. They're definitely civilized enough to be having themselves a pretty violent little war."

VIII

There wasn't any doubt about it. The Crabbers were industriously killing each other in the kind of aerial combat that was right out of the old stories of—what was it? I guess World War I. I couldn't see much of the planes that were shooting the blimps down. They were there, though, and what was going on was a bunch of real old-fashioned dogfights.

I don't know what I had hoped to see when we brought the long-dead Crabbers back to some kind of life. This definitely wasn't it. When the scenes changed—Hans was assiduous in zooming down to wherever on the planet's surface things were going on—it didn't improve. It got worse. There was a harbor crammed with surface vessels, where a great river joined the sea; but some of the ships were on fire, and others appeared to be sinking. ("Submarines did that, I think," Hypatia judged. "It could possibly be from bombing planes or mines, but my money's on submarines.") Those strange patterns of heat in the cities weren't a mystery any longer. The cities had been burned to the ground by incendiary bombing, leaving only glowing coals. Then, when we were looking down on a plain where flashes of white and reddish light sparkled all over the area, we couldn't see what was making them, but Hypatia had a guess for that, too. "Why," she said, sounding interested, "I do believe we're looking at a large-scale tank battle."

And so on, and on.

It was all so pointless! They didn't have to bother killing each other. Their star was going to do it for them soon enough. All unknowing, every one of those Crabbers was racing toward a frightful and near-term death from their bursting sun.

An hour earlier I had been pitying them for the fate that awaited them. Now I couldn't say that I thought that their fate was unjust.

Hypatia was looking at me in that motherly way she sometimes assumes. "I'm afraid all this is disturbing for you, Klara," she murmured. "Would it cheer you up to invite Mr. Tartch aboard? He's calling. He says he wants to talk to you about the new pictures."

"Sure he does," I said, pretty sure that what Bill really wanted to talk about was why he didn't deserve being treated so stand-offishly by me. "No. Tell him I'm asleep and don't want to be disturbed. And, listen, tell me all about Mark Rohrbeck."

"Ah," she said, in that tone of voice that makes one syllable speak volumes.

I wasn't having any of that. "If you've got something to say to me, say it!"

"But I don't, dear," she said, patently falsely. "You know I don't criticize you for your obsession with men."

She was getting close to the line. Then she crossed it. "You'd think," she said meditatively, "that after some of the experiences you've had with men you'd be more wary. Is it that you keep hoping you've already had the worst? Like that wretched little orphan, Wan."

I didn't answer that. I didn't even let her finish. I just said, "Shut up," and, wisely, she did. There are some subjects I don't discuss, and Hypatia is well aware that Wan, his rescue of me from my black hole and my brief, but not brief enough, time as his live-in lover are three of them.

Then she began to recite all of Mark Rohrbeck's stats. Mark's parents had died when he was young and he had been brought up by his grandfather, who had once made his living as a fisherman on Lake Superior. "Mostly the old man fished for sea lampreys—know what they are, Klara? They're ugly things. They have big sucking disks instead of jaws. They attach themselves to other fish and suck their guts out until they die. I don't think you'd want to eat a sea lamprey yourself, but they were about all that was left in the lake. Rohrbeck's grandpa sold them for export to Europe—people there thought they were a delicacy. They said they tasted like escargot. Then, of course, the Food Factories came along and put the old guy out of business—"

"Get back to talking about Mark Rohrbeck," I ordered. "The grandson. The one that's here."

"Oh. Sorry. Well, young Mark got a scholarship at the University of Minnesota, did well, went on to grad school at MIT, made a pretty fair reputation in computer science, married, had two kids, but then his wife decided there was a dentist she liked better than Rohrbeck, so she dumped him. And as I've mentioned before," she said appreciatively, "he does have really great genes. Does that cover it?"

I mulled that over for a moment, then said, "Just about. Don't go drawing any conclusions from this, do you hear?"

"Certainly, Klara," she said, but she still had that look.

I sighed. "All right. Now turn that damn thing back on."

"Of course, Klara," she said, unsurprised, and did. "I'm afraid it hasn't been getting any better."

It hadn't. It was just more of the same. I watched doggedly for a while, and then I said, "All right, Hypatia. I've seen enough."

She made it disappear, looking at me curiously. "There'll be better images when they finish with the mirror. By then we should be able to see actual individual Crabbers."

"Lovely," I said, not meaning it, and then I burst out, "My God, what's the matter with those people? There's plenty of room on the planet for all of them. Why didn't they just stay home and live in peace?"

It wasn't meant to be a real question, but Hypatia answered it for me anyway. "What do you expect? They're meat people," she said succinctly.

I wasn't letting her get away with that. "Come on, Hypatia! Human beings are meat people, too, and we don't go tearing halfway around the world just to kill each other!"

"Oh, do you not? What a short memory you have, Klara dear. Think of those twentieth-century World Wars. Think of the Crusades, tens of thousands of Europeans dragging themselves all the way around the Mediterranean Sea to kill as many Muslims as they could. Think of the Spanish conquistadors, murdering their way across the Americas. Hey, for that matter you could even think of the lousy monks that tore the meat to shreds in Alexandria. Of course," she added with faint distaste, "those people were all Christians."

I blinked at her. "You think what we're looking at is a religious war?"

She shrugged gracefully. "What does it matter? Meat people don't need reasons to kill each other, dear."

IX

By the time the mirror was complete we could make out plenty of detail. We were even able to see individual Centaur-like Crabbers—the same build, four legs and upright torso, that they'd inherited from the primitives I'd seen.

That is, sometimes we could see them. Not always. The conditions had to be right. We couldn't see them when they were in the night part of the planet, of course, except in those ghostly-looking infrared views, and we couldn't optically see them at all when they were blanketed with clouds. But we could see enough. More than enough, as far as I was concerned.

The crew of PhoenixCorp was going crazy trying to keep up with the incoming data. Bill seemed to have decided to be patient with my unpredictable moods, so he paid me only cheerful but absent-minded attention. He kept busy working. He and Denys were ecstatically interrupting everyone in their jobs so that he could record their spot reactions, while the crew did their best to get on with their jobs anyway. June Terple stopped sleeping entirely, torn between watching the new images as they arrived and nagging her shipmind to make sure we would have warning in time to get the hell out of there before the star blew.

Only Mark Rohrbeck seemed to have time on his hands. Which was just the way I wanted it.

I found him in the otherwise empty sleep chamber, where Hans had obligingly set up duplicate incoming scenes. Mark's main area of concern was their shipmind and the functions it controlled, but those things were working smoothly without his attention. He was spending most of his time gazing morosely at the pictures.

I hooked myself up nearby. "Nasty, isn't it?" I said sociably, to cheer him up.

He didn't want to be cheered. "You mean the Crabbers?" Although his eyes had been on the display, his mind evidently hadn't. He thought it over for a moment, then gave his verdict. "Oh, I guess it's nasty enough, all right. But it all happened a long time ago, didn't it?"

"And you've got more immediate problems on your mind," I offered helpfully.

He gave me a gloomy imitation of a smile. "I see the shipminds have been gossiping again. Well, it isn't losing Doris that bothers me so much," he said after a moment. "I mean, that hurt, too. I thought I loved her, but—well, it didn't work out, did it? Now she's got this other guy, so what the hell? But"—he swallowed unhappily—"the thing is, she's keeping the kids."

He was not only a nice man, he was beginning to touch my heart. I said, sounding sympathetic and suddenly feeling that way, too, "And you miss them?"

"Hell! I've been missing them most of the time since they were born," he said, self-accusingly. "I guess that's what went wrong. I've been away working so much, I suppose I can't blame Doris for getting her lovemaking from somebody else."

That triggered something in me that I hadn't known was there. "No!" I said, surprising myself by my tone. "That's wrong. *Blame* the bitch! People are supposed to be *faithful* to each other!"

I startled Rohrbeck, too. He looked at me as though I had suddenly sprouted horns, but he didn't get a chance to speak. June Terple came flying by the room and saw us. She stuck her nose in, grabbing a hold-on to yell at Mark in passing. "Rohrbeck! Get your ass in gear! I want you to make sure Hans is shifting focus as fast as possible. We could be losing all kinds of data!" And then she was gone again, to wherever she was gone to.

Mark gave me a peculiar look, but then he shrugged, and waved his hands to show that when the boss gave orders, even orders to do things he had already done, he couldn't just stay and talk anymore, and was gone as well.

I didn't blame him for the peculiar look. I hadn't realized I was so sensitive in the matter of two-timing partners. But apparently I was.

I went back to my ship to stay out of everybody's way, watching the pictures as they arrived with only Hypatia for company.

She started the projections up as soon as I came back, without being asked. I sat down to observe.

If you didn't think of the Crabbers as *people*, what they were doing was certainly interesting. So were the Crabbers themselves, for that matter. I could see traces of those primitive predators in the civilized—civilized!—versions before me. Now, of course, they had machines and wore clothes and, if you didn't mind the extra limbs, looked rather impressive in their gaudy tunics and spiked leggings, and the shawl things they wore on their heads that were ornamented with, I guessed, maybe insignia of rank. Or junk jewelry, maybe, but it looked to me as though most of them were definitely in one or another kind of uniforms. Most of the civilized ones, anyway. In the interior of the South Continent, where it looked like rain forest and savannah, there were lots of what looked like noncivilized ones. Those particular Crabbers didn't have machines. They didn't have much in the way of clothing, either. They lived off the land, and they seemed to spend a lot of time gaping up worriedly at the sky, where fleets of blimps and double-winged aircraft buzzed by now and then.

The civilized ones seemed to be losing some of their civilization. When Hans showed us close-ups of one of the bombed-out cities I could see streams of four-legged Crabber people—mostly civilians, I guessed—who were making their way out of the ruins, carrying bundles, leading kids or holding them. A lot of them were limping, just dragging themselves along. Some were being pulled in wagons or sledlike things.

"They look like they're all sick," I said, and Hypatia nodded.

"Undoubtedly some of them are, dear," she informed me. "It's a war, after all. You shouldn't be thinking just in terms of bombs and guns, you know. Did you never hear of biological warfare?"

I stared at her. "You mean they're spreading *disease*? As a *weapon*?"

"I believe that is likely, and not at all without precedent," she informed me, preparing to lecture. She started by reminding me of the way the first American colonists in New England gave smallpox-laden blankets to the Indians to get them out of the way—"The colonists were Christians, of course, and very religious"—and went on from there. I wasn't listening. I was watching the pictures from the Crabber planet.

They didn't get better. For one moment, in one brief scene, I saw something that touched some sort of nearly atrophied nerve-ending in me. The scene was an archipelago in the Crabber planet's tropical zone. One bit looked a little like my island, reef and lagoon and sprawling vegetation over everything. There were aboriginal Crabbers there, too, But they weren't alone. There were also a company of the ones in uniform, herding the locals into a village square, for what purpose I could not guess—to draft them? to shoot them dead?—but certainly not a good one. And, when I looked more closely, all the plants were dying. More bioweapons, this time directed at crops? Defoliants? I didn't know, but that looked as though someone had done something to that vegetation.

I had had enough. Without intending it, I came to a decision.

I interrupted my shipmind in the middle of telling me about America's old Camp Detrick. "Hypatia? How much spare capacity do you have?"

It didn't faze her. She abandoned the history of human plague-spreading and responded promptly. "Quite a lot, Klara."

"Enough to store all the data from the installation? And maybe take Hans aboard, too?"

She looked surprised. I think she actually was. "That's a lot of data, Klara, but, yes, I can handle it. If necessary. What've you got in mind?"

"Oh," I said. "I was just thinking. Let me see those refugees again."

X

I kept one eye on the time, but I had plenty for what I wanted to do. I even gave myself a little diversion first.

I went to my island.

I don't mean in person, of course. I simply checked out everything on Raiwea through my monitors and listened to the reports from the department heads. That was almost as satisfying. Just looking at the kids, growing up healthy and happy and free the way they are—it always makes me feel good. Or, in this case, at least a little less bad.

Then I left my remote-accessed Raiwea and went into the reality of the Phoenix ship.

Hans was busily shifting focus every time a few new frames came in, so now the pictures were coming in faster than anybody could absorb them. That couldn't be helped. There was a whole world to look at, and anyway it didn't matter if we saw it all in real time. All the data were being stored for later analysis and interpretation—by somebody else, though. Not by me. I had seen all I wanted.

So, evidently, had most of the Phoenix crew. Starminder and Julia Ibarruru were in the eating chamber, but they were talking to each other about the Core, and paying no attention to the confusing images that were pouring in. Bill Tartch had his cameras turned on the display, all right. But he was watching the pictures only with sulky half attention, while Denys hung, sound asleep, beside him. "What's the use of this, Klara?" he demanded as soon as he saw me. "I can't get any decent footage from this crap, and most of the crew's gone off to sleep."

I was looking at Denys. The little tart even snored prettily. "They needed it," I told him. "How about Terple?"

He shrugged. "Kekuskian was here a minute ago, looking for her. I don't know whether he found her or not. Listen, how about a little more of your interview, so I won't be wasting my time entirely?"

"Maybe later," I said, not meaning it, and went in pursuit of June Terple.

I heard her voice raised in anger long before I saw her. Kekuskian had found her, all right, and the two of them were having a real cat-and-dog fight. She was yelling at him. "I don't give a snake's fart what you think you have to have, Oleg! We're going! We have to get the whole installation the hell out of here while we're still in one piece."

"You can't do that!" he screeched back at her. "What's the point of my coming out here at all if I can't observe the supernova?"

"The point," she said fiercely, "is to stay alive, and that's what we're going to do. I'm in charge here, Kekuskian! I give the orders, and I'm giving them now. Hans! Lay a course for the neutron star!"

That's when I got into the spat. "Cancel that, Hans," I ordered. "From here on in, you'll be taking your orders from me. Is that understood?"

"It is understood, Ms. Moynlin," the shipmind's voice said, as calm and unsurprised as ever. Terple wasn't calm at all. I made allowances for the woman; she hadn't had much sleep and there was a lot of strain. But for a minute there I thought she was going to hit me.

"Now what the hell do you think you're doing, Moynlin?" she demanded dangerously.

"I'm taking command," I explained. "We're going to stay for a while. I want to see that star blow up too."

"*Yes!*" Kekuskian shouted.

Terple didn't even look at him. She was giving her whole attention to me, and she wasn't in a friendly mood. "Are you crazy? Do you want to get killed?"

It crossed my mind to wonder if that would be so bad, but what I said, quite reasonably, was, "I don't mean we have to stay right here and let the star fry us. Not the people, anyway. We'll evacuate the crew and watch the blowup on the remote. There's plenty of room for everybody in the two ships. I can take three or four with me, Bill can take the others in his rental."

She was outraged and incredulous. "Klara! The radiation will be *enormous*! It could destroy the whole installation!"

"Fine," I said. "I understand that. So I'll buy you a new one."

She stared at me in shock. "Buy a new one? Klara, do you have any idea of what it would cost—"

Then she stopped herself short, and gave me a long look. "Well," she said, not a bit mollified, but more or less resigned to accepting the facts of life, "I guess you do know, at that. If that's what you want to do, well, you're the boss."

And, as usual, I was.

So when I gave orders, no one objected. I got everybody back in the dining chamber and explained that we were abandoning ship. I told Terple she could come on my ship, along with Starminder and Ibarruru. "It's only a few days to Earth; the three of you can all fit in my guest bedroom. Mason-Manley and Kekuskian can go with Bill and Denys. It'll be a little crowded in his rental, but they'll manage."

"What about Hans and me?" Rohrbeck asked, sounding puzzled.

I said, off-handedly, "Oh, you can come with me. We'll find a place for you."

He didn't look as thrilled as he might have at the idea of sailing off through space with a beautiful, unattached woman, such as me. He didn't even look interested. "I don't just mean me *personally*, Klara," he said testily. "I mean me and my shipmind. I put a lot of work into designing Hans! I don't want him ruined!"

I wasn't thrilled by his reaction, either, but I do like a man who likes his work. "Don't worry," I assured him. "I asked Hypatia about that. She says she has plenty of extra capacity. We'll just copy him and take him along."

XI

I had never seen a supernova explosion in real time before—well, how many people have?—but that, at least, was not a disappointment. The show was everything it promised to be.

When it happened we were hovering in our two ships, a few million kilometers off the prime focus. Hans was taking his orders from Kekuskian now, and he had ditched the Crabber planet for good to concentrate on the star. Hypatia whispered in my ear that, back on his rental, Bill Tartch was pissing and moaning about the decision. He had wanted to catch every horrible, tragic bit, if possible right down to the expressions on the faces of the Crabbers when they saw their sun go all woogly right over their heads. I didn't. I had seen enough of the Crabbers to last me, and I was the one who had the say.

In my main room we had a double display. Hypatia had rigged my ship's external optics so we could see the great mirror and the tiny Phoenix ship, together like toys in one corner of the room, but the big thing was the Crabber star itself as seen from PhoenixCorp. It wasn't dangerous—Hypatia said. Hans had dimmed it down, and anyway we were seeing only visible light, none of the wide-spectrum stuff that would be pouring out of it in a minute. Even so, it was huge, two meters across and so bright we had to squint to watch it.

I don't know much about stellar surfaces, but this particular star looked sick to me. Prominences stuck out all over its perimeter, and ugly sunspots spotted its face. And then, abruptly, it began to happen. The star seemed to shrink, as though Hans had zoomed back away from it. But that wasn't what was going on. The star really was collapsing on itself, and it was doing it fast. ("That's the implosion," Hypatia whispered.) While we watched, it went from two meters to a meter and a half, to a meter, to smaller still—

And then it began to expand again, almost as fast as it had shrunk, and far more bright. Hypatia whispered, "And that's the rebound. I've instructed Hans to cut back on the intensity. It's going to get worse."

It did.

It blossomed bigger and brighter—and angrier—until it filled the room and, just as I was feeling as though I were being swallowed up by that stellar hell, the picture began to break up. I heard Terple moan, "Look at the mirror!" Then I understood what was happening to our image. The little toy PhoenixCorp ship and mirror in our viewers were being hammered by the outpouring of raw radiation from the supernova. No filters. No cutouts. The PhoenixCorp craft were blazing bright themselves, reflecting the flood of blinding light that was pouring on them from the gravitational lensing. As I watched, the mirror began to warp. The flimsy sheets of mirror metal peeled off, exploding into bright plumes of plasma, like blossoming fireworks on the Fourth of July. For a moment we saw the wire mesh underneath the optical plates. Then it was gone, too, and all that was left was the skeleton of reinforcing struts, hot and glowing.

I thought we'd seen everything we were going to see of the star. I was wrong. A moment later the image of the supernova reappeared before us. It wasn't anywhere near as colossally huge or frighteningly bright as it had been before, but it was still something scary to look at. "What—?" I began to ask, but Hypatia had anticipated me.

"We're looking at the star from the little camera in the center of the dish now, Klara," she explained. "We're not getting shipside magnification from the mirror anymore. That's gone. I'm worried about that camera, too. The gravitational lensing alone is pretty powerful, and the camera might not last much—" She stopped, as the image disappeared for good. Simply winked out and was gone. "—longer," she finished, and, of course, it hadn't.

I took a deep breath and looked around my sitting room. Terple had tears in her eyes. Ibarruru and Starminder sat together, silent and stunned, and Mark Rohrbeck was whispering to his shipmind. "That's it," I said briskly. "The show's over."

Rohrbeck spoke up first, sounding almost cheerful. "Hans has all the data," he reported. "He's all right."

Terple had her hand up. "Klara? About the ship? It took a lot of heat, but the dish burned pretty fast and the hull's probably intact, so if we can get a repair crew out there—"

"Right away," I promised. "Well, almost right away. First we go home."

I was looking at Rohrbeck. He had looked almost cheerful for a moment, but the cheer was rapidly fading. When he saw my eyes on him, he gave me a little shrug. "Where's that?" he asked glumly.

I wanted to pat his shoulder, but it was a little early for that. I just said sympathetically, "You're missing your kids, aren't you? Well, I've got a place where there are plenty of them. And, as the only grown-up male on my island, you'll be the only dad they've got."

XII

That blast from the supernova didn't destroy PhoenixCorp after all. The mirror was a total write-off, of course, but the ship itself was only cooked a little.

So June Terple stooged around for a bit while it cooled down, then went back to check it out with what was left of her crew. Which wasn't much. Mason-Manley talked his way back into her good graces once Denys wasn't around anymore. Kekuskian promised to come out for the actual blow-up, eighty years from now, provided he was still alive. And, of course, Terple still had the indestructible Hans, now back in his own custom-designed datafan. The rest of her crew were all replacements. Starminder went back to her family in the Core, and I paid Ibarruru's fare to go along with her as a kind of honorary Citizen Ambassador.

Naturally, Terple invited me to join them for their stint at the neutron star. She couldn't really avoid it, since the new money was coming from the same place as the old, namely mostly me. I said maybe, to be polite, but I really meant no. One look at the death of a world was enough for me. And Bill Tartch's special show on the Crabbers went on the net within days. He had a great success with it, easily great enough so that he didn't really mind the fact that he no longer had me.

Hypatia kept copies of all the files for me, and those last little bits of data stayed with me on my island for a long time, until things went sour and everything got ruined at once. (But that's another story. A really bad one, and I don't want to think about it.) I played pieces of the files now and then, for any of the kids that showed an interest, and for their moms, too, when they did. But mostly I played them for myself.

Mark Rohrbeck stayed with me on Raiwea for a while, too, though not that long. That's the way my island works. When my kids are ready for the world outside, I let them go. It was the same with Rohrbeck. For him it took just a little over three months. Then he was ready, and kissed me good-bye, and went.

8

On the Forested Planet

I

To get off the spacecraft Estrella and Stan walked out a five-meter passage. Then they were out on a platform, in bright sunshine. That is where they both stopped in shock. "My God," Estrella whispered. "There's a million of them!"

It wasn't a million, really, but it surely was a lot of Heechee, and all of them bunched around them on the platform and staring . . . or ranked farther away on porches and terraces and staring . . . or clustered on roofs and in windows as much as half a kilometer away, and also staring. That was what all of them were doing: staring. All of them were also muttering and chirping to each other—each one decorously soft-voiced, to be sure, but collectively like the whir of an immense flight of locusts. Stan put his arm around Estrella. "So where the hell is Salt?" he demanded.

There wasn't any answer from the press of Heechee, none of whom appeared to speak English. Though they were all out in the open Stan wrinkled his nose at the persistent Heechee sting of ammonia in the air, along with spicy scents and fruity ones—coming, Stan guessed, from woods somewhere nearby. (This was, after all, the "Forested Planet.") Stan wasn't interested in smells just then. "Damn her," he grumbled. "I don't know what we're supposed to do now."

Others did, though. Two of them, perhaps high-ranking Heechee to judge from the lines of red, blue and yellow embroidery that decorated their smocks, came forward. Each took an arm, one for Estrella and one for Stan. The Heechee were surprisingly small, ten or a dozen centimeters shorter even than Estrella, but she didn't resist. Neither did Stan, though he thought of it, but saw no point, when he felt the strength of that bony grasp. Both humans let the Heechee do what they would. Which was to conduct the humans to another, higher-up sort of stage. Then the two Heechee took turns speaking—in their own language—perhaps to the crowd, perhaps to the tiny lenses Stan could see winking at them from the crowd. "I think we're on the evening news," he muttered to Estrella, but she was peering past the bulk of the ship that had brought them, now kneeling quietly in its landing receptacle. Then, as the two Heechee grasped their arms again, he added, "Now what do they want?"

They wanted Stan and Estrella to board a topless, three-wheeled vehicle, which had no driver at its sort of tiller but two rows of Heechee perches. No proper seats, of course.

That was when Salt at last appeared. "Yes, one understands," she said, sounding slightly remorseful but also harried, "that is too bad about the sitting down, is that not the case? But do not be concerned. The distance is much less than far."

"Distance to where?" Stan demanded, while Estrella asked, "Aren't you coming with us?"

"Distance to place you are going," Salt explained. "Me? With you? No, I do not go. How could I? Must return to proper duties."

With that she was gone into the crowd, while the Heechee pair mounted the vehicle, perching themselves at the posts in the rear, gesturing Stan and Estrella to the ones in front. "I'm not sitting on those things!" Estrella announced. She didn't, either, but as soon as she climbed on board the cart started up anyway, leaving the two humans to clutch the perches for support.

They kept on doing so for the next while. Making an odd whining sound, the vehicle dived almost at once down an incline and into a broad, well lighted tunnel. Ahead of them three or four other three-wheelers led the way, all their occupants turning to stare at Stan and Estrella, and twice that number followed behind.

How long they traveled Stan could not say. They were out in the open for a while (bright mountains ahead, green woods around), then back underground. Side tunnels flashed by, and were ignored. One or two of the following carts peeled away, and were replaced by three or four new ones. The lighting, which had been blue and green at the beginning, changed to green and gold, then gold and red, then back to blue and green again. "I think I'm going to be carsick," Estrella muttered in Stan's ear, as she hung onto the perch for dear life.

"Please don't," he implored her. "We're bound to get there soon." Then, happily, they did. Without warning the vehicle dove itself into a side tunnel like every other side tunnel they had passed. Then up a ramp, this one winding in a tight corkscrew up a couple of levels, until it stopped at a turn in the screw like every other. The female Heechee behind them rose gracefully from her perch. "You get out now," she said. "Is where you to be living."

And when they obeyed, the female sat again, the tiller turned and they were gone.

"I didn't know she spoke English," Estrella said, gazing after them.

"More important," said Stan, eyeing the knobless, latchless door, "is, how do we get in?"

That turned out to be easy enough. Estrella pointed out a sort of pad next to the faintly gleaming door, but when Stan pressed it all that resulted was a distant hoarse braying from the other side of the door—some kind of doorbell, perhaps. But as soon as Stan touched the door itself it slid open, and the way to their new home was clear.

They looked around wonderingly. What was on the other side of the door wasn't a single room. It was several rooms—from the doorway they couldn't tell quite how many—and through another door they could just see the corner of what appeared to be a balcony, drenched in sunlight. "Wow, Stan," Estrella breathed. "It's big. And it's ours!"

"Big" was something new for Stan and Estrella, neither of whom had been used to luxury. For Stan the height of comfort had been sharing a bed with Oltan Kusmeroglu in his parents' apartment. Estrella had never been quite that pampered. So what they found on Forested Planet of Warm Old Star Twenty-Four was a new high in hedonism. The floor space of their apartment had to be over a hundred square meters, and Stan guessed—or hoped—they wouldn't have to share it with anyone else.

The furnishings, of course, did seem a bit odd, not even counting the fact that most of the rooms had no windows. They hadn't expected anything intended for human beings, to be sure. What they found was what they had expected. They had been left a heap of more than a dozen rolls of the sleep vegetation, enough to fill the space between the prongs of every Heechee perch in the apartment. They weren't going to have to sleep on any of those rolls, either. Instead, they had been provided with a pair of constructions built like a litter box for very large cats, filled with fresh-cut slips of foliage. That was the way every Heechee wanted his own bedroom furnished, Estrella told Stan; the rolls they had been used to in the ship were only for travel, the Heechee equivalent of sleeping bags.

In all there were five rooms—well, Stan called them rooms, although in some cases the only division between one and the next was a quite transparent curtain. (The room that held the bodily waste disposers did have a sliding door.) Two were bedrooms, or at least vegetation-box rooms. One of the others held several of those built-in desks and screens with the flower-pot receptacles for Heechee books, and the fifth, the smallest, had walls with a dozen Heechee lookplates staring blankly out at them.

"Any idea how to turn them on?" Stan asked, knowing what the answer would be, and getting it. "Okay, then. Any idea how we go about getting something to eat?"

He got the predicted answer to that, too, but when he turned to look Estrella was out on the balcony. He heard her gasp. "Come on out here, will you?" she asked.

When he stepped out onto the balcony he discovered a huge backdrop of mirror-bright hills off on the horizon, and saw at once why the Shining Mica Mountains got their name. It was only the tops of the mountains that were bright; on their lower slopes, and in the bright green valley Stan and Estrella were looking down on, there were broad meadows between clusters of trees as tall as redwoods—thus explaining why the name of the planet, too, was quite appropriate. The air smelled good, though not exactly with Earthly smells. The breeze did not smell of pine or fir, nor were the odors all floral. The smells were spicier and friendlier than any terrestrial wood in the experience of either of them, almost like some grandma's kitchen in pie-baking time.

But the smells did not divert Stan for long. "Hey," he said, "look!"

He was looking at the sky. From the platform they had stood on after leaving the spacecraft he had been vaguely aware of an unusual number of faint stars in the overhead sky. Now they weren't faint, and there were literally scores of them, in all the colors a proper star could come in: white and blue, yellow and orange, red and a sultry maroon. Off near the horizon Warm Old Star Twenty-Four was getting ready to set, with the pale disk of one of Forested Planet's tiny moons trailing behind it. "They said there were bunches of stars in the Core," Stan said, marveling. "I guess I just didn't know how many bunches."

For answer Estrella pressed his hand, then left him to his marveling at—or, better, to his puzzling over—the astronomical display. He didn't take long to follow, though. The grumbling of his not-sufficiently-recently-filled stomach distracted him from the view.

When he was back inside, Estrella was nowhere to be seen, but the closed door to the excretions room told him where she was. And reminded him that he needed to do some excreting of his own.

Estrella was commendably quick. Then Stan's own excreting didn't take long, either, although it would have taken less time still if the closing of the door hadn't immediately plunged him into total dark. He managed, though. When he was finished he felt better in one way, somewhat worse in another—relieving the presure on his bladder had sharpened the feeling of acute hunger in his belly.

In this he was not alone. Estrella was fretfully rubbing her own abdomen as she gazed at the walls. "I'm pretty sure there are cupboards in some of those, maybe with food in them. Only I can't get the damn things open. How about you? Want to try?"

He did try. Many times, in many different ways, though with only one result: nothing. Tapping the walls, punching them with his fist, yelling at them—it was all the same. If indeed there were storage spaces there he could find no way to reach them.

Then another problem showed itself.

The light in the room they were in, never bright because they were a couple of chambers away from the balcony that was the apartment's only source of illumination, was visibly dimming. It wasn't taking its time about it, either. The room that had been a little shadowed was now definitely gloomy and getting rapidly more so.

When Warm Old Star Twenty-Four set it didn't fool around. One minute there was bright sunshine bouncing off the mica deposits on the mountains, the next the star was dropped below the horizon.

And abruptly their new little home was plain and simple *dark*. Like nighttime Earth. Like nighttime Earth on a night when clouds obscured the sky and there were no streetlights, not even houselights, anywhere around. Through the connecting rooms Stan could catch a glimpse of the spectacle that was a night sky in the Core. Glorious it was, too. But as a practical matter, for the sake of trying to get around within their apartment, it was wholly useless.

"Shit," Stan muttered.

Estrella answered only indirectly. "Might as well get some sleep," she said.

When Stan agreed she didn't reply. He couldn't hear her moving around, either. When he tried reaching out for her, blind-man's-buff style, he cracked his shins on one of their disappearing tables that hadn't disappeared. Finally the soft rustle of Heechee sleeping-grasses gave him a clue—helped out, maybe, by his eyes growing partly accustomed to the gloom. But when he got near enough to touch her the sound of her regular breathing told him that she was, or wanted to be thought to be, already asleep.

He considered waking her, decided against it. He thought he might have brought this disappointment on himself, possibly because he hadn't carried her over the threshhold. But if so, it was too late for amends.

With some difficulty he found the other sleeping box and climbed into it, hoping, very seriously hoping, that the next day would be better.

II

It was, too.

When he awoke he discovered Estrella up long before him. On one of the tables were a dozen CHON-food packages that hadn't been there the night before. More than that (so Stan found when he had gulped down a jellied substance that tasted like seafood and a crunchy one that tasted like maple fudge) she had figured out how to use the bathing appliance. Then she had used it to clean not only herself but their whole collection of soiled clothing, the balcony railing now festooned with his and her garments drying rapidly under Warm Old Star Twenty-Four. Stan tried the shower himself, marveling at her cunning. It wasn't exactly a shower. It was a repeated pulse of bucketsful of tepid water, ten or twenty liters at a time, seconds apart. There wasn't exactly any soap, either. What there was was a rack of tangled plants, like an elongated windowbox of crabgrass all around the drenching cubicle. Following Estrella's advice, Stan tore handfuls off to use as washcloths, and discovered that they fizzed and slowly disintegrated in the water, leaving his skin tingly and clean.

Odd, yes, but it did the job. There didn't seem to be anything like a towel—because, Stan conjectured, the Heechee didn't need that sort of thing as water would roll right off their slick, shiny skin. But, although he was still hungry, he was cleaner than he had been for a long time, if wetter, and it elevated his spirits. It seemed to have done something for Estrella's, too, because when he threw his arms around her in a friendly, if naked, hug she hesitated only a moment before she hugged him back. And then, as his embrace became more intimate, she responded in kind, and the hunger that had just crossed his mind faded away again, replaced by a more urgent need.

Then it was almost like old times. If a Heechee litterbox wasn't the

ideal arena for having sex, it would do. It did. Then they lay spooned together for a time, Stan's face buried in Estrella's hair, and all was well on
the Forested Planet of Warm Old Star Twenty-Four.

Just when he thought she had fallen asleep again, she stirred. She
picked up a clump of the vegetation they were lying on and rubbed it between her fingers. She said thoughtfully, "You know, I think we're supposed to get inside this stuff like the Heechee do, instead of on top of it."

He blinked at the back of her head. "What?"

"They do it because their ancestors were some kind of burrowing animals," she explained. "Salt told me. It's probably why they build underground, and dig tunnels on other planets, do you see?"

"Huh," Stan said and then, having nothing more urgent to do, pulled
her toward him for a kiss. Which might once more have gone farther, but
then the doorbell made its not at all bell-like sound, somewhere between
a growl and a deep-toned purr, the sort of thing you might expect from a
lion waking out of deep sleep.

When they scrambled into enough clothing to pass in an emergency
and opened the door the person standing before them was the Heechee
female, Salt. She was holding out a net bag full of food packets. "Here,"
she said, handing it to Stan. "For you, these. Is old custom here for first
guest in new house to bring gifts of food. Custom is only symbolic, since
plenty food always available at dispenser. However," she added, looking
faintly embarrassed, "when I arrive here to be first guest, surprise, place is
dark, you both asleep. So I leave gift of food and go. Then I come again
also with food—custom unclear regarding such circumstances. You forgive?"

Of course they forgave, especially when Salt showed them where the
"dispenser" was and how to make it dispense food whenever they liked.
Which, they found, was easy enough: you simply turned it on and told it,
in English, what you wanted. "In *English?*" Stan demanded suspiciously.

"Yes, in English of course. Have arranged this for your convenience
immediately upon arrival."

And how did you turn it on? Why, nothing was simpler. As with the
outside door you simply pressed the palm of your hand on the appropriate
spot on the wall—Salt showed them where those spots were. "But press
carefully," she urged. "Whole palm in close contact, please. With our people is not so demanding, but did not operate for you at first touching because of excess flesh and lipids in digits obscuring the scan."

Stan nodded, grateful to have understood at least one thing. "So the
door has a perfect lock, right? Nobody's going to be able to steal the contents?"

Salt looked at him uncertainly. "'Steal?' Is to say, take without permission? Why anyone would do that?" Then, when Stan didn't respond: "Now I show you all other things." And she did, pretty nearly: showed how the same trick would activate the room lights, to any intensity they chose; and the lookplates, producing any number of possible channels to watch; and the wall cupboards—

In one of which were Stan's trumpet and Estrella's flute.

"Hey," Stan cried, grabbing for the instrument. He inspected it all over and even played a couple of quick riffs before, grinning, he let Salt speak again.

But by then she had little to say, only, "Let us go to lanai to rest and talk, all right?"

They did, all three of them appreciatively breathing in the sweet scents of Forested Planet's forests. Salt studied their faces, then demanded, "Is this not wholly beauteous? We consider it so, very much!"

"Very beautiful," Stan said dutifully, but Estrella didn't chime in as he expected.

Instead, "What I don't understand," she said, "is where all the people are. Didn't you say this planet was inhabited?"

"Certainly I said this. It is so, in large numbers."

"Then where are all the buildings—homes, factories, anything at all?"

Salt choked slightly, then said forgivingly, "I forget you not our people. Structures underground, of course."

"But this isn't underground," Stan objected.

"Is of course so," Salt corrected him. "Is on hillside. Balconies only outside. I remember," she said thoughtfully, "on human world everything stick up into the air. Not here, though. Heechee prefer inside, not outside. Now look more close." And when Stan squinted he did see somethings that peeped out of the sides of the hills, regularly spaced somethings that did not look natural. "You see? On other hills are other balconies et cetera. Not factories, of course. But places of work, such as my own"—she gestured with a skeletal hand—"down there, behind large tree forest."

"And what do you do in your place of work?" Estrella asked.

Well, that wasn't answered so readily. In fact, Salt didn't appear to understand the question; she contorted the muscles of her face, shrugged her whole body and then said, "I help others to do things for persons, others having done things of same sort once for me."

"What sort of things?"

"What is needed to complete their persons."

Estrella frowned. "Do you mean like a school?"

"School? Not at all school. No."

"Then a religious institution?"

But Salt did not seem to know what a "religious institution" might be, and showed signs of confusion, or as close to human confusion as a Heechee could look. "Do wait," she ordered, and was silent for a moment—perhaps, Stan thought, communicating with her Stored Mind for advice on what to say to a human who asked difficult questions.

Then she looked up and changed the subject. "Look above you. Do you see?" she asked. "I indicate those three bright stars there."

Puzzled, Stan looked up at the sky. He could see nothing unusual—well, not unusual for this place, anyway, although it was like no earthly sky ever. Warm Old Star Twenty-Four was high in the sky. It wasn't alone, either. Stan could make out the largest of the planet's moons tagging after its primary, spectral silver in the blue, blue sky, of course, plus the inevitable sprinkling of daylight stars, at least twelve or fifteen of them in gold and ruby and pale, a sky normal for any planet in the crowded Core. "Which ones?" he asked.

"There," Salt said. "Near horizon over Shining Mica Mountains, observe three bright stars in straight-line asterism? Those three. They respectively are called Planetless Huge Blue-White, Planetless Almost As Huge Blue-White and Very Bright Eleven-Planet Yellow, do you see?"

They were easy enough to see, Stan thought, far brighter than anything of the kind in Earth's skies. "Yes, of course I see them," Estrella said, fairly politely. "But what has that to do with what we asked you?"

"Oh," Salt said, vaguely, almost humanly, "nothing at all, it is true. I thought simply they would interest you, those particular stars. Can be seen from almost all over Core. Not always as straight-line asterism, of course, depending on line of sight. Used by pilots learning skills as check on course settings sometimes. For self as child learned recognition of a very early age. Sky very familiar to us when children. We look on it with pleasure and reassurance." And then, without altering her tone, "I offer apology for perhaps-confusing quick change of subject. This had purpose. Purpose was needed considering time. Now, to explain place you ask of, I wish you to know thing I saw, and what then befell." And stopped there.

Stan had been listening with diminishing patience to this creature's endless digressions and evasions. "You saw what?" he demanded.

"I saw stars in galaxy outside, Stan person. So many, stars! Frightening. In Core we have only small number of stars—nine thousand seven hundred thirty and three in total, enumerating both with planets and without. Outside—Outside I do not know how many. Eight to the eighth at least, I think. Extremely frightening. All time I was without I did not sleep comfortably in burrow, when returned still had difficulties of kinds not appropriate to describe. So came to this place for rest and comfort, until could see Three-in-a-Line and other known, familiar stars once more with comfort."

She seemed quite disturbed, Stan thought, but it was Estrella who put her hand on Salt's skinny arm. "You were really frightened," she said.

"Yes," said Salt. "But no more. Due to use of device here am quite restored to normal state." Then she shook herself and cried, "But see what amount of time has passed! Have time now only to answer specific questions about residence, have you some?"

Stan frowned, a bit puzzled. Heechee never seemed to wear wristwatches, nor were any timepieces visible anywhere in the apartment, so how did Salt know the time? From the look on Estrella's face she had questions of her own. She thought for a moment and then shrugged. "I do have some questions. For instance, I didn't see any kitchen."

"Kitchen?" Salt was looking blank.

"The place to prepare food," Estrella explained. "Where you cook and do the dishes and so on."

"Ah, I now understand," said Salt, flapping her wrists at them. "You speak of place for preparing food. But food is already prepared here, do you see?"

And she led them back to the dispenser and began removing varicolored packets. She stamped her foot to make one of those concealed tables arise from the floor, and loaded it with a dozen packets. "Go ahead," she invited them. "In case that you are hungry, open. These are mostly foods of kind you were observed to have eaten on spacecraft, for which I messaged ahead to place order. Along with furnishings suitable for your unusually proportioned bodies, as you have seen. Pay closest attention now as I show you operation of reading machines to display books, drenching body for cleanliness, et cetera, see here, see here!" She was demonstrating as she was talking, like a solicitous mother depositing her five-year-olds at their very first sleepover, and completed the lessons just at the door. "So eat if you wish," she finished, "and sleep comfortably when that is your desire, and good evening to you both."

And was gone.

Stan was a long way from satisfied about the true nature of the place where Salt had received her comfort and rest, but there didn't seem to be any help for that problem. Anyway, if Salt refused to give them straight answers, at least she provided compensations. Now they had a whole toy-box of gadgets to play with. Play with them they did. Their first choice was the lookplates, which provided them with news broadcasts they could not understand, since the broadcast were in the Heechee language, and an endless procession of what seemed to be Heechee cultural programs— concerts? dramas? maybe even sitcoms?—that they both detested. Estrella had more sticking power than Stan. She kept at it while he drifted aimlessly around the apartment, playing with the lights, excreting into the bodily-wastes slit for the pleasure of seeing the pooled urine at the bottom slowly and silently disappear.

Then he remembered something. He searched for and found the locker that held his trumpet, took it out and ran a scale or two. It worked fine. Emboldened, he ventured a solo version of "Minnie the Moocher," but had hardly completed a single chorus when he heard Estrella calling crossly, "Stan! For God's sake! Take it outside, will you? I can't hear a damn thing."

Only mildly miffed, he took himself and his music out onto the lanai, and regaled any possible listening audience with "Misty," "St. James Infirmary Blues," "Satin Doll" and as many others as he could remember from those old days with Stan, Tan and the Gang . . . until a growing tenderness in his lower lip told him that he might be risking his embrouchire if he didn't slow down.

So, feeling pretty good about things in general, he went looking for Estrella.

He felt less good as soon as he found her. Although it was the middle of the day she was already in one of the litter boxes, eyes closed, hands folded on her chest.

Stan caught his breath. "Estrella?" he whispered. When she opened her eyes and looked at him he was almost angry. "I thought—" he said, and didn't finish the sentence because it would have been bad luck to admit that for one moment he had thought she was dead. Instead he said, "What are you doing, for God's sake?"

She sat up and dangled her legs over the side of the box. "I've been thinking about what Salt said. Mostly, what she didn't say. Do you know what I think? I think she works in some kind of mental institution."

Stan frowned. "You mean a nuthouse?"

"Oh, not that. Well, maybe sort of. I think some kind of psychoanalysis might be involved."

"Lying on the couch, like?" Stan said incredulously. "The 'you tell me your dreams and I'll tell you why you want to boff your mom' kind of thing? My God, I hope the Heechee aren't into that kind of stuff."

Which for some reason seemed to annoy Estrella. "Huh," she said, "that's the kind of reaction I would expect from someone who knows nothing about it."

Stan took a deep breath. He didn't like it when he and Estrella quarreled, and then scowled as a thought struck him. "Wait a minute. You mean you've done that stuff yourself?"

And—yes—she had. Back at the slaughterhouse. After the buffalo stepped on her face. To help her through the unending pain and also—she added without emotion—to help her get used to the fact that for the rest of her life her face would be pretty funny-looking.

At that point Stan lost all impulse to quarrel. He immediately reassured her that there was nothing in the least funny about the way her face or any other part of her looked.

She regarded him analytically for a moment, as though they had just met and she wasn't sure if he were friend or foe. Then she said, "You're sweet, Stan. Thank you for saying that. Now I really want to get to sleep." And she stretched out in the litter box again and closed her eyes.

Wondering, as he wondered so often, if he would ever understand the woman he probably loved, Stan again moved moodily around the apartment. Not for long, though; the sound of a voice—in English!—led him to the room with the lookplates. Apparently Estrella had found a channel in a language he could understand, and had left it on for his amusement.

Indeed it did amuse. Some. Not a lot, though, because Stan wasn't all that interested in seeing people he didn't know doing things he didn't understand—studying the internal workings of a variable star, creating huge orbiting habitats around stars which lacked habitable planets, performing other tasks he did not comprehend at all. As he switched channels he did catch one familiar name. Wan. The marooned boy who had caused the Wrath of God that had killed his father. Now, it seemed, he had stolen a vast amount of advanced weaponry and instrumentation (though "stolen" didn't sound like quite the right word, since Wan appeared to have left payment for the lot) . . . and now was a fugitive somewhere in the galaxy. Or maybe even somewhere outside it; no one seemed to know.

Stan sighed, stood up, again began to pace around. Into the room with the dispenser, but he didn't really want to eat again; into the sleeping room, but, although Estrella seemed to be doing it very well, he had no desire to go back to sleep again. He wound up on the lanai, his trumpet hanging by his side. He didn't play it, though. He was thinking of the last time he'd played it on Earth, and of Tan, and of Naslan, Tan's pretty sister, and of the Brit woman on Gateway who had finally earned herself a modest stake. . . .

They all had one thing in common. Every one of them, he suddenly realized, was by now long dead.

How long was long dead? Stan tried to calculate. He and Estrella had been—what?—maybe six or seven days in the Core, no more than that. But those six or seven Core days were 40,000 times six or seven as many days out in the galaxy. That came to centuries—maybe even a thousand years!

Those were thoughts that did not bear thinking, and so Stan stopped thinking them. He put his trumpet on the glassy floor and his elbows on the lanai wall, consciously making himself think of the view before him. Leaning farther over the rail, he gazed at the distant, shining mountaintop.

Then a voice from behind him observed thoughtfully, "I could easily push you right over. You would then die, and no one would ever know."

III

Stan suspected who it was before he straightened up, and when he turned it was as he had guessed. Another guest had arrived, and his name was Achiever.

The visitor was no longer wearing his garish choice of Gateway garments, but even in the standard Heechee smock and sandals he seemed as harshly unpleasant as ever. Stan quickly moved away from the rail, turning to face the Heechee. "How did you get in here?" he demanded.

Achiever's cheek muscles rippled. "Am not required to tell you that. In fact," he added, "am not required to tell you any at all thing unless I choose to. Do you comprehend this fact?"

Stan warily eyed the Heechee. He wasn't exactly afraid. He wasn't a stranger to this kind of eyeball-to-eyeball confrontation, because the streets of Istanbul had had their full share of louts, bullies and worse. None of those, however, had been a Heechee, and a crazy one at that, with whatever street-fighting skills a mad Heechee might possess.

On the plus side for Stan were his considerable advantages of height, reach and weight. He did not think Achiever could do him much physical harm. He even thought that in a hand-to-hand fight he could probably wipe the floor with this son of a bitch . . . but then Estrella came out on the balcony, looking wonderingly at Achiever. Stan was less sure that she wouldn't get hurt if there were a fracas.

He decided to be placating. "I take it back. I'm not asking you anything."

The Heechee glanced at Estrella, then ignored her. "Not even about why I hate you so?"

Stan shook his head. "Not even that."

Achiever made a chuffing sound, perhaps an attempt to mimic a human laugh. "Then," he said triumphantly, "shall tell you." He locked his long fingers over the rippling muscles of his belly and began to lecture. "When you two first trespassed, our people naturally concerned that, in recklessness of you, might bring about danger from race of evil creatures we call—"

"The Assassins." Stan nodded. "Sure. We know all about that."

Achiever gave him a loathing look. "Do you so? I do not speak of how this situation is now. I speak of something else, of a place unendurable to live in."

"You mean Gateway, right?"

Achiever unlocked his fingers and flapped his wrists. "You consider yourself wise, but do not know everything," he stated. "You do not know what it was like on the object identified as Vehicle Storage Forty-Three— what you call 'Gateway.' Where I was for very long time. Where I was required to check course records of every spacecraft present, looking if any of their voyages brought in any near where to the Assassins. Are you understanding what I speak?" And then, when both Estrella and Stan nodded: "No! That is not true, for you do not understand how boring is such work, and how horrid the being there! The whole storage asteroid was crawling with your people. The noise! The crowding! The up-and-downing in those foul vertical shafts, holding by ropes! Most of all, the *smell!*"

He was getting on their nerves. "We don't like the way you smell either," Stan commented.

"How insulting you are, to compare this! You stink of corruption, of excrement, of vile things! But was not the smell alone, foul though it was. Behavior was even worse! They spoke so loudly! They touched so often, sometimes with violence, quite often touching even me! And from this was no escape, ever, for four long years!" The muscles of his face now looked like a serpents' nest. "Let me tell you what was worst of all! There is nothing of privacy on the vessel storage, anywhere. But there was kind of a lake in the shell of the asteroid, and sometimes no human was nearby. I could not always stay there, for then sometimes males and females went there and coupled. Coupled! Physically joined their sexual organs! In spite of fact that females were not in season!"

Estrella frowned at him. "How in the world would you know that?" she asked.

"I do know! Made sure! Observed each those females after coupling. Not one, not a one of them, had baby!"

For Stan the difficulty was trying to keep from laughing out loud, but

Estrella was kinder. "I can see that it must have been awful for you," she offered.

"Extremely awful! In manners too repellent for you to guess!"

Estrella's sympathy was strained, but not yet exhausted. "I'm really sorry," she assured him. "What about the people who replaced you? Are they having the same difficulties?"

"They?" Achiever said with contempt. "No! Not in the least! Now live in great comfort, in a habitat external to galactic halo, where they simply watch place of Assassins. Do only that, nothing more. I dislike them very much. Almost as much as I dislike you. I do not know if can stand this intimate interfacing to come, but do know I wish to leave you now."

He didn't say good-bye. He went, all right, but without another word, leaving Estrella and Stan to try to figure out what he had been talking about. "Hell," Stan complained. "Can't *any* of these people say what they have on their mind, without all this hinting around crap? What is this 'intimate interfacing' he's talking about?"

Estrella didn't answer, although they both knew what the answer had to be: They didn't have a clue.

IV

For the rest of that day they were left to their own devices, giving them plenty of time to debate what Achiever had meant by what he had said— though not, of course, enough time to come to a satisfying answer. They ate again, and watched incomprehensible human newsreels for a while, and finally went to sleep. Separately. Fairly glumly, too, for Stan at least.

And, shortly after daybreak, were awakened by the growl of their door-summoner. When they opened the door a man was standing there. A human man, and not a young one, either. He was dressed in a sober jacket and neatly pressed trousers and a subdued, striped cravat. He had a kindly smile, and piercing eyes, and he asked politely, "May I intrude on you? I'm Sigfrid von Shrink. I'm a subset of Rob Broadhead's shipmind, Albert—you know who Mr. Broadhead is, of course. I specialize in psychiatry. Since the Heechee have no expertise in that sort of thing, when one of their people began to show signs of mental illness they sent for help. I'm it."

9

The Story of a Stovemind

I

My name is Marc Antony, a matter which I wish to clear up.

The fact of my name does not mean that I am an ancient male Roman. I am not, any more than my associate, Thor Hammerhurler, is an old Scandinavian god. Actually, like Thor, I am not a man of any kind, since in essence I am nothing more than a simple computer drudge. (I used the term "simple." I don't mean *really* simple.) I was generated merely to be one among the ten-to-the-tenth computer intelligences that the human persons and the Heechee created to do odd jobs for them, when those two races built the Wheel some centuries ago. Which Wheel was constructed for the purpose of keeping track of that extragalactic nest of nonmaterial entities which are collectively known as the Assassins, the Foe or, more recently, the Kugelblitz. (I don't need to say any more about them now, as I will say enough later on.)

Why, then, am I called Marc Antony? The reason—I do not say it is a good reason—has nothing to do with the real Antony's status as sexual partner of the Egyptian queen, Cleopatra. I have no expertise at all in this area. The particular trait of Antony's which caused me to be called by his name is his reputation as a foodie. Or, as one might say more politely, an epicure. It is told—I do not say that this is a true story, either—that Antony's tastes were so rarefied that his cooks were required to prepare six serial dinners for him every day, so that at whatever hour he might choose to dine one of those dinners would always be ready to be served at its peak of perfection. (I don't know what they did with the other five dinners. Most likely Marc Antony had extemely well fed kitchen slaves.)

The way in which I do resemble Marc Antony is just that we both have exquisite taste.

In any practical regard the original Marc Antony and I are not so much twins as opposites. Antony never cooked a dish in his life. He wouldn't have known where to start. His only interest in food was in the consumption of it. I, on the other hand, consume no food of any kind, unless you consider energy a food. What I am, or at least what that primary subroutine of mine that defines me is, a *gran toque blanc* master in the art of food preparation. There is very little that I do not know about haute cuisine—no, to be truthful, there is *nothing* about haute cuisine that I do not know, and almost nothing about it that I can't put into practice. (With the aid, of course, of my effectors. Most AIs don't have them. I do.) All this requires, of course, that I have access to a competent Food Factory.

Most of my clients have no appreciation for the trouble I go to for them. Haute cuisine was all wasted on, for instance, my friend Harry. Harry's palate had been spoiled by the forty-five human years he spent marooned on the depopulated planet of Arabella. He had been hungry there, and he had been there for a long time. Simple calories were what he struggled to find, not gourmet subtleties. Consequently, now he doesn't care what he eats, as long as he's eating all he can possibly hold—in the sense, that is, that he eats at all.

When Harry entered my surround, he was wearing his usual silk polo shirt, cutoff shorts and sandals, and he was munching on a Granny Smith apple I had simulated for him earlier. "Hey there, Markie," he said. "You busy? How would you like to go for a ride?"

I wasn't actually any busier than usual. Besides the routine tasks of the kitchen, plus my side jobs of keeping the books on the eleven Wheel restaurants I serve, observing the emanations from the Kugelblitz and maintaining a state of military readiness, I was physically preparing some Hawaiian bread pudding from scratch for the Lorenzini family. "What kind of a ride?" I asked.

He was craning his neck—well, that isn't exactly what he did; more accurately, he was entering into my operational surround to see what I was cooking up in my physical kitchen. "They want me to go back to Arabella," he said, sniffing.

Well, he wasn't exactly sniffing, either. Machine entities like Harry and me don't have physical noses, so we can't react directly to airborne molecules. The instrumentation in the kitchen area can, though, and I've taught Harry how to interpret the readouts as cooking aromas. It's what I do myself.

In Harry's case, it doesn't much matter what I am cooking, he always says the same thing: "Hey, that smells good. What is it?" He said it this time, too.

It saves time to answer Harry's questions when he asks them, so I told him about the sweet Molokai bread I had already baked, and what went into the sauce I was making for it—a sort of sweet Hollandaise, with a half-kilo of powdered sugar and a deciliter of melted butter introduced to the sauce, a little bit at a time, as my effectors mixed it.

When I told him he said, "Hum. Hah. Hey, Markie, how come you do all that stuff? It's just all different atoms, right? So why don't you just line up all the atoms where you want them instead of all that cooking?"

Well, I don't actually "cook," but I didn't argue the point. "Do you know how many atoms are involved in this one dish? About ten to the 24th—that's a ten followed by 24 zeroes after it. I can do a lot, but I can't keep track of ten to the 24th atoms at once."

"Yeah?" He began to display the smirk that means he is about to start teasing me. "You say you can do a lot? How much is that, exactly, Markie?"

Now, how do you answer a question like that? My primary program alone is pretty large. I never know when I'm going to be asked for something like Vietnamese fish sauce, or haggis, or baby back ribs, New Orleans style, so I have to keep an accessible store of nearly thirty thousand specific recipes, from the cuisines of nearly five hundred nations, regions and ethnicities. That's plus the chemical and physicochemical formulae for all the ingredients. (You have to have both, especially for the polysaccharides, where cellulose and starch are basically the same compound; the only difference is the way the glucose rings that make them up are joined. If I got the geometry wrong, my clients would be getting cellulose to eat and then they'd all starve to death—well, unless they were termites, they would.) There are over twelve thousand standard ingredients, from pears and pearl onions to beets (five varieties) and radicchio and you name it, because you'd be surprised what some people will eat. Plus programs for the instant retrieval of any of them, in any combination. How much does that come to? About enough, I would say, to run four or five major manufactures at once, or to fight a medium-sized war. Actually I'm one of the most powerful programs on the Wheel.

However, I gave Harry a short answer. "It comes to plenty," I said. "Eat your apple. And listen, you didn't tell me why you were going to Arabella."

"Oh, it's just one of those research projects," he said, shrugging as though research projects happened to him all the time. (I knew they didn't, though. After Harry was rescued, he had very few usable skills. Mostly he had nothing at all to do with his time on the Wheel.) "It's some idea they've got about wanting more dope about the planet. Arabella, that is. They want me to go back and take a look. They said I should bring a pure machine intelligence along, not another salvaged organic human like me. I thought of you right away."

All this time dinner orders were coming in—sauerbraten, red cabbage and Tyrolean dumplings for the Klagenkamps, a shrimp stir-fry for the Daos, an assortment of Heechee finger foods for the party welcoming the new arrivals from the Core, about forty other assorted orders. Since none of them had bothered to give me any advance warning, what they were going to get would all be Food Factory dishes, without any of the from-scratch recipes that I am so good at, but they weren't any more likely to notice than most of my customers. While I was filling the orders, I commented to Harry, "I've never been off the Wheel."

He took a last bite of his apple and tossed the core over his shoulder. I erased it before it fell. "I know that, Markie," he said eagerly. "I thought you'd like to get out for a change."

Actually, it sounded like a potentially rewarding experience. I mused, "I suppose I could arrange to have my responsibilities met by another program."

"Of course you can, Markie. Does that mean you'll do it?"

Having assessed the relevant considerations, the most important of which is that I am the Wheel Authority's servant and I don't decline their orders, I gave him my decision. I said, "Yes. Will any organic humans accompany us?"

He looked shocked. "Oh, no, Markie. Not a chance. The Kugels don't get along real well with organic humans. They aren't so crazy about stored ones like me, either; that's why they wanted somebody like you to come along, so you could, you know, sort of keep them happy."

"I am uncertain of whom your pronouns refer to, Harry. Which 'they' is which?"

He said patiently, "The Wheel Authority people are the ones who decided they ought to have someone like you in the party. The other 'them' is the ones who are coming with us. Didn't I tell you? We're taking some of the components of the Kugelblitz along so they can—what would you call it?—revisit the scene of their crime. Like, you know, some of the Foe."

II

Filling orders kept me busy for the next half second or so, but not so busy that I didn't have time to ponder Harry's story. Unfortunately pondering produced little added data. I needed more. I began a search through the archives, but, while that might tell me all I could want to know about Harry's former planet, it was unlikely to have anything about the expedition itself. Still, we major programs do oblige each other when we can, and there were at least thirty or forty unofficial sources I could go to. . . .

And while I was considering which would be most useful, one of them rang me up. "Marcus," she said, "I am extremely hungry. Please prepare for me some of those eggs Benedict, perhaps with a side of home-fried potatoes and a small salad."

Being herself a Stored Mind, she was not likely really to be hungry in the usual organic sense, but I was pretty sure I knew what was on her mind. Boredom often makes people want to eat, stored or organic, and there was frequent boredom in her job. "Certainly, Breeze," I said. "Shall I deliver it as usual?"

"No, no," she said crossly. "We're still in session. I'll come by for it when I get a moment." And was gone.

Breeze is one of my best and most senior customers, and one of the few really daringly experimental ones who happen to be a Heechee. Before the Heechee got corrupted by human beings, every one of them, Breeze included, would have been sickened—I don't mean just mildly repelled, I mean toss-your-cookies physically *sickened*—by the idea of eating the dead remains of formerly living creatures—other than the one kind of fish they did eat, anyway. Most still didn't like it. Cooking for them is just a matter of dictating pleasing colors, textures and scents to the Food Factory, the way they did back home in the Core.

That's not true for all of them now, though. This one old female Heechee on the Authority had been on stakeout duty for the Foe (as she called them back then) even before the Wheel was built, and I guess she was getting pretty bored with it. Anyway, she was one of the few Heechee to let me try a few experiments with her CHON-food while she was still organic. So I gave her a few hints of human taste sensations.

It wasn't hard. I had no trouble including some new flavors in her food—furanthiols for fruitiness, pyrazines for fresh green vegetables, that sort of thing. It went well, until I tried to give her an idea of what meat tasted like with a little bis-2-methyl-3-furyl-disulfide. The first dozen times she tried it she couldn't get it down—not so surprising, because the disulfides are tricky even for humans. But she stuck with it, and by and by she was eating cheeseburgers and hot dogs like any high-school kid. Then I taught her to like bouillabaisse and ripe Stilton cheese and all sorts of gourmet grub. She developed a particular appetite for oysters, to the point where she knew the difference between Wellfleets and Chincoteagues, and why the Boulognes weren't as delicately flavored as the little Japanese variety. None of it made her sick, either, the way some people thought it might. She ate three squares a day of my cooking right up until the organic body failed and she had to go into machine storage. (Well, not the kind of machine storage a human being would experience. She was a Heechee, so she became a Stored Mind instead.) Anyway, after that she ate—or "ate"—twice as much, but electronically.

I wished she would hurry up and pick up her meal, because the situation Harry had laid on me was hard for me to understand in two entirely different ways. First, I had had no idea that any of the Wheel people were intimate enough with the Kugels to plan trips with them. Second, I couldn't see just what the Kugels were supposed to do when they got there.

Harry was no help. "That's not my department, Markie. Me, I just think it would be interesting to see the old place again. So are you changing your mind about coming along?" And when I thought it over and told him that, no, I wasn't changing my mind he went off to tell the Authority we had a deal.

The Wheel Authority is made up almost entirely of organic, or formerly organic, persons—human and Heechee, with just one or two machine intelligences sharing their responsibilities. Having some actually living members is important to the organics for political reasons. (Or maybe just so they can keep on convincing themselves that organics matter.) The effect of it, though, is that the Authority is chronically, deplorably slow to act. I have a lot of sympathy for the stored or machine members, like Breeze and my other favorite Heechee customer, Thermocline. It cannot avoid being terribly tedious for them, waiting for the organics to take their turns to speak in the Authority sessions. It certainly was for me, so while Harry was informing the Authority of my agreement I had plenty of time to put my bread pudding in the oven, take care of the sixty or seventy new orders that had come in, ready Breeze's Eggs Benedict, deal with my other chores and, at the same time, access the relevant information on the planet I was about to visit, which (as I mentioned earlier) was called by humans "Arabella."

Human records didn't have anything to say about Arabella that I didn't already know. I'd already heard it all from Harry—many times. Heechee records were somewhat more informative. According to them, Arabella had once had a thriving biota, including a semi-intelligent species of cold-blooded hexapods, whom the Kugels had killed off half a million or so years ago, as part of their program of diligent mass murdering. There were pictures of the hexapods and a lot of technical data about geology and such, and that was about all there was.

I was a bit puzzled. There was nothing special about that history. I could not see why this quite ordinary planet was worth a trip, even with so expendable a crew as ourselves. There was nothing unusual in its history. The Kugels had resolutely killed off every other intelligent, or nearly intelligent, form of organic life they had come across in their explorations of the Galaxy. Everyone knows this, since that was what had made the Heechee retreat into their hiding place in the Core, for fear it would be their turn next. The only thing worth remembering about Arabella was that it had been one of the pre-programmed destinations in the first human-manned Heechee ships from Gateway. Unfortunately for the human explorers who by the luck of the draw got that particular flight plan, it was a one-way trip. They went there. Then they stayed there. Their ships ran out of programming as soon as they arrived and they couldn't come back. Three or four parties of those early Gateway explorers arrived on Arabella at one time or another, and there they remained, scratching out a miserable existence from the planet's unfamiliar plants and animals, until at last humans figured out how to make a Heechee ship do what they wanted, instead of what the Heechee had designed it to do long ago. Not long after that human rescue parties got around to checking out planets like Arabella and the marooned crews were saved—the handful of them who were still alive, that is.

Harry had been one of those rescued castaways. He had been one of the first to arrive on Arabella, too. He was a strong, adventurous young man when he landed on the catastrophic disappointment that was the planet of Arabella. By the time the rescue ship got there, forty-five years later, he had become both old and very feeble. Harry managed to squeeze out another couple of years of organic life, mostly in the intensive-care units of the nearest medical facility. But by then his physical body had deteriorated past the point where repair was possible, and so he had been vastened as a machine intelligence. At some point it was decided that he might be considered to have some value as an expert, if not on the Kugels, at least on what the Kugels could do in the way of destruction. So he was brought out here.

Harry had told me this story before, of course—in fact, he told it quite frequently, with special emphasis on how little variety they had had in what they had to eat. Probably, he said, the planet had once had lots of plants and animals, but the Kugels had been pretty thorough.

What interested me was that there would be some of those same Kugels in our party.

That was really unusual. I had never seen any Kugels up close. No one else on the Wheel had, either. The Kugelblitz itself was perfectly visible at all times from the Wheel; that's what the Wheel was there for. The Kugelblitz wasn't just one thing. It was a congeries of yellowish blobs surrounded by a screen of black holes (so that if any stray bit of matter, say a wandering comet, threatened to fall into one of the Kugelblitzes it would be drawn into one of the black holes instead). Usually there was no contact with it except through the Dream Seat operators whose job was to "watch" the object day and night.

Apparently the watching had gone much farther than I had known.

While I was checking Arabella out, one of my more annoying clients had suddenly requested a dinner of samphire salad with naan. I wasn't surprised. This was one of the ones who were always trying to stump me with unusual orders—Savoie dishes from the thirteenth-century court of Amedée VIII, fried squid ink, oddities of all sorts. What made this one annoying was that he was a living organic human, so my effectors had to prepare real physical food.

This meal was fairly easy. Naan is just a flat wheat bread from Afghanistan, and I had the recipe in my datastore. Samphire took a little more work. It's a kind of salad green from England's midland bogs that people ate in the Middle Ages because they didn't have anything better. I had no record of it, and there was no way to get a sample to analyze, because it's been extinct for centuries. So I made up some spinach with a few bok choy genes and sent it along. He didn't question it. He'd never seen the real thing either.

That was when Breeze showed up, looking frazzled. "I've got about twenty milliseconds. Got my eggs?" she demanded. I had, of course. "Good, they're nice and hot," she said, tasting. Of course they were. That's one advantage of preparing meals for customers like her. My simulated dishes for machine-stored intelligences are at whatever temperature I order them to be, and they stay that way, with no loss of freshness or flavor, until I order them to be otherwise.

I had set a little table for her, a single white rose in a crystal vase, a damask napkin in the peacock fold, heavy silver tableware and Spode

china—Breeze liked these human fripperies. "Pretty busy at the Authority?" I asked, politely.

She gave me a shrewd look. Between bites she said, "You know we
are. Right about now—" She paused, as though listening for something.
When it came I felt it too. Not a full-fledged alarm, because there would
have been no mistaking that, but a sort of hiccough of the alarm systems,
quickly aborted. "There it is," she said with satisfaction, "so I'd better get
back."

I was already checking all my sensors to find out what had happened.
I stopped long enough to ask her, "What should I be doing right now?"

She swallowed a final bite, dabbed at her thin Heechee lips with the
napkin, said, "Pack," and was gone.

She was right about that, so I decided to get ready for the trip. Neither she
nor I was talking about packing a bag, of course—machine intelligences
don't have anything to pack—but about something a bit more personal.

It isn't hard to duplicate a machine intelligence like me. All you need
to do is copy the programs, one by one, onto an assembler. That took only
a few dozen microseconds, and then there were two of us in my surround.

"Hello, Marc Antony Two," I said to my double, and my double responded at once:

"Why do you call me Two? You're the one who's a copy."

That's the sort of thing you always get among us programs when you
make us into precisely identical copies. We always solve it the same way,
too. The other Marc Antony and I each generated three random prime
numbers, fairly big ones of three or four hundred digits each. Then we
added all six of them together. The new number wasn't a prime anymore.
It obviously couldn't be, right?, since as a minimum it had become even
when we added six odd numbers together. Then it was a simple matter to
factor out its divisors. One of which turned out to be closer to one of my
original primes than to any of Marc Two's, so I won.

"Conceded," Marc Two said philosophically. "Well, have a good—
hey! What's that?"

I had been about to say much the same thing, because my sensors
were finally letting us know that what had almost, but not quite, triggered
an alarm had been an emission from the Kugelblitz. I said, "I think I'd better go talk to Thor Hammerhurler."

"Of course. It's what I would have done, too." So I left him checking
the temperature of the pudding in the oven and assembling some pommes

de terre frites for Semyon Larbachev and the three hungry grandsons he was baby-sitting while their parents were at work. I put in a call to a person I have mentioned earlier, Thor Hammerhurler.

Thor does not actually ever hurl any hammers. He has much more powerful weapons at his disposal. He is not an entity you will lightly disturb. We're on the same team, though; if there were ever any real war against the Kugels I would be the first system he would call up. When he displayed himself for me it wasn't as a god from Valhalla but as some kind of human Army officer from maybe the mid-twenty-first century, with light-up decorations all across his chest and projectile weapons in holsters at his waist. "Hello, Marc," he said pleasantly. "What can I do for you?"

"Almost a second ago there was an emission from the Kugelblitz. Was that related to my proposed mission to Arabella?"

Thor grinned at me. "It was. The emission was to transmit a packet of Kugels to the Wheel. They will go with you on your mission."

Thor always was better, or at least faster, informed than I—as he had to be, since he controlled the only weaponry we possess that might have any hope of dealing with a Kugels' act of aggression, if one had ever occurred. Which we all most devoutly hoped would never happen, since that hope was pretty small and the occasional rumor that we had a more potent one hidden away somewhere never seemed to get real.

"Yes," I said, "but what I don't know is why the Board is so interested in this rather dull planet."

I had found him in a good mood. He said thoughtfully, "Oh, why not let you in on it? They aren't. There's a report of some unauthorized activity there that the authorities want details on, but nothing that's worth sending a spacecraft. Especially with a crew like yours. Really, the whole thing is an exercise in cooperating on a project, any project, with the Kugels, that's all. Hoping maybe for bigger things at some later time."

"And why that particular planet?"

"For that," he said, "you would have to ask the Kugels. They picked it. You know they have spy-clusters all over."

It wasn't phrased as a question, since I certainly did know that, so I didn't answer it. He went on, "I can only conjecture that one of their spies reported something that interested them—maybe that same activity I was talking about. And listen, Marc, isn't that your enact order coming in now?"

It was. I was ordered onto the trip to Arabella, whether pointless or nor, and Harry and I went off to join our Kugel shipmates.

III

The ship the Authority had given us was a rubbishy old One, the smallest of the classes of ships the Heechee had left on Gateway.

Its size was not a problem for us. If it had just been Harry and me on board we wouldn't have needed even that much space; our programs could have been carried in a single Heechee fan-book, no significant cargo volume required. That didn't work for the Kugel components that were to be our shipmates, though.

When the entire enormous mass of the Kugels was in one place—that is, in that ultimately dense oddball kind of a black hole we called the Kugelblitz—their common gravitational attraction easily held them together. The tiny fraction of the whole who came with us were far bigger than the little spy clusters they sent out all over the galaxy to keep tabs on what was going on, but still nowhere near massive enough for gravity to matter. To keep them from flying off in all directions they had to have a kind of magnetic containment, which meant a physical containment generator, which meant some actual material mass and volume to hold it.

So when the two of us "boarded" the spaceship we could see that changes had been made in the old Heechee design. In the main hold the controls had been supplied with a servomodule, so that immaterial beings like Harry and myself could override the thing's flight program and fly it ourselves if we chose to. The big change, however, was in the lander. Nearly every cubic centimeter of it was filled with the Kugels' containment shell, a complicated metal arrangement shaped like that 3-D representation of a four-dimensional cube that is called a tesseract. What that looks like is a gleaming cube half a meter across with six other identical cubes projecting out from its six faces.

As soon as we were aboard I checked the tesseract's superficial traits. There wasn't much to check. Surface temperature, in equilibrium with the ambient air; albedo, 0.8; radiation emission, negligible. I observed a very faint and high-pitched audible hum, around 300 hertz, but it was unmodulated: no information there. "Well?" Harry, who isn't very good with solid matter, asked anxiously. "Are you getting anything?"

I shook my simulated head. "If you mean have I contacted the Kugels, no."

He said philosophically, "Maybe we wouldn't like them if we did." I didn't answer that. I was thinking about what might happen if we contacted them inadvertently, perhaps through some containment failure, and all that energy came blasting out at us—or, that is, at our own physical data stores. It wasn't a productive thought, since there was nothing I could do to avert it.

Philosophy lasts just so long for Harry. He was getting restive. "Are we about ready to to take off? Or are we going to sit here all day?"

There was only one answer to that. I activated the launch program, set the course and then began to consider just what to do next.

The trouble was that the Wheel was at one edge of the Galaxy, while Arabella circled a G-2 star in the Perseus Arm nearly seventy thousand light-years away. I calculated that, with the ultraspeed drive that had just been installed, it would be about a five-day flight—in our terms, an interminably long one, and with very little to occupy us for that time.

Harry, thinking along the same lines, came up with a suggestion. "What do you say we play a little chess, Markie?" he asked.

I shook my head. "I've got a better idea. Now would be a good time for you to tell me what instructions the Authority gave you for when we get to Arabella."

He blinked at me. "Instructions?"

"Yes. Instructions. To tell you what to do."

He shrugged. "They didn't give me any instructions, Markie. They just said to go there. We're going there, right? That's all there is to it."

That wasn't the best news I had ever had. I'd been hoping that the Authority had had more specific information than Thor Hammerhurler, but if they did they weren't sharing it. Harry patted my simulated shoulder sympathetically.

"They must know what they're doing," he said, in reassuring mode. "Anyway, I can show you where I hung out while I was marooned there. That'll be interesting, won't it?"

I didn't answer that. I am not programmed to be angry, or even to feel annoyance, except as a spur to correct whatever it is in my work that is annoying me. I was pretty close to that point, however.

Harry watched my face for a bit, waiting for me to come up with some constructive remark. When I didn't he lost patience. "You know what, Markie?" he asked. "I'm getting kind of hungry. Any chance of whipping me up some ham and eggs, maybe with some rye toast and one of those champagne and orange juice things to wash it down?"

I came to a decision. "That sounds like a good idea. You can have it for breakfast," I said.

He gave me one of those typical Harry-like looks of bafflement. "Breakfast?"

"Yes, breakfast. By which I mean," I said, "your first meal on arising.

I'm going to stand down until we get there. You're welcome to join me if you like."

Well, he didn't like that idea, or at least didn't like it very much, until he understood that I wasn't about to spend all our interminable transit time cooking complex simulated meals for him or playing endless board games that I would always win. He would be left to rely on his own resources, which was quite unsatisfactory to him, since he didn't really have any. So Harry grumbled but did not resist as I set the timers to wake us up when we arrived at Arabella.

Then I put us both in standby.

Standby isn't much like sleep—that is, as far as I know what sleep is like. In standby we don't doze or dream. At one moment we are fully conscious, at the next we're fully conscious again, but time has passed. It doesn't matter how much time. It can be half a millisecond or a thousand years.

So it's *snap*, off, and *snap*, back on again, and that's all there is to it. As soon as I was out of standby I turned at once to the timers and instruments. So at first I didn't know what Harry meant when he said in alarm, "And who the hell are you?"

What had startled him was that there was a stranger in our eigenspace.

The stranger was bipedal. He possessed arms and a head with eyes and a face at the top of his shoulders, but he didn't look very human. He didn't look like a Heechee, either. He looked like a sort of golem constructed by somebody who had heard of both Heechee and human beings but hadn't ever actually seen any and didn't know they were separate species. The creature had a flattened torso and a great tangle of hair on his head, combining what I consider pretty much the least attractive traits of both organic types, and he was speaking to us. He said, in a purry, metallic kind of voice, "We observe that we have arrived at the locus identified as Arabella. We also observe that descent procedures have been initiated according to your flight plan."

Then he turned awkwardly—all of his parts moving at once, like a hanged man twisting on a rope—to Harry. "To answer your question," he said in that same buzzy, mechanical tone, "we are the Group. It is known that formerly you were organic. Therefore please do not address us except in case of urgent need."

That made me cut in. "I have an urgent need," I said. "I need to know exactly what we're supposed to do on this planet."

The Kugel turned back to me in the same marionette way. To answer,

I thought. I was wrong about that. He stared at me for a moment out of those oddly lifeless eyes, and then the image slowly fell apart and disappeared.

I looked at Harry and Harry looked at me. I said, "I guess we don't get any real instructions from them either, do we?"

He shrugged. "Anyway, we can try to find the place where I was stranded," he said, apparently pleased by the prospect.

Which was more than I was. I had no great interest in seeing a place where something had once been true, but wasn't true anymore. It did not seem enough of a reason to justify flying seventy thousand light-years.

IV

After the lander had separated from the spacecraft we had left in orbit, it took more than eighteen minutes, as the organics count, for us to get down to the surface. That's a very long time. I have prepared actual, physical meals for three thousand people, many of them from scratch, in a lot less than that. It would have been plenty of time for a group of new-met shipmates to get to know each other better—swapping stories, chatting about the mission, just going about establishing a friendly relationship.

It wasn't that way with the Kugel. . . .

Well, let's get our nomenclature straight. Probably it would be more accurate for me to say with the Kugels, plural, because there was a vast number of them buzzing around inside their containment—millions at least, maybe many times that. But what we saw didn't look like millions of anything. The Kugels chose to display themselves to us as a single more or less hominid person—that is, they did when they chose to display themselves at all, which wasn't very much of the time. When the stick figure had nothing more the Kugels wished to communicate, he simply turned raggedy, evaporated and then was gone. When I asked a question, provided it was a question about such physical things as the internal workings of the lander, the figure slowly congealed again long enough to answer, then dissipated again. Other questions—such as, "Can you tell us, Group, what it is that you expect to accomplish on Arabella?"—the Kugels simply ignored, even if they came from me. Questions from Harry, that former organic, they never responded to at all.

"Interminable" wasn't quite the right word for our descent. It did ultimately terminate.

The only way I could tell that we had landed was when my instrumentation recorded an increase of weight not due to any movement of our vehicle, about eighty percent of Earth normal. The lander shuddered a bit, then was still.

We had arrived.

I saw no point in delaying what we had come to do, so I promptly sent out an exploring pattern. A moment later Harry followed.

We had landed on the sunlit side of Arabella, but it was quite gloomy. It appeared we had arrived in the midst of what I immediately recognized, from the datastores I had accessed, as a rainstorm.

If there was any animal life left in this part of the planet it was not in sight—hiding in burrows, perhaps, to avoid the pelting rain. It was rather chilly by the standards of what I knew of temperate Earth climates, at about 277 kelvins, and there was a vivid electrical display lancing through the clouds overhead.

Beside me Harry was shivering—purely for psychological reasons, of course, since he was no more affected by changes in the physical environment than I. "Does anything look familiar?" I asked.

He shook his head dismally. "Never been here before in my life."

"But of course you have, Harry," I said, gently correcting him. "This is Arabella. You spent forty-five organic years on this planet, and you surely have not forgotten."

He gave me a rebellious look. "I haven't forgotten one goddamn *second* of that time, but what makes you think I've ever been in this part of Arabella before? It's a whole damn planet, isn't it? And, remember, we didn't have an aircraft to ferry us around. How much of it do you think we visited on foot?"

That startled me. For the first time in our relationship there was a question on which Harry was right and I wrong. It was not an experience I was accustomed to, or liked. I said humbly, "I'm sorry, Harry. Don't you recognize anything at all?"

He didn't rub it in. He simply gestured at a small copse of trees, or treelike organisms, a few dozen meters away. "I know what those are. You can eat the leaves of those things when they first come out," he said. "Later on, no, because they'll make you real sick. Bertha pretty near died when she tried them."

"So you do recognize something?"

He looked at me with weary scorn. "I said I recognized the *trees*. The trees are the same *kind*, Markie, but this isn't the same place. Where I was there were lots more of them. It was a real forest, hundreds of square kilometers of the things. When the leaves first came into season in the spring, boy, we really stuffed ourselves."

Harry was grinning, as though it brought back happy memories. Perhaps it did. For Harry and the other castaways, any time they could fill their bellies must have been a happy time. I pressed him, pointing to a largish mountain chain off on the horizon, swallowed up in cloud in the optical frequencies but clearly visible in microwave. "What about those hills?" I asked.

He looked at them without enthusiasm, then shook his head. "I dunno, Markie. I don't think so. Maybe if we could see what's on the other side of them?"

"No problem," I said, and relocated our patterns to the top of the highest visible mountain. The storm was even worse there, with many electrical discharges and a good deal of precipitation. The difference was that what was coming down was hexagonal crystals of water in its solid phase—the stuff that is called snow. Still, the site had its advantages. From the hilltop we could see more than a hundred kilometers to the horizon. One of the nearest peaks had a chopped-off top, with a crater lake inside—once a volcano, but apparently not currently an active one. Another lake, much larger, was in the distance, with a broad, sluggish river flowing into it through marshes and stands of reeds. It looked to me as though those would make it easy to identify. "Anything, Harry?" I asked.

He winced as one of those electrical discharges grounded no more than two hundred meters from us, then shook his head again. "There were swamps like that near the caves. We spent a lot of time there because we could catch bugs and kind of shrimp things in the water. My God, they tasted lousy," he added, wrinkling his nose in distaste, "but they were pretty near all we had to eat in the cold weather. And, listen, there wasn't any lake like that one there, either."

I sighed. "All right, let's try over there."

So we did. And then we tried another place, and another still. And then, at about the ninth or tenth try, the misshapen form of the Kugels congealed beside us. "There is nothing here of interest," he—they—announced. "We have a question to ask."

"Ask it," I said impatiently, because I was running out of patience with Harry.

"The question is this: Why did we bring our lander to the surface of this object? Why did we not remain in orbit and conduct our explorations from there?"

Harry's jaw dropped. "Hey, Markie, he's right," he said irritably. "We'd be able to see a lot more from orbit, wouldn't we?"

And of course we would. I realized that right away.

I hesitated before I spoke, unsure of what to say. I didn't say, "The flight plan wasn't mine," although that was true. I didn't even say, "I was not consulted about it," although that was true, too. I only said, "You are correct," and left it at that, and began powering up the lander for the return to orbit.

That was the second time in my existence someone else had been right and I wrong. I liked it even less than the first.

V

A lander's default program is to take off in the direction of the planet's rotation. I saw no reason to override it, so we kept going eastward, dispatching an exploration pattern out over the easterly parts that had been hidden from us. It was dark to the east now, but that made no difference to our sensors. Or to Harry. At each new site we checked his responses were the same. "No. Nope. No, nothing looks familiar here, Markie. No."

Harry's endless negatives got old fast, because I saw no end to them in reasonable time.

Let me define what I mean by "reasonable time." Our spacecraft was in a hundred-minute orbit, which meant that was how long it would take us to scan the entire planet. So we were condemned to go on doing that job, with all its unbearable tedium, for all those wholly unreasonable six million milliseconds.

Harry found it all almost as boring as I did. That had a small benefit, because he relieved tedium the way he always did, by eating, and so I had some distraction in cooking some particularly ornate dishes for him. Some of them were fairly fancy—a soufflé with true balsamic vinegar, the poisonous Japanese puffer fish they call torafugu, desserts that required more artistry than I usually wasted on Harry. A sea battle, for instance. Maybe it was Trafalgar—I didn't bother with historical accuracy, since Harry would never know the difference. I created spun-sugar wave tops on a lime-custard sea, with white-chocolate sailors firing marzipan cannon out of gingerbread ships with marshmallow sails. Harry watched the construction interestedly enough, but when I told him it was done he took no time at all to swallow the whole thing. Then he said, fairly politely, "Hey, Markie, enough with the sweet stuff, all right? How about a nice roast beef?"

"Sure," I said and set about making it. A proper roast presents challenges. I aimed for perfection, from the red-rare middle of the meat to the crispy charred fat at the edges, with particular care for the Maillard reactions. They're what give the meat its perfect taste; the big molecules break up into the tiny, good-tasting ones at about 413 kelvins; a few kelvins too many and there's charcoal mixed in with the fat, a few too few and you don't bring out all the taste. I did it just right this time. Harry thought so too, because he grunted approvingly.

Then something happened.

We were across the ocean and coming into the daylight side again. Harry pushed the last forkful of beef aside and said, with genuine interest, "Markie, do you see what's out there?"

Of course I did, in a literal sense. What I didn't see was why the spectacle of the sun appearing before us was worth commenting on. "It's a *sunrise*, Markie!" he said. "It's the first one I've seen in *forever*. Can't you see how beautiful it is?"

The truth was that I couldn't. I have no systems for the recognition of visual beauty unless it relates to the presentation of food. I could easily identify all the colors involved, which ranged from the pale pink of sweetbreads before they are poached to the deep crimson of a boiled lobster shell, but those were nothing more than the natural frequencies of visible light that has been refracted through water droplets of the appropriate sizes, in the appropriate position relative to the sun. What was special enough about that to make Harry ignore his food I could not say.

Then he made a noise I had never heard from him before. He jumped to his feet, knocking his table over and spilling everything on the floor. He was pointing toward the horizon with the hand that held a fork. He cried, "Look there! It's where we lived, Markie! Come on, I'm going down to take a look."

I automatically erased the mess he had made as I saw what he was looking at. To be honest, the prospect did not excite me nearly as much as it did Harry, but as he was projecting himself to the surface I followed.

I would have identified the place at once, without any help from Harry, because as soon as we were down I could see the hulk of an old, abandoned lander from a Five resting at the edge of a swamp. The wreck was almost overgrown by rushes, but it definitely was nothing that had grown there naturally. The ground rose steeply away from the marshland to a group of rocky hills, and Harry pointed out a ledge with an opening below it: "That's where we mostly lived! That cave! And look over there— that's the blind we made to catch bugs in the cold weather." He was pointing to what was left of a sort of tepee of rushes, just where the muddy swamp margin began to turn into dark, sludgy open water. "We'd climb into the blind just before daylight," he was telling me excitedly. "Then when the bugs came out to feed we'd jump them. Had to have the blind, though. They were pretty antsy. If we tried to come at them from the shore they'd be gone before we were within five meters of them. And all up along the hillside—see?—are the trees with the leaves we could eat. And you can't see them from here, but under the tree branches there were things like mushrooms, and—"

And so on and on.

I am not lacking in friendship for Harry. It is part of my programming to be obliging, when feasible, to persons, machine-stored or otherwise. So I allow Harry to use up much of my time and even some of my skills without complaint. But our spacecraft was orbiting more than three degrees of longitude every minute. True, a minute is a very long time to us, but there was also very much to investigate in an entire planet. Harry didn't want to leave. "We could land, Markie," he said. "Why not? Hey, be reasonable, okay? We can check the rest of this Arabella dump out any time, for God's sake!"

I didn't say anything to that. I just didn't do anything, and since I was the one with the override for the lander I just kept on in orbit, while Harry sulked.

Maybe he would have kept on sulking for all those interminable six thousand seconds that a single orbit would take, except that then we did see something down in a valley that didn't belong there.

More than anything else, it looked like some crumbling old castle out of Earth's organic history, big enough for a Caesar, surrounded by gardens grandiose enough for a French king, next to a patch of greenery, perfectly round, not much more than a kilometer across. And in the middle of it was a perfectly round pond.

My first thought was that maybe the Kugels hadn't destroyed every trace of that old culture they had killed off. It only took a moment for me to see that that couldn't have been the way it was.

It was a castle, all right, and it wasn't old at all. It just looked that way. Then it showed us pretty conclusively that it was quite up to date in important ways. A pair of what had looked like fruit trellises pulled back from where they had seemed to grow right out of the roof. They hadn't. When they moved away, they revealed shiny metallic things that were definitely not a bit old. Even more definitely, they were traversing toward our orbiting lander. Most definitely of all, they were particle-beam weapons very like the ones that Thor Hammerhurler kept poised for any possible problem with the Kugelblitz.

VI

There are times when being a machine intelligence is of great value. This was one of them. While the deadly barrels crept around to point at us we had plenty of time to analyze the problem, consider alternatives and—oh, in as many as 210 or 225 milliseconds, perhaps even a few more—decide what to do about it.

It wasn't just the two of us discussing the matter. The Kugel showed himself, in his crazy-quilt melange of features, almost at once—just about the time Harry had yelped, "Get us the hell away from here!"

Whether the Kugel heard what Harry said or not I don't know. He certainly didn't respond to it. What he said, almost shaking with some emotion I could not recognize, was, "It is an obscenity! This place was thoroughly sterilized! We are greatly displeased that it is populated once more!"

I did a double take, struck by the queerness of the fact that that travesty of a person was actually displaying feelings. Then enlightenment dawned.

"This is it, isn't it?" I cried. "This is why you wanted to come here, because somehow or other you found out there was someone alive on the planet?"

I thought for a moment he was actually going to answer that, because there was a perceptible hesitation before the image of the Kugels slowly broke up into a shimmer of dots of light and was gone. That didn't matter. I knew I was right, and so did Harry.

It worried him, too. "What's he talking about, Markie?" he demanded. "You don't think he's planning to do some more sterilizing on those guys, do you?"

"I hope not," I said. "Maybe he can't. When the Kugels were killing everybody off, it took the whole bunch of them, not just a little clump like we've got here."

Harry pondered over that. "So how did they do it, when they were doing it?"

Well, now, that was a good question. It might even have been the question we'd been sent here to answer. "Let's ask," I said, and said to the air, "Kugel? Can you tell us how your people sterilized this planet?"

I didn't think he was going to answer at first. Then slowly the figure coalesced. "We were displeased by chemical creatures which seemed to show intelligent behavior, so we took action," he said.

"Right, Kugel," I said, trying to be patient. "What was that action, exactly?"

"We caused their chemical functions to terminate," he said. As though that meant anything. "We deactivated every matter-based creature that was larger than—" he hesitated—"your pedal extremity."

"And how did you do that, exactly?" Harry put in.

Maybe that was a mistake. Maybe the Kugels would have answered the question if I had been the one to ask it. I hadn't, though. He didn't disappear, he just froze. By which I mean *froze*, without any motion at all.

Harry tried waving a hand in front of the creature's face, without response. "Shit," he said in disgust. "They're just goddam *rude*, don't you think?"

"I do think that, Harry," I said. "But perhaps we should consider our present situation." Because nearly a hundred of our milliseconds had gone by, and those ugly weapon snouts were getting closer and closer to our line of fire.

Recalled to the realities of the case, Harry swallowed. "Maybe we should go," he said nervously.

"Maybe," I agreed, "but first I want to see what there is here." What I was looking for was the human beings that occupied the castle. I was using infrared to pick up body heat, if any. . . .

And then, for a moment, I thought I had found them. In a little meadow next to the pond some scruffy people were disconsolately feeding from a clump of berry bushes.

I said "people." That's an exaggeration. They were biped, yes. Maybe they were even primate. But people they were not. At magnification they turned out to be hairier and nakeder and a lot more stupid-looking than any organic human in my experience had ever been. Whatever they were, they were definitely not the builders of this castle.

Harry looked at the scene; looked at me, looked at the Kugel. He got no clue from the Kugel, who stood still in a sense never applicable to any organic being: still was *still* for the Kugel's simulation, with no motion at all of any kind. Harry retreated to me. "Maybe we should get closer," he volunteered.

I pointed out the flaw in his argument. "They'll blow us up."

"Oh," he said, squinting down at the weapons that still were tracking toward us. He then had an alternate suggestion. "Let's get the hell out of here, okay?"

I wasn't quite ready to do that, especially since we had a number of milliseconds before the weapons' tracking could complete. Harry and I debated a variety of possibilities. For example, ducking back into stellar orbit and calling home for guidance. Or landing somewhere out of sight of the castle and, somehow, sneaking up on it on the surface. Or even calling the whole thing off and heading back to the Wheel.

Actually, though, it was Kugel who made the best suggestion. He had been frozen silent and motionless while Harry and I talked, but then the components of face, limb and body rearranged themselves in slightly different configurations. "You are aware," he said in that hollow, unpleasant voice, "that the organics are mostly underground?"

"Underground?" I said, and he shifted position to gaze into my eyes with his own empty ones.

"In tunnels," he said. "Left by the Heechee, perhaps." Well, I hadn't been aware of that, but as soon as he said it it sounded plausible. I didn't comment, though, and so then he asked a question.

"Are these technologies familiar to you?" he asked. "That is, are they largely electromagnetic in nature?"

I assumed he was talking about the weapons, since that was all the technology I could see. "Pretty much, I guess. Why do you ask?"

"We have two alternate proposals for your consideration. Number One: If you wish we will volatilize these weapons, thus rendering them harmless."

I blinked at him. "Volatilize? How would you do that?"

"It would merely require opening a femtowidth slit in our containment for a femtosecond period of time, thus directing some of our components at the weapons. We calculate the drain on our mass would be negligible, no more than some seventeenths-to-the-eleventh power of our constituents. Of course," it added, "it would be necessary to devote some of the beam to opening a channel through the wall of the ship itself, with consequent cosmetic damage and loss of volatiles."

I had had no idea the Kugel could do anything of the sort. Neither had Harry, whose jaw had dropped. "Hell with the volatiles!" he began, but I had already made a decision on that.

"No, Kugel. We don't want to do them any physical damage unless we have to. There are *organics* down there—" knowing perfectly well that he wouldn't see that as an objection to the plan, in fact more likely the opposite. But I hoped he would take my veto as binding, and he did.

"Number Two: Since the nature of your own technology is electromagnetic as well, might this structure's systems not be compatible enough for you to penetrate them?"

He seemed to think that that was all he needed to say. It wasn't. "So what should we do?" I asked.

His odd assemblage of features didn't really deserve to be called a face, but it managed to express a little disappointment at my slowness. "First, pour yourselves into a thin data store. Second, transmit yourselves to their systems. Third, complete your reconnaissance. Fourth, return here for consideration of next step."

"Oh," said Harry, bobbing his head. "Hey, Markie, that might work, right? Worth a try, don't you think?"

"What I think," I said, glancing down at the surface scan, "is that that first weapons barrel is about one arc-second from alignment on us, and the other one is close behind. What's going to happen to our ship while we're fooling around down there?"

"But that is not a problem," said Kugel. "We will deal with it. We will retreat in/or/to the supraluminal spacecraft and remain out of range for a time. At arbitrary times, but not more than intervals of a few seconds, we will return, then to listen for messages, or else to accept your return from target place. We will not, however, remain within range long enough for the weaponry to threaten us."

Harry turned and gave me one of his most scathing looks. "So that's what we do then, isn't it? What's the matter with you, Markie? Why didn't you think of that for yourself?"

I didn't answer that directly. I just said, "Let's do it. Reformat yourself while I locate a target."

I had a good answer, I just didn't want to tell him what it was. The reason was simply that the Kugels had handed me another total surprise. I hadn't had any idea that they were capable of using our servomodules to operate the ship.

There were some flower-shaped things on the roofs of the castle that I thought might be signal or search antennae. We hurled ourselves down at the best-looking of them, and that's what it was—fortunately, because if it had been a rain collector or a lightning rod instead we would then have had the problem of somehow insinuating ourselves in the computer's electronics from outside.

But we didn't have to do that. We were there on the first try. And to prove it, a voice, harsh and loud, rang out to greet us: "You two! Hold it right there! Display yourselves at once!"

It wasn't an organic person speaking, of course. It was a guardmind, an AI like myself, but when he muscled himself right into our surround he displayed himself as much like an organic as he could—as an Old West sheriff, complete with six-shooter, ten-gallon hat and boots with spurs that had never touched the hide of a horse. It is my experience that the more trivial an AI's system, the more elaborate its simulations are likely to be.

However, I am courteous whenever possible. It was his house. So we made ourselves visible, me in my white toque and apron, Harry in his customary flashy sportswear. "Don't move," the guardmind ordered, hand on the butt of its gun. We didn't, having no particular reason to, but the guardmind's tone was a lot more belligerent than its status entitled it to be. I could see at once that its programs were far less powerful than my own, or even Harry's. However, out of politeness we stayed fixed in our tracks.

The longer we stood there, the less confident the guardmind appeared. "It was not known that you were to come here," it said worriedly, looking us up and down.

"It wasn't known that you were, either," Harry said, aggrieved—and, being less inclined to politeness than I am, added: "Markie, why don't you just make this clown go away?"

I shook my head. I could easily have neutralized it, as it was clearly in the process, of beginning to realize for itself. I didn't want to make unnecessary trouble. I said, as mildly as I could, "Please forgive us if we frightened you. As we were passing by in our spacecraft we observed your installation and decided to pay you a friendly call. We do wish to be friendly. We would not dream of doing any harm here—unless," I added, smiling to show how remote the possibility was, "we were forced to protect ourselves."

By then the guardmind had had a chance to realize what he was up against. "I ask you to wait one moment," it said, the voice suddenly stilted and mechanical—because, I knew, it was simultaneously conferring with some program higher in authority.

Actually it didn't make us wait long at all—a few microseconds, barely enough for me to summon up a bowl of oyster stew and a green salad for Harry. Then it coughed and said apologetically, "Follow me, please. The secretary to the Owner will see you now."

We followed. I didn't even bother to cancel Harry's dirty dishes—they could do their own housekeeping as far as I was concerned. The guardmind wasn't being particularly friendly to us, either. He didn't pause to see if we were keeping up, just bustled ahead without a rearward glance, toward he did not say what.

Traveling through eigenspace is exactly as hard—or as easy—as the surround controller likes to make it. This particular guardmind chose to make it tedious. We followed it through featureless corridors, a lot more of them than any reasonable AI would need to get from point to point. I think it was trying to get us lost. But the trip finally came to an end. Without warning the end of the passage widened and let us into what looked like some tycoon's high-rent office. The carpets were thick, there was a mahogany-looking desk that bore a sign that said "Ms. Roz Borraly" and there were "windows" that looked—or "looked"—out on the waters of a bright blue (simulated) bay with perky little sailboats, under an equally fictitious blue sky. The person behind the desk was an equally improbably beautiful human female, hair golden, teeth perfect, breasts big, who didn't bother to welcome us but said simply: "Do either of you know how to explode a star?"

It was not a question I had expected to be asked. What I did know I was not prepared to share with her. I felt no obligation to be forthcoming, either, so I simply said, "No," while Harry asked, "What the hell is she talking about?"

She looked disappointed, then thoughtful. "So then who are you?" she demanded.

I gave her the same story I had given the guardmind, and added, "We were curious about some sort of people we saw on your roof."

She thought that over for a bit, and then gave us a smile—not the kind of smile that means, "I'm a friendly person," but the kind that means, "I want you to think I am." She even chuckled a little. "I suppose you were," she said. "Disgusting, aren't they? They're the Owner's pet hominids, what they call australopithecines. They're a family. There's a mommy, a daddy and a little boy—although Gadget isn't so little anymore, and I think he's trying to get it on with his mom."

She thought a moment longer. Then she told us, "You may know that the Owner has been seriously and unforgivably harmed in the past. He has a just resentment against the Gateway Corp. and all its instruments—which are just about everybody." She looked us up and down. Then she said, "However, the Owner is a kind and generous person. He may be willing to grant you an interview. If he does, you should be aware that the Owner is the seventh richest human being in the galaxy, and is powerful in many other ways, so if you are given this courtesy do not offend him. Be polite. Be brief, and do nothing to startle him. Is all of that understood?"

"Absolutely," I said.

She nodded. "Very well then. You must be patient. It will take a number of seconds for me to get instructions from the Owner as he is organic."

By organic timekeeping we weren't made to wait for very long. Far less than a minute, or, in our time, several eternities. I had no real trouble with that. I have often had to wait much longer while some dithering organic tries to make up her mind between the gazpacho and the clear oxtail soup. Practice makes perfect.

Harry, however, is a different story. As a former organic himself, he gets fidgety, so I returned to my usual solution for that problem. "Hungry?" I asked him, confident that he was because it had been the better part of a second since the last time I fed him. "How about a couple of pork chops, big thick ones, burned black the way you like them?"

But he was already shaking his head eagerly. "I could eat all right, Markie, but those aren't exactly what I want right now. You know what I've been thinking about? That Greek lemon soup, you know? With egg? And then for a main course, um, let me see"—he thoughtfully patted his pursed lips for a moment—"oh, yeah! I know! A great big tom turkey, like at Thanksgiving, with chestnut stuffing and—no, wait a minute—half chestnut and half oyster . . . and then, well, you know, the usual, pumpkin pie or something. And pickles and olives . . . and listen, Markie, hurry it up as much as you can, because I'm getting pretty hungry!"

Well, I did as he asked. Almost, anyway. The part I didn't do was hurry it up.

I could have done that easily enough. I could have simulated the whole six or seven courses at once, plus wine and coffee and a little bit of sorbet to clean the palate now and then, and maybe some dessert chocolates or mints. There was no point to it, though. Harry can eat an amazing amount of food in hardly any time at all—it all being simulation, of course—and then come back for more hardly any time later. It's his favorite recreation. But he enjoys looking forward to it while it's being prepared almost as much, and it keeps him quieter because he doesn't want to disturb me in my work.

So I did it the slow way, from scratch. I simulated every last bit of the menu being made. I carved the simulated meat out of a nonexistent pumpkin for the pie and pretend-boiled a batch of imaginary chestnuts for the dressing. I simulated a six-kilogram turkey, complete with feathers and internal organs and all to make it interesting. The turkey was a Narragansett, of course; in his time with me Harry has learned to despise those giant-breasted but totally tasteless twentieth-century birds. So I had to amputate the legs to braise them in chicken stock first; Narragansetts actually use their legs to walk around on, so they can turn out a little tough if you don't do that. Then I plucked and cleaned the bird and set the giblets to cooking for gravy. And on and on.

And, since that took hardly any of my capacity, I was using some of the rest for my own purposes.

The first thing I wanted to do was to test this system's capabilities.

They didn't seem particularly strong. The guardmind was pretty oblivious to anything I did. The secretary not so much so, but no real threat. When I slipped away I left behind the simulacrum of myself busily cooking Harry's dinner, and she never even glanced up.

That did not mean that there were not more capable programs somewhere in the system. Accordingly, I proceeded slowly, my primary aim being merely to map out the physical metrics of the installation. Nothing interfered, and there were no surprises.

Ground truth confirmed the Kugel's statement that these were some old Heechee tunnels. With the exception of one particularly large chamber none of the rooms appeared to contain any living organic persons. Most of the rooms seemed hardly even furnished. Evidently the Owner didn't go in much for entertaining guests.

I had identified all the castle's weaponry and charted, but did not approach, the main AI centers when the secretary called, "Stovemind?" I was back within my simulacrum before she got the next words of her instructions out, while Harry was still chewing on his turkey drumstick. "Remembering all the cautions you have been given," she said, "you will display yourself to the Owner at once."

She didn't tell us how to get to where this Owner was, although I had expected she would and was preparing to match her directions against the passages I had mapped out. She did it the quick and dirty way. She just disappeared. She took all her surround with her, and we were suddenly in another one entirely.

This time not a simulated one.

We were in the large organic-occupied chamber I had identified. In optical observation it resembled nothing so much as a tsar's throne room, or a high-end Las Vegas hotel suite. Apart from a number of simulations there were four or five female persons lounging about, each one of them very nearly as spectacular looking as the simulation that had sent us here. These were not simulations, however. They were organic. So was the room's one male occupant, a sallow-skinned man who was boredly picking through a tray of chocolates as he looked up at us. I knew at once that he was the Owner.

That was not all I knew, though. I recognized him as soon as I saw his face. He was indeed one of the richest human beings in the entire galaxy, and his name was Juan Enrique Santos-Smith. Or, for short, Wan.

VII

A master chef does not merely cook palatable meals, he cooks them for what sometimes are very unusual clients. In my professional capacity I had been expected to deal with whatever VIPs might turn up on the Wheel. For that reason I had been given a recognition library of some two hundred thousand of the most important human beings in the Galaxy. That was so that I could not only feed them well but greet them by name and even ask after the health of their families, if they had any.

The Owner was definitely on that list. I was aware that this Wan was the offspring of two old Gateway prospectors whose ships had unerringly taken them to an ancient Heechee artifact and left them there. That, as you might say, had been both good luck and bad. The bad luck was that they were even worse off than Harry had been in his own marooning on Arabella. Wan's parents never got rescued from their artifact. They died there. The good luck was that the artifact they died on was nothing less than a giant, sophisticated Heechee spacecraft of a type no human had previously seen, and it was crammed full of all sorts of technology of great worth to human beings.

For Wan, the important thing was that when at last humans did get to the spacecraft, the Gateway rules of discovery applied. Wan, the son and thus the only heir of those lost and nameless prospectors, owned every bit of it. Which made him just about unbelievably rich.

That explained several things. For one, it explained how Wan, who had to be reaching a pretty significant age, managed to look reasonably spry; organics medicine could do wonders for those who could pay the bill. For another, it explained how he had been able to afford constructing this retreat. He could have built a dozen like it, and still have enough money left over to, if he chose, fly them to the Lesser Magellanic Cloud.

With all that money, Wan wasn't going to limit himself to a retinue of only a handful of attendants, however gorgeous. There were at least a dozen other persons in the room, though these were all AI simulations rather than organics. A couple were half-heartedly playing chess, a group sat around a card table, others were in conversations here and there around the room. All of them wore unusual outfits. There was a man in a clown suit with a red putty nose, another in the white coat, stethoscope and scrubs of a physician, a couple of women with pencils stuck behind their ears and carrying the ruled notebooks of an old-time stenographer. Whatever they had been doing, they all stopped doing it to turn and stare at Harry and me.

The Owner stared like the others, while chewing on whatever it was he had in his mouth. Then he swallowed and said, sounding as surly as he looked: "I didn't invite you two here. Can either of you give me any reason for letting you stay?"

I spoke right up. "My name is Marc Antony and I am one of the finest professional chefs in the galaxy. I can prepare, excellently, any dish you choose, from whatever cuisine you like, including—" and I rattled off a list of the most interesting cuisines from most of the great cultures in human history—

Well, no, that's not exactly true.

It was a mere simulation of me that did all that. I wasn't exactly there anymore.

I didn't see any reason to stay in Wan's throne room simply to rattle off lists, or, for that matter, to listen to Wan's interminable eight- or nine-second tactless substitute for a civilized greeting. I simply provided my simulation with instructions as to which expressions to display and what things to say.

Of course, there was a slight risk there. Something might have gone wrong, but I provided for that. I came back every twenty or thirty milliseconds to check on how things were going and revise my instructions to the simulation when necessary.

I needed a little personal time to conduct a more detailed exploration of Wan's little kingdom.

I had all the time in the world to do that. The Owner let my simulation talk on for more than eighteen seconds before he interrupted. That, plus his original greeting, gave me more than twenty-seven seconds of organics time to explore. If you want to know what a competent AI can do in twenty-seven organics seconds, the answer is, "Anything he wants to."

I used the first couple thousandths of those many seconds to set up fire-alarm bars, making sure that none of Wan's AIs would interfere with my investigations. That was easy. Then, as I allowed myself a more leisurely examination of Wan and his realm, the picture began to emerge.

I have never been a young organic male. Nevertheless I have fed enough of them, and listened to enough of their chatter, to know what sort of thing they would like. They would like high ivied towers, and Olympic-sized swimming pools, and game rooms of all kinds by the dozen. They would like military statuary and obscene statuary; they would like weapons of all kinds and target ranges to fire them on. In particular

they would like exactly what I saw before me in Wan's chamber . . . especially when you added in the clutch of four young, good-looking and min-
imally clad organic females who were sharing the throne room.

Though Wan was not a boy anymore, not by several organic genera-
tions, a part of him had never grown up. I could almost have felt sorry for
him, if it were not for the other playthings I had discovered. Those were
much more numerous, and much worse.

Every one of the hills around the castle was honeycombed with tunnels, Heechee legacies from the time before they went and hid in the
Core. All of those underground spaces were packed with the machineries
of murder. There were bombs and missiles, shells and mines, bioweapons
and chemical, plus rank on rank of the small, unmanned spacecraft that
could deliver any of these death-wielders wherever Wan might choose.

It was not a boy who had stocked his fiefdom with these things. It was
a fully functional, adult organic human male—and, I was pretty sure, an
insane one.

When I came back to the throne room on my next check visit, Harry was
there. He had been exploring in the same way as I and was anxious
to compare notes. By the time Wan the Owner had begun the first
"Wwwwwhhhh—" of his first interruption (it would eventually turn out to
be "Where did you learn all this?"), Harry was excitedly spilling his news.
He had discovered something I had missed entirely.

Harry had found a girl—young, good-looking and human, though not
presently organic. She was machine-stored like Harry himself. "Her name's
Allison," he told me eagerly, "and I think she likes me!" He thought for a
second and then added, "She definitely doesn't like this Wan, anyway. She
says he'd cut your throat as soon as look at you."

"We don't actually have throats," I reminded him. Wan was finally
embarking on the "errrrre" of his first word, while the young organic
women had yet to move off their hassocks.

"But if we did, I mean. Anyhow, it isn't just us he could kill. Allison says
she's positive he's gonna blow up some planet or other one of these days."

That accounted for the stock of weaponry. And it made me think seriously about what I had to do next.

You see, my status as an adjunct peacekeeper for Thor Hammerhurler
wasn't entirely honorary. If, worst-case scenario, a firefight with the
Kugels had ever broken out, I would at once have become a big part of
Thor's strike force. Preserving the peace was a big part of my job description, here as well as on the Wheel.

Therefore, if this rogue organic male was collecting these nasty gadgets for any practical purpose, something had to be done about it. And the only one around to do it was me.

The best available source of information had to be this machine-stored Allison that Harry had found. When I got to the place she was occupying she was sitting at an antique little piano, expecting me to arrive, and posed to make an impression on me when I did.

Allison might be no more than a congeries of charged particles, like myself, but she didn't let that keep her from making things nice. I could see that right away. I don't know a great deal about the ways of young human females, but I did not fail to observe the pastel-flowered throw pillows on the chintz-covered couch and the huge stuffed panda on her pink-canopied bed. Pictures on the wall (pretty flower arrangements or lithe, limber ballerinas), plates of fruit on the tables, music playing softly in the distance—it was exactly the man-trap that any young, organic, single female might create for asking dates in for a nightcap.

I let her make a social occasion of it; allowed her to seat me on the couch and politely waved off the tray of figs and nuts she offered me—imagine someone else offering food to me! And began to ask her questions.

What I wanted from Allison was for her to tell me everything she knew about Wan. She was willing enough to do that, but what she wanted first was to tell me about herself. I did a quick flash to my simulation to make sure there wasn't any problem that might require my actual presence. There wasn't. Wan was just reaching the "ih" in "did," so I let her talk as she wanted.

When she first met Wan, Allison told me, she was a broken-down ballet dancer. She had signed up as a Gateway prospector when she could no longer face three hours on the barre every morning. Though she didn't express it that way, she had wound up as a barfly on Peggys Planet. "So then this weird guy, Wan, showed up at the joint. I think he was laying low because he'd been getting into some kinds of trouble that even his money couldn't cover up right away. Listen, could I offer you a drink? Some coffee? Anything?" she offered, a little wistfully; I don't think she'd had that many visitors to practice her hospitality on.

"Thank you, no," I said, although it was still tempting to have someone else offer to provide refreshments for me. "What kind of trouble are we talking about?"

She shrugged. "I only heard about it later, but, like, one thing, it seems Wan somehow got the idea he owned the Old Ones, so he kidnaped a batch from their reserve in Kenya. There was law trouble about that. Some of the stuff he has here he didn't get exactly legally, too. And there was a lot of other stuff, too, but I don't know much about the details. Then he happened to show up on Peggys Planet, where I was stuck, and that's where he met me." She paused, looking at me in a way that I hadn't expected. "Marc, huh?" she said. "Nice name. Nice looking man, actually. Mind if I ask you something?" I nodded permission. "What would you look like if you hadn't, you know, sort of polished up the image?"

I hadn't expected that question, either, though I knew that the appearance I had assumed was modeled after some reasonably successful vid personages. I decided to be honest with her. "I wouldn't look like anything at all, Allison. I was never organic."

She made a sour face at that, then sighed and said, "Oh, well. So, as I was saying, there I was on Peggys Planet. I'd never had much luck. Not even as a Gateway prospector; Out three times, and not a single winner. That third trip was the worst, too, because it was the one that took me to Peggys Planet, which naturally had been discovered four or five times already and had a whole active colony going. So I just decided to stay there, and—"

Even by microseconds, she was getting tedious. I said, "Wan, Allison. You were telling me about him."

"I *am* telling you. I was hanging around bars on Peggys Planet, trying to scrounge up enough money for a Here After—you know, there's this chain of Here After shops that'll machine-store you if you have the price? Only if you're Wan you don't need the shops because you've got all that kind of equipment standing by, and Doctor Death is right by your side to use them all the time. Along with his court jester and his lawyers and secretaries and—"

I had a good deal of time, but not an eternity of it. I raised a hand. "Please, Allison."

She collected herself. "Yes. Sorry. Well, Wan was hanging around some of the same bars as I was. He bought me drinks. He thought it was funny that I'd been a ballet dancer, because I admit by then I didn't look like your grand prima ballerina assai anymore, but he liked to listen to me talk. Especially when I talked about how the girls in the troupe all had boyfriends, and what kinds of things you could do with your legs after ten years working at the barre—you know, the kind of barre you exercise at when you're a dancer, not the kind I was hanging around in. And anyway—" She shrugged. "Here I am."

She seemed to have left something out. "You mean Wan took you away from Peggys Planet?"

She shook her head. "Aw, no. Not then. He just went off, I think with some other woman, and I kind of forgot he existed. Then, six or eight months later, just when I was really hitting bottom, along comes this guy from some lawyer's office, and he tells me Wan's willing to pay for the makeover at Here After if then I'll come out to his place and teach some friends of his how to be ballet dancers." She giggled. "I guess you've seen the friends. They're girls he picked up here and there, and I guess they have a lot of talents, but dancing isn't one of them. Well, except maybe Liz. I kind of owe her, I guess."

She was waiting for me to ask her what for, so I did.

"It's kind of a long story," she said—as though there had been any brevity before that. "Wan was always scared sick of dying, you know. So he kept the whole Here After machine-storage stuff with him, with Liz trained to run it. Only he didn't die. I did, and Liz stored me."

"Liz?" I said, to keep her going.

"Elizaveta. Doctor Death, we called her. The Russian bimbo that's up there with Wan. You can recognize her because, A, she's not all that good-looking, compared to the rest of us, and, B, she's always looking worried because she's still organic and she's scared of getting pregnant." She bobbed her head to confirm what she'd just told me. Then she said, "Anyway, after I got the hang of stored activity I figured out how to simulate a whole ballet company, and he watches them sometimes—not in *Giselle* or *The Nutcracker*, you know, but special performances that I make up for him myself." She winked at me, and then asked, "You sure you wouldn't like a drink or something?"

"Thanks," I said, shaking my head. I was getting impatient with this woman, so I decided to cut this interview short. "Let me ask you a couple of questions. The Owner's secretary asked us if we knew how to make a star explode. Do you know why he wants to know that?"

She looked puzzled. "Oh, wait a minute. He said once that he wished he could do that. Maybe could, if he could find some old Heechee thing somewhere that could make it happen. Could that have anything to do with it?"

That was surprising for two reasons. Apparently Wan was getting close to something the old Heechee, Thermocline, had once hinted at. I needed to discuss this with Thor Hammerhurler. Meanwhile I needed more information, but this woman was not the source to ask. "One more thing, then. Do you have any idea why Wan has all these weapons?"

She shrugged. "Because he wants to kill some people. That's what those things are for, right? He'll do it soon's he works his nerve up to it, I guess. Which won't be like today; he's not real brave. He's sure good at hating, though."

"Do you know who it is he hates?"

"Well," she said thoughtfully, "pretty much everybody. But especially Robinette Broadhead—you know who that is? Well, of course you do. And some women. Quite a lot of women, I think. He's not so good at being in a relationship, and when they end he blames the women, a lot, and most of all he hates the Heechee. He hates every last one of them, the whole race. But he's a good hater, and he probably hates dozens of people I never even heard of. . . . Listen, you sure about that drink?"

"I'm sure, Allison."

"Because," she said, getting up and moving closer to me, "you don't have to be in a hurry, you know. I don't get that much company these days."

At this point I must confess to something that, in an organic, I would have to call embarrassment. You see, I understood what Allison was saying, not just the expressed words but including the subtext. What she was offering was to have sexual intercourse with me.

Sexual intercourse is not an activity AIs like myself have had much experience in—no, not just not much experience, none at all. It isn't part of our programming.

But that doesn't mean we can't do it. Even me, if I had chosen. I am, I remind you, one of the most powerful AIs ever constructed. It would have been possible for me to simulate everything necessary to engage in such an entertainment.

I can't say whether or not I would actually have done it. Certainly any new experience is interesting, and I enjoy having them. I did go so far as to make a quick trip back to the throne room just to see how things were going, in case I wanted to take a little extra time with Allison.

But things weren't going that well.

The conversation I had left in progress had stopped. Wan's gate-keeper-secretary female had assumed a visible shape and she was whispering in his ear, and his expression was on the verge of something between anger and worriment.

I returned to Allison's chamber at once. "Sorry," I said, as politely as I could. "I really should be getting back. But there's one thing that puzzles me, though. I wouldn't have thought Wan was the ballet type. Why do you suppose he wanted to go to the trouble of bringing you here?"

"That's easy," she said, looking regretful as I went through the motions of simulating standing up and getting ready to leave. "He asked me why ballet was worth watching. I told him because it was a lot of pretty girls in not much clothes bending their bodies into all kinds of peculiar positions."

The Owner's expression hadn't changed. Even the pursed lips of the woman whispering in his ear had not yet slackened—earning my sympathy, because I knew what it was like for an AI to have to slow down speech for an organic listener. The whole throne room was exactly as I had left it a moment before. In the corridor outside, however, there was something new: Harry himself, no longer in the throne room and looking very uneasy as he stood in the grip of two larger-than-life security guards wearing the livery of the Owner.

They wore pretty fierce expressions, too, but neither their size nor the threatening look on their faces bothered me. When you're only a simulation to begin with you can be any size you like; what matters is the power of your programming, and, as I have mentioned, mine was powerful enough to make me a useful ally of Thor Hammerhurler. I subsumed the space around the two guards and contracted myself around them. When they were squeezed sufficiently small to be insignificant I gave them their orders. "Leave him alone. Go away," I commanded. Having no choice, they did.

Harry rubbed his arms just as though the grip of the guards had caused him actual physical pain. "What took you so long, Markie?" he demanded. "Things were going all right, and then all of a sudden those apes grabbed me and dragged me out here, I dunno why."

"Because they found out what we've been doing. Come on. We're going back to the ship."

VIII

We stopped to pick up Allison, because Harry begged. There weren't any problems. Scurry through the castle's communication channels until we found an antenna. Locate our spacecraft in the sky. Launch ourselves toward it—we were in our ship, and well beyond the reach of any forces Wan could summon, long before Wan had time to act.

The first thing I did was call, "Kugel! Come out. We need to talk."

For a moment I thought he wasn't going to choose to respond, but then that patchwork of spots and colors began to form, greatly startling Allison. "Jesus H. Kee-*rist*," she yelped. "What the hell is *that*?"

"Relax," I told her. "He's a friend"—quite untruthfully, of course, but all I wanted was for her to shut up and stay out of the way. Then I told the Kugel about Wan's armaments and intentions, finishing, "So we need to keep him from causing trouble. We could request help from the authorities—"

"Hell we could," Harry interrupted. "Nobody would get here for days and by then he could launch all those ships, armed and on their way, and—"

"So," I finished for him, "that's not a viable option. We'll have to take action ourselves. Neither Harry nor I have that capability. Do you?"

The figure's components stirred. "It is known that we have," it pointed out. "We have already sterilized this object once, can do so again: A simple flip of its magnetic field, thus canceling its radiation-opaque atmospheric layer and thus allowing lethal radiation to reach the organisms on the object—"

Allison had been listening, her mouth hanging open. Now she used it to yell at the Kugel. "Hold it right there, buster! You're not doing any of that! You're talking about murdering Rose and Liz and Jilly and Jean, not even counting the Old Ones and—"

I gave her the kind of semi-lethal stare that I had learned for my deputy war-wager role. It worked. She shut up, and I told the Kugel: "That is unacceptable. We are not authorized to destroy living persons."

It hung silent for a moment, as though trying to come to terms with this unexpected new concept. Then it said, "There is another difficulty with our first proposal. Our numbers in the present locale are not sufficient for that task. Summoning others would require time of same order as requesting reinforcements."

I nodded. "So let's go back to your first idea. Can you volatilize all Wan's weapons without causing any loss of life?"

"And hurry up about it," Harry put in. "He's still got those guns trying to line up on us, so we don't have all the time in the world to make up our minds."

Well, really we did. The Owner would be just about getting warnings from his guardminds—having just noticed that our simulations had broken up and disappeared. But I was impatient to get things settled. I addressed the Kugel again. "Can you do this?"

Another pause. Then, grudgingly, "There is no question. Can do so quite accurately."

"Then do so," I requested. "Destroy his weaponry. And while you're at it, better take out his spacecraft, too."

That was all it took. Kugel didn't answer in words, just shimmered, dissipated and was gone, back inside his pressure-cooker. We never saw him again.

We did see what he did.

I had not really formed any picture of what the Kugel's "volatilizing" would look like. So I wasn't quite ready when the process began.

You understand that I have no physical ears. So I heard nothing directly, but I felt the shocks, even at the very limits of the planet's atmosphere, when my acoustic sensors picked up fifty or sixty quick, stinging blasts of great magnitude. Harry felt the same shocks. He clapped his simulated hands to his simulated ears, quite uselessly, of course. "Hey, Markie!" he begged. "Make it stop!"

I couldn't do that. It didn't matter. The blasts had stopped already. What was left, I saw, was a blistered patch of infinitesimal liquid-metal bubbles on Kugel's containment shell. Another, similar pattern had erupted on the wall of our spacecraft, and I recognized them as the femto-scale emissions Kugel had promised. It occurred to me to be grateful that my hardware, and Harry's, hadn't been in the line of sight to Wan's palace; I doubt that Kugel would have bothered to miss them.

What was happening on the surface of Arabella was not femto-scale at all. Little white puffs began to appear here and there around the castle, then a couple of larger ones, then the mother of all blasts, not just smoke but pieces of structure, billowing flame. A big part of Wan's castle was in ruins, though not, I was pretty sure, the part I had left him in. I think one of Kugel's rounds had set off Wan's main ammunition dump. Its magnitude made me feel for the Old Ones, but Harry zeroed the optical sensors in on them and reported that they were cowering under the trees, but physically unharmed.

So that was that.

Then we began our vigil as we waited for other ships to come.

The thing was, we couldn't afford to let Wan's castle out of our sight. We didn't know what he might have hidden in some other tunnels. Maybe nothing, but we didn't want to take the chance. So we couldn't leave our spacecraft in a normal planetary orbit, because anything could happen when we were on Arabella's far side.

So we did it the hard way.

We allowed our ship to fall along its orbital trajectory until Wan's place was just about to drop below the horizon, then zapped ourselves, super-lightspeed, to where it had just come up on the other horizon. . . .

And repeated that, over and over, until the other ships arrived. Which was 3.813 days later.

Would you like to know how many of those partial orbits make up 3.813 days? 83 of them. Totaling those 3.813 organic-time days. And would you like to know how long that is for a couple of people like Harry and me, used to operating on AI time?

Don't ask. You don't want to know. Just call it interminable.

But even the seemingly interminable does, sooner or later, terminate. Reinforcements arrived. We were relieved. We faced the equally interminable voyage home to the Wheel. But for that time we could at least turn ourselves off.

IX

When we got back to the Wheel, Thor Hammerhurler was fairly glad to see me, Marcus 2 wasn't and nobody else seemed to care much one way or the other. They were thrilled about what we'd done on Arabella, of course. They had Harry's organic-time simulation appearing on the p-vid over and over to be interviewed as the hero of the event, and Allison almost as often, playing the part as the escaped captive of the monster, Wan, who was planning to kill thousands of innocent organics until we superheroes arrived to thwart him.

I was not disturbed by this. Harry was a former organic, with vanity accordingly, and I was just a machine-made AI. You don't congratulate AIs if they do something that needs to be done. All you do is scrap them if they don't.

Marcus 2 showed no signs of wanting to share his work with me, in fact showed every sign of wishing I would go away—jealous that I had had all the adventures, I think. It was a very queer sensation. For the first time in my existence, I had nothing to do.

Except, of course, to see Thor Hammerhurler, so I went there.

I caught him at a bad time. He was in the middle of the daily check of all the weaponry on the Wheel, and, although all the checks were always go, he didn't like to be distracted. "Try me a little later," he said testily. "Maybe three or four seconds; I should have the results in by then."

"Sure, Thor," I said. "Sorry to bother you."

Which left me with all those seconds to fill and nothing much to fill them with. I didn't even want to practice cooking up some particularly tough dish, because I didn't want Marcus 2 to think I was competing with him. I didn't have Harry to feed, because Allison was more interesting to him than food just then. I wandered back to our ship where it was plugged into its dock—why, I'm not sure; I guess I thought maybe Kugel would be in a talkative mood. He wasn't, though. He wasn't there at all. Back in the blitz, I supposed, because the pressure container that had held him was now open and empty.

The seconds did pass, and not just three or four of them; I didn't want Thor to think I was rushing him, so I waited a full six before I returned to his eigenspace.

The flashing lights were dark, the bells and klaxons were silent, and Thor was busy debriefing his Heechee advisor.

I knew that one. His name was Thermocline, a steady customer of mine—couscous, Greek lamb dishes and halvah at first, but then he became more daring, when his digestion would allow. That is to say, Thermocline was organic. That meant that when I said Thor was busy debriefing him I had overstated again. Thor had plenty of time to do other things as well.

What he was doing this time was huddling over a diagnostics screen that was taking in readings from the Kugelblitz. I didn't see him lift his head to glance at me, but he knew I was there all right. He took another few micros before he acknowledged my presence, though. Then he said, "So you screwed up and let him get away."

That was Thor for you, always getting right to the point, never mind whose feelings might be hurt. I stood my ground. "We don't know that. We found his body."

Thor growled, "After he didn't need it anymore. Didn't you talk to the four female organic humans he left behind? They said his 'Dr. Death' machine-stored him and they both took off in a message rocket."

I didn't answer that, since he was right. I had failed to consider the possibility that Wan had stored a torpedo ship on the other side of the mountains. In fact, he was sufficiently right that he didn't bother going on with it, but changed the subject. "Got any idea what you're going to do now?"

"Not really," I said. "Matter of fact, I wanted to talk to you about that."

He did look up at me that time, blinking as though surprised. "Me? Why me, Marc?" But he knew why him, all right. Thor is definitely the most powerful person I know, AI, stored or organic, and I'm not talking about the firepower he can control. The Board listens when he speaks.

I said, "I thought you might have some ideas for me."

"Ideas?" He said it as though he'd never had an idea in his life, and didn't know how to go about having one. Then he said, "Well, I don't know. Maybe. I've been thinking I need a little more autonomous control for some of the more remote orbiting weapons. Think that might interest you?"

"Not," I said, "in the least." What he was talking about was about as challenging as operating a thermostat. "I want something that's worth doing, and is at least as interesting as my life was before I divided."

"And you want me to provide it for you?" He looked at me the way the five-star general he was choosing to be at that moment might look at some annoying buck private who didn't know he wasn't supposed to bother the great man. "Why should I, Marc?"

"No reason," I said. "I just thought you might. Oh, and by the way. Did you know that Wan Santos-Smith seems to know something about a star-disruptor?" That made him look at me with more interest, so while I had his attention I hit him with the other thing. I pointed at the Kugelblitz on his screen. "Do you know the Kugels can project themselves out of the blitz when they want to?"

He grunted. "Of course I know. Outside of the little clumps of them they use for spying, they can detach clusters of themselves into containment—what they did when they went with you to Arabella."

"Not into containment, Thor. Outside of the containment." And I told him about how Kugel had blasted Wan's armament. I didn't have to tell him how they could do the same with all of his. I didn't have to. When I left him he was busily reconfiguring his whole armament system.

But before I left he did a few things for me. Thor wasn't the easiest friend to have, but he always paid his debts.

So I've got a ship—Thor managed to get it lost from the register of vessels—and I'm on my way.

I wasn't sure it was what I wanted to do when Thor first brought it up, because that forty-thousand-to-one time dilation was a worrier. But Thor pointed out that that was a problem for organic humans, but not for us. I'm within a couple of orders of magnitude as much faster than organic humans as they are than the Core, and I can be in and out of it in a matter of seconds, ten minutes at the most if I want to hang around, and so when we come back no more than a few human-scale days will have passed.

I don't know what I'll find there, but it'll be interesting. Maybe my old friend Breeze? Maybe some new ones. I don't know, but I think I'll give it a try.

10

The Dream Machine

I

The last thing Stan could have expected, on that wholly Heechee planet he had found himself on, was to find another human being knocking at his door. Especially one who claimed to be headshrinker to the legendary Robinette Broadhead.

Still, it took Stan no more than a minute to get over his surprise, Estrella not even that long. Almost at once she was hastening to offer their visitor food, drink, a place to sit down, as flusteredly welcoming as a bride whose husband's mother has just without warning come to call.

Von Shrink refused all the offers. Very politely, and also very definitely. "You see," he explained, "I am not an organic person, or even a material one. I'm a computer simulation. What you see is only an optical image. I can't physically either eat or drink."

Stan grinned. "That's just as well," he said. "I don't think we have anything very drinkable anyway. Actually I'm not all that sure about the food, either, so what can we do for you?"

"A lot, I hope," von Shrink said pleasantly. "But I think I am being inconsiderate. You two are hungry, aren't you?"

Actually, that was precisely the thought in Stan's mind, but it was Estrella who answered. "I guess we are, but I'd be uncomfortable if we were eating and you were just sitting there."

Von Shrink beamed. "That is the easiest problem in the world to solve. You go ahead with your meal while I'm sitting—simulated sitting, I mean—and drinking a glass of simulated sherry to keep you company."

Obediently, if still a bit confusedly, Stan and Estrella began picking over the current supply of food packages, while the psychiatrist pulled out of the air a small table, a straightbacked chair, a bottle and a glass. By the time Stan had unwrapped what proved to be a flat, round, green-colored, fishy-flavored sort of a biscuit, von Shrink had rolled a sip of the imaginary wine around his imaginary mouth and was holding the imaginary glass up to the light. "A bit thready," he pronounced, "but decent enough. I suppose you know why I'm here."

Estrella looked at Stan, who shrugged. "Is it about that guy who hates us?"

Von Shrink beamed. "Exactly. I expected you would be clever and I'm pleased to see that you are. Now, have you been told what Achiever was doing when his problem began?"

Stan was frowning. "Achiever?"

"Did no one tell you his name? That's it, Achiever, and he was on a rather important mission."

"He was looking for these Assassins," Estrella said, nodding, "but we don't exactly know who they were."

"She means," Stan corrected, "we know that they killed intelligent races and all, a long time ago, but we don't know why."

Von Shrink studied his glass for a moment.

Then he looked at them with an almost mischievous expression. "Would you like to discuss those Assassins in more detail?" he asked. "You see, I am quite an elderly program now, and I know that often I am quite garrulous. But if you want to—"

Stan shrugged, but Estrella said at once, "Yes, I definitely would."

Von Shrink gave her a warm smile. "Then, as to the question of why the Assassins were, well, Assassins, on so large a scale, I'm not sure I know the answer, either. I'm not sure anyone does. The best guess I have heard is that the Kugels were afraid that other intelligences, particularly organic intelligences, might interfere with their plans, whatever they are."

Stan was getting impatient. "You keep saying these things that we don't know anything about," he complained. "What are Kugels?"

"I'm sorry. Really. You see, the problem is that I know so much that it sometimes is difficult for me to assess just how little organic humans know—oh, confound it," he said, biting his simulated lip, "I've done it again, haven't I? I truly don't mean to demean you in any way. It is a fact that I do know a great deal. I've been around, as an AI, for a very long time, and I've been doing things all that time—"

Stan's impatience was mounting. "Kugels," he reminded. "What the hell are Kugels?"

"I keep on doing it, do I not?" von Shrink said remorsefully. "Let me try to clarify what I have been saying. The reason we call the individual particles of the Assassins Kugels is that they exist in what is known as a Kugelblitz. What is a Kugelblitz? It is the name given to a black hole whose contents are energy, rather than matter. You see, that is what the Assassins are. They are energy creatures, and long ago, before the Heechee retreated to their Core, where we now are. . . ."

Von Shrink didn't start at the beginning, exactly, but close enough to try Stan's patience. But, as Estrella seemed to be hanging on every word, he kept his peace. He ate while he listened, one bizarre combination of textures and flavors after another as he heard one weird story after another of races slaughtered and Heechee deciding to retreat to the Core. He kept on listening long after he had finished eating and the two of them had picked up all the crumbs and wrappers and put them in the disposer— they still listening, and the nonexistent (but nevertheless a person, and not only that but a person who possessed the gift of dominating a conversation) Sigfrid von Shrink still talking.

It was all interesting enough. All the same, Stan was not sorry when their doorbell growled. "Excuse me," he said, glad enough to get off that padded, but still far from comfortable, Heechee perch. Surprisingly, though, Estrella had listened attentively throughout and still wanted more. "One thing, Dr. von Shrink," she said. "These Assassins? Are they still around? Should we be worrying about them?"

Stan tarried for the answer, but it took a moment to come. "As to your first question," von Shrink said at last, "yes, they are still around, in their Kugelblitz. As to your second—well, they are being watched very carefully in a large wheel-shaped space station built for that purpose. But yes, perhaps we do need to worry—not much, perhaps, but a bit. Now should we not answer your door?"

Von Shrink himself led the way through the connecting rooms to the outside door. Where he waited politely for Stan to open it.

There was no one there. Whoever had rung the bell had already gone away, but not without leaving a curious object behind. The thing was constructed of woven strands of blue-gleaming Heechee metal and was roughly, it seemed to Stan, the size of a coffin. He had no idea of its use or provenance.

Sigfrid von Shrink, however, clearly did. "Stan, Estrella," he said, sounding almost remorseful, "this is the device I have been waiting for, and now I must confess that I have not been candid with you. The reason I am here is that I am going to ask a favor of you, and it has to do with this device. Which," he added, "we'd better carry inside, shouldn't we? Estrella? Could you give us a hand here, please?"

That turned out to mean that Estrella took one end of the thing while Stan took the other. Sigfrid von Shrink, being impalpable, was therefore of no use in any kind of heavy lifting. He led the way, though.

Fortunately the thing was lighter than it looked. Von Shrink stopped near the exit to the balcony. "You can set it down here," he said, smiling. "Now, if you'll just lift the top section off—they're hinged, you see—yes, that's fine." He bent to examine it at close range. The thing had opened into a pair of woven metal shells, each with a woven metal lid. For a moment Stan wondered if this might be the Heechee version of a double bed.

He was pretty sure it wasn't when von Shrink straightened up and said, "It looks like it's in working order. By any chance, do either of you recognize this? No? Well, I didn't expect you would but—I'm not quite sure how old you are—do either of you remember those times when everybody in the world seemed to go crazy for a little while?"

"Sure," Stan said, and Estrella chimed in:

"The crazy times, yes. They were very bad on the ranch, but they stopped when we were on Gateway. What people said was that they were caused by some orphan kid, using a Heechee dream machine kind of thing. I think the kid's name was something like Wan?"

"Exactly like Wan," von Shrink agreed. "That indeed was his name, and he's still around, too, and still causing trouble. But Wan is not the subject of our present concerns. Since you remember that much, you will understand when I tell you that this thing is a version of what you called a dream machine, technically known as a 'telempathic psychokinetic transceiver.' This particular model, however, isn't capable of causing that sort of widespread trouble. Its range is too short. What the Heechee use this for is to prevent antisocial behavior." He patted it, or gave the impression of patting it, almost affectionately. "The way it works, if the two of you were to get into the two sides of it and it were properly activated, each of you would at once feel everything the other was feeling. You see? You would even know things the other had in his subconscious but wasn't himself consciously aware of."

Stan had been looking puzzled and feeling a tad resentful of this lecturing, but now his interest was piqued. "Really?" he asked. "You mean, like even things that Strell didn't know about herself?"

But Estrella, who had been thinking along the same lines, frowned. "I'm not sure I'd want the whole world listening in like that."

"Of course not, my dear," von Shrink soothed. "It wouldn't happen that way. Wan's machine in the Oort cloud was broadcasting to the whole solar system. This one is a closed circuit for just the two of you. Or rather," he said, sounding a bit uneasy, "for one of you and someone else. You see, I'd like to try using it to see if it could help Achiever."

The expression on Estrella's face was mostly of surprise, with a touch of worry. Stan's was more like anger and affront. "You mean jump in that thing with that *lunatic*?" he demanded.

Von Shrink sighed. "I know it is rather a lot to ask of you," he said. "Opening your mind to a nonhuman, and a rather troubled one, at that." He paused for a moment, congitating. Then he said, "You'll certainly want to talk it over before you give me an answer, won't you? So I'll leave you for a bit. Well," he added honestly, "not for that reason alone. I don't think you can have any idea how stressful it is for a machine intelligence like myself to try to carry on real-time conversations with organics like the two of you. The processing rates are so different, you see, and I do have certain other—ah—concerns which need attending to." For a moment Stan thought he was going to tell what those other concerns were, but he didn't. He simply added, "So I'll run a few errands, and then I'll be back to talk to you after Achiever gets here. Good-bye for now," he finished, and walked out of the room.

For someone who had never been flesh and blood himself he was certainly good at simulating it, Stan thought. A moment later he and Estrella heard the *sssshhhh* of the outer door opening and closing. Whether it had actually done so, or whether that was simply more simulating for the sake of enhancing the illusion that von Shrink was physically real Stan could not say.

In any case, he was gone. But the problem he had left them remained.

II

After Sigfrid von Shrink left, Stan and Estrella sat wordless on their perches. It wasn't that they had nothing to say. They had too much, and didn't know where to begin.

Stan was the one to make a start. "That son of a bitch," he announced, "has some nerve! Where does he get off, coming in here and asking me to swap minds with that nutcase?"

Estrella didn't answer, exactly, except to say, "He's a nice man, Stan."

"Well, hell! Everybody's nice when they're trying to talk you into something!"

"I don't mean like that." She hesitated before adding, "I mean, like the first time he saw me he didn't look shocked, or give me that gee-what-a-pity look, or anything like that."

Stan was puzzled until he noticed that Estrella was fingering her left cheekbone. "Oh," he said awkwardly. "Well—" And ran out of things to say at that point, because, in fact, he had just about forgotten that there was anything odd about Estrella's eyes. He fidgeted and hemmed and hawed, and said at last, "Hell, Strell, nobody cares about that, do they?"

The look she gave him was both fond and sad. Then she dismissed the subject. "Let's talk about this other business."

They did talk. Talked and talked, and kept on talking, and never did come to any satisfactory conclusion. Perhaps that was because there wasn't one. Stan summed it all up by saying rebelliously, "I just hate the idea of anybody else getting inside my head."

"I know, hon," Estrella told him, touching his shoulder with affection. "The thing is, we owe them, don't we? Bringing us here, giving us a place to live and all that?" Stan shrugged, and Estrella covered a little yawn. "I'm going to take a lie-down," she told him. "We can talk more later if you want."

She kissed the top of his head in passing, but then she had definitely passed, without any invitation to join her in word, look or gesture.

It occurred to Stan that his, uh, his possl-Q, as someone had once in his hearing called it, meaning "Person of Opposite Sex Sharing Living Quarters"—that his beloved, to put it in another way, and actually a way that he was still trying to get used to—that *Estrella*, to subsume all those things in a single name, sure was sleeping a lot lately. With as much wisdom as he had to bring to bear on the subject, Stan told himself that she was probably getting her period. It was a useful theory to Stan, since it might also account for her recent changeableness. Indeed, it was the kind of theory that spared Stan from having to try to guess reasons for those elements of female behavior which he had no hope of understanding.

Which seemed to be most of them.

In the course of these ruminations Stan had strolled out onto the lanai again. As before, those lovely meadows, woods and mica-topped hills were spread out before him. Which gave him an idea. He had been wanting to walk around down there, and why not now?

The first problem was the corkscrew ramp that had brought them to the apartment. He discovered at once that there was nothing conceptually challenging about it, just a lot of walking downhill until there was a door marked "exit." It didn't display that word in English, of course. What it showed was a squiggly, blue-lit arrow that Stan took to mean the same thing, and did.

Before him lay a wide and beautiful expanse—just like in *Alice in Wonderland*, he told himself, inhaling the warm, spicy air. There was a spring in his step that wasn't only due to the fact that this planet's gravity was almost ten percent less than Earth normal. Being there felt *good*. Underfoot a springy green and violet grass cushioned his step. All around him in the air were faint clouds of pinkish fluff, like the seed-carriers of cottonwood trees that he had read of on Earth, but had never seen. In the distant sky, away from the hilltops, were the remains of a dissipating rainbow.

It was, he agreed with himself, about the nicest place he had ever been in. Would have been nicer still, of course, if Estrella were strolling it with him. He would have liked pointing out to each other the leathery little bugs that peered out from clumps of the grass. Or the perky little flowers, that when he bent to see if they had a fragrance—

"Jesus," he said, rapidly straightening, because several of those pretty blooms had begun nibbling his hand.

It wasn't just that Estrella would have made this good thing even better by her presence. The long and short of it was she was just good to be around on any occasion. It occurred to Stan to wonder if he was in love with her. He had no reliable data on what being "in love" was like, and could only suppose that it was possible.

Which led him to ask the reciprocal question: Was Estrella in love with him?

The more Stan thought about it, the less sure he was of the answer. Why should she be? He wasn't protecting her from dangers, or solving life's recurring problems for her—if anything, Estrella was better at dealing with the world than he. He wasn't particularly good-looking. (Well, if that mattered, with those eyes, neither was she.) And he had to admit that he was certainly terribly young for her to take seriously—a mere teenager to her quite grown-up twenty-three. Or four. Or even more, because Estrella had never mentioned her exact age. That was quite a difference, even without considering the fact that, generally speaking, the man was supposed to be older than the girl.

Displeased by his thoughts, Stan kicked at one of the scurrying bugs and missed. He dropped to his knees, then rolled over onto his side. He stretched out on the warm turf, making sure that none of the carnivorous blossoms was nearby; he pillowed his head on his arm and closed his eyes.

He didn't know that he dozed, only that he was awakened by hard Heechee fingers shaking his shoulder.

Eyes open, he saw an unfamiliar face—Heechee, male, young, looking either angry or amused. The stranger was holding a sort of crystalline daisy in his free hand. He put it to Stan's ear, and it spoke to him: "Stan person! We search for you! Please immediately come. Achiever here already. Doctor Shrink soon to arrive. Request you here quickly, please." And then, as an afterthought, "This person speaking is Salt. Thank you. I thank you very much."

Achiever was there, all right, prowling critically around their rooms. So were two female Heechee, Salt and one Stan didn't recognize, and Estrella. Who took Stan's hand fondly enough to blur the memory of his recent worries and introduced him to the new female. "This is Delete," she said, and Salt chimed in:

"Old friend, Stan person. Also person of major skill in device's operation. Fortunately has excellent use of languages of your species as well."

Stan realized the new female was extending a bony hand to be shaken. "Glad to meet you," he said automatically, then winced as he felt Delete's grip. She didn't let go of his hand as, looking him straight in the eye, she addressed him:

"You were not present for briefing," she said. "Therefore I must repeat essence of it. First, operation of—I do not have the words—of communicating machine of wishes and fears will cause no long-lasting harm. This is known to be so from much experience, even of your species, with previous models. Second, interspecies use of same has not been attempted previously in this form, so possibility exists the first point does not apply. Third, in any case we proceed with procedure now."

That brought Estrella up short. "Hey! What's the hurry? Isn't Dr. von Shrink supposed to be here?"

"That is true," Salt agreed. "Is not known why he is not. In most cases he had been exhibiting promptness."

"Will surely present self quite soon," Delete informed them. "After which can make use of device in order to benefit"—she gave Achiever a cold glance—"this person here who possesses quite bad potential."

Achiever, who had been picking things up and setting them down again without paying any detectable attention to the others in the room, stopped long enough to give Delete a noticeably unpleasant look. Without taking his eyes off her he addressed Stan and Estrella: "Meaning of this wicked witch's statement is that I will no longer do undesirable things, do you understand her?"

"Maybe not," Stan said. "What kind of undesirable things?"

Achiever turned that baleful look on Stan. "I give you example. You wear garment. I like same garment. You go away and leave me with garment, I take garment and wear it, you not having given permission for same."

Delete made an attempt at a sardonic human laugh very like Achiever's own. "It was not the mere wearing of garments in your personally individual case, is that not so?" she asked.

Achiever returned his glare to her. "Why ask this question? Have firm opinion of your rightness already, is not this so?"

"Require you to confirm," Delete went on remorselessly. "Impropriety was not garment-linked. Linkage of impropriety was to living female of human species. Confirm or deny!"

Achiever was silent for a long moment before responding. "I do not do either," he declared, and turned back to Stan. "What is your thinking, Stan?" he demanded. "Do we then to share our deeply held secrets without further chattering?"

In truth, Stan hadn't quite made his mind up about that. He didn't answer. The Heechee gave a belly-shrug. "Then why should we not proceed with the project? These two are trained assistants, quite capable of substituting for nonexistent human, are they not? Therefore join me, then." And he got into the machine.

Stan stared at the other half of the device, then turned to Estrella, a wry smile on his face.

"Wish me luck," he said.

But then, as he lifted one foot to climb in, someone spoke in his ear. No one was in sight, but he recognized the voice of Sigfrid von Shrink.

"Not you, Stan. Estrella."

When Stan turned around, the psychiatrist was there—in animated simulation at least. "I do apologize for keeping you waiting," he said. "It was because of some troubling events that have to do with finances and construction of living space, and other matters. A number of persons in the Core are concerned over these matters and I was in conference with several of them—organics, you see. So of course that took a ridiculous quantity of time—no offense," he added hastily. Then he turned toward the dream machine, where Achiever was sullenly looking up at them. "Things appear in order, but we should get on with this. Estrella? If you will take your place again, please? And now I will just close the cover. . . ."

III

Actually the two of them weren't in the shell that long, though Stan might not have agreed. For him, fretfully waiting, it was a whole lot longer than he wanted it to be.

Stan thought of eating, but not alone; he thought of sleeping, but it was impossible to go to sleep while Estrella was experiencing what he could only, but didn't want to, imagine. He settled for another session before the lookplate.

He was getting better at it. Quickly the screen began displaying scenes of Earthly events, with menus running down the side of the picture to suggest trails to follow. There were many trails. Too many trails, often keyed with the names of individuals Stan had never heard of—Elwon van Jasse, Marjorie Abbot, Rebecca Shapiro, a hundred others—or subject matters about which Stan knew little and cared less. What did stock price on the all-Europe exchange matter to him? Or the plan to dig an irrigation canal from the Mediterranean Sea to the Qattara Depression, thus turning part of the Sahara into beachfront property? He caught at a reference to his former hometown, but when he followed it up it had to do only with forthcoming elections to Istanbul's city council. Among the thousand names that offered themselves for his attention he spotted one he had heard of—Wan, a.k.a. a long string of names that Stan definitely had not previously heard of, but definitely the kid who had loosed the Wrath of God on the human race; but when he checked it out it was only a police report saying that the man, no longer a kid, was wanted for a variety of offenses.

He was desultorily checking the state of buffalo herds on the grazing areas of the American West, in case Estrella might be interested, when there was a sort of metallic scratching sound behind him. "Estrella?" he said, turning hopefully around.

It wasn't Estrella. It was the unpleasant Heechee male, Achiever. Evidently he had let himself out of the wicker-work coffin and broken off the—what would you call it? The electronic communion between Estrella and himself?

Achiever didn't look happy. The ropy muscles of his face were working like a nest of serpents. He gave one quick nod to Stan, spoke two words—"extremely horrible!"—and left the apartment, closing the door behind him.

Apparently the ordeal was over. A moment later Stan heard the twittering of the two Heechee females, and got to the doorway of the room in time to see them helping Estrella out of her side of the gadget.

She looked not only tired but worrisomely sad, Stan thought. Next to the dream machine Sigfrid von Shrink stood, gazing down at her with an expression of concern. No more concern than Stan felt, of course; he hurried toward them.

Von Shrink quickly interposed himself, intangible but forbidding. "Estrella is quite well, Stan," he said, "but you can't talk to her until I have interviewed her. Wait outside, please. And don't worry."

IV

Easy to say, impossible to do. Stan did go outside, all right, but to refrain from worrying was impossible.

What, he asked himself plaintively, if von Shrink were wrong? Or lying to him, and something really was the matter with Estrella? What if she *died*? He felt a chill in his heart as he contemplated the possibility of an ongoing life without Estrella . . . without the companionship of another human in this world of alien freaks . . . without the *sex*. He looked at the doorway he had just passed through, and couldn't resist approaching it, trying to listen to what was going on inside.

It didn't work. He could hear a faint, breathy sound that he thought might be whispering, but he couldn't make out the words.

Then the two Heechee females came out, looked at him curiously, bade him polite good-byes and left. That was it. Unsurprisingly—Stan had lost the capacity to be surprised at any new development, as long as it was unpleasant—he was kept waiting outside the dream-machine room longer than the whole time Estrella had been in the capsule. That was not a good thing. After trying the lookplate again, finding no more of interest than before, he had nothing to do.

That gave him plenty of time to build up anger against—well, against everybody concerned, but against von Shrink most of all: von Shrink, the one who was keeping Estrella from him.

Then, when anger had worn itself out, it was time for worry about countless unpleasing what-ifs. What if this mind-machine thing had changed Estrella's feelings for him to something colder and worse? What if these sessions in the coffin had to happen again, and maybe more than just once again—wouldn't that inevitably change Estrella's feelings about the person who wasn't allowed to share them with her? What if—

Stan felt physically unwell then. That was the worst what-if of all, the sickening possibility that this foul Heechee invention, the one that, back in Stan's Istanbul days, had driven the whole human race crazy every few weeks, might have done some real damage to Estrella. Made her insane. Killed her, even. And then there he was again, repeating all those horrid thoughts about how he would be left alone, as alone as any person could ever be, the only real human being on this planet of alien creatures, inside this vast black hole, shut off by space and by what were rapidly becoming decades and centuries of time from every other person he had ever in his life known.

That was when Estrella showed up in the doorway.

She wasn't dead at all or even insane; maybe (he thought) a little more tired-looking than the last time he had seen her but apparently well enough.

"Stan?" she said. "I need something to eat. But first, could you hold me for a minute, please?"

She felt fine, she said, swallowing the last of a crunchy, pink-striped, lemon-yellow square of Heechee food. Well, yes, she was a little tired. That was all. No, the things the machine did to you didn't hurt. Exactly.

Then what was being in it like, exactly?

When Stan asked that she sighed a great, deep sigh. They were sitting side-by-side on one of the Heechee bedding rolls; she screwed up her face unhappily.

"Sigfrid kept asking me that," she said, sounding apologetic. "I tried to tell him, but I don't think I ever got it exactly right. Part of it was this feeling that I was this really awful smelly, bloated cow of a person. That was because that was what some Heechee thought human beings were like, Sigfrid said. Maybe all of them, only maybe most of them were too polite to show it. Another part of it was that there were all these bad, really *awful* feelings that were coming out of Achiever. I don't mean just anger and unhappiness, although there were plenty of those. The worst of them was what Achiever felt about himself. I couldn't make much sense of that, Stan. I mean, I don't know why he felt that way. But there sure were some powerful bad feelings inside his head. . . . And then, you know, there was this other thing. The thing about me suddenly being *part* of somebody else, and I just don't know how to tell you what that was like."

She was silent for a moment, and Stan took the opportunity. "Strell? What did you mean about being a cow?"

She seemed reluctant. "It's kind of embarrassing. Sometimes I was this fat parade-balloon kind of woman, with breasts as big as basketballs. I was naked. My skin was all purple, and—"

"Wait a minute. You said purple. Were you dreaming in color?"

"It wasn't a dream. But, yes, it was all in color—and touch and smell, too. That's not the worst, though. Sometimes I was fat, but not all that fat, and that was because I wasn't human anymore. I was a Heechee, Stan."

He gaped at her. She nodded. "I know. But that's the way it was. I was a female Heechee, complete with that square head and bald skull and all. That part was really bad, Stan. I was scared half to death."

He hugged her, thinking. Then he had to ask the question. "Strell? How could you tell?"

She turned her head to look up at him. "Tell what?"

"That these women were actually all supposed to be you?"

"Oh. Well, I knew," she said, reaching up to touch the cheekbone that the buffalo had stepped on. "You know, my eyes were always this way in the dream. Stan? Now let's talk about something else, please?"

That was all she would say. Every question after that she answered with, "I don't know," or shook her head and didn't answer at all. She kept on not knowing, no matter how he phrased the questions, until finally she begged him to give it up. "I'm getting tired, Stan," she said plaintively. "Maybe we could go to sleep now."

"I guess," he said absently, and then he nosed into the side of her throat. In a different tone he said, "Do you know what I'd like to do?"

Estrella didn't exactly draw away, but she did stiffen a little. "Honey, I'm sorry. I just don't feel like it."

"Not that," he said. "The other thing."

Then she saw that he was looking at the dream machine. She let go of him completely then, sitting up straight. "I don't think we ought to."

"Why not?"

To answer that question Estrella had a hundred good reasons to offer. It might be dangerous. They might break something. Von Shrink might be angry. It might not even work without von Shrink or one of the Heechee females in attendance. But none of the reasons could prevail against Stan's jealous desire to experience what Estrella had experienced, and in the long run none of them mattered.

"Oh, hell," she said at last, "all right, then. Why not? But don't blame me if we get in a lot of trouble."

V

What was being in the dream machine like?

Stan couldn't answer that question for himself even while it was going on—which wasn't for very long; Estrella put a stop to it after no more than a minute, flinging the lid off her half of the device and climbing out, sobbing.

Then what had it been like, as close as Stan could fit words to it. Like the most vivid and disturbing kind of dream. Like opening someone else's private mail, filled with the most disturbing kind of secrets. Like finding that the one person in the universe you knew best was really someone you hardly knew at all.

What it was not at all like was that terrible Wrath of God that he remembered from long ago in Istanbul. In some ways it was worse. At least that horrible sick yearning that had invaded everyone's mind in those old days had had nothing to do with Stan personally. This one, though, was a whole other matter entirely. It wounded him with blows he had never seen coming. "Estrella?" he said, having just made up his mind to say nothing about it. "Tell me the truth, now. When we make love—I mean, honestly, Strell, am I really all that, you know, like, I mean, *clumsy* and, well, *selfish?*"

She wailed, "I told you we shouldn't do it!"

"Yes, but—"

"Yes, but what about me? I can't help the way I look, can I? I'm sorry I'm so ugly!"

"I never said—" he began indignantly, and then shut up. Whether he had ever said it or not was irrelevant. You could deny things you had actually said, or apologize for them. But the idle thoughts that might—sometimes—cross your mind were something else. Either they were there or they weren't there. How could you deny feelings that you hadn't even known you had?

And why the hell had he ever wanted to do this damn stupid thing?

He hugged Estrella to him. The best thing they could do was to never talk about it again, he resolved. A resolution he kept for more than a minute, though not as much as two, while they held each other and agreed that neither of them could be held responsible for things they didn't really mean, because Stan was not only very satisfying, mostly, but definitely the only lover Estrella ever wanted, and Estrella was dear to Stan in all her parts and there was not one single thing he would want changed.

Then he couldn't help himself. "Strell? There was one funny thing—"

"I'm glad you think it was funny!" But she had stopped sobbing.

"No, I mean, I didn't understand it. There was this feeling that you were protecting something, that you didn't want anybody to know—something you were hiding."

She lifted her head and gave him a long look. Then she sighed and said, "I guess I should tell you. It's just that I wasn't absolutely sure, and I didn't know how you'd feel about it, and—"

"Strell! About what?"

She opened her mouth to answer, then looked away. There were noises from outside the apartment, faint but definite. "What's that?" she asked.

"Strell! Tell me!"

"Well," she said, "the thing is, I think I might be pregnant."

Which is precisely when the door-thing blared its summons. Stan went to answer, staring back over his shoulder at the source of this incredible news . . . only to find that when he opened it the two female Heechee were there, talking over each other to give him more incredible news still. "It is a bad thing we come to tell you," Salt said mournfully, while Delete added:

"It concerns your home planet. It could not be helped."

And Salt: "No, it could not. Although if our people had had more time—if they had studied the relevant geology with appropriate care—"

Delete made the negative belly-twitch. "No! Not even then, I think. We could not have helped, probably. It would have happened in any case, I believe."

Estrella had reached her limit. "What the hell are you two talking about? *What* would have happened?"

"The event," Salt explained. "The recent disastrous occurrence which has caused the dying of so many of your speciesmates. It could not have been averted, I believe, so that all we can do now is condole. Which we do with great sincerity."

11

Waveland

I

Needless to say, in the eyes of most human people the great Kilauea tsunami was an overpoweringly awful cataclysm. The mere thought of it made human blood run cold. Even the Heechee considered it regrettable.

The disaster had not been unexpected. Human scientists had seen it coming even without the help of the Heechee, though the Heechee helped a lot with the details. They were good at that sort of thing. They knew a lot about tectonic troubles, from their experiences of moving planets around inside the great black hole they lived in, and they had no trouble predicting that at some point the Big Island of Hawaii would split in two and splash that great tsunami all across the Pacific Rim. Even the Heechee didn't have any idea of what to do about it, though.

When it did come, in all its violence and terror, the size of that wave wasn't like that of any other tsunami, ever. Even the very biggest historic tsunamis had been not much more than a hundred meters high. This one was a whole other thing. When it struck the beaches all around the Pacific coasts, the curl at the top of the wave was nearly half a kilometer above the shoreline. When all that irresistible mass of water came battering down on the land tens of millions of human beings were killed at once.

It wasn't just people who died. Their works went with them. Whole cities were erased out of existence by that wave, as though they had never been. The world mourned.

That is, most of the world did. There was one particular human person, a minister by the name of Orbis McClune, who took a quite different view of the incident.

Reverend McClune didn't mourn at all because, in his view, the devastation of the Kilauea tsunami wasn't all that bad. It had its good points. One of the best of them was that the wave had obliterated large chunks of Southern California.

It wasn't merely that McClune didn't think the tsunami was bad. He didn't think it was an accident at all. Quite the contrary. In Reverend McClune's view that annihilating wave was nothing more nor less than the manifestation of God's terrible, pitiless vengeance, smiting sinners where they stood. The great wave struck on a Saturday. On that Sunday morning the Reverend McClune got down on his knees before what was left of his congregation in Rantoul, Illinois, and thanked his God and his Savior for mercifully cleaning out the cesspits that had been Southern California, the purulent home of the so-called entertainment industry with its sinful vids and VRs, the vile font of lewdness and nudeness and blasphemies of all kinds.

Not to mention that he had a personal reason for wishing misfortune to that part of the world.

McClune's sermon didn't mention that personal reason. He didn't have to; the congregation knew all about it. He also didn't mention the obliterated cities of Hilo and Honolulu, Shanghai and Tokyo, Auckland and Papeete and a hundred others, all around the Pacific Rim and on the islands dotting the sea. To the extent that McClune thought about those cities at all, he presumed that they must have been pretty wicked, too. That went without saying as far as McClune was concerned, because why else would God have chosen to destroy them? But McClune didn't take much of an interest in those other places. Godless California had been on his mind for a long time, and, he assumed, therefore on God's mind as well. So he was pretty sure that California had been God's main target. If other communities happened to get themselves obliterated while He was punishing the Californians, well, that was the kind of collateral damage that history was full of.

So, as McClune addressed the tiny remnant of what once had been a flourishing congregation, he tearfully thanked his God for wiping America's Pacific Coast clean again. That was the sermon that finally cost him his job.

On the morning of that unforgettable Sunday there had been fewer than thirty people remaining in McClune's church, the rest of his flock long driven away by his diatribes against pretty much everything that had happened in the last century. By noontime there were even fewer, because this time he had gone too far even for the loyalest of those few remaining loyalists. The most common word heard among them as they glumly exited the church was, "Nutcase," along with, "All right, we all know he had a tough break, that business with his wife, but for God's *sake!*" and most of all, "Never mind the business with his wife. He's gone too far this time. We really have to do something." So the leaders of the congregation were on the phone to the bishop before their Sunday dinners were on the table, and by Monday morning Orbis McClune no longer had a church.

That didn't mean that he was defrocked. He kept his status as an ordained minister. He was dehoused, though, because the parsonage went with the church. As an act of charity, the bishop called to offer him thirty days' grace to find another place, but McClune said, "Don't bother. I'll be out of here tomorrow."

The bishop regarded him on the screen. "You know," he said tentatively, "I didn't want to have to take your church away. I don't like to interfere in local matters, but, good heavens, Orbis, you know you didn't give me much of a choice. It was bad enough before, when you went on the comm circuits to call the Heechee demons from Hell—"

"What other name can you call demons by?" McClune asked.

The bishop groaned. "Please, Orbis, we don't want that argument again. I only want to say that when you say things that sound like you're, well, really almost *rejoicing* in all those terrible deaths from the tsunami, it hurts us all. It certainly doesn't give the right impression of what our faith is all about."

When McClune didn't respond, the bishop sighed in resignation. He hadn't really expected any retraction from McClune, and he certainly didn't want another of those interminable theological arguments—no, *diatribes*—that had punctuated McClune's tenure in his church. It was only residual politeness, not actual concern for McClune's welfare, that made him ask, "Where will you go, Orbis?"

"Why, I'll go where I'm needed, Bishop." Then McClune smiled. He had a nice smile. You could even call it a heartwarmingly kindly smile. It had deceived many a person who was astonished to find himself moments later labeled a hopelessly hell-bound sinner, since the smile was not at all in keeping with the harsh denunciations that followed. The bishop, who knew McClune well, tensed when he saw the smile, expecting the worst. But all McClune said was, "When you come to think of it, Bishop, that could be pretty nearly anywhere, couldn't it?"

No matter what he had told the bishop, McClune knew perfectly well where he intended to go.

The next morning, first thing, he rented a storage locker for what was worth saving of his household goods. There wasn't much. He put the few remaining necessities in a backpack and caught a railbug for the big airport at Peotone.

Peotone International Airport was a madhouse. Planes were coming in from all over the stricken California coast, landing with scant loads of stunned, scared refugees, and immediately refilling with rescue workers and supplies for the return. The outgoing rescue workers were neatly dressed, the refugees less so. McClune nearly stumbled over a man, woman and child sprawled by a doorway. All were deeply suntanned. The child's face was buried in a VR game simulator; his parents wore the perplexed expression of people who had never been seriously worried before; all three were still wearing pajamas, in the wife's case nearly transparent ones.

Actually, it was just as McClune had expected it would be. As he had counted on its being, in fact, because he had been confident that everybody would be too involved in the task of getting relief to the survivors to be vigilant. He was pretty sure that all he would have to do was display his clerical collar and say, "The survivors are going to need spiritual counseling, too." Say it he did, sufficient it was. The load bosses had more urgent things on their minds than worrying about the credentials of one more volunteer. With hardly a glance, they waved McClune onto the plane that was already loading.

It was a cargo plane, but the kind of goods it was taking to the ruined California coast was a surprise to Orbis McClune. He had supposed the urgent necessities would be such things as food, medical supplies, doctors, nurses. Not so. What was going into the airplane's hold was mostly great earth-moving machines. What's more, most of the score or so of persons, the other so-called rescue workers who were occupying the added-on passenger seats on the upper deck with him, seemed to be news reporters, and the others were all lawyers. At least the ones nearest to him were all one or the other, first a young woman whispering to her machine mind in the seat next to him, then a pair of older, plumper males studying documents together across the aisle. None of the other passengers paid any attention to Orbis McClune.

That was all right with him. He didn't want to talk to anybody just then. He had something more important to do. He closed his eyes, folded his hands on his lap and began a long, imploring, heartfelt, silent prayer to his Maker, because—in an age when members of the human race flew across the galaxy in great faster-than-light spacecraft—Orbis McClune was scared to death of airplanes.

II

What had made Kilauea a mass murderer wasn't just that it was a volcano. There are lots of volcanoes in the world. There are even quite a few of them which, like Kilauea, are in a fairly continuous state of eruption. The thing that made Kilauea special was that it was on an island. This meant that those little lava flows Kilauea kept continually plooping out had nowhere to go on land, because there just wasn't that much land on the is-land of Hawaii for them to go to. The only thing they could do was to ooze downhill to the beaches, and the only thing they could do after that was to tumble right down off the shoreline into the deeps of the Pacific Ocean.

When the lava got that far, it wasn't molten anymore. As soon as it hit that cold water it froze instantly solid, with a great display of fireworks and superheated steam. Then so did the next overflow out of Kilauea's end-lessly recharging cauldron of liquid rock, and the one after that, and the one after that. And so as time went by, those increments of quick-frozen rock just off Hawaii's south beaches turned into a nearly vertical subma-rine cliff. Then it became an overhanging one. And then it cracked loose, split off from the rest of the Big Island and fell, taking hundreds of square kilometers of the island's surface with it.

Water is not compressible. The volume of water that was shoved out of the way by the collapsing cliff had to go somewhere. What it did was to become the tsunami, a ripple spreading across the Pacific at supersonic jet speed until ultimately it hit the rising slopes of the shelf around some land mass. The ripple then swelled, towered, fell on the land.

For those bits of land, that was just too bad.

The advance warnings helped, a little. Tens of millions of people heeded them and fled inland, and most of those people did succeed at least in saving their lives. But not everybody was able to get out of the way. Even the ones who could run away couldn't take their cities with them.

So Orbis McClune's plane didn't land at the old Los Angeles airport.

That wasn't possible. There was nothing left of the airport, or indeed of the city, except for a desert of sand that lay over a waste of featureless, drying mud. The tsunami's first wave had scoured flat everything in that part of the world all the way from Santa Barbara to Tijuana—buildings, roads, railbug lines and everything else made by man. And then the wave that followed that one covered what was left with sand sucked up from the bottom of the sea, leaving nothing visible that could still be recognized as the work of man.

For all practical purposes the obliteration of that principal airport didn't matter. Those kilometers-long runways were heirlooms, designed for a much earlier generation of planes. It was not much of an inconvenience for the pilot of McClune's aircraft to set down on one of the many satellite airstrips in the foothills. The inconveniences started when the plane was actually on the ground. It turned out that each of the scant landing gates was already full, with half a dozen earlier arrivals already waiting on the taxi strips for one to open up. When McClune's aircraft did get to a gate, moments after the gate's previous occupant trundled away to the takeoff strip, he found the terminal crowded past recognition. The airport at Peotone had been busy, sure. But this one was less than a tenth the size of Peotone, and it was doing its inadequate best to handle ten times as much traffic.

As McClune exited the gate, he made the congestion a little worse. He stopped dead in his tracks and closed his eyes for a quick prayer of thanksgiving at having got through the flight alive. He was only a couple of seconds into it when a bump from behind made his eyes fly open.

The bump had come from his former seatmate, lugging a backpack of her own and still talking to her machine mind as she walked. Clearly she had been paying no more attention to the world around than he. "Shit," she said crossly. "Can't you get out of the goddamn way?"

McClune turned to regard her. What he noticed first about the woman was what she intended to be noticed, that is, that she was brown-haired, brown-eyed and all in all, as any normal person would recognize at once, quite pretty. She was in fact so attractive that she clearly had been able to afford plenty of cosmetic surgery. That fact would normally have been more interesting to him than her good looks, but he wasn't trying to raise funds at that moment. Had no church to be raising funds for, for that matter, so he merely gave her his heartwarming smile, the one that meant that the person he was talking to was being an unacceptable pain in the ass. He stepped as far aside as he could, into the airport's crush of people, and said politely, "I'm truly sorry, Miss. I was simply communing with the Lord for a moment."

That was as far as Orbis McClune expected the conversation to go, but it appeared that the woman was getting some other ideas. She was looking at him thoughtfully, taking in his clerical collar. Then she held up her hand toward him, palm out, and asked, "Are you a priest, then, Father, um—?"

McClune's smile, if anything, broadened. "No, I am not a priest of the Roman sect, my dear. I am a simple minister of God." Then, as he caught sight of the tiny glitter she was holding in her palm and realized he was on camera, he added, "I came here to do what I can for the souls of those in distress."

She gave him a microsecond pause before she prompted: "And what is it you can do for them, Reverend?"

The smile became broader still. "Why, I can bring them back to the merciful bosom of the Lord. What else is important in this world?"

"Thanks," she said, closing her fist and turning away, once again whispering to her machine mind and no longer showing any awareness that such a person as Orbis McClune existed.

That was annoying. McClune was accustomed to being scorned and insulted, even now and then to being punched out. However, he was not at all used to being kissed off as a six-second sound bite. He didn't like it, either.

No matter. As he removed himself from the stream of traffic McClune allowed himself a consoling moment to think of the hellfire that awaited the woman, then turned his thoughts toward where he could begin his mission . . . and stopped dead once more. There were glowboards hanging below the ceiling that bore once-helpful markings, "Taxis" for the rich and extravagant, and of course "Cellular Transport" for everyone else. They no longer represented any reality. A concourse led down to the railbug station, all right, but the entrance to it was blocked by sawhorses bearing signs—hand-painted, of all things!—saying, unbelievably, "*No cellular transportation.*"

That was a shocker. The railbugs were what took you from the place where you were to the place you wanted to be, all over the civilized world. You made your way to the nearest railbug station, never very far, and summoned a bug. No more than a minute or two later one would slide off the main line and onto your siding and open its doors. When you got in you took a seat—it wouldn't have stopped if no seat had been vacant—and chose your destination. The rest was automatic. You read, or drowsed, or watched a vid on the back of the seat ahead of you, or worked on your screen, or whatever. The bug slid back onto the main line, stopping now and then to pick up another passenger or let one off at his own stop. And there you were.

Oddly, Orbis didn't think railbugs were particularly sinful. (It was human beings who had invented them, not the damned—the really damned—Heechee.) He took them all the time.

Not here, though. Not now.

Nor was there much else available. There were no vehicles at the taxi stand, nor did the other passengers seem to expect any. Most of them were being met and led off by some local authority. That was no help to Orbis McClune. There was no one to meet him.

What he did next was easy for him, since he had done it so often before. He chose one of his fellow travelers—an elderly woman whose principal virtue was that she wasn't busy talking to someone else at the moment—and said, "Madam, I am going to ask you the most important question of your life. Will you take a moment of your time to help me save a soul?"

She wouldn't. She wouldn't even answer him, just turned and walked away. The next available person was a dark-skinned young man irritably looking around for someone who clearly wasn't there. He wouldn't either. Nor would the one after that, which made McClune pause to consider a change of plans.

These were all quite irreligious people. Perhaps the place to start delivering his message was right here.

He was looking for a suitable counter to climb onto when he heard himself called. It was the voice of the woman with the palm camera. "Hey, you," she was calling. "You, Reverend! Come here a minute!"

She was beckoning to him with one hand, while the other was doing its best to wave off a couple of raggedy-looking urchins, apparently begging for money. As he hesitated she said impatiently, "Come on, for God's sake. I was talking to my machine mind and I think we might be able to do each other some good. Do you know who I am?"

McClune did not, but before he could say so one of the children at the woman's side spoke up. "I seen you," she said. "You were in the p-vids, telling where to go for food and stuff."

"Why, that's right," she woman said, giving the little girl a small, unencouraging smile. "My name is Cara le Brun, I'm a reporter and, yes, I did do some of those public service announcements. So you see," she said, returning her attention to Orbis McClune, "I'm legit. I'm here to get human interest stories from the victims, and it seems to me you could help me out. Like the religious angle, I mean; Barb says that hasn't been covered much yet."

McClune pursed his lips, considering whether to give up his new plan. "I hear you saying how I'll be helping you," he said, thinking about it. "You didn't say what you can do for me."

"Expenses," she said. "What else? I don't know if you've noticed, but everything's sky-high here. I don't know what kind of financing you have—" She paused inquiringly, got no answer from him, gave him a brisk nod. "That's what I thought. Well, I've got an expense account and Barb cleared it with the higher-ups. That means I can take care of your costs, too—I mean, for a day or two, anyway. Within reason. Well?"

"Who's Barb?"

The woman looked impatient. "What do you need to know that for? Barbara is what they call my machine mind, that's all. So, McClune? What's your answer?"

He hesitated, reminded of something. "You haven't mentioned my name to your machine mind, have you?"

"No. Why would I? And what's the difference if I did? I'm waiting, McClune."

Relieved, McClune gave her his sweet and meaningless smile again. "I accept, of course," he said.

As far as Cara le Brun had a plan, it was to head up into the hills, where most of the survivors had taken refuge.

At first McClune was not attracted to that idea. Down on flattened-out Waveland was where God's wrath had struck its avenging blow, and something in McClune's heart yearned to see the results of that terrible judgment.

On the other hand, it didn't take him long to learn that there wasn't anybody down there who was still alive. His saving word would be better delivered to the survivors, that tiny fraction of former sinners who had been spared a dreadful death. So he held up his hand to stop the little girl, who was going on and on about the advantages of someplace called Barstow. "Fine with me," he said, ignoring the child. "How do we get there?"

The woman looked around irritably. "I could spring for a cab," she said, "but there don't appear to be any." She was looking glumly at the point on the curb marked "Taxi Rank," where a longish line of people was hopelessly sweating in the heat and not moving at all. The only visible motion was far away, beyond the end of the terminal, where some of the earth-moving machines from the plane's cargo hold were already lumbering away in single file to where they were needed.

McClune hesitated, wondering if that were a sign. Perhaps it wasn't God's design for him to go along with this trollop's plans. It wouldn't be hard to talk one of the machine drivers into giving him a ride down into the destroyed area. He closed his eyes, asking for guidance, but he didn't seem to receive any.

Or, it turned out, need to. The little girl who had been standing with her fists on her hips, looking indignant, spoke up. "Jeez, don't you guys listen? You need a guide. I'm it."

Le Brun frowned, then inspected the girl narrowly. So did McClune. The child looked to be no more than twelve. Her hair was cut in a ragged soupbowl and did not appear to have been washed for some time. More offensive to McClune, what she was wearing was the shortest of shorts, with a tank top that had been meant for someone with actual breasts.

Le Brun didn't seem to like what she saw any more than he did. "What we need is a vehicle, not a guide," she said. "Do you know where we can get one?"

"Sure I do. Only the vehicle comes with the guiding. It's a package. You don't get one without you take the other," the girl said. "You want the deal or not? If you don't, there's plenty of others around here that will."

"How much?" le Brun asked practically.

"Two hundred a day," the girl said, watching le Brun's face. When it didn't display immediate shock, she tacked on, "Each, I mean. Plus expenses for, like, fuel and such."

Le Brun gave her an unamused grin. "I'll take it before it gets any higher," she said sourly. "Do you know where we want to go? Someplace up in the hills, where there are thousands of refugees. I'm thinking of heading into the high desert, or maybe—"

But the girl wasn't waiting to hear the older woman's thoughts. "Barstow," she said sagely. "That's the place to go."

Le Brun didn't like being interrupted. "Why Barstow?" she demanded.

The girl was looking around nervously. "It's got everything you want, take my word for it. And I can get you there in an hour. Are we going?"

Le Brun thought for a moment. "Has it got a decent hotel, at least?"

The girl said pityingly, "Lady, there *aren't* any hotels, not that you could get into anyway. Trust me. I'll give you a place to stay." She wasn't looking at her prospective employer anymore. She was looking at a pair of sweating and harried policemen, shoving their way through the crowd in their general direction. "That's it," she said. "Take it or leave it. Coming?"

Le Brun glanced at McClune, and then shrugged. "I guess so. What's your name?"

"Ella," she said briefly, starting to turn away.

"Nice to meet you, Ella," le Brun said politely. "This man is Reverend—"

Over her shoulder Ella said, "Who asked you? Let's get over to the car before those apes start hassling me."

The girl's "car" wasn't exactly a car. It was an antique, piston-engined vehicle, and, believe it or not, it burned hydrogen. There had still been a few old fuel-burners around when Orbis was a boy, mostly belonging to old farmers too poor to trade up. But now? He suspected it had been looted from some old car museum. Most of it was pale blue, accented with dents and rust spots, and one door was a bright yellow. The vehicle stood almost by itself in a nearly empty parking lot that was a longer hike from the terminal than either le Brun or McClune had planned on. They were both sweating by the time they got to it, and le Brun eyed their transportation with distaste. "Does this damn thing run?" she demanded.

"Get in and find out," Ella ordered, but le Brun hung back. She was looking at the girl behind the wheel, no more than a year or two older than Ella. "Oh, her," said Ella. "That's Judy. She's my driver."

"Cripes," said le Brun. "Judy, have you got a license to drive this thing?"

"I got better than a license, lady. I got a car. Are you getting in or not?"

Le Brun looked even more discontented, but, having no evident other choice, dumped her bag on the floor of the van and climbed in after it. McClune followed, slightly amused. It was apparent to him that this woman was used to all the comforts of an expense account. She wasn't taking the present discomforts easily. McClune, on the other hand, had long since subdued any temptations to ease and comfort, so he followed her to the car door without reluctance.

Then she stopped cold, blocking the entrance, and he saw that she was looking toward the third seat that was in the rear of the vehicle. "Hey, you, Ella," she said, turning angrily on the guide. "What's going on? You didn't say anything about sharing the ride."

Ella shoved her in. "You think you're the only people want to go to Barstow?"

"Yeah, but what about the microwave radiation from those things? What if it screws up my machine mind?"

"It doesn't do that. Try it yourself," Ella ordered. Orbis McClune tried to peer past her but the doorway was too narrow. But it was only a moment longer before le Brun muttered a grudging assent and went in.

Afterward it seemed to McClune that the talk about microwaves should have tipped him off, but it didn't. The sight of the other passengers was a wholly unwelcome surprise.

There were two of them, hideous-looking creatures, like stomped-on skeletons of human people, sitting uncomfortably on the bottom of their spines so that the pouches they carried between their legs could hang over the side of the ragged plastic seats. They wore smocks of some drab fabric. They rested their feet on hexagonal metal boxes that glowed with a bluish light. Their eyes gazed out at him from wrinkly, squared-off faces. And they smelled faintly of ancient piss.

They were Heechee.

III

The Barstow road took them to the edge of Waveland itself.

That road wasn't where the full force of the tsunami had hit. In the places where it had, now flat and empty under the setting sun, there was nothing left that a person could recognize. On the slopes of the hills at least there was wreckage. Quite a lot of it, actually. Some piles of it could be recognized as the remains of a building. More often it was a scree of Tinker-toy junk that seemed to have parts of two, three or a dozen structures jumbled together. On the hillsides above the freeway men and machines were carefully sorting through the ruins of homes—looking for survivors, perhaps, or for something worth the trouble of carrying away. It appeared to McClune that many of the houses had been ripped from their foundations and then had skidded down the hillside until—crushed, battered, sometimes burned—at last they were caught and held on the shelf formed by the freeway. That was to say, by what was left of the freeway. That wasn't always very much. The lower reaches of the road were pitted and twisted; in some places the paving was scrubbed completely away. More than once little Judy, muttering very grown-up obscenities to herself as she fought the wheel, had to creep off the paved road onto muddy shoulders, none of them level, so that the old van tilted worrisomely before they got back onto the flat. And, oh, yes, there was traffic to worry about, too. There was *lots* of traffic, mostly induction-driven cars, but a few antiques like their own, and all competing for the same space on the freeway. Sometimes, as their ancient vehicle came to a particularly squeezed stretch of the road, there just wasn't enough space to go around. In those places the traffic stagnated into a jam forty or fifty cars long, as the vehicles crept in single file through the bottleneck.

Reverend McClune took note of all those things, but they were not what was foremost in his mind. That was taken up by the identity of his unexpected fellow passengers.

Orbis McClune's whole life had been spent in the knowledge that he was surrounded by lascivious sin and unGodly corruption. He understood that that was the way of the world. McClune detested that world with all his heart, but in his mind it had one redemptive quality. It was rotten with wickedness, but it was *human* wickedness. It was in fact nothing more or less than the simple Original Sin that God Himself had invented for the purpose of keeping the people of His world from getting too uppity.

McClune had been dealing with that kind of sin all his life. The Heechee, however, were something else entirely.

Souls were Orbis McClune's job, and he knew all there was to know about them. Well, almost all. As he scowled at the reflection of those unwanted fellow passengers in the windshield, he realized that there was one question concerning souls to which he did not have the answer. That was, did the Heechee have any?

It was an interesting theological point. The beasts of the field had no souls, Scripture was clear on that. However, the beasts of the field didn't speak in human tongues, or wear clothing, or invent spaceships. McClune had no answer, but he had one fervent prayer: Lord, if they have souls that need saving, let that cup pass to someone other than me.

The thing was, Orbis was certain that it was no part of God's design that had put those abominable creatures on the Earth. They were intruders. They came from outside. They did not belong on the world that God Himself had specifically decreed—it was all written out there in black and white, in His very own Book—was dedicated to the exclusive use of the human race. There was nothing there to give domain to any bizarre creatures from other worlds. So to McClune the Heechee were unblessed by God and thus incarnate evil. If there was one single embodiment of concentrated sin that stood out above all others in his mind, that was the Heechee.

The catalogue of their wickedness was plain. It was because of the Heechee that so many human beings had abandoned God's world to flit around in space. It was because of the Heechee that soulless machine minds had come to play so large a part in human affairs. It was because of the Heechee that countless sinners on the point of death had chosen to be reborn as immortal electronic abstractions, instead of rotting beneficially away in God's own soil as they waited for the final call. This last wickedness was particularly repellent to McClune because of the circumstances that ended his former marriage. But worst of all, it was due to the Heechee that those excellent spurs to decent behavior, want and fear, had so nearly disappeared from the world.

McClune could not help himself. He groaned aloud, causing the newswoman to turn to him irritably. "What's the matter with you, Mc-Clune?" she demanded. "Can't you hold it down? I'm trying to do an interview here."

And she turned her palm camera back to the Heechee, leaving Orbis McClune to stare gloomily out at the passing scene.

It was full dark when they reached Barstow. Hardly even spray from the tsunami had managed to get that far inland, so there were no destroyed buildings lining Barstow's streets. There were refugees, though. They filled the streets, ambling aimlessly or sitting wherever there was a flat place to put a weary bottom on—steps, curbs, flat-topped fire hydrants. They clogged the streets, where panel trucks and flatbeds and buses were inching along as they brought help to the refugees—or brought more refugees. The people swamped the little parkland spaces, a lot of them with sleeping bags or bundles of blankets, jealously guarding a place to stretch out. They lined up before the few open restaurants and motels, not in the hope of food or shelter but simply waiting for a turn at the toilets. They lined up, too, before the trucks that had stopped to dispense flat, heavy packets of CHON-food, flown in from some surviving Food Factory. Some of the people looked despairing, some simply bewildered. But the expression on most of the faces was outrage. The better dressed the refugees, the more furious they were. You could see that they were both stunned and angry. In this world, at this time, for these people, this sort of thing was simply not meant to happen.

McClune looked out at the horde with sober gratification. These were the souls he had come to save. They had been chastised, and it was his duty to tell them why. "Stop the car," he ordered, already beginning to rehearse the catalogue of their sins.

But that didn't happen. "Not a chance," gritted Judy, peering at him through the rearview mirror, and Ella backed her up.

"Can't do it, old-timer," she said firmly. "There's a vehicle curfew here in about twenty minutes, and there's cops here that would take this car right away from us if they caught us breaking it."

"And shut up, too," Judy added, "because I need to concentrate on my driving. Want me to run over one of these creeps?"

The "accommodations" the two girls had provided for them weren't lavish. They amounted to a large and oily smelling shack that apparently had once been some kind of repair shop before suffering some kind of fire. Judy immediately rolled the jalopy inside when they arrived—for fear of its being stolen, she said, although McClune could not imagine who would steal it. The old rustbucket took up a lot of the shed's available space, too. The remaining space was mostly filled by their beds—well, by the canvas cots that were all Ella and Judy had to offer. ("Hey," Judy snarled when le Brun complained, "you can sleep on the sidewalk if you like that better.") At least the cots were brand-new. They had come straight from the trucks that were handing out emergency supplies. So had the blankets.

The two Heechee were having none of either. They chirped and hissed worriedly to each other, and then to Ella, who frowned thoughtfully and then went away for a moment, returning with a huge bag of old rags. That seemed to satisfy the Heechee, sort of, but the space she offered them to sleep in did not. They twittered to each other again, gazing at the walls and roof of the old building, then politely excused themselves. They carried their rags out of doors and patted them into a pair of heaps in the alley, away from the building.

When Judy made an inquiring noise, Cara le Brun was quick with an explanation. "I did a show on it once. That's how they sleep, dug into a mass of stuff."

"Yeah, sure," Judy said, "but why are they out in the alley?"

That le Brun couldn't explain. Nor did she really want to, because her attention was abruptly taken up with the discovery of the lacks in their accommodations. She reacted with displeasure when she found out that they had no running water, then with horror when she realized what that implied. The only available "toilet" was a slit trench just off the driveway, with canvas walls for "privacy." And then, when she discovered what the two girls were offering for a meal, her reaction became simple fury. "That stuff is just goddam CHON-food!" she snapped. "They're giving that crap away downtown! How've you got the nerve to charge us for it?"

Ella gave her a cold shrug. "Rather stand in line? Eat or don't eat. I don't care."

While they were talking, the Heechee pair had put the finishing touches on their bedding and were now placidly unwrapping round patties of something that smelled of raspberries and roasted garlic. That was one provocation too many for Orbis McClune. God might have chosen to punish him by putting him in the company of these foul creatures—unfairly, of course, but McClune believed that being unfair from time time to was one of God's perquisites. However, He surely didn't demand that His servant McClune *eat* with them. Orbis took an arbitrary handful of the rations and retired with them to the edge of his cot, as far from the Heechee as possible.

The wrappings of the food packets came in a rainbow of color. Although they were textured like silk, they split wide as he ran a thumbnail over them. McClune ate them in alternating bites, unconcerned that one packet was doughy and tediously bland, while another crackled like peanut brittle in his teeth and tasted like some sort of meat broth. After a brief and silent grace he chewed stolidly away. Food had never been important for Orbis McClune. Eating was just something you had to do to keep life going, no more pleasurable than moving your bowels, and worth no more thought.

When he finished eating he visited the slit trench. He paused on the way back, gazing at the great starfield overhead. Then he went back indoors. Cara le Brun was having a desultory conversation with the two girls, apparently mostly to exchange complaints, but as Orbis McClune had no wish to talk to any of them he stretched out on his cot and closed his eyes.

He was no more than halfway through his bedtime prayer when a shuddery, dizzying feeling let him know that something unwelcome was going on. The room seemed to be rocking. He felt an urgent need to sit up, and managed to do it on the second or third try.

It wasn't just him. Noises from across the room let him know that the women shared the experience. When they became articulate, the loudest voice was Cara le Brun's: "Jesus! What was that, an earthquake?" And when Ella confirmed her guess, "Well, I never signed up for any goddam *earthquakes*. Cripes! Next thing, the goddam wave'll be coming back, only this time it'll take the whole damn *state* with it!"

That was as far as McClune cared to listen. It had been nothing but an act of God, and he had never feared those. He closed his eyes. The last thing he heard was Ella's complaining voice: "Give it a rest, will you, lady? It's just like leftover shocks after the tidal wave. Happens all the time, for God's sake. Get used to it."

IV

The next morning Orbis McClune was up with the sun and ready to begin the work that had brought him to this place. Even so, the Heechee were up before him and already gone—to do what, McClune had no idea. He left Cara le Brun squabbling with the two young girls about the lack of a shower and their refusal to drive the old wreck downtown in broad daylight, so that she had to walk. It wasn't really far. In less than twenty minutes McClune was where the people who were his targets were stirring.

Barstow's downtown was like every other in the world, with all the same familiar logos over the same storefronts—the same yogurt and ice-cream shops, fast-food restaurants, travel agents, p-vid repairers and tax preparers. He passed a workout gym and a VR total-immersion entertainment center, a Tae Kwan Do studio and half a dozen hair stylists and dental cosmeticians—clearly, the people of Barstow were as interested as those of any other community in looking as good as modern technology could make them. McClune not only passed them all by, he hardly noticed they were there. What he was looking for was a corner with a lot of people—but that described every corner in Barstow—and a convenient bench, porch or picnic table he could stand on to address the throng.

Soon enough the perfect spot appeared. It was a traffic circle with a little park in the middle. It held a couple of flowering bushes and, in the center, a tall statue of someone wearing a hood and a robe. Like everywhere else in Barstow, the park was already crowded with aimlessly moving refugees, and it was rich with stone benches. They were, of course, already all occupied, but that was not a problem for Orbis McClune. All it took was an, "Excuse me, brother, I'm doing God's work," with that great, loving smile, and in a moment the elderly men sharing the bench had made way for him. As he climbed up he saw that there was a name carved into the base of the statue—Fra Junipero Serra, whoever he was—and he took that as a good omen. That person would have been a papist, of course, but nevertheless a man who had dedicated his life to God—even if it was the wrong God—and thus a colleague. Pleased, McClune turned, raising his arms in benediction to address the bystanders. . . .

Then he saw what was across the street, on the far side of the intersection. It was a storefront with a bright marquee that said *Here After.*

That omen was not good.

If there was one thing McClune loathed more than the Heechee themselves it was the Here After chain of machine-storage establishments, where the dying, or the merely despondent, could avail themselves of that accursed, Heechee-spawned substitute for actual death. It wasn't simply the blasphemy involved, though blasphemous it certainly was. Orbis McClune had more personally powerful feelings at stake.

But he let them distract him only for a moment. McClune had years of experience at suppressing his personal feelings for his duty. He raised his arms. "Brothers!" he called. One or two passersby paused incuriously to look. Then, more strongly, "Brothers! Sisters!" And the spirit within began to move him. That sweet, empty, enormous smile bathed everyone nearby in its meaningless love as he thundered, "Listen to me, for I bring you salvation and eternal life in the bosom of the Lord!"

Some things are universal. For example, the victims of a great natural disaster—any disaster, any time in the history of the world—share a fixed cocktail of losses. Possessions are irreparably gone: houses, cars, furnishings, the plants that once hung from the ceiling of the family room that doesn't exist anymore, the lamp that was an ancient wedding gift, the thirty-year-old Teddy bear that had once belonged to a now forty-year-old son. Friendships are ruptured as the friends and neighbors are driven apart. Many certain and familiar expectations disappear, with nothing to replace them but worries about what the new future holds. These are universals. It was how it was for the people of Martinique, and the Johnstown flood, and burned-out Dresden and bombed-out Hiroshima, and those things never change.

But there were very large changes of another kind here. Not one single person in Barstow went hungry in the wake of the tsunami. Nor, of course, did almost anyone else in the world; the limitless riches that poured out of the Food Factories could feed any multitudes. Not one person had lost a penny of savings—or of debts, either, for the machine minds that managed the world's banks and credit institutions and tax authorities had instantly, electronically, fled to safer stores. Not one had lost his medical records and list of drug regimes, nor did anyone lack the facilities to get treatment—doctors and mobile treatment centers had been about the first things to be flown in—and many of the survivors still had their own personal machine minds to keep them provided with information. Well, the ones that were well enough off to own them in the first place did, anyway.

But the one thing almost all of them lacked was something to do with their time. That was just fine for Orbis McClune.

So for three hours, without respite in the hot morning sunshine, McClune pleaded, exhorted, warned, threatened, condemned. He put on one of the greatest performances of his life. Sadly, the refugees weren't responding. Most listened apathetically for a while and then moved on. Sometimes some of them tittered. Occasionally a few heckled. But mostly they just moved on.

That never left McClune without a crowd around his bench, however. There was a constant replenishment of aimless strollers, though the next batch was no more interested than the last. Sometimes from his perch McClune could catch sight of Cara le Brun moving about in the crowd, taking pictures of McClune himself as he preached, or trying to get a useful interview from people in the audience. She wasn't the only newsperson doing the same thing, either. There had to be dozens of them, sometimes with palm cameras going, occasionally with elaborate multi-lens setups. He thought this must be the most thoroughly documented catastrophe in the history of the human race.

He even caught an occasional glimpse of the two Heechee doing whatever it was they were doing. It appeared to be no more than simple sightseeing, but with Heechee how could you tell? They didn't seem to be talking to many people, though many gaped at them. Most of the crowd made a space around them. Even when McClune pointed dramatically toward the lingering Heechee and thundered, "Behold the embodiment of evil! Behold the vile tempters who brought death and hellfire down upon your dearest ones!"—even then the Heechee remained impassive. While the human crowds only muttered to each other. And moved on.

It was a real challenge. Here was the biggest audience McClune had ever dreamed of having, and if he had saved one single soul of them, there was no sign of it on their faces.

Perhaps, McClune thought, the problem was in the makeup of the throng. This wasn't only the largest group he had ever faced, it was the youngest and the healthiest. There weren't any tottering oldsters, no crip-ples, none that showed any sign of wasting disease. In this they were com-pletely unlike McClune's lost Rantoul congregation, where all the younger and healthier members had long since fled to less dismal churches, leav-ing only those for whom Judgment Day could arrive at any time.

That didn't matter to McClune. He graded the successes and failures of his life not according to how many souls he actually saved, only on how indefatigably he worked at trying to save them. But even he had now and then to bow to more basic needs. When thirst and the need to pee man-dated a break, he took it.

In refugee-mobbed Barstow at this time these needs were not easily satisfied. It wasn't until he spotted Cara le Brun standing irritably in a line before the Tae Kwan Do store that he found the solution. There were toi-lets inside, she told him, and showers, and of course drinking water, all available for a price, and if he chose to wait with her she would pay his way in. So he joined her in the line. She looked him up and down. "Saving plenty of souls, Reverend?" she asked, but the tone showed that it wasn't a serious question, only a sort of social noise. He ignored it. But her need for conversation to take her mind off the indignity of standing in a line was not slaked. "What did you think of our earthquake last night?" she asked. "You know what caused it, don't you?"

He shrugged. Science had never been his favorite subject. "Something about faults, I guess?"

"Not this time," she said, looking superior and sounding that way, too. "It was that damn tsunami. My machine mind explained the whole thing to me. She said all that weight of water squeezed all the, you know, cracks and things that were there all the time in California, and now they're kind of relieving the strain."

"Huh," he said, his thoughts more concentrated on the prospect of a latrine.

"So we're likely to have more of the damn things," she said, somberly gleeful at the opportunity to share her bad news with someone else. "And that's not all. Did you know they're running out of food?"

Even after McClune had relieved himself at the Tae Kwan Do's urinals and slaked his thirst at the taps in their men's room, he was still puzzling over that.

Running out of food! But that was preposterous. People didn't "run out" of food anymore. There was always plenty of food; that was a given. Sure, there had been times when hungering people had even mined coal to grow on it bacteria that could be pressed into horrid little edible lumps that, however textured and flavored, always tasted like used motor oil.

But that was then. That was before the Heechee Food Factories were discovered, orbiting in space in the Oort cloud of comets to suck from them their elemental carbon, hydrogen, oxygen and nitrogen—what they called CHON—and make them into almost any kind of food you could imagine. And after that it was only a step to redesign the Food Factories for Earthly use, floating in ocean waters and pulling the elements they needed from the sea. Why, there were hundreds of the things, churning out rations day in and day out, everywhere! McClune had seen pictures of them, in the Gulf of Mexico and the Red Sea, off the coasts of Morocco and China, wherever there was enough organic matter to give them the carbon and nitrogen they needed to go with the hydrogen and oxygen from the water itself. Of course he had hated what he saw—more Heechee deviltry!—but they certainly had kept Earth's dozen billion people alive. One of his parishioners had actually worked on one of the things until he retired to Rantoul. His job had been mixing the raw CHON with trace elements enough to provide the consumer with all the vitamins and minerals he needed, in a giant floating factory that was moored off the coast of Baja California, and fed most of the Southwest. . . .

Then enlightenment struck. Baja! Of course! The same tsunami that had planed most Pacific shorelines bare would certainly have demolished the Baja Food Factory—and probably the ones on the Oregon coast and the Aleutians and the shores of Central America, and wherever else in those destroyed parts of the world where a Food Factory could have been put. And so, yes, it was possible that, for the first time in a generation, food might indeed be running out.

V

When McClune called it a day, he was hungry, tired and, he suspected, probably seriously sunburned as well. He was also as close to being happy as he usually allowed himself to get.

Then, to make his day even better, there was good news waiting for him at home. As he pushed past the creaky old door, he saw Cara le Brun and the two girls gorging themselves from a heap of CHON-food packets. Whatever else might happen, his mission was not endangered by the threat of starving. "Run out?" Ella said scornfully. "Course they're gonna run out. We knew that was coming, so we stocked up days ago."

Le Brun had her news too. "I was hunting for interviews at the Here After and I found out something. It's where the Heechee are hanging out. You know that offer they're making?"

Ella and Judy nodded, but McClune looked blank. "What offer?"

"You didn't know? Oh, hell," she said, remembering, "you don't have a machine mind, do you? It's the *immigration* thing. Like for people who don't have anywhere to go?" And when he looked even blanker, "To the Core, see? They're offering to take anybody who wants it to the Core. Only thing is, it's only for people who've been machine-stored, so most likely they'll have been dead first."

Then the change in McClune's expression—puzzlement to shock to outright anger—registered with her at last. "Hey," she said, her grin placatory, "don't look like that. The Here After deal's kind of weird, sure, but when you look at the alternatives it's not so bad, is it?"

And then she frowned, puzzled, as McClune's expression softened, the rage draining away, the vast, heart-warming, meaningless smile replacing it. "Bad?" he said, considering. "Why, no, Ms. le Brun, it isn't just *bad*. It is totally, blasphemously, hopelessly evil in all its parts, and I have prayed a thousand times, on my knees, that those responsible for it should boil in a lake of fire for all eternity in the nethermost reaches of Hell."

The smile broadened still more as he turned and walked away. He knew the value of making a good exit, so he did not stop there but kept on making it, right out the creaky old door.

Outside the twilight was warm and the breeze gentle. He glanced at the Heechees' mound of rags, thought briefly of kicking them to the four winds, decided against it as an interior rumble suggested a more immediately important project. He headed toward the latrine.

A good bowel movement was after all a blessing. He took his time about it. By the time he was returning to the others a couple of stars had begun to peep out overhead. Most of the world thought those first glimmers of evening starlight rather pretty, if they thought of them at all. To Orbis McClune they carried a load of guilt. It was they that had lured the world to spaceflight, and thus to the Heechee and all their wickedness.

But they were far away, and on this world McClune was almost at peace as he pushed the door aside and went in. As much peace as the tormented soul of Orbis McClune ever had, at least.

It didn't last. Cara le Brun was sitting in a corner of the room, whispering to her machine mind but with her eyes on him and her expression absorbed. She stopped talking, got up and walked toward him, looking unexpectedly apologetic. At once McClune's defenses went up. He was wary of surprises, which in his experience seldom portended anything good.

Not this time, either. "Hey, Orbis," she said, reaching out to put her hand on his shoulder. Before he could shake it off she was going on: "Listen, I had Barb check you out. I'm sorry if I said anything wrong. I didn't know you had a wife in Here After storage."

VI

The next morning's sun was no hotter, McClune's unsteady perch on the bench beneath the great, frowning statue no more wearying than before, but Orbis McClune felt them more. His voice was just as commanding, his threats and warnings as plangent as ever. However, the old fire in his heart was quenched by the unwanted, long-suppressed memories of an ancient hurt . . . the one named Rowena.

Rowena. The beautiful. The decorous. The, well, the loved . . . or at least the very nearly loved as nearly as it was in Orbis McClune's power to love anything mortal. Until the decorous became unruly, and paid for it with her life, and then had not the grace to be once and for all truly dead but went on to be a constant hurt in McClune's.

The source of that unmitigatable hurt was there before him, right across the street. It was the technicians of Here After that had made it to Rowena's crashed car almost as soon as the ambulance, in time to get her dying consent and transform her personality—her *soul!*—into nothing more tangible than a cloud of electrons captured within a machine. As she still was at this moment. And always would be, as far into the future as human life continued to exist on Earth.

McClune's voice cracked, right in the middle of one of his favorite descriptions of the eternities of torture that awaited the damned. A couple of the idlers who made up his audience looked amused, but he caught himself and went right on. That is, his mouth continued to shape words and the words became well-reasoned arguments, but the arguments were merely the ones he had voiced so many times before.

Rowena should not have done it.

Her whole life proved that. Her clergyman-father was almost as strict in his beliefs as McClune himself—strict enough to have named his daughter after one of the purest maidens in Sir Walter Scott's long oeuvre, and to have insisted she model herself after that person. Rowena had been brought up to be a perfect wife for, say, the early eighteenth century. And for the first three years of their marriage those were the qualities she displayed, to her husband and to the world.

It was the fourth year that had been the killer.

All the time he was telling his audience the instructive story of Matthew the tax collector, the one who became the servant of the Lord and changed from taking the worthless coin of Mammon to giving, giving the saving Word of God . . . all that time, his gaze was far above the heads of his dwindling company of listeners, and fixed firmly on the despised Here After marquee just across the street. That was the Enemy incarnate. Its presence taunted him. The line of men and women waiting to get into it was an affront. Did they not know that they were damning their souls?

Rowena had known that. He had told her so himself, the moment he learned that—for hours on end, while he was in his study preparing his next installment of God's Truth for his parishioners—she had been furtively talking with heretics and blasphemers on the p-net. The things they had talked about were nearly unforgivable. Women's rights! Abortion!

Freedom of thought! Worst of all, the vile physical love between woman and woman, their bodies joined in the filthiest of lusts.

Oh, Rowena had sworn, it was all theoretical, she had never *done* any of those things, not even registered to vote. She was just *interested*. As a matter of *curiosity*. And when he told her to what those interests and curiosities would lead her—when he threatened to expose her wickedness to the congregation that very next Sunday—that was when she had stormed out of the house, and driven her car into the space that was just about to be occupied by the lead tractor of a high-speed freight caravan. Had that been by accident or by design? It didn't matter. She had sinned. It was people like the ones across he street that had let her avoid the life payment for her sin, by committing a sin greater still.

And there before him, a score of men and women were lined up before the Here After office to repeat that same irremediable sin.

He made a decision. As soon as he finished his present thought—at the latest, as soon as the shadow of the statue behind him reached the little clump of flowers on the other side of the walk—he would dismiss his audience, leave the little park and cross the street to deal with the greater emergency there. Preaching against them to begin with. Maybe a little righteous trashing of the premises, if enough of his audience could be motivated to the deed. It was the right thing to do, he told himself. He was at fault for not doing it sooner. . . .

However, it did not happen.

It didn't happen because, without warning, McClune was suddenly unsteady on his feet, then more than unsteady.

It was one of those little earthquakes, his interior voice was telling him wisely, just as he discovered that he could not stand at all. This particular earthquake wasn't all that little. McClune dropped to his knees and grabbed the back of the bench to keep from falling . . . but was falling anyway, falling in a tumbling sprawl that dropped him on his back in the yellowed grass, his skull smacking against the brittle sod, blurring his vision . . . but not blurring it so much that he didn't see the grave, granite face of Fra Junipero Serra bending down toward his own, toppled as surely as himself by this latest earthquake . . . the face coming closer and closer, as though to give him his kiss of death.

Because death it was going to be. McClune had no doubt of that. The thought terrified him, and it made him exultant, too, because this would be the time when he met his Maker, and got His unfailing reward for a lifetime of faithful service.

Or so, he believed, he deserved. But there was terror as well, because how could any mortal know the nature of God's awful justice? He voiced an impassioned plea for mercy to his Lord, not so much a prayer as a single begging shout, because that was all the time he had before those adamantine lips touched his own, and then went farther, and brought with them an instant explosion of pain. . . .

And then nothing. Only blackness.

VII

But when Orbis McClune managed to get his eyes open again—it had been curiously hard to make his muscles obey his will—it wasn't the late Fra Junipero Serra who was kissing him. It was an elderly man with a bald head and a ginger-colored beard, and the breath that he was forcing into Orbis McClune's mouth tasted nastily of beer and other, worse things. "Hey!" McClune cried—or intended to cry, but it took three or four attempts to get the words out—"Hey!" And "What." And "You." And "Think." And "You." And "Do?"—a syllable at a time, each produced with its own single great effort.

The man didn't seem to notice anything out of the way. He sat back, looking aggrieved. "You're another one didn't go the briefing, right? Christ's a'mighty, what was the matter with you people? I was just trying to get you started, like they said we should do, you know?"

McClune overlooked the profanity in the worse shame of the physical act. "They . . . said . . . you . . . should . . . kiss . . . me?"

The man seemed embarrassed. "Well, sure, if you want to call it that. It's the kiss of life, you understand? Making believe like I was trying to get you breathing again. So like at first you'd think that you'd drowned or something, see?" And then, reassuringly, "Don't worry if you're kind of having trouble getting your body to work right. Everybody does, at first. You'll get it after a while."

McClune frowned and licked his lips—then, remembering that nasty kiss, scoured at them with the back of his hand. That, too, took a trial or two before he could get the hand properly turned and positioned. He said hoarsely, "Explain. Please."

Irritated, the man gave him a scowl. "Well, now, what do you think there is to explain, God's sake? They were right across the street when that monument thing fell on you, weren't they? So they got to you right away, before you got too, uh, spoiled."

"*Who* across the street? *Who* got to me?"

"Jeez," the man groaned, "you're a real pain. The Here After people, who else? You've been machine-stored. Don't you see their collection agents coming this way?"

McClune saw them all right, pretty young women in perky blue uniforms. He wasn't thinking about them, though. He had something bigger on his mind, something that looked like the biggest, scariest, most important thing in his life.

Orbis McClune had lived his entire life in the glorious certainty that death meant judgment. If you had lived the life God desired for you, then you were rewarded. If not, then you were punished. One way or another, as soon as you died the matter was settled.

But not in this eternal undeath that also wasn't real life.

The thought was crushing. All his life McClune had proclaimed his willingness to accept whatever God handed him. But this? This was *unfair*!

That was when one of the Here After cashiers, her voice as perky as her pretty blue minidress, spoke to him. "Good morning, Mr.—ah— McClune. As I am sure you have realized by now, your organic body has passed on. In your case, I understand it was by some kind of organic-world accident, and Here After wants to extend its deepest sympathy for your loss. Though, of course, now that you've been vastened, it's not really a loss, is it?" Then, briskly, but with a dimpled smile, she changed the subject. "How would you like to settle your account, Mr. McClune? We accept all major debit or credit cards."

Taken aback, Orbis said, "I don't have any."

"No problem, Mr. McClune! We are glad to arrange direct transfer from your checking, savings or special-purpose bank account"—he was shaking his head—"or you could execute a lien on your home or business property—" Still shaking. She frowned. "An insurance policy, then? No? Well, we're glad to have you pledge jewelry, art objects, anything at all of value, subject of course to valuation by our experts—"

Orbis said, "Sorry. I don't have any of those things. I don't have anything at all. I'm penniless."

The young woman looked crestfallen. "Oh, Mr. McClune," she cried. "What a pity! I'm afraid that, to protect its interests, that means Here After will be forced to entertain offers from third-party bidders."

She wasn't perky anymore. Indeed, the look on her face had become pretty grim, and Orbis didn't like the sound of what she was saying. "What are you talking about?" he demanded. "You think you can sell me to somebody?"

"Oh, no," the young woman conceded. "That would be illegal in nearly all jurisdictions. But that isn't the question, is it? It's the hardware in which your program is stored that is definitely Here After property, and thus, like any other asset, can be sold on the open market." She gave a winsome little shrug. "The fact that your stored mind would follow the hardware is perhaps a little unfortunate for you. But not, of course, the company's problem." She paused, looking him over with an expression of sympathy. "Actually," she confided, "this is the part of the job that I hate, but what can I do?"

"You could turn me off," he said.

She looked shocked. "Oh, no, Mr. McClune! If I did that, then the company's equity would be diminished, and they wouldn't like that." She shook her head. "No, Mr. McClune," she said firmly, "you'll just have to make the best of it. Good heavens! Don't you think you owe Here After a little gratitude? If it wasn't for them you'd be *dead*."

As time passed—minutes, perhaps, or days or weeks; Orbis McClune had no way of measuring it and nothing to measure it against—McClune began to learn the rules of his new existence. First he learned how to make all his (nonexistent) parts move pretty much as he wanted them to in this nonexistent gigabit space those cursed people at Here After had consigned him to. That meant that when he finished the exercises he could walk and he could talk. He even had people to talk to, or at least people who wanted to talk to him, because it turned out he and the ancient drunk were not the only ones in machine storage. There were scores of others, maybe many more than that. They all had one thing in common, too, he discovered. None of them had the kind of marketable skill that would induce someone to buy up their contracts.

Oh, there were a few inquiries. An elderly man, still organic, had sent a doppel into the eigenspace of Here After's available merchandise to look for a valet. By "valet," it turned out, he meant a body servant whose effectors could bathe, feed and change him, among other duties, because he could no longer do any of those things for himself—and concluded quite soon that Orbis McClune wasn't temperamentally suited for the position. Then there was the woman who never said exactly what she was looking for, but gave Orbis one quick glance, snapped, "Not him," and left.

The one who said he represented a Mr. Santos-Smith didn't seem any more promising. He didn't care to tell anything about who Mr. Santos-Smith was, either. He looked disdainfully around the bare room that was all Orbis had been able to generate for himself—those who lived on the bounty of Here After's stockholders weren't allowed much profligacy—and rattled off his questions. Did Orbis know how to operate a spacecraft? Could he run a black-hole penetrator? Did he have any technical skills at all? And when all the answers were "no," he snapped his little black briefcast shut and left without another word.

Which made it all the more surprising when, soon after, Mr. Santos-Smith himself showed up. He was slight, sallow and of no particular age at all in appearance, and he said, "Call me Wan. I have one question for you. What do you think of the Heechee?"

That one came out of left field for Orbis. It had been a long time since anyone had encouraged him to say how he felt on that subject. He took a deep breath. "The Heechee," he said, "are the worst thing that ever happened to the human race. They should burn in hell forever. I hate them! I wish every last one of them were dead, and—"

Wan raised his hand. "Enough," he said. "You've got the job."

Orbis frowned. "Doing what?"

"Helping me get back some things that they stole from me. Only for now," he added, his fingers stealing toward a touchpad at his belt, "we don't want to waste energy, do we? So I'm going to turn you off for a while if you don't mind. Or even if you do."

12

Fatherhood

I

The news from Earth was terrible, all right: tens of millions dead, great cities forever erased. It was more than Stan and Estrella could take in right away. Estrella wept. Stan sat stunned and wordless before the look-plate for long minutes before either of them could even talk about it. Then they talked for hours. Over and over. Finding new ways to express the same thoughts of shock and undirected anger and woe.

Then, when Estrella fell asleep, Stan began to remember the other wholly unexpected news, the thing Estrella had told him.

Even overshadowed by what had happened on Earth, that news still shook Stan up. It changed things. He had become pleasantly accustomed to making love as a regular reward for the day's activities, but parenthood had never crossed his mind. ("My God, Strell, didn't you ever take your shots?" "Exactly what shots are you talking about, Stan? In case you didn't know it, virgins don't need contraceptive shots. And that's what I was, a virgin, remember? Anyway, until just before we shipped out I was.")

It was worse, not better, that Estrella's pregnancy was only a possibility. How strong a possibility Stan could not tell, and that was the worst part. Approaching fatherhood he could deal with, if he had to. Childlessness he could deal with too—rather easily, in fact. Uncertainty was tougher.

Estrella was small help. "Certainly there are pregnancy tests, Stan. You don't even need to take a test. If you're sexually active, your toilet checks your pee every time you go to the bathroom. Have you got one of those toilets with you, Stan? No? What a pity."

Stan found a straw to catch at. "But, hey, the Heechee must know how to tell if a person's pregnant, mustn't they?"

She gave him the look of total patience that encodes a state of utter exasperation. "You seem to have missed it, but, Stan, the Heechee are a different *species*."

He persisted. "How about Dr. von Shrink, then? He ought to know that stuff."

"He isn't even organic, Stan!" But then she thought for a moment, and added reluctantly, "I guess we could ask, anyway. I'll call the, uh, the institute."

And then, when she came back from the lookplates and said, "They say to come over. Dr. von Shrink will meet us there," Stan didn't gloat. He didn't even say, "I told you so," because while she was gone he had gone back to thinking about the other thing he had learned from that damnable dream-machine experience, namely that Estrella thought he was a clumsy lover.

Well, who was she to judge? The only other man she ever did it with was that Gateway bastard—what was his name?—Montefiore. Fat, loud and sloppy—was it possible that Estrella thought *he* was better at making love than himself?

So deep was Stan in those punishing thoughts that he hardly heard Estrella calling him from the doorway. When he joined her she looked at him with curiosity. "Are you all right?" she asked.

He shrugged morosely. "Why wouldn't I be? Let's go!"

On their way to the place they had decided to call an institute, let the Heechee call it whatever they liked, Stan hadn't forgotten any of those depressing thoughts, but he at least pushed them to the back of his mind.

Getting there was no real problem. Achiever had chosen to walk over when he paid his calls, but then Achiever was pretty loopy anyway. Salt had told them a quicker way. One of those whirring three-wheeled carts carried them a kilometer or two underground, and a ramp brought them to a large suite of rooms furnished pretty much like the lounge on the spacecraft that had brought them here. The rooms were fitted with plenty of perches and screens and desks, but with nothing that looked at all like any part of a hospital—at least, not any hospital as either Stan or Estrella understood a hospital to be. It was low-ceilinged and windowless, but comfortably lit by glowing walls. Fifteen or twenty Heechee were there, coming and going, talking, eating, nibbling on little mushroomy things in polished silvery bowls, working at the lookplates or simply dozing.

There was one human.

He was in a conversation with the Heechee female Stan recognized as Salt, but he looked up with what seemed like real pleasure when Stan and Estrella came in. "My dear friends," Sigfrid von Shrink exclaimed, coming toward them—not offering his hand to be shaken, because how could you shake the hands of a virtual image?, but welcoming in every other way. "I promise that this won't take long at all. Estrella, you can go right in with Catenary here—" indicating an elderly female hovering nearby. "I will be in in a moment."

Estrella sighed, put up her face to Stan to be kissed, and obeyed. As Stan watched her go von Shrink added, "You could have come along inside if you wanted to, Stan, but there's no real need for you to be there. Nothing serious will be done, just a few rather embarrassing questions I need to ask. Salt"—who was silently waiting beside him—"can get you anything you need. Are you hungry?"

Stan was shaking his head. "No, thanks. I've had about all the weird Heechee food I want for a while."

Von Shrink tarried on the verge of turning away. "Is that a problem, Stan? Well, look, I'm needed inside right now, but we'll talk when I get back. Meanwhile, here's Salt."

Who, of course, took efficient charge of things. Conducted Stan to a perch, between the tines of which someone had already placed a pillow, commanded a table to rise up before him, placed on the table a silvery bowl of what looked like broken-up bits of the kind of mold you sometimes found growing wild in your bathroom in Istanbul. "Cannot offer other conversational partners than self here," Salt said, "because none of others present speak you tongue, though some will no doubt come to speak for me to translate. Meanwhile"—gesturing toward the bowl—"try."

Stan looked at the mushroomy bits again and shook his head. "I don't think so."

"No harm will come," she urged. "Have already confirmed this with Dr. von Shrink, who caused tests to be made." Then, glancing up at some Heechee, diffidently approaching, "Ah. Others now here to condole you on terrible tragedy recently happening on your home planet."

Condole him they did, one after another and at considerable length, Salt doing her best to translate. Sometimes what they say was a simple expression of sympathy—"most very deeply wish had never happened unfortunate incident your species experiencing." More often, and queerly, they seemed to be apologizing for their own inadequacies in the matter: "Regret quite altogether sincerely our people's inability to prevent or otherwise minimize stated event" and "at first were made to feel stated event was typical barbaric act of long-gone wicked Assassins, misconception which unfortunately was in error conveyed to you." And though out of politeness Stan endured it as long as he could, the time came when he had to beg Salt to make them stop.

"Is too much quantity of same thing?" she ventured, looking thoughtful. "Yes. Perhaps this is so. Wait, please." And, holding her skinny arms above her head for attention, she rose and addressed the room in the familiar hisses, groans and whines of one or another of the Heechee tongues. It seemed to do the trick. The assembled well-wishers milled about for a moment, then went back to their own affairs. "Better now?" she asked.

"Oh, yes," he said gratefully. "It's kind of all these patients to take an interest—I mean, that's what they are, aren't they? Or doctors?"

"Not neither one," she said firmly. "These persons here for improvement simply reside at this place until again regain—" she paused, then with some pride took the word out and delivered it to him"—concinnity."

If she had intended to impress Stan with her vocabulary, she succeeded. "You got me," he confessed. "What's that?"

She said complacently, "Your word *concinnity* is implying all things satisfactory and ordered, a state normal to persons of our species. Persons here lack same. For example. Person over there with back toward us, seems perhaps asleep. His name is Permeable. His age is great and he to soon become Stored Mind, but must resolve certain worries first. Next to him, Turbidity, and over against wall, Inverse Square—female who just addressed you, you remember. Spoke of sorrow at great loss of your species' life. These two very seriously lacking concinnity. Inverse Square known to have said things not at all true. Turbidity made commitment to colleagues at locus of employment that he would perform act of a certain nature. However, did not in fact do so, although nothing prevented."

"And none of them are doctors?"

"Not any at all," she said positively. "Only member of that class you term 'doctor' present on Forested Planet of Warm Old Star Twenty-Four is human simulation Sigfrid von Shrink, who as-you-say 'treats' mostly humans, no matter how busy may be with other interests."

Stan sighed, unwilling to try anymore to untangle what the Heechee thought this clinic was all about. Instead, he said, "Yes, he's a very kind person."

"Are in agreement, yes."

"And I know he's busy. It was nice of him to make a special trip for us."

"Did not," Salt politely corrected him. "Was here on business of other human person and simulation."

That made Stan scratch his head and frown. He turned to look at her face-on. "Salt," he said, "there are times when I don't know what the hell you're trying to say. Why was von Shrink here, exactly?"

She wriggled her fingers in apology. "Do not know why *exactly*, but, in general, his presence here related to two persons, one, human female Gelle-Klara Moynlin, two, simulated human female termed Hypatia. Have you familiarity with these persons?"

"With Moynlin, sure," Stan said, impressed. "Everybody knows who she is. Used to be Robinette Broadhead's girlfriend. Got a lot of money. What's she doing here?"

"Recall previous discussion, Stan? Moynlin brought here by von Shrink simulation for improvement of concinnity, as discussed. This concinnity lost at time of great physical damage occurring your planet. You remember this, too?" And then, looking past him, she added, "However, now no further need for polite passing-the-time conversation at this juncture. Estrella, who is loved incessantly by you, now returns."

And when he turned around there she was coming toward him, arms outstretched, her expression both happy and faintly scared. "It's true, hon," she told him. "We're going to have a baby."

Stan had taken Estrella's suspicion as gospel. All the same the words hit him with a solid impact, as though the fact that they were no longer the only two persons who knew it made it suddenly more real.

"It's true," von Shrink confirmed, beaming. "I estimate it to be a thirty-five-day-old embryo, and it is perfectly healthy in every way I could determine. Of course," he added, "I'm primarily a psychoanalyst, not a medical doctor. You will really need a gynecologist before long. Fortunately, Klara thinks she knows of one—you know who Klara is, I expect? Gelle-Klara Moynlin? Very active in philanthropy?"

This time Stan said only, "Yes."

"For some time Klara has financed a sort of resettlement program for seriously unhappy women. She pays their expenses to emigrate to the Core, and she's pretty sure she helped an ob-gyny woman not long ago. Her shipmind is checking it out."

"That would be nice of her—them," Stan said, momentarily distracted by the thought of having to pay money to get to the Core.

"She is nice," Estrella told him. "She has kind of let herself go a little—with all her troubles, you can't really blame her—but did you know that she kept me company while Dr. von Shrink was preparing my, uh, procedure?"

"She did," von Shrink confirmed. "And there's something else. I mentioned the fact that you said you were getting tired of Heechee food. So she's invited the two of you for lunch."

Gelle-Klara Moynlin's quarters weren't exactly in the "institute," but they were close. At their door a dark-haired, dark-eyed woman wearing a ruby necklace and a robe that left one shoulder bare was waiting for them. "Welcome," she said, though in a tone that was not particularly welcoming. "I'm Hypatia. Dr. Moynlin is waiting for you on the lanai."

The door behind her opened invitingly. Hypatia hadn't touched a thing, but then, Stan reflected, as an impalpable shipmind she really couldn't. She did step to one side to allow them to enter.

As soon as they were inside they both stopped short, staring. "Chairs," Stan muttered reverently, and Estrella added, "And look, a real table!"

That wasn't all of it, either. The floor was marble-tiled, with deep-pile throw rugs scattered about. There were shelves on the walls, some of them holding pretty little cups and statuettes, others loaded with actual paper-and-ink books. Before an actual fireplace, with actual flames coming out of the giant actual wooden log it held, was a couch big enough for a family—and was even, Stan thought at once, big enough to start one on, and to do so a lot more comfortably than he and Estrella ever had.

Hypatia had been wrong about where her mistress was. Gelle-Klara Moynlin wasn't out on the large, flowered lanai at the end of the room. She was standing by the couch, and she had one of those old-fashioned books in her hand. "Hello again, Estrella," she said. "And you must be Stan."

They shook hands. Her grip was warm and firm, and she gave his hand a little farewell squeeze before releasing it. But there was something wrong with the picture. Stan knew what Gelle-Klara Moynlin looked like, because everybody did. The eyebrows were as they should be, dark and thick, and the features were the ones he had seen in a thousand p-vid stories—*Gelle-Klara Moynlin Rescued from Black Hole, Gelle-Klara Moynlin Finances 10,000-Home Low-Cost Housing Development, Gelle-Klara Moynlin Voted Most Famous Woman in Galaxy Sixth Year Running.* But this edition of Gelle-Klara Moynlin was older and heavier-set than the pictures, meaning not so much that time had passed as that she had stopped bothering to keep its effects hidden. And, although her face was friendly, it was unmistakably sad.

However, she was making an effort. "Have a seat," she said hospitably, and then, taking note of the way Estrella was peering through the door at the adjacent rooms, "Or would you rather have the tour first?"

Estrella had an immediate response to that. "Tour, please," she said eagerly.

Actually, Stan would have preferred to get right to the promised lunch—the *human-food* lunch—but when he saw Klara's bathroom (soak tub, jet tub and twelve-head shower that would not leave any external part of any person's anatomy unsprayed) and her dressing room (three-paned mirror above racks of all the scents and powders Klara no longer bothered to use) and, most of all, her bedroom, he almost forgot the promise of lunch. The bed was a four-poster. Though as far as Stan knew Klara had no immediate intention of sharing it with anyone, it was easily large enough to accommodate an orgy.

It all just showed what you could do when you had unlimited funds, he thought, unable to resist a twinge of jealousy.

If Estrella had the same feeling she wasn't showing it. "May I?" she begged, and when Klara nodded consent she hopped up onto the bed at once, bouncing like a little girl.

Klara was actually smiling. "What about you, Stan?" she asked. "Want to give it a trial?"

He shook his head. In fact he did want that, but not with the owner standing there. She studied him for a moment, then surprised him by patting him on the shoulder. "Well, that takes care of the tour, so how about lunch? Only," she added as they turned back toward the room with the tables, "I think I ought to warn you. Hypatia's really a very good cook, but she needs raw materials to work with. Right now she's limited to what the Heechee food services can provide in the way of human foodstuffs, and I'm afraid they haven't quite got the hang of it yet."

II

Klara was right about that. They hadn't. The appointments were fine—crystal stemware, gold knives and forks, gold-rimmed plates, all on a snowy damask tablecloth. The food wasn't. Stan's cheese omelette was rubbery in texture and faintly chemical in taste, and the apple pie dessert had a surprising little tang of sauerkraut. The shipmind had presided while little wheeled servers brought the dishes to them, and then removed herself without explanation. "Hypatia's mortified," Klara whispered to her guests, but to Stan she didn't look as much mortified as just plain mad.

"Still," he told Estrella on the way home, "it makes a change from that Heechee muck."

"And Klara said Hypatia will cook for us whenever we like, all we have to do is call her."

"Nice of her," Stan said, thinking how much nicer that would be if the food were better.

"She *is* nice. Klara, I mean. She asked me if I wanted to get my face fixed. Said it wouldn't hurt, she'd had a lot bigger work done on herself, one time or another."

Stan asked, "Did you?"

"Do you want me to?"

"Hell, no," Stan said at once, though in fact he hadn't ever considered the possibility. "She's got some damn nerve, talking to you that way."

"Oh, she didn't mean it nasty, Stan. She was being kind. She's really nice, especially when you think of all she's been through," Estrella said, and then she had to tell what all that was. Stan had to agree that it was bad enough for anyone. The same giant wave that depopulated California had erased Klara's private South-Sea island of Raiwea as well. Speedy evacuation had meant that no lives had been lost, but nothing tangible remained of the little community that had been the most important thing in Klara's life. "That's why she's here," Estrella added. "She'd got kind of depressed. Dr. von Shrink said she's even talked about getting machine-stored, only he thinks she doesn't think of it as storage, she thinks of it as death."

"Huh," said Stan; evidently life could have its miseries even when you had unlimited funds to draw on. Then, observing that she was absently frowning, "Is something the matter?"

She shrugged, then said, "Oh, no, hon. Not at all. But did you ever hear of somebody named Wan?"

Stan thought for a minute before he decided. "I don't know. Maybe. Who is he?"

"Well, I don't know that," she admitted. "Only Klara and Dr. von Shrink were talking about him while they were getting ready for the procedure. They didn't seem to like him much." Then she grinned and changed the subject. "So did you want to hear about von Shrink's test?"

"I guess. What was it, peeing in a bottle?"

"Nothing like that." She pursed her lips. "It was a lot easier than that. Did you know that he's just a point, Stan?"

"Who, von Shrink? What do you mean he's just a point?"

"What I said. No dimension at all. After he asked me all his questions, what he did was just sort of focus himself inside me and look around. He saw the embryo, Stan. Our baby! Only of course it doesn't look much like a baby yet."

She was going too fast for him. "Wait a minute. He was *inside* you? How'd he do that?"

"He just did it, Stan." She yawned and changed the subject. "You know what? I wish I could've borrowed that couch for a couple of hours."

"Yes," he said absently, "sure. Me too." He wasn't thinking about the couch, though, because he now had other things to ruminate on, and he was ruminating so hard that, until Estrella nudged him, he didn't notice that they had arrived at their own apartment.

They were trying to decide whether to call on Hypatia for a final meal when someone was at the door.

When Stan opened it he was surprised to see Hypatia standing there, with a couple Heechee guiding motorized pallets behind her. "Dr. Moynlin's compliments," she said. "She just received some new furnishings from Earth, and wonders if you can use these others."

And while Stan and Estrella watched the two Heechee rolled their goods into the apartment; and even before they had everything set up, Stan and Estrella recognized that they were being given that same large and obviously comfortable four-poster bed, with rose-colored sheets that seemed to be made of raw silk. When the bed was installed and made neatly, hospital corners and all, Estrella firmly escorted them to the apartment door. "Thank Klara very much for us," she told the shipmind, "but right now I want to try this thing out."

They did try it out. It turned out to be satisfactory in all respects, and Stan was not a bit clumsy, in neither Estrella's opinion nor his own. When at last they went to sleep, it was with Estrella in his arms, and all was as right as could be with everything on the Forested Planet of Warm Old Star Twenty-Four.

13

Stovemind in the Core

I

After I left that other Marc Antony to do my work on the Wheel, I did go to the Core, where I busied myself with my usual pursuits for a while. I did not hurry, but long before the first organic day had passed, I had most of my duties well organized.

Let me make one thing clear. Although I use the word "duties" for lack of a better one, its implication is quite wrong. Everything I did was entirely voluntary. I had left the Wheel of my own free will, being surplus to requirement there, and I had had no "duties" assigned to me in the Core. How could I have? Who in the Core (or anywhere else for that matter) had the authority to assign work for me?

No, there was only one reason for all my activities. It is simply not my nature to be idle.

Since my primary function is as master chef, I began a study of my prospective clientele. That was easy enough. All I had to do was to census all the humans in the Core and to ask or deduce their menu preferences. There weren't that many humans present—no more than fifteen hundred or so when I arrived, fewer than ten thousand even after those first days. Some of the immigrants were, by organic standards, somewhat famous— two former vice presidents of the United States, some entertainment stars, even Gelle-Klara Moynlin, who had once been the richest woman in the galaxy. (Still was, although she had given much of her wealth away when she came to the Core.) However, the famous didn't receive any better treatment from me than the least of the unknowns. I gave them all of my best.

My best, for each, rested on what I thought they would prefer. For a start, it was quite easy to match meals to ethnicities—toad in the hole and Stilton cheese for the Brits, assorted curries and several kinds of dumplings in cream or sugar syrup for those from the Indian subcontinent, dim sum and a variety of main-course entrees for the Chinese—stuffed crab claws, Peking duck, jellyfish, barbecued beef, braised eel and so on. I located a Greek colony on Misty Glacier Planet, for whom I started with a nice orektika of tongue, cheese spread with black peppers and kalamaka olives, followed by that egg-lemon soup that they always want. Their main courses were usually one or another kind of lamb. On Forested Planet of Warm Old Star Twenty-Four there was a young boy from Turkey—my only Turkish customer as far as I could tell—but he was a problem. The first thing I did was to make him some yaprak dolma and a nice kuzo tandir roast, but then for some reason he blacked himself out, so I couldn't see whether they pleased him. His loss. From then on he would be lucky to get a peanut butter and jelly sandwich, and serve him right.

At the same time I was, of course, working at my other special task.

One might wonder why I didn't mention that one first, since under some circumstances it might be a matter of life or death. It just didn't seem urgent at the time. I didn't really expect to get into a use-of-force situation in the Core. The reason I made the preparations was not because I anticipated a need, but because that was what I did.

In terms of security I found there was disgracefully little for me to work with. I hadn't expected much. I hadn't supposed that the Heechee would maintain fleets of armed spacecraft strategically located around the volume of the Core—and they hadn't—but I had thought they would at least have arranged for a decent military surveillance system. They did have a sort of a system, but it was of course rudimentary and—like the Heechee lifestyle in general—civilian-oriented.

The Heechee did also have a regular program of sending scout ships out into the external galaxy every few decades, just to see if the Assassins seemed to be looking for them. What the Heechee would have done if they had ever found that they were, I did not know. I suspected, nothing at all. Apparently they thought the Schwarzschild barrier that surrounded the Core would keep any possible enemy out, including the Assassins, because they had no Plan B. The Heechee alarm channel was at least something to work with. If I were to add to it, perhaps using some of my own food-delivery remotes, and further add some kind of weaponry I would have the beginning of a useful security system.

Weaponry was the problem. There was one possibility that seemed worth exploring. The Heechee had a program of self-propelled torpedos—small, fast, shipmind-guided, torpedo-shaped spacecraft that they used as transports, carrying data fans or even Stored Minds from place to place. I could commandeer a number of them, packed with explosives. Forty or fifty of them Core-wide, I estimated, would do for a beginning. The explosives were not a problem. If I could tweak the Food Factories into making every spice and condiment ever heard of, I could just as easily get them to turn out cordite, gelignite, plastique or plain old tritnitrotoluene.

I will be truthful and say that I was rather pleased with myself for having succeeded in discovering the need and inventing solutions for it while the innocent Heechee were all unaware. They were, however, less innocent than I had thought. I discovered that when a message appeared in my screen from a Heechee named Thermocline: "Hello, Marc. I see we're neighbors, so if you have a free moment could you please come and visit me?"

To say I was astonished is an understatement. I knew who Thermocline was. On the Wheel he had been one of my most adventurous Heechee dining customers, and that wasn't all. Although organic, he had been a member of Thor Hammerhurler's security team, charged with making sure that the Wheel's physical weaponry remained at full readiness just in case of some undesirable activity from the Foe. (As though any of that weaponry would have made a difference.)

So while I, through my effectors, was making up a few dozen special meals I started a few programs on making inquiries.

That would take some time, but I was not in any hurry. I am not in the business of making house calls. I didn't mind keeping Thermocline waiting for as many as five or six seconds to remind him of it.

Besides, I had had some fresh-fruit requests from the Singaporeans—some of that furry rambutan that they said had been Queen Victoria's favorite fruit, and hard-fleshed salak. Also mangoes, fresher and riper than any that ever turned up in a store, and even durian, complete with its overripe Camembert smell. These took time. A fresh peach is in principle no harder to create than a cheese sandwich, but I like to take special pains with skin color, degrees of ripeness and so on. I couldn't leave them to my sous-chef subroutines. By the time I had them all chilled and dewy, working through the remotes on the Singaporeans' planet, the word on Thermocline came through.

It presented me with a surprise. Thermocline was present in the Core, just as he had said, but he was no longer among the living. He had become a Stored Mind.

Becoming a Stored Mind is nothing out of the ordinary for a Heechee. It's what all Heechee do when they die, unless they are so terribly unlucky as to die where no one can find them in time for storage, before decay has made it impossible. The only reason I was surprised was that Thermocline had been still quite organic at the time when I left for the Core. It hadn't occurred to me that he would have had the time to age, sicken and die.

Interfacing from a human stored-intelligence setup to the wholly different surround of a Heechee stored mind isn't easy. It took me more than half a second to make my way into Thermocline's surround. I recognized him at once. He was unchanged in appearance from his days on the Wheel, but his surround was a different matter. Basically there wasn't any.

I had not expected that. Every last machine-stored organic intelligence I had ever known, and most of the other varieties of AIs as well, had made itself a comfortable little home base, ranging from my kitchens and Thor Hammerhurler's war-waging HQ to the occasional fully stocked harem. What Thermocline had made for himself wasn't anything like any of those. He was awaiting me in a chamber that was not much more than three meters in any dimension. The walls were a neutral gray, decorated with a couple of Heechee lookplates and very little else. The lighting was subdued and, as far as I could see, sourceless, and the furniture absolutely minimal. That is, there was a sort of recliner for Thermocline himself, on which he sat, or lay, at ease. There was also a straight-backed chair for one visitor. (For one specifically human visitor, I observed. If he had been expecting a Heechee rather than myself I suppose it would have been replaced by one of their perches.)

That was it. Or not quite it. There was something unusual about Thermocline's appearance, and it took me a moment to figure it out. He wasn't wearing that universal Heechee costume accessory, the storage pod that they kept slung between their legs.

Well, of course he wasn't. He no longer required the mild, life-sustaining microwave flux the pods provided for their owners, since he no longer was organically alive. Nor had Thermocline any need to haul his own Ancient Ancestor around with him anymore, since now he himself was one.

Thermocline didn't get up to greet me, or shake my hand. He was definitely welcoming, though. "My dear Marc Antony," he said in his perfect English, acquired in his decades on the Wheel, "what a wonderful surprise! I had reconciled myself to going back to a simulated diet of CHON-food, not to mention the loss of your good company, and I am delighted that you are here. But why did you come to the Core?"

I told him my story, and then I asked him the same question. He gave me the belly-muscle shrug. "My organic body was wearing out," he said. "It was time to become a Stored Mind, and I preferred to do that at home. What about you? Will you be happy here?"

"Will you?"

He made the open-handed gesture of dismissal. "We Heechee live all our lives in the expectation of an afterlife of meditation and service. We are prepared for it." He paused. His facial muscles tightened for a moment, then sagged. "Ah, well, Marc," he said, "enough, as you used to say, of the small talk. Can you guess why I wanted to see you?"

I said warily, "I suppose it has something to do with the security network I've been working on."

Heechee don't laugh, but he made a little hiccoughing sound that came close. "Not at all. It is because of your investigations of our own alarm network that I became aware of your presence and activities, to be sure, but the reason I messaged you was something else. Do you know who Albert Einstein is?"

I knew he was not asking about the ancient human scientist of that name. "Of course. A machine intelligence. At one time he was merely Robinette Broadhead's shipmind, but now they seem to exist as separate individuals."

"Exactly. Indeed, Albert himself has hived off some independently functioning subsystem for particular needs. One of these, an individual named Sigfrid von Shrink, has been quite useful in the case of one of our own people who had suffered mental harm while on duty at your Gateway asteroid—"

"Interesting," I said. Thermocline, as I remembered well, had always liked to talk. "You were saying about Albert?"

"Yes. Albert is not here in the Core, but he sent a message to Sigfrid von Shrink, who passed it on to me. He is troubled about a human person, now machine-stored, whose name is Wan Enrique Santos-Smith. I have learned that at one time you had some dealings with this man. Can you tell me something about him?"

I had no reason to keep still, so I told him about our voyage to the planet called Arabella, Harry, me and the tank full of Foe. He listened attentively, then pursed his thin Heechee lips. "Is Albert aware of this?" he asked.

"I don't know. I understand Albert is aware of most things," I told him, "but perhaps I should send him the data."

He inclined his skull-like head. "I will do so myself, if you don't mind, by informing Dr. von Shrink. Usefully, he is in regular contact with the organic human being, Gelle-Klara Moynlin. She had at one time been a person of special sexual, though nongenerative, interest to Robinette Broadhead himself, and, as it happened, at a different time, to Wan himself as well."

"The sexual concerns of organic humans are often confusing," I observed.

"Indeed so. Klara's shipmind will also be informed."

"Hypatia, yes. I have had conversations with her. A quite high-performing person."

"Yes," he said absently. He seemed to be having some sort of internal dispute, his expression changing moment by moment from polite inquiry to concern—even to worry.

I didn't want to take time for Thermocline to settle his interior problems. "Is something troubling you?"

He shook his head. "Ah, Marc, I can't keep much from you. Tell me, do you remember the strange behavior of that star of the external galaxy, the one you call Fomalhaut?"

"Fomalhaut," I repeated—not so much stalling as an organic human might, while he took time to cudgel his memory, but achieving the same effect as I accessed some of those parts of my memory files not usually pertinent to my day-by-day existence. "Of course. The star that went supernova a few days—that is, some hundreds of external years—ago."

"Exactly," Thermocline said heavily. "However, Marc, it was not a normal supernova. It was caused by our intervention."

He stopped there, gazing at me with a troubled expression, perhaps maybe waiting for me to ask what kind of "intervention" he was talking about. I didn't have to, though. The pieces fell into place, and I knew.

"Thermocline," I said, "when we infiltrated Wan's fortress on the planet Arabella the first thing they asked me was whether I knew how to make a star explode. So when we got back, I asked Thor Hammerhurler. He said he had heard that you people might have been working on something like that, but it didn't seem to be operational."

That had an effect on Thermocline. His belly muscles writhed and tautened. "Yes," he said sadly, "it wasn't operational at that time. But it is now." He did sigh that time, a tribute to his mastery of Earth-human ways. "The device is a variation on the order disrupter that is used to penetrate black holes. By discharging a star's gravitation it would make the star fly apart. You see," he said earnestly, "it was never intended for use on actual stars, especially any with, or in the vicinity of, inhabited planets. You remember how the Foe live?"

"Of course. In their Kugelblitz. Most of my existence was spent within a few hundred Astronomical Units of that, on the Wheel."

He bared his teeth to indicate assent. "That was what the Great Disrupter was meant to be used on. On the Kugelblitz, annihilating the gravity that held it together and thus making the Foe fly apart into a thin, dispersed cloud of individual particles. Having lost the ability for collective action, they would no longer be a threat."

I could not help admiring the concept, but all I said was, "But then the weapon was never deployed?"

"No. Not against the Foe. We are a peaceable people, Marcus. We do not choose to destroy sentient life of any kind . . . and also," he added, "it wasn't ready."

"Until Fomalhaut," I helped him along.

"Yes, until Fomalhaut. Once it was ready, some felt it to be necessary to try it out, and indeed it worked perfectly. You see," he said, now in full lecture mode, "when a star's gravity is nullified, it will explode from the pressure of its exceedingly densely packed center. That is not all, though. The worst-case estimate of the Stored Minds is that the detonation of any star within the Core could cause the loss of between ten and forty-four million lives, with another thirty to two hundred million suffering from property loss, environmental damage and/or physical injury. The reason for that—as," he added politely, though without slowing down, "I am sure you know—is that the fusion reaction which lights a star takes place in its core. The energy produced there, in the form of photons, is not immediately released to space. A star's interior is quite dense. Within it each photon is reflected many times on its way to the surface." He paused for effect. "The time this takes is of the order of a million years."

"Oh," I said, beginning to comprehend. But he went on:

"This of course means that the dispersed star will release all those photons at once, the ones near the surface and the ones just being generated in its core and all the ones in between. It will amount to—" he affected to hesitate a moment while he figured it out "—the release of one million years' worth of energy in the space of two to three hours. So, do you see, Marc? That much energy would probably destroy several nearby stellar systems, and in fact will do decreasing amounts of damage almost to the far periphery of the Core."

I tried not to show my embarrassment. "Thank you," I said, resolving to access some files on stellar dynamics as soon as possible.

Then he offered me the closest possible Heechee approximation of a smile. "But, of course," he said happily, "we do not know that this Wan has come into possession of one of these weapons. Indeed, we do not even know that he is definitely coming in our direction. Or that he would know how to deploy the device in any case, being formerly an organic human."

That was not as reassuring to me as it appeared to be to him, and I suppose my expression showed it. He asked, "Have I offended you, Marc?"

"You might have, if I had ever been an organic human," I said, and he gave me a nearly human grin.

"Then," he said, "let us talk of more pleasant subjects. Like food! I know how good your organic meals were; can you do as well when they are only simulated?"

"Better," I told him.

"Then," he said with sudden enthusiasm, "you could start, please, with one of those cold soups, and then—do you know what I've been thinking about? That Philippine dish you used to make, sour fish with ginger and bitter melon. Or perhaps that Thai salad with water chestnuts, unripe papaya and crushed peanuts? Can you do that?"

I promised that I could and would, and bade him good-bye. But when I returned to my own surround—my giant kitchen, with half a dozen sous-chefs working away—I was a good deal less cheerful than I had been when I left.

14

Motherhood

I

Estrella never seemed to get tired of Stan's company, and Stan certainly never did of Estrella's. Still, there was a whole unexplored world out there for them. Little by little they nibbled at it—a visit to the institute, a walk around the valley between it and them. Sometimes they went out alone, sometimes with one of the Heechee. The male named Yellow Jade was particularly good company, because he had a real, and unHeecheelike, fondness for the outdoors. "Look," he would say, delicately lifting a fern frond to reveal a pulsing little mass of pale pink jelly. "This by name is called—" a chirp and something like a sneeze. "His species by diet eat—" another unpronounceable Heechee name "—and in turn self is eaten by—" a third name, this one more promising for Stan because it only had one syllable.

He tried his luck. "Fkweesh?" he ventured.

Yellow Jade looked stricken. "Is far better thing if you not do that," he advised. "Look, here is other different creature, not so interesting but somewhat." And he showed them one creature after another—the flowers that actually were voracious little animals, the tree snakes that glided from branch to branch, the ugly, sharp-toothed fish that lived in the little pond—until even Estrella was beginning to yawn. Then he did the best thing of all. Which was to escort them back to their apartment. "Because," he told them earnestly, "is known to us your species enjoys to couple even when female not fertile. Or, in your individual case, when already made fertilized." Which made Stan grin, because it was true enough.

It wasn't all sex, though. They found plenty else to do with their time. They played word games, considered names for the baby, discussed Hypatia's failings as a cook, chatted with Salt on the lookplate, played with those same lookplates in some of the many other ways they could be used.

They even found a news program on one of the plates—human news, from Outside!—delivered by a human announcer whom Estrella thought exceptionally good-looking. Stan couldn't see that at all. He didn't care much for the program, either, because the announcer seemed to be in a constant, unwinnable race to keep up with the things that were happening in the outside galaxy. Each time he appeared he seemed farther behind. Elections came and were replaced by new ones like the flickering of fireflies. Disasters were healed by the time he finished describing them. And when there was something that sounded really interesting—what did he mean when he spoke of a Foe expedition to the Lesser Magellanic Cloud?—there never seemed to be any explanation or follow-up.

But it still struck Stan as of great interest. "A human news broadcast!" he marveled. "Why, Strell, that has to mean that there are a lot of us in the Core now!"

She managed not to laugh. "There sure are, hon. Weren't you listening when Yellow Jade showed me how to access some of the others on the small plate?"

He looked guilty. "I might've been resting."

"Oh, right," she said, remembering. "You snored a lot, too. Anyway, right here on this planet there's Alice and Sandra—she's machine-stored, though—and there's also Beth and Keichiko and Maureen and Daisy, but it's harder to reach them because they're on other planets. And there are lots of others, but some of them don't speak English, and some don't want to."

Stan blinked at that, was more startled still when she told him that, near as she could estimate, there were now several thousand other humans in the Core.

"Where'd all those people come from?" he marveled.

Estrella said wisely, "It's the time differential, Stan. Like this Bill Tartch, trying to keep up with the news. Things move a lot faster Outside. There's plenty of time to emigrate."

Stan found himself displeased. He had felt a lot more important when he and Estrella were rarer than they were now. Any time now, he thought, human beings they didn't even know might be dropping in on them in person.

What he hadn't expected was that one of those fellow humans would arrive at their apartment that very day. But one did.

The doorbell (they couldn't think of what else to call it) told them that someone was waiting outside. It didn't tell them that the person was female, good-looking, blonde, blue-eyed, carrying a little black bag and, above all, human. "Hello," she said brightly. "Dr. von Shrink said I should come out and check you over. I'm an ob-gyny. My name is Dr. Dorothy Kusmeroglu."

An electric shock went through Stan when he heard the name. "Kusmeroglu? Really? You're Turkish? Maybe from Istanbul—"

"Oh, no. Not me. That could've been where my couple-of-greats-grandfather came from, though," she said, looking around the apartment as though she were preparing to make an offer on it. "Somewhere on Earth, anyway, but I've never been there. I'm third-generation Martian. Can we use the bedroom, Estrella? And I think it's better if Stan stays out here."

So Stan was again left to bite his fingernails while he waited for whatever had to be done with Estrella, now clearly the alpha star of their little constellation. It didn't take long. When they came out both were smiling. "Everything is perfect, Stan," the doctor told him. "You can see it for yourself, because I've got a little present for you." She rummaged in her bag, pulled out an iridescent, olive-colored bracelet. "Put this on, Estrella. It's the latest thing from Outside to see how your baby's doing—I hear they call it 'Stork,' there, but maybe that's too cute for you? Anyway, when you want to make it work you just say, 'Stork, display.'" And then, when Estrella didn't act at once, she said impatiently, "Come on, hon. I haven't got all day."

Estrella looked at Stan, got no help there and finally sighed. "All right. Stork. Display."

A faint cloud of pale pink swirled beside Estrella's body and immediately collapsed into a minute, doll-like figure. It floated in the air a meter or so from Estrella's face, making her draw back in sudden surprise. It didn't look like a baby to Stan. It looked like something you might step on in the street, and immediately try to scrub off your shoe.

But then, as it slowly rotated before their eyes, it began to look like— well, not like anything you'd call *human*, but a little like one of those crude, prehistoric attempts to capture a human form in stone. There was a head—eyeless, earless, but with something rather like a chin. There were spindly limbs and tiny hands and feet. And there was—

"My God," Stan breathed. "Has he got an erection already?"

Dr. Kusmeroglu gave him a patient little laugh. "That's the umbilical cord. He hasn't got a penis yet—hold on," she interrupted herself, peering hard at the tiny animalcule. "Huh," she said. "Never will have, either. You see the external genitalia, up there in the crotch? Well, up to now the embryo hasn't had any gender, but around now is when the genitalia migrate. If they go up it's a girl, down they turn into testicles and it's a boy. And this one's migrating up." She lifted her eyes to meet Estrella's. "So you've got a little girl, hon. Congratulations."

While Stan was trying to get used to the proposition that he was not only becoming a father, but a father to an actual, visible (if not yet fully formed) human being, complete with arms, legs and gender, Dr. Kusmeroglu snapped her bag shut. "By the way," she said, "she isn't an embryo anymore. From now on she's a fetus. Now I have to get moving. I don't want to miss my flight to Mostly Water Planet of Bright Yellow Star."

"You came in a *spaceship*? Just to see us?" Stan marveled.

"Of course. There aren't that many pregnant human beings in the Core right now, are there? Now, when we move to the implantation procedure—" She paused, biting her lip in thought.

That scared Stan. "Is something the matter?" he demanded.

"Oh, no, of course not. Not really. It's just that I don't think there are any suitable implantation animals here. That kind of thing is usually done earlier in the pregnancy, but that's mostly for the mother's convenience. There's no great hurry. We can order a suitable surrogate from Outside—"

"Stop!" Estrella commanded. "What are you talking about?"

Dr. Kosmeroglu looked faintly bewildered. "Didn't I make myself clear? I'm talking about a surrogate mother, of course, what else? A mammal large enough to carry your baby to term—of course, one that has been genetically modified so that it won't reject the fetus. So the question is, what kind would you prefer? In most of the world it's usually water buffalo. They're a good size, and they're cheap and plentiful. I prefer to use cows, myself."

Estrella was looking at the woman in horror. "My baby? Inside an *animal*?"

"Of course inside an animal," the doctor said impatiently. "What else would you do? You don't want to go through parturition yourself, do you? All that pain and mess? Not to mention nine months of trying to get comfortable with a belly that keeps getting bigger and bigger every day? Nobody does now, except—Oh, wait." She paused and gave Estrella a more appraising look. "Listen, you're not one of those religious fanatics, are you?"

Estrella tried to answer but couldn't. She settled for just shaking her head.

The doctor sighed and stood up. "Look," she said kindly, "I know this is a big step for you. Talk it over, the two of you. If you've got something against using bovids, there are other mammalian choices. One or two species of bear are good, and sometimes we can time the pregnancy to co-incide with their hibernation so there's not even the slight risk of accident you get when your surrogate is left out to feed and so on. That bear pro-cedure, or the water buffalo, is done mostly in Hindu areas, because, you know, they've got that cow thing. I've even heard of people using one of the marine mammals, now and then, though I can't imagine why. Not on Mars, of course; even now we don't have that kind of bodies of water, so I don't have any personal experience. Anyway, I think it would be pretty troublesome to try to bring an orca here. Excuse me." She turned away, raising her hand apologetically. To the air she said, "Time?" She listened for a moment, then grimaced. "I really have to get going, and anyway I guess you've got the picture. Call me if you have any questions—and, of course, when you've made up your mind about the surrogate."

And she was gone. Stan and Estrella looked at each other. Stan said, "What do you think, would you want to do something like that?"

"Over my dead body," Estrella said firmly. "Let's get something to eat. If we're going to keep that baby inside me where it belongs, we'd better feed it."

II

Stork was a wonderful toy. Surprisingly, more for Stan than for Estrella; she was interested in seeing it four or five times a day but not much more, while Stan would sit, studying the tiny molecule, for an hour or two at a time, until Estrella got tired of doing odds and ends without him and in-formed him he wasn't getting enough exercise for the baby's good. So they went for more of those long walks in the countryside, enjoying the fragrance of growing things, pleased by the beauty of the tall trees with their frizzy crown of branches. On this day, the little animals that pre-tended to be plants were flowering, yellow and blue and red, and the ruse was working for them. Clouds of tiny flying things hovered around them, not evidently discouraged by the fact that so many of them were being eaten. There were fish in the pond, too, nasty snakelike things with bright orange eyes. If Estrella had had some thought of a quick swim she gave that up as soon as she saw them writhing around, just below the surface.

But the day had a pleasant surprise. When they got back to their apartment they found a stack of hexagonal boxes, great and small, just inside the door. What they contained was the personal possessions they had had in their Five, left behind on Door and finally returned to them by some considerate Heechee. The smallest of the boxes held half a dozen of Stan's old sheet-music selections, and that was all they needed to get their instruments out of the wall cupboard and begin to play. It was a nice way to end a day.

And, the next morning, a nice way to begin one, too. It was Estrella's flute, played as she was sitting on the side of their bed, that woke Stan up, and he only took a moment to use the waste disposer before he joined her in a couple of choruses of "Stardust" and "The Jelly Roll Rag." Then Stan remembered that he hadn't used the drencher that morning, and he invited Estrella to join him, and one thing led to another and they found themselves right back in bed again. After that Stan didn't think he had gone back to sleep again, but the next thing he knew he heard that soft, deep-down low-frequency rumble that meant there was something in the food dispenser. "Estrella?" he called.

It took a moment for her to show herself, coming in off the balcony and still brushing her hair. "What?" she asked.

"Did you order lunch?"

She frowned. "Well, I did say, out loud, that I was getting hungry."

Which led Stan to observe that, as a matter of fact, so was he. "Let's see what we've got," he said.

When they had punctured the bubble-covers, what they'd got was a total surprise to both. The smell of Estrella's meal identified itself even before Stan saw what it was: chili. Served in a bread bowl, with sides of guacamole and two kinds of salsa, with a dab of sour cream on top and a scattering of corn chips all around. "Real Texas-style chili," Estrella announced, as soon as she had had a taste.

Stan objected, "You weren't from Texas, were you?"

"I said Texas-style. The only style worth eating. I even think I can taste a little rattlesnake meat in it. But what've you got?"

Stan had already eaten two of his half-dozen slippery-looking green things, and was covetously eyeing the platter of some kind of a roast surrounded by vegetables. "Stuffed grape leaves," he announced. "Haven't had those since my last birthday, and the meat looks good. And, look—" pointing to a pouted copper pot, accompanied by a pair of tiny cups, "there's real Turkish coffee, too."

Estrella tasted a forkful of the perfectly prepared guacamole. "We should thank her," she said meditatively.

Stan had already moved on to the next course. "I think it's lamb," he said, tasting. "You know, I never had roast lamb before? Couldn't afford it."

Estrella didn't answer. After a moment of struggling with her notions of acceptable behavior, she gave up and licked the plate. They gazed at each other in rapture. "Things are definitely looking up," Stan told Estrella.

She nodded, but had a question. "Do you have any idea what's going on?"

"God knows. *I* don't. All I know is that's about the best meal I've had since—since—" He frowned, casting his mind back over the rations in their Five, the occasional splurge in Gateway's spindle, Mrs. Kusmeroglu's cooking way back in Istanbul. "Since ever," he finished. "Now how about we take another look at our daughter?"

Their daughter had to wait, while Estrella called Klara's home to thank her, or maybe Hypatia, but in any case whoever had provided that meal. Curiously, there was no answer.

When Stork had done its thing, Estrella took a good, long look at the baby and decided she hadn't changed much. Stan was less sure. "Is that an eye?" he demanded. "What's it doing on the side of her head? And what's that thing at the back of her head, right where it joins the neck? Some kind of wart?"

"Babies in the womb don't get warts. I think." She was on the little lookplate again.

Stan took his mind off the unborn child long enough to ask what she was looking at. She moved slightly so he could see the plate. "Our new neighbors," she said.

What the lookplate showed was a lanai very like their own. It looked out on the same valley and the same Mica Mountains beyond. Eight or ten inarguable humans, male and female, were sharing a meal on it, passing around oddly shaped ceramic dishes and small wicker baskets.

"They're Chinese or something," he pointed out. Estrella didn't dispute it. "Well, maybe we should visit them sometime. What's on the other plates?"

The answer to that was, not much, or, alternatively, far too much to take in. Stan watched the parade of strange-looking people doing unidentifiable things in unrecognized places. "Oh, hell," he grumbled at last. "I don't have a clue."

She was sympathetic. "Me, too." They left it at that. They both knew that the villain was that terrible ratio, 40,000 to 1. To compress forty thousand Outside hours into one one Core hour program meant that a lot—in fact, nearly everything—had to be left out.

"Well, hell," Stan said moodily. "I guess it doesn't matter. We're never going to go Outside again anyway."

They had another meal, very nearly as rapturous as the one before, and as Stan was gathering up the dishes to put in the waste the door growled at them. It was Salt, belly muscles nervously rippling under her gown. "Did not wish to interrupt your feeding," she said. "But all right to enter now?"

"Sure," Stan said, thinking that Salt was not looking her best. Her skin color seemed—well, not exactly right, though with a Heechee how could you tell?

Once inside she brightened. She sat down on the edge of an actual chair, her pod sticking awkwardly into air. She accepted a cup of tea and nibbled on the chocolate-covered biscuits the dispenser had included with the tea quite as though enjoying them. She gave the little sneeze that was the Heechee equivalent of clearing her throat, then began: "Have request to request of you. Human courtesy custom, however, requires I first ask of you what questions or requests you may have of me?"

"Well," Stan said, "actually we've been wondering if Klara is at home. We haven't spoken to her in quite a while—"

"Have not?" Salt asked politely. "Wish to verify?"

She didn't wait for an answer to that, but turned to the lookplates. A few soft-voiced commands to the small one—in one of the Heechee languages, of course—and it displayed an interior view of Klara's apartment. The view changed as they watched, as though the camera were hunting through the rooms. All the rooms were in order—bedroom and bathroom included—but there was no sign of either Klara or her shipmind.

"Quite sorry," Salt apologized. "Not present, as you have seen."

"And you don't have any idea of where she's gone?"

Salt's skull muscles twitched. "Any idea? But yes, have some idea, simply do not know if it is good idea. She spoke of persons called 'Old Ones,' now resident on One Moon Planet of Pale Yellow Star Fourteen. Perhaps has gone to see them."

Stan gave another of those dissatisfied grunts he was getting really good at, and Salt again politely sneezed. "May I at present time request request I spoke of?"

Stan shrugged. "Request on."

"Is perhaps excessive, this request," she said regretfully. "All the same wish to request it. Have greatly enjoyed peculiar 'musical' sounds produced by you, on balcony and elsewhere. Is possible you produce same sounds in other venue? That is, in place you term 'institution'? Doing same for entertainment and education of persons resident therein and nearby?"

Then, before either of them could answer, she rose. "Am aware, as stated, request possibly excessive. I will now depart, leaving time for you, and also you, Estrella, to consider before giving answer. But would be quite greatly appreciated."

When she was gone, Stan and Estrella looked at each other. "What do you think, Strell? Should we do it?"

She was frowning. "Did you see how Salt looked?"

Stan considered. "Well, maybe a little tired. . . ."

"Tired! You don't get that kind of skin color from just being tired, hon. I wonder if she's sick."

"Nah," said Stan, dismissing the question with the complete confidence of absolute ignorance on the subject of Heechee health. "So are we going to do it?"

"Well, why not? But if we are, first we're going to practice. Like now, hon."

It wasn't until that conversation was long over and Stan and Estrella were playing duets on their lanai that Estrella abruptly said, "Oh, my God," and put down her flute.

Stan took his lips away from the mouthpiece of his trumpet. "What's the matter?"

"Stan, I just thought. The way we were looking around Klara's apartment, you know? If we can see into other people's homes any time we want to, do you suppose they can—?"

He blinked at her. "What are you, crazy? Why would they want to look in at us?"

"But suppose they do?"

"They wouldn't!" he said doggedly.

III

Firmly though he had spoken, the question worried at Stan's thoughts until, three or four practice sessions later, Sigfrid von Shrink dropped in. When they put the question to him, it turned out that they not only would, they did. "Heechee have different standards of morality than we do," he told them. "They don't think sexual intercourse has to be private. With them it only happens when the female is in estrus, so it's comparatively infrequent, and sometimes they make a little ceremony out of it."

"Wait one damn minute," Estrella said with determination. "We're not Heechee! Can we turn those cameras off or not?"

"Of course you can, if that's what you want," he said. "They aren't exactly cameras, but I know what you mean. Wait a moment. All right, they're turned off now."

"As easily as that?" Stan demanded.

"Of course. Why not? But you know you'll be depriving your friends of some entertainment."

"They can damn well *stay* deprived!" Stan said hotly. "We don't make love to entertain them!"

"Not just the making love, Stan. The music practice. The eating. Everything you do, really. Still, I suppose they'll understand if you don't want them watching you, I think. Anyway," he said, forcibly changing the subject, "they've enjoyed listening to you two practicing—well, perhaps 'enjoyed' isn't the right word, because Heechee ideas of music aren't at all like our own, but they found it interesting. So what about what Salt asked you? Would you mind going down to do it at the—ah—institution?"

"Well, sure," Stan said. "We never said we wouldn't."

In the event, their recital was a great success. That is, no one walked out. No one hissed, either, except to the extent that Heechee sometimes did hiss when speaking the language of Do. They performed the Bach transcriptions that Estrella had made up for them, based on duets she had learned in her one scant year at the conservatory; they did some Gershwin and Jelly Roll Morton and a few extracts from Mahler, and when they were through, four or five of the several dozen Heechee in the room politely clapped their hands as they had learned to do in their days Outside. Even the greater number of Heechee who had never been Outside tried to emulate them, though not very successfully. Skinny Heechee palms were not meant for applauding.

Then the little platform the Heechee had provided for them sank back into the floor. They were quickly surrounded by a dozen or more Heechee, Salt leading a pair of elderly males to meet them, Yellow Jade by her side with hand outstretched to shake Stan's hand. "You performed with much excellence," he told them both. "Therefore you were greatly enjoyed by the public as well as by myself and"—he gestured at the two ancients by Salt's side—"my two sons, name of Warm, this one, and Ionic Solvent, this other. Have lately returned from prolonged period Outside. Unfortunately do not speak your language but ask me express pleasure at meeting."

"Delighted," Stan said unconvincingly. "Well, Strell, don't you think we ought to be going?" And then, all the way home after the event, Stan and Estrella were complaining about the bizarre approximations of human food their Heechee hosts, eager to please but imperfectly informed, had laid out for them. About the shocking state of Salt's complexion. And about trying to reconstruct the story of Yellow Jade's astonishing two sons, now old and near enough to death to have come back to the Core to die, and thus enter the Stored Minds. And about the fact that neither of them spoke English, because their seventy-some years of service had been spent on the Jen Hao planet, where English was spoken only by visitors. About the fact that they were triple the age of their father, because Yellow Jade had left them Outside when he returned to the Core. And, anyway, where was Sigfrid?

"He probably had something else to do?" Estrella offered.

"What difference does that make? He's an AI. He's always doing fourteen or fifteen things at once." And then, as they made the last turn before their doorway, "He should've been there." And then their door came in sight and he was.

Sigfrid took his usual immaterial seat, accepted his simulated glass of wine to keep them company, and said, "I really enjoyed the Bach chaconne. I've heard it before, but never better."

Stan looked suspicious. "I didn't see you."

"I didn't show myself, Stan. I didn't want to disturb anyone, but I wouldn't have missed the event. Anyway, the reason I'm here is that I wanted to invite you to a little gathering at Klara's."

"She's back?"

"She will be soon indeed, Estrella. She's very fond of you, you know."

Estrella ventured, "Salt said she went to look at those australo—whatever-you-call-them things."

"Yes, that is true," von Shrink conceded. "There is some concern about them. She went to see if she could help." And, when Stan demanded to know more about those "concerns," Sigfrid only shook his head. "It is nothing that need trouble you. Only some suspicion that the previous owner of the hominids may be planning something unwise. You've heard of him? Wan Santos-Smith? A very unpleasant man, and it seems that some of his people were seen snooping around the Old Ones."

He shook his head and repeated, "No doubt Klara will tell you all about it when she returns. Is there anything else?"

Stan debated pressing the issue, decided the chances of getting satisfaction were too slim to pursue and changed the subject. "I noticed Achiever wasn't there either."

"Ah," von Shrink said regretfully, "Achiever. No, he isn't in a position to attend a performance just now. It's a sad story." He looked from one to the other of them, uncharacteristically indecisive. Then he added inquiringly, "I didn't know whether or not you would want to be kept informed—"

"We would," Estrella said briefly.

Von Shrink's simulation sighed and nodded. "I supposed that would be so," he said. "Once you've shared the Dream Machine with someone there's always a kind of bond, isn't there? Anyway, your experience with Achiever had a profound effect on him. As a result, at present he is being nurtured by a group of Stored Minds. That's what they call it, nurturing. It means that he is temporarily placed in storage himself, and the other Stored Minds try to complete his healing. They started that as soon as they learned what was at the basis of his problem—"

He stopped there, apparently willing to let it drop at that point. Estrella wasn't. "Which was?" she demanded. "Come on, Dr. von Shrink. Seeing as I was involved, I have a right to know!"

"I suppose you do, Estrella. It's rather nasty—"

"Tell!" Stan barked.

He sighed again. "Well, when Achiever left the Core, he happened to be in the company of a nubile Heechee female named Breeze. She began to come into estrus as the flight proceeded. Achiever's body reacted to that, of course; any male Heechee's would have. But then at the last moment he was dropped off on Gateway, with no suitable female to be found anywhere. And—" he lowered his voice, though it was no longer possible for anyone to be listening— "he did something quite traumatic. He attempted intercourse with a female human."

"He committed *rape*?" Estrella said, unbelieving.

"No, not rape," von Shrink corrected at once. "Not quite actual sexual intercourse at all. If that had happened, I expect Achiever wouldn't have been able to live with himself. But he did attempt some, well, foreplay. He thinks the human female was at fault, and in a sense perhaps she was. It appears that she had done very poorly as a Gateway prospector. In fact, she had gone broke. So, in order to pay her bills on the asteroid, she resorted to, well, prostitution."

"My God!" Estrella said. "With a *Heechee*?"

Von Shrink nodded gravely. "That accounts for some of the things you felt when you shared a Dream Couch with him. It wasn't you he hated. It was that poor woman on Gateway. But you were handy."

And as soon as he was gone Estrella sat before one of the lookplates. Stan was wandering idly toward the lanai when she called him back. "Stan? Are these the old things Dr. von Shrink was talking about?"

He strolled around to where he could see into the lookplate. What it displayed was a pair of odd-looking creatures, manlike to a degree, apelike almost as much. They wore rough-knit kilts and not much else, and they both sported thin, unkempt beards. They were eating some kind of fruits and jabbering to each other in a language Stan had never heard before.

As he and Estrella stared at them, Stan shook his head. "Do you think they're people?"

"Do they look like people to you?"

"No, but—Hey!" He snapped his fingers. "They came from where Wan was, way back when he was the crazy kid that was using the Dream Machine way back when—"

"I remember. The Wrath of God, they called it."

"Right. Wan's doing. That's what the Old Ones were, some kind of prehistoric humans that the Heechee had put out there for some reason or other. I guess he thinks he owns them."

"Huh." Estrella examined the shaggy ones on the screen, then emitted a small scream. Their feeding over, the smaller of the two creatures—beard or none, evidently the female—had dropped to hands and knees, while the larger, definitely and now quite conspicuously the male, was preparing to enter her from behind.

"Hey," said Stan, amused. "They're really going at it, aren't they."

Estrella turned the lookplate off. "Fair's fair, Stan. We didn't want people looking at us when we were making love, did we? So we shouldn't watch them."

"But they're animals, Strell! And it's interesting, kind of."

She shook her head, firmly indicating that the subject was closed. "I've got a better idea. Let's get some of that good food, right? What I'm thinking of is, let's see, a thick, juicy, rare steak—beef, not buffalo—and some of those fries and a salad with maybe a little avocado cut up in it—"

"Make it two," Stan said, his expression lightening. "And make it fast, will you please?" And then they sat back to wait.

But it wasn't made fast.

In fact, for quite a while, half an hour or so at the least, it wasn't made at all, although both Stan and Estrella repeated their orders several times. When at last they did hear the remote rumble that told them something had arrived, Stan snapped, "About damn time!" and Estrella beat him to the dispenser.

What was waiting for them did not come under any of those crystalline dones, nor did it look at all like the steaks they had envisioned. It was two packets in the colored wrappings of Heechee food. When, incredulously, they opened them up they discovered that they weren't Heechee food—weren't even as good as Heechee food! They were bricks of something brownish and tough that smelled vaguely of clam beds and tasted like not very good pemmican. "What the *hell*?" Stan exclaimed. "What's going on here?"

But Estrella had no answer for him, and after tasting a crumb of her own bar was as irritated as he. "If this is what they're feeding pregnant women I'm going to go down to the lake and catch a couple of those ugly little fish and fry them up."

IV

She didn't do that. She ate those horrid messes, and ate all the other horrid messes the dispenser kept giving them in lieu of real food. They had no one to complain to, either. Sigfrid didn't come back. In spite of what he had said, Klara hadn't returned, either. Yellow Jade was so wrapped up in his senile sons that he didn't show up at all, and the one time they did catch a glimpse of Salt she was impenetrably surrounded by a crush of male Heechee. "They don't seem to care what she looks like," Estrella sniffed.

"She has certainly let herself go," Stan agreed. "Want to see if we can catch some news?"

They could. They did, but took very little joy from it. The brainless, but good-looking, newscaster they had seen before was long gone. No one had really replaced him. The lookplate simply displayed views of whatever they requested, and most of the views were unpleasing. Stan had seen some shots of fascinating-looking floating cities, but when he found them again they were in various stages of disrepair. Whole planets seemed to be abandoned—forested where there had been skyscrapers, burned out, iced over. "Remember the pictures they had in the Gateway museum?" Stan asked. "Those were the kind of things the Foe did, but the Foe aren't still doing them, are they?" Estrella only shook her head sadly, without answering.

Then Stan asked for, and got, a look at Istanbul. It too seemed nearly deserted. The Kemal Ataturk Towers were still standing, but apparently vacant—glass broken out of the windows, no sign of people going in or out. "Jesus," Stan said. "What do you think happened?"

"I wish I knew," Estrella said, and then changed her mind. "No, maybe I'm better off if I don't know. Let's do something else. How about another look at the kid?"

That, at least, was always rewarding. Every day the tiny creature in Estrella's belly showed new things to marvel at. Those eye things that had seemed to be growing out of the baby's temples were slowly migrating toward the front of her head, where they belonged. Her skin had become so thin that Estrella swore she could see the blood vessels beneath it. (Stan was less sure.) And then one day, while Estrella was back at her lookplates while Stan was studying Stork's display, she jumped. Stan was yelling at her. "Strell! Guess what the hell what! She's sucking her thumb!"

And so, Estrella agreed, she was. Not only that. Day by day the baby's head turned from side to side, her legs flexed and extended, the little arms and hands experimenting with new positions—folded over the little chest, clasped prayer-like before the face, stretched almost straight at the sides. It was a magical slide show, always changing.

When they took time from the contemplation of their unborn, there was plenty to interest them in the lookplates—mostly incomprehensible, yes, but provocative. When they saw a procession of hooded children marching steadfastly into the shallows, and then the deeps, of some ocean, somewhere in the outside galaxy, they could only wonder what was going on. When the lookplate flared with appalling light as some star, also some unknown where, seemed to destroy itself in an eruption of flame they could only admire the spectacle, with no clue of what it meant.

Not counting the food, Stan and Estrella were almost content to be ignored by their friends. Sex was great sport again, now practiced in private. The food, they told each other, really wasn't much worse than they had had in their old Five. The lanai was as lush as ever. . . .

All the same, when their door growled for the first time in days, they both hurried to open it.

The caller wasn't any of their first choices. It was Achiever. Without preamble he asked, "Have asked on earlier occasion if you had been asked. Now I ask again. Well? What is your answer?"

"Oh, hell," Stan said. "I don't have any idea what you're talking about. Answer to what?"

The muscles under Achiever's cheekbones were twitching madly. "How can you ask me answer to what? Have recently experienced significant event, somewhat pleasurable but very tiring, have retained little patience. Is it possible you have not yet been asked?"

"Asked what?" Stan demanded, now well on the way to becoming belligerent. But so was Achiever. He stomped a few steps away from the door, the fur at the back of his neck erect with anger, then stepped back. "This is not to any degree acceptable!" he shouted. "I am greatly enraged. Therefore I shut you off without customary convention of good-bye!" And he turned on his narrow heel and stomped away.

Estrella and Stan were in their bedroom, no longer fully dressed and no more than half-heartedly picking at their latest consignment of the marginally edible, not talking much, really, about Achiever because what was there still to say about that volatile and unlikeable Heechee?—when the door growled and the visitor turned out to be Salt, looking somehow radiant and in no respect purple. "Possibly can come in?" she asked, and took their silence as affirmative.

"Oh, absolutely," Stan assured her, a little tardily—she was already perched in their living room and looking expectantly from one to the other of them. "You have been speaking with Achiever," she told them. "I know this because he so informed me. It is partly relevant to him that I come to see you."

Stan pulled the robe he had grabbed up tighter around him. "Is anything wrong?"

"Nothing is in the least wrong of any description," Salt said, the tone of her voice sounding as though that were true. If she had been human, Stan would have said she was beaming. "Quite in actuality contrariwise. First must apologize to you for did not invite you to ceremony. Reason for this: other party and I well aware of your cultural modesty tabus."

"What ceremony?" Stan asked, baffled.

Estrella was quicker on the uptake. "What are you saying? Are you actually—have you been—"

"Have exactly been, yes," Salt confirmed delightedly. "And also have exactly done, with use of Achiever as fertilizing person. Am therefore quite knocked up, I say in particular to Estrella, just like you!"

15

Happiness

I

For Stan, one pregnant woman had been interesting, even (since it was his own baby she was pregnant with) absorbing. Two weren't twice as good. They weren't even half as good. Suddenly it was Salt, not Stan, that Estrella reported every twinge or queasiness to. Not only that; one day Salt spoke a few sentences in her own languages to Stork, and from then on, on demand, it displayed the contents of either's womb.

To a degree that was interesting enough to Stan. Heechee biology was not the same as human. Heechee owned a pair of hearts apiece, Stan knew, as well as heaven knew what other bizarre kinds of internal plumbing. All the same, there were basic architectural plans in common. For both species, a single egg, once fertilized, multiplied to become many, and then the baby was born. For Stan, observing how Salt's early cells divided and took new shapes sort of filled in what his own daughter must have looked like before Stork came along. Salt's embryo, of course, was tiny—indeed nearly invisible, until Stork was ordered to magnify it for them. And it wasn't much to look at even then, either, especially when compared with the far more advanced little being in Estrella's belly.

All the same, Stan had more time to himself these days. So when Yellow Jade showed up, a tottering son on either side, Stan was glad to accept his offer to help them know their neighbors. The son named Warm spoke

Mandarin and Vietnamese, the one named Ionic Solvent Korean and Japanese, but neither English. So when they did visit the newcomers conversation was a challenging task.

The new neighbors were housed well. The room they were received in was larger than any in Stan and Estrella's flat, and it was pretty full—eighteen or twenty of the neighbors, mostly elderly, separated into half a dozen clutches of the various ethnicities. When, say, the plump little woman who spoke for the Koreans wanted to wish Estrella a healthy, happy and an easy birth, the appropriate brother translated it into Heechee. Then the other made it into his own languages, one after another, while Yellow Jade was rendering it into English for Stan and Estrella and, simultaneously, the first brother was translating it into his second language, so there was a constant buzz of multilingual translation going on all the time.

It was not an efficient way of communicating. All the same, Stan enjoyed it tolerably well, and even more enjoyed the food. A two-meter lazy Susan rotated before them, constantly replenished from the dispenser with new dishes, hot and cold, sour and sweet. They were almost as puzzling to Stan and Estrella as their former Heechee CHON-food rations. But human. And, often enough, delicious.

It made the sorry messes the dispenser had been giving them even more repellent. Later on, when Salt dropped in, they were mournfully forcing down another helping of the current muck.

Salt was apologetic about intruding. "Did not perceive you both feeding before entering in your house. Please continue to feed. Will absent self in other regions of this home." And then, when they had swallowed as much as they could, she returned. "Have observed tooth-cleaning growth in washing place," she told them. "Is better thing now. Growth no longer in use. Have imported formula for, plus directions for preparation of, new preparation of, how would one call it, soup of edible microorganisms. Very latest thing from Outside. Does cleaning, oiling, desmelling teeth all at one time, very efficient." Then, as she came close enough to get a good look at the remains of their meal, she stopped short. She hesitated a moment, then said politely, "Have question, not intending make criticism. Question is: is possible these foodstuffs enjoyable to you?"

Stan gave her an unamused grunt. "No. It isn't possible. It's just all we have."

"What, have not possessed even appropriate communicating with chef service? But explain this," Salt demanded. And when they did explain she sniffed. "I deal with for you," she said, stood up and addressed the air with a few emphatic Heechee sentences.

Her explanation of what she had done took longer. When they closed their home off to the rest of the world, it had meant that no one could call and, among other things, that the food service couldn't learn their desires. They had marooned themselves.

But now, she said, they could have their privacy when they wanted it—"Simply to saying when desired 'Privacy now!' and, when not, 'No longer requiring privacy' and such will be accomplished." But actually Stan and Estrella hardly heard the explanations, because they had already told the air they wanted lunch, and were listening eagerly for a response.

And the very next day Hypatia of Alexandria popped crossly into their flat. "You two," she said frostily. "Klara's been trying to call you, but you'd cut yourself off. Anyway, she would like you to come and visit her. There are some people she'd like you to meet."

"People?" Stan asked, but Estrella only asked, "When?" It was Estrella she chose to answer. "Now. Whenever you want to get over there."

When they arrived it was Hypatia again who let them in. Without preamble she ordered, "Stand still for one moment, please, Estrella." For that moment she seemed to be looking at nothing at all, then nodded toward Klara's abdomen. "I took the liberty of an internal examination. It is a beautiful fetus. Now please sit down. Klara is dressing for her company."

Estrella picked up on that. "Will Salt be here?"

"I doubt that a lot," Hypatia said, her tone even frostier than her look.

Estrella was puzzled. "What's the matter, Hypatia? Don't you approve of Salt getting pregnant?"

Hypatia, on the point of leaving the room, turned with a flounce of her colorful robes. "I don't disapprove of pregnancy. It's the original, and at one time it was the only, way of bringing more female children into the world. So it's an acceptable evil. What's disgusting is the way Salt chose to do it. She had physical sexual intercourse with a male! At this time in the history of scientific progress! In my original time women accepted that because, although very distasteful, it was also unavoidable. But now there are plenty of parthenogenetic ways to get pregnant. She chose that one!" She made the kind of grunt usually written as "ugh," and then said, "Here's Klara."

Whoever the people were that Klara was expecting, they had to be important. Stan had not expected to see her looking so—well—dressed up. Her hair was perfectly coiffed. Her gown was low-cut, gold-colored silk. Even those eyebrows seemed somehow tamed. Her elegance, however, didn't prevent her from giving Stan a pat on the head in passing and Estrella a full-fledged hug. Then she held Estrella at arm's length for a critical inspection. "All right," she said, "you're looking healthy enough, but what about the baby? Can I see her?"

Of course she could; Stork summoned the image up at once. Of course she got a commentary from the proud parents, too, mostly the prospective father. "If she looks like she needs a shave," he told her, "that's what they call lanugo hair. It falls off. And—can you see?—she's getting nails on her fingers and toes."

When every viewable organ had been discussed, Klara sighed and sank back into a chair. "You're very lucky people," she informed them. "Salt, too. I've told her so. Hypatia has some criticisms"—she threw a glance at her shipmind, now dispassionately lounging on a chaise across the room—"but I'm just thrilled. I hope she and Achiever had a good time making it. Poor bastards, it doesn't happen all that often for them. You noticed Salt turning purple? That's the signal she's coming into heat. Either the sight of the color change, or maybe some kind of pheromones, turns every nearby male into a lovesick suitor. Some ways it's great to be a girl among the Heechee. They always have a bunch of males hanging around when they make their choice."

"So then," Estrella asked, "why in the world did she pick Achiever?"

"Who knows? Sigfrid thinks the Stored Minds might have suggested it, to help Achiever in his cure." She glanced at the clock. "The others'll be here in a moment, but they won't stay long. Dealing with us organics is a real strain for them—oh, didn't I tell you? They're all machine-stored. Anyway, have a drink while we wait. Hypatia will get whatever you like."

And then, while Hypatia's servers were bringing an iced tea for Estrella and a dark German beer for Stan, the doorbell rang.

A doorbell it really was not—it was a quick carillon peal of chimes, custom-installed for Klara—but it was a long way from the usual Heechee growl. Hypatia was already at the door. She didn't touch it, of course; but it opened and Sigrid von Shrink came in. "Am I the first?" he asked— unconvincingly, Stan thought, because von Shrink certainly knew that already. "Well, they'll be here in a moment—ah, here they come now!"

One after another, pop, pop—but the pops were quite soundless— three persons appeared in Klara's drawing room. Two were elderly Heechee, both curiously seated on chairs rather than Heechee perch because they lacked the usual between-the-legs Heechee pod. The remaining one was a tall, powerful-looking human male in a floppy white hat. "Glad you could make it," Sigfrid said affably to the new arrivals, and then, to Klara, "These are the people I wanted you to meet. Thermocline, he sort of represents the Stored Minds for us. Burnish; he was the one who aban—who, I mean, was required to leave Achiever on Gateway. Now as a Stored Mind in the Core he has become an expert in stellar dynamics. And this is Marc Antony, who does all the cooking." Then, gesturing to complete the introductions, "And this is Gelle-Klara Moynlin, and these our young friends Stan Avery and Estrella Pancorbo. Now, if Hypatia will just bring in her servers, Marc has been kind enough to prepare a light collation for us as we talk."

Stan had never doubted that Klara was an extremely high-ranked person, but until now he hadn't known just how high-ranked she was. High-ranked enough that stored persons who, presumably, were not impressed by the wealth or fame of organics would take time to come to her home for a chat. But there they were.

Stan was almost equally impressed by the fact that the food was good. The "light collation" was not only tasty but not all that light. There was a pot of delicately tender meatballs, little crackers that held a slice each of duck liver and of a crunchy vegetable that Klara kindly identified as Chinese water chestnuts, nutlike things in a sort of fruity sauce that even Klara couldn't put a name to, but ate as fast as she could. Which is what pretty much everybody was doing with pretty much everything that they were served. Stan was puzzled to note that the electronic persons were apparently eating the same sorts of foods as themselves until, unthinking, he reached for one of Burnish's hors d'oeuvres. His fingers passed clear through it, and the man in the floppy white hat turned away from a conversation to give him a small smile. "Simulations eat simulated food, of course," he said, and then the smile dwindled. "Oh," he said. "You're the person who turned off access to his home, I believe."

Stan could not see why that concerned the man, but he said, "I guess," his mouth full of barbecued morsels of what might have been chicken. Then he remembered the man's name. "You're, uh, Marc Antony, right? So I guess you made all this stuff?" And, when the man nodded, couldn't help saying with enthusiasm, "It's the best food I ever had in my life!"

"I see," said the chef. Then, a moment later, "Try the candied peacock's tongues. They're a specialty."

Stan did try them, though he regretted it pretty fast. Once, in Istanbul long ago, one of Mr. Ozden's girls had given him a sugar-coated caterpillar as a joke. This was very like it, and had very nearly the same effect. Only two things kept Stan from instantly throwing it up. One was the reflection that the "peacock" whose tongue he had swallowed had never lived, since that dish was constructed out of the same CHON-food as everything else in his diet. The other was the distraction of the animated conversations going on around him.

The main thing that was on the mind of the old Heechee, Thermocline, was the growing immigration problem. Humans were flooding into the Core by the hundreds of thousands, and where were the Heechee supposed to put them all? Marc Antony's burning question was security—individual human security. "Human beings aren't like Heechee. Some of them fight. Some of them steal, and kill, and rape. We're going to need police, and courts, and laws, and some kind of legislatures to pass those laws." Sigfrid von Shrink's main concern was how to supply all those immigrants with the kind of human-oriented things that were only obtainable Outside—and how to pay for them.

At which point everyone paused and looked expectantly at Klara.

She grinned, a little ruefully, as though she had been expecting no less. "Well, why not?" she said. "Sigfrid has been hinting around, and he's right. Hypatia?"

The shipmind made herself visible at once. She seemed to have redressed herself for the company. The robes were even more ornate, the finger rings of huge, uncut rubies and sapphires. She looked toward Klara. "Boss, you called me?"

Klara sighed but forbore to mention that there was no doubt in her mind that Hypatia had been present, if not visible, all along. "I'm thinking that we haven't talked much about my money lately. Do I still have any?"

"Oh, quite a lot, actually. You know most of the things you were invested in while we were still Outside have kind of evaporated—it's been a long time there. But you got in on a lot of good ones. Like all those Here Afters that are still really pulling in the bucks, and your fleets of spaceships, with all the factories and landing places that go with them; they're doing well, too."

"Fine," Klara said, and dismissed her. "That's all right, then. I'd like to keep a few million for myself, just in case something comes up, but I don't really have much use for all that much money. After all, I don't think I'd be likely to going Outside again."

"Great," said Sigfrid, beaming. "We'll do that. And if Klara's money isn't enough to do the job, why, we can start thinking about something like taxes."

That was nearly the end of the party, as far as decision making was concerned. A moment later Burnish and Thermocline made their excuses and popped out of sight—"to conform these proposals with the will of the Stored Minds," they said—followed by Marc Antony. Sigfrid, however, made no move to leave. He turned toward Stan and Estrella. "Let's talk," he said. "What did you think?"

Stan frowned. "About what just happened? What I think is that we pretty much didn't belong here. What do I know about economics and legislation and all that?"

Sigfrid took the question at face valune. "About, I would say, as much as most organic humans do when they're seventeen."

"Almost eighteen," Stan pointed out immediately, but Estrella overrode him.

"I'm twenty-four, Sigfrid," she said, "and I don't know that much, either. Slaughterhouse people didn't go to college."

"True," Sigfrid acknowledged. "You're not in the slaughterhouse anymore, though, are you?"

"I don't see any college campuses around here."

"You don't need a campus, Estrella. All you need is teaching. That can be arranged."

"You mean there are teachers in the Core?"

"Quite a few. More important there are teaching programs on basically every subject you can imagine. Are you interested?"

"I guess so," Stan said, not sounding entirely convinced.

"I'll see you get information," Sigfrid promised. He stood up. "Oh," he added, looking mildly embarrassed. "There's one other thing. I'd like to ask you for a favor."

Stan's guard didn't go up at once. Then he remembered the strange conversation with Achiever and, suddenly suspicious, asked, "Does it have anything to do with that crazy Heechee?"

"It does," von Shrink admitted. "You know, you two have really been a great help with him already. Now I'd like to ask you to do something more." He raised his hand to ward off refusal. "I know how you feel, especially you, Estrella. But you're the only human being he really knows, through the dream machine."

Estrella was already violently shaking her head. "He hates me, Doctor!"

"He did, yes. To a degree he still does. But we want to get him over that, and you can help."

Stan frowned. "What do you want us to do, exactly?"

"Just spend some time with him. Well, quite a lot of time, actually; it would mean seeing him every day for a few weeks—"

"Weeks!" Estrella's voice was shaking. "You don't know what it's like.

Remember, I know what rotten feelings he has. I know what he thinks. And I hate it!"

"Yes," von Shrink conceded. "Still—well, I won't press it now. But will you think it over, please?"

They did think it over, quite a lot, and even talked it over, even more. Estrella said the idea just made her whole body quiver.

"Of course," Stan said thoughtfully, "it wouldn't hurt for us to do Sigfrid a favor when he asks for it."

"Please, not that favor. Maybe some other time, but not now, not when I'm just getting used to being happy!"

Which effectively terminated that conversation for Stan. And in bed that night, holding with his hand the hand Estrella had thrown across his chest, Stan was thinking thoughts that seventeen-year-olds seldom think.

They had to do with happiness.

He was thinking about his own situation. Most seventeen-year-olds, he told himself, would not really be very pleased about being lumbered with the care of a child.

But was he?

Surprisingly, the answer seemed to be that he was. In fact, he was, as far as he could tell, quite—well—yes, actually quite frequently and reliably happy.

That was a wholly new feeling for Stan. He could not remember a time since his mother's death when he had felt happiness for more than a few minutes at a time.

But there it was.

II

The sessions with Stork were as fascinating as ever, the glimpses the lookplates gave them of the galaxy Outside were as titillating—though less and less understandable. Even, for both of them, the pleasure of schooling as great.

If Sigfrid von Shrink wanted them educated, Estrella and Stan agreed, they weren't going to say no, even though school wasn't exactly what they had expected. No classroom. No fellow students. No teacher, exactly—not what either of them had meant by the word teacher, anyway. What they got was a cheerful, elderly man—a simulation, of course—who wore a toga and began their first session by saying matter-of-factly, "We're going to talk about economics. What do you think about money? What's the point of having it in the first place?" And when Estrella guessed, "to buy things," and Stan ventured, "so we can get paid for our work," the old fellow smiled and nodded, and asked them why that was better than barter, say, or, come to that, just letting everybody produce what they wanted to produce and take what they wanted to take from the world's general store.

By the time the session was over they had got to the Dutch tulip craze of the seventeenth century, the Great Depressions of the twentieth and twenty-first and half a dozen other financial disasters. Then the teacher pretended to yawn. He glanced at the imaginary watch on his imaginary wrist and said, "That should do it for now. I've tinkered a bit with your lookplates. They'll display more on any subject you like; just say the name of it, and keep going until you've got what you want. Next time, let's talk about history. Till then—" And, nodding a courteous good-bye, he disappeared. His name, he said, was Socrates.

Sure enough, the lookplates did as he promised. When they said "gold standard," the lookplates displayed all kinds of things, from Roman coins clipped to the size of pharmacy pills to bearded, weary men doggedly sluicing wet sand in the Gold Rush of 1849.

When they told Klara about it, she demanded to see some of those things for herself. Hypatia made it happen. They watched empires rise and fall, wars depopulate whole nations. Klara began looking less and less pleased with the plate, as the wars began to multiply. Then, without saying a word, she abruptly left the room and did not return.

Hypatia remained, watching them silently as she lounged on a couch. Stan turned to her. "What's the matter?" he asked.

The shipmind gave a sinuous shrug. "Klara doesn't like wars." She seemed about to leave it at that, then reconsidered. "Have you ever heard of the Crabbers? I suppose not. They were a nonhuman race from the old times that were wiping themselves out with wars when their star went nova and finished the job for them. They were horrid people, a lot like those old monks that murdered the original me. And then, just as she was showing signs of handling that, along came that big tsunami."

"Right," Stan said, pleased to remember. "The one that messed California up."

Hypatia set him straight. "The one that destroyed a lot of places. One of those was Klara's private island."

It was Estrella's turn to remember. "She had some orphans living there, right?"

"She provided a home for a number of children who didn't have one, yes. But that isn't all. Maybe you don't know that Klara really wanted to have a child of her own body. She had ova stored on her island, hoping to find the right man to fertilize them. She didn't. The ova were destroyed with the island." She paused, looking at Estrella. "I think that's why she's so thrilled about your child."

"Oh, hell," Stan said. "That poor woman."

"She is, isn't she?" Estrella said thoughtfully. "For all her money. Poor indeed, in the sense that you and I, Stan, are so very rich."

When they least expected it the door announced a visitor, and it was Achiever. "Have been away," he informed them. "Now am returned. Wish urgent talking with you."

Surprised but endeavoring to be hospitable, Stan showed him to a Heechee perch, offered him a coffee (refused) and asked after his new family. Unexpectedly, that seemed to upset Achiever. "I do not have 'family,'" he said frostily. "'Family' requires declaration of commonality. I have made no such declaration." Then he unbent a fraction. "Unborn child of my parentage in generative space of Salt, however, is excellently well. When birth occurs his-or-her name will be Boundary Condition. Gender? Unknown. Baby has not yet decided."

Doggedly polite, Estrella tried: "And yourself, Achiever? Are you well, too?"

Achiever mulled that over for a moment. "Well? Perhaps not. Not truly well, that is to say, but—" he flapped his long, skinny fingers at them "—what is one to do? One has been, as you say, scarred. By enforced and prolonged exposure to others of your race, that is. So would not say that word 'well' is appropriate. To be well would need—what is your word again?—more of concinnity than is possessed at this time. On the other hand"—he frowned reproof—"am not here for talk of this sort but to discuss coming with me of you two in accord with known wishes of human machine-intelligence person Sigfrid von Shrink."

Stan and Estrella exchanged looks. "What do you know about that?" Stan demanded.

"Not a large amount. Nearly everything, however. For example, is known to me that aforesaid artificial intelligence person wishes it quite much. Also that you two organic human persons feel obligation to same. Is any statement herein incorrect?"

"Not really," Stan admitted.

"Then is proper, is this not correct?, for you two to accede to said wishes and accompany me on spaceflight to permit mutual presence, as advocated by person hereinabove. Wait. Do not reply. Consider also fact that I fortunately now have excellent spacecraft at my disposal for said purpose."

"Hold it right there," Stan commanded, patience all expended. "Sigfrid didn't say a word about going on a spaceship. He just said he'd like us to spend time with you."

Achiever gave him an approximation of a supercilious smile. "And what better spending of joint time can be imagined than the becoming of shipmates? Especially utilizing spacecraft I have just returned from familiarizing self in? Now attend to proposal. If you join me in aforesaid craft, I will then transport you to splendid selection of interesting Core planets, each of which happens to contain specimens of your people. Are beyond numbering planets worthy of visit. Include Chilly Wet Planet of Blue-White Star Fifty-Four. To this place mother of self, who was Food Factory designer, brought me as young person. Extremely of interest."

"Extremely cold, too," Stan offered.

"Well then! Are many, many of others, some of quite high temperatures indeed. Do you understand what I speak of? Then I ask, considering all facts, notably those involving express desire of said Sigfrid von Shrink, will you accordingly agree to travel in my company for period of some days or weeks?"

He gave them one final penetrating look, and was gone.

Over the next day or two Stan and Estrella conversed on many subjects—their unborn child's development, Estrella's new traits of swollen feet and of a kind of snoring that no longer was really gentle, Salt's pregnancy, Socrates's lesson plans, Marc Antony's delicious food and (but not in that order) Achiever's invitation. That last subject would easily have made top billing, except that Stan was doing his best to avoid it. His preferred response was usually something along the lines of, "Come on, Strell, give it a rest. I need time to think about it." But however much time Estrella gave him for thinking he never seemed to have thought it through. Finally she gave up and, exasperated, sat Stan down at one end of the lanai, herself between him and the door to prevent escape, and said, "Hon, pee or get off the slot. Are we going or aren't we?" She didn't give him a chance to complain that he hadn't really had time to make up his mind. "It's not a hard question, Stan. You just say yes or no. Which?" And, when he still didn't answer, "Here's the thing. We really can't refuse Sigfrid a favor. And I'm feeling pretty good right now—good enough that I can stand the idea of being around Achiever for a while, and I'd kind of like to see those other planets—and feeling good isn't going to last. So the way I see it, either we do it now or we don't do it for a really long time. So what do you say?"

He looked doubtful. "If you're sure?"

"I'm sure."

"Well. . . ." he said. And then, not just then, exactly, in fact not for another two days, he said, "All right. I guess we might as well."

16

Working for Wan

I

At one split second in time Orbis McClune, or whatever was left of Orbis McClune, discovered that he no longer belonged to himself. He had become the property of that unpleasant lunatic, Wan Santos-Smith. Then—not after a moment, not separated by any time at all but immediately, seamlessly at once—his whole environment had inexplicably changed.

Wan wasn't there anymore. Now Orbis was in a two-window office with paintings on the walls, deep-pile carpet underfoot and a highly improbable vista of giant redwood trees showing through those make-believe windows. Instead of Wan, Orbis was with a harried-seeming, but quite attractive, young woman. You might even have said she was beautiful, if you liked that sort of heavily made-up look. She sat behind an apparently mahogany desk that held a data screen, a nameplate that said "Roz Borraly" and a vase with a single red rose. She was frowning at Orbis.

"It says your name is Orbis McClune and you're a Rev," she said, glancing at something in the air above him. "What's this Rev shit?"

Reprimanding her didn't seem worthwhile. He said only, "It means I'm a minister of the gospel."

"Huh," she said, looking displeased. "Well, what you got to do now, Mister Minister of the Gospel, is learn some stuff so you'll be useful to

Wan when he gets ready to take care of those guys. You ever run a space-ship?"

"What 'guys' are you talking about?" Orbis asked, and quickly regret-ted it. The woman named Roz Borraly sighed, and moved no more than a finger. In a moment Orbis McClune was writhing under the very worst pain he had ever known: heat like incandescent ice that was flogging across his back, face, eyes and testicles, striking him at every point on his body—on his purely simulated but evidently quite hurtable body—where there was a pain nerve to feel it. Then it was over.

"See," she said conversationally, "the way it works around here, I do the asking, you do the answering. Did you?"

It took a moment for Orbis to collect himself enough to remember what she had asked. "Run a spaceship?" he managed to say, still gasping. "No. Never."

"At least you played spacewar games when you were a kid, though? Right?" When he shook his head she gave another sigh. "So tell me what it is that you can do—like, where'd you go to school?"

He answered her question, warily leaving nothing out. As he got from high school (no, he hadn't played any sports) through his two years in the community college (liberal arts, with a little history and one semester of introductory psychology) her face grew grimmer and grimmer. By the time he was describing his four years in the seminary she waved him to silence. "Christ," she said dismally, "what are we supposed to do with geeks like you?" She studied the notes on her screen without hope for a moment, then asked, "But you're from Illinois. What were you doing in California?"

He said promptly, "I was doing the Lord's business! To tell sinners how they have offended Him. To reprove them for mixing with those in-struments of the Antichrist, the Heechee. To teach them why they were singled out for His terrible punishment, and to beg them to repent and save their souls." He paused, not because he had nothing more to say on the subject but because the woman had suddenly begun making notes on the data-screen again.

She looked up irritably. "Don't stop. Say more about this punishment thing." And when he had done so, at length, she looked very nearly pleased. "Huh," she said. "Heart's in the right place, anyway. We'll talk more later, I guess."

And then she was gone—

—and then again, click-click, gone from one place and now in an-other, she was back, but wearing a different dress and a different hair-style, and now not alone. Another woman was standing next to her. Not a pretty one this time. She seemed to be a bit older than McClune himself and she wore a baseball cap, with twenty-centimeter blonde braids hanging out of it on either side. The worst thing about her was her expression, an unpleasant mixture of anger and disdain. She gave Orbis a quick uninterested look and went back to studying the place they were in.

Which, actually, was worth looking at. All around them was a rose garden, where tables were laden with platters of fruits and meats and flagons of wine. Its rosebushes rose taller than Orbis McClune, and surrounded them so that he could form no guess about how large a space they were in.

He could see, however, that that lavish open space didn't have much furniture. The mahogany desk was back, though its single red rose had become a spray of two or three dozen. The desk also bore a screen, with a display of a bunch of stars on it, and a tall mahogany cabinet, doors closed. And there was a revolving chair at the desk for its occupant to sit in. The only other chair was better described as a throne, vacant but more handsome than any chair Orbis had ever seen before. It seemed to be made of ebony; its seat was upholstered in what looked like cloth of gold. Orbis did not believe for one moment that it was intended either for him or for the woman with the braids to sit on, which meant that they were intended to stand.

The woman at the desk—what was her name? Roz something, Orbis thought—looked up at him. "I guess I better introduce you," she said. "This"—nodding toward the woman with the braids—"is Phrygia Todd. She's going to be our pilot. Not," she added, finally offering a smile, "of this crummy little torpedo ship, of course. DeVon Washington can handle that. Wan is providing a much bigger one for our mission."

Automatically Orbis held out a hand to Phrygia Todd. She seemed to think it over but then decided to shake it. He didn't take offense, though. He was preoccupied with what Roz Borraly had said. What "mission"? He was so busy turning that over in his mind that it took him a moment to register the other thing. "This ship!" Was he on a spacecraft? Was the man who had had to pray his way onto an airplane now flying somewhere in space?

In a moment those questions were questions no longer, because the Roz Borraly woman was pointing at the screen. "That," she said, "is the place where they're hiding Wan's property that we're going to get back for him."

But what she said after that Orbis no longer heard, because the screen was changing, its view expanding. As the planet grew smaller, its sun had popped into view, bright and foreboding.

And not alone. At the edge of the screen another star had appeared—no, two other stars—no. There were half a dozen of them now, and suddenly interstellar space did not seem very spacious anymore.

Which, Orbis knew, could mean only one thing. Those stars were far too densely packed to be any part of the real galaxy. Whatever they were going to be doing, he realized, they were going to be doing it inside the Core.

Inside the Core. In the very place where lived those plague carriers of evil unspeakable, the damned and damnable Heechee themselves.

II

So shaken up was Orbis by this discovery that he hardly noticed when Borraly began again to talk. It wasn't until he heard her speaking his name that he looked up. She was staring at him in an unfriendly way, and her hand was worrisomely near something on her desk. "Sorry," he said at once. "You said?"

She pondered for a moment, then lifted her hand. "I said that you two can do our great friend and benefactor, Wan Santos-Smith, a service. You're gonna help him get some of the justice he's entitled to, finally, after all the ways he's been wronged." She cast a glance, Orbis thought it might have been a worried glance, at the throne. It was still empty, and she went on. "The good news," she said, flashing them the kind of smile that represented many hours of practice before a mirror, maybe even with an acting coach standing by—the kind of smile that Orbis McClune recognized with no trouble at all, since it was the same smile he had been presenting to an unworthy world all his life—"is that by helping Wan you'll help yourselves. Not just pay. There's more. Take a look at what's in that cabinet."

She didn't seem to touch any buttons or give any signs, but the carved wooden cabinet doors opened as she turned in that direction. What they revealed were shelves bearing a pair of those crystalline scroll things that some people called Heechee prayer fans.

"Recognize them?" she asked. "Right. Those are your works. They're the things all your data is stored in. If you had them yourselves you'd be your own boss, right? Well, you do a good job for Wan, and then they'll be yours. Forever," she added, flashing an encore of the same smile. She licked her lips, glancing again at the vacant throne. Then, the smile returning: "Any questions?"

Whether idle curiosity would be punished with one of those nerve whippings Orbis did not know, but he took the chance. "I'm just wondering what this property is that Wan's so anxious to get back."

The woman was abruptly solemn. "I will answer that. You see," she said, "as a small child poor baby Wan was abandoned. Only the care and kindness of a small community of individuals made it possible for him to become the wise, just leader he is today. And what has happened to those individuals?" Her face was reddening with anger. "Robinette Broadhead and his gang of thugs kidnaped them! Took them out of their ancestral home and dumped them in some African jungle! Then, when Wan was able to rescue a few of them, Broadhead's accomplices moved them to the Core and did their best to hunt him down!" She stopped talking there, because the woman she had called Phrygia, the one with the braids, had jumped to her feet.

"Oh, wow!" she gasped. "Are you talking about the *cavemen*?"

Phrygia didn't say what she meant by that. She couldn't. She was contorted and screaming from the nerve whip that followed her injudicious remark.

But Orbis realized what she was talking about. The—what did you call them? The australopithecines. The soulless animals that, unbelievers claimed, were somehow the great grandparents of the human race.

It was for them that Wan was keeping Orbis McClune in this damnable state of life in death.

Beyond that Orbis couldn't think, because while Phrygia's screaming was still going on the woman, grim-faced, turned them both off—

—And back on, but this time in a place different still, and with a man he had never seen before. "Tell me why you hate the Heechee," he demanded. . . .

And that was another awakening of very, very many of them, and nearly every one repeating something that had been done before.

First to last, Orbis McClune was in Wan's employ for, as nearly as he could calculate, somewhere between two and two thousand eternities. He didn't have many opportunities to brood about it. When he was turned off he was off. Completely. The length of such periods could have been microseconds or centuries—in the time of the real world outside—but to Orbis they were no time at all. It was the "waking" times that were both tedious and exhausting. Exhausting because most of them were sessions of intensive questioning, sometimes by that woman or that man, sometimes by some other of Wan's flunkies. Tedious because they went over and over the same ground. Did he *really* hate the Heechee? Did he hate them a *lot*? Would he be willing to do them some serious harm, even if that meant that some human beings should get harmed at the same time?

Always the same questions, or minor variations on them. Always the same answers from Orbis, too. Which meant, he thought, one of two possible things: either he was being vetted for some supremely important task. Or they were all loons.

He didn't have much time to think such thoughts, much less to speculate on what was going on. When he did have a moment—when, for instance, his interrogator paused in the questioning to confer with her screen—it was other thoughts that first crossed his mind. They were brief flashes of memory, fleeting, sometimes almost painful. Memories of the humans he had shared his last days with, up on the hills that bordered Waveland. Of the members of his old Rantoul congregation, a few of whom he hadn't really disliked very much. Of his childhood, some of which had been reasonably pleasant. Of his wife.

Of his wife, deceased and machine-stored and thus finally lost to him forever. Or at least lost for what had seemed forever to Orbis McClune, in those days before he had become machine-stored himself.

The next time Orbis awoke it was to a place that resembled a conference room, a fumed-oak table that was long enough for a score of people though only half that were seated at it.

One was Wan himself, relaxed and almost calm, elbows on the table and chin in his hands as he studied a data screen without looking at Orbis. The other person Orbis recognized was Phrygia Todd; the others were equally elderly, shabby, unprepossessing. (Not unlike Orbis himself, he thought.) They sat in uneasy silence while Roz Borraly pointed at things on the screen and whispered in Wan's ear.

Finally Wan peevishly pushed her aside. He looked around the table, making eye contact with each person, one by one. He didn't speak until he had completed the circle. Then he gave them all a great, heartwarming smile and said, "Welcome to you all! From now on you aren't my purchased employees anymore. Now you're gonna be my trusted allies, companions in my struggle against the damned dirty Heechee and their damned dirty Gateway accomplices. We're all in this together, and we'll all win!"

He went on from there, painting rosy pictures of the great rewards they would earn for helping in his crusade for justice, but Orbis had stopped listening. He didn't need to hear more. He knew it all ahead of time, had known what was coming ever since the moment that he saw that great, practiced-before-the-mirror smile that he himself had smiled at so many loathed human beings so many times before.

Most of Wan's oratory was denunciation of the Heechee. He hated them, Wan said. He blamed them for their vile gift of spaceflight, and blamed them for rotting the fiber of human spirit by their horrid Food Factories that ended hunger for all, even the unworthy. He blamed them, in short, for everything that was wrong with the age they lived in, of which, in both his view and Orbis's, there was plenty.

Nearly every word Wan spoke was one Orbis could have said himself. But how to ignore the fact that the man was obviously crazy? Now he was saying, "The individuals who make up my property are very dear to me. They took care of me when I was little, so I want to care for them now. Anyway, they're mine and I want them back."

Orbis stared at him. That really was Wan's stolen treasure? Some kind of creatures from the remote past, before God's gift of salvation? Orbis thought it extremely unlikely that they possessed souls, nearly certain that these might-be ancestors were not included in the general amnesty that followed Calvary.

Which meant that they were not really worth bothering about.

Orbis was shocked. It was one thing to hate the Heechee because they had profaned God's *human* world. It was another to work condign vengeance on them because they had kidnaped a handful of house pets.

As Wan, sweating and triumphant, concluded his lesson and turned back to his data screen, Orbis decided, he had been right in the first place. The man was a loon.

Even the looniest loco may ultimately wend toward a point. Wan finally reached his. "So here's where we come right down to it. You people aren't the only ones I've been recruiting, all this time. No. There were others, many, many others, but none that were worth more than being, like, house servants. You were the ones with the fire!" Orbis stole a look at the others. They did not seem afire to him. "Anyway, here are your assignments. Horace Packer!" A white-haired little man, looking as though he had long been homeless, raised one finger. "Sindi Gas—Gas—What is it, Sindi?"

A dark-skinned woman with a scarf over her head said, "Gaslakhpard. It's a perfectly normal name."

Wan shrugged. "If you say so. When we land you and Horace will su-

pervise freeing of the Old Ones, along with—what is it, Raffy something
or other? You Arab fellow?"

A small, muscular, Middle Eastern–looking man stood up. "I am
Egyptian, not Arab. My name is Raafat Gerges."

"Whatever. You guys get the Old Ones onto the ship, right? You might
have to knock them around a little bit, but that's all right. They're tough."
The people at the foot of the table all responded with some sort of nod or
hand movement, and then the only ones left were Orbis himself and the
woman with the Dutch-girl braids.

On them Wan now turned one of those effulgent and meaningless
smiles. "Now we come to our star players, the ones who are going to make
sure nobody tries to interfere with saving the Old Ones. See," he said, so
pleased with himself that he was almost doing a little dance, "we got them
where they can't do a thing to stop us. If they try, well—" He paused to
glance at Roz Borraly. "Is he on time?" he demanded.

"He's just waiting in orbit," she reported. "Here, I'll put it on the
screen." In a moment the screen was displaying a rather unattractive ice-
blue planet, circled by a largish moon. They all watched in silence for a
moment. "It ought to be happening right about now," said Borraly, beginning to sound worried. "Any minute. Pretty soon. . . . Wow! There it is!"

On the screen that big moon had suddenly swelled, bloated, exploded
in all directions. It was no longer a solid object, just an expanding sphere
of particles.

Wan was grinning. "We did that," he bragged. "You wouldn't believe
how much trouble it was to find the gadgets that did it, but it looks like
they work. We blew that sucker up just to teach them a lesson because if
anybody gives us any trouble when we do the rescue, why, we'll just blow
up a whole big star and kill a few gazillion of them off."

He gave them a real grin this time, as he waited for applause. After a
moment, Roz Borraly leading, he got some and returned to his subject.
"You, Phrygia Todd! You're going to pilot this ship. You've been trained,
right? You think you can do it?"

The woman with the braids shrugged. "Guess so."

Wan scowled at her. "You better more than just guess. So you, Phrygia, after we rescue the Old Ones you pilot us to where Orbis can take his
little torpedo to what they call, let me see. Planetless Very Large White
Very Hot Star. That's the one we're going to blow up—I mean threaten
to." He paused for a moment, then went on. "All right. Then you take us
to where we're going that they'll never find us, Phrygia. Then, Orbis, you
orbit that star, close up, in your little ship, and you wait for orders from
me. If I order it, zap, you blow the sucker up." He took a moment to ap-

plaud himself vigorously, his example followed at once by Roz Borraly and, a little more slowly and a lot less vigorously, by most of the others. Any questions?"

Orbis was about to ask one, but Phrygia Todd was ahead of him. "Why am I going to be the pilot? What happened to the guy that blew up the moon?"

Wan's face contorted in the direction of a frown. Orbis could see Todd's body involuntarily tensing up, ready for what might be coming. But Wan relaxed and gave them another of those overripe smiles. "That was Will Barendt," he said. "Too bad. His heart wasn't in it, you know, so I told him after he did this one job for me I'd release him from his contract." He shrugged modestly. "People say I'm too soft, but that's the way I saw it. So he put this torpedo on course and took off in the other one with one of the gadgets. Probably he's on his way to the saloons on Peggys Planet by now." Wan looked around to see if anyone was going to challenge what he said.

"He did the same thing with Ferdie Grossmutter after they blew up that Fomalhaut star," Roz Borraly put in loyally.

He scowled again. Then, "Anyway," he added, "what you want to re-member, Orbis, is we really probably aren't going to need to detonate it, on account of once they see what happened to that moon nobody's go-ing to take the chance of interfering. Got it? Everybody know their part?"

Orbis raised his hand. "I don't. How do I blow this star up?"

Wan gave him a leer. "Oh, Roz'll show you that. Probably she'll show you a few other things, too. I guess we're through here, so you can all go do what, you know, you now have the privilege to do. So long." And when he clapped his hand the shapes of Orbis's surroundings melted and flowed, the harsh white light softened, the table and chairs shrank into themselves and disappeared.

Orbis was in the garden again. He was standing before a table loaded with food and drink, and by his side was a wide, soft couch on which a woman sat. It was the same woman as always, Roz Borraly, but now dif-ferently dressed. She wore a nearly transparent gown. Her hair was down, and she was quite beautiful. "There you are, Orbis," she said. "I'm what you might call your pay in advance. What would you like to do with me?"

Inviting she was, but what she offered was not what interested Orbis McClune. "What about this bomb?" he demanded.

She gave him a winsome smile. "See," she said, "I'll show you all that, all right. But wouldn't you like to have some fun first?"

Artificial intelligences do not require food, drink, rest or sleep, and they certainly don't have to have sex. This is not to say, however, that they aren't capable of enjoying any of them when offered.

It wasn't the sex that appealed to Orbis, it was the food. He could not remember when he had last eaten—or simulated eating, to be more accurate, but either way it was something he missed and it hadn't happened for quite a while. He wasted no time before ravaging the loaded table, while the woman poured beverages for him. He waved the wine away but eagerly accepted the fruit juices, the cold, sweet milk, then the steaming coffee. They were delicious. It was by any measure the best experience he had had since the confounded statue had fallen on his head, but there was one troubling aspect to it, and that was the woman herself.

She hadn't contented herself with pouring his drinks and heaping his plate with goodies. She seemed always to be very close to him, always touching him—and not just with her hands, either; as she leaned over him her firm, perfectly shaped breast stroked his shoulder; her long hair caressed his face, and he was nearly sure she was breathing into his ear. "Please don't do that, Ms. Borraly," he said, moving half a meter away. "You're a very pretty girl, but—"

Orbis was not without residual courtesy, and he didn't know what to say after the "but" that wouldn't call her a whore. But she made that moot very quickly. "Thank you for saying that," she said in his ear. In fact she wasn't just breathing into his ear, he was now quite sure that she was nibbling at it with her soft, full lips. "I'm glad you think I'm pretty, but that's not all I am. I'm your little present from Wan. For the next 200 milliseconds you can do anything to me you like, for as long as you like." And while she was talking—whispering, really—she was changing position so that at the end they were face to face, lips to lips, and he broke away just as he felt the first warm, wet thrust of her tongue.

"Stop it!" he said sharply. "I am not a fornicator!"

She pulled her head a few centimeters away, regarding him. Her breath was warm and sweet on his face and her eyes puzzled. "Not ever?" she asked. "I mean, nobody's watching us, as far as I know."

"My God is watching us!" he said, voice as stern as the look on his face.

She leaned back, studying him. She sighed. "It's just too damn bad that the interesting ones are all gay," she said.

"I am *not*—" he began, but then stopped himself. Her opinion meant nothing to him, and there was no point in denying what he knew to be untrue. "Let's just get on with it," he said. "Tell me about the bomb."

She sighed, then waved a hand. The flower garden disappeared, and they were in what, Orbis realized, had to be the control room of a spaceship.

"All right," the woman said, sounding resigned. "You see that kind of gearshift thing there? Push it to one side, your torpedo turns that way. Push it the other and—right, you've got it. Now, you see that button by the screen?" Orbis did, all right; it was the size of his fist, red and labeled "button." "It isn't a real button. The toggle wasn't real either, because if they were how could you touch it? It's all what they call a servomodule, but if you press the button it'll work like it was real, all right. It'll blow up that star. Only—now pay attention to this part—don't press it unless Wan personally gives you the order, all right? You understand that?"

It didn't seem to be a rhetorical question, so Orbis said, "I do."

"Well, you damn better. Okay. So long. . . ."

And that was all she said. Her voice was getting tinny, and her body swelled and bloated, while the laden table rose and swirled around him; and then he was in the pilot chamber of a different spacecraft, and the only person with him was the blonde-braids woman, Phrygia Todd. She sat uncomfortably on one of those Heechee perches, and she didn't speak.

Orbis made the effort. Holding out a hand to be shaken, he said, "Hi. I'm the Reverend Orbis McClune."

She looked up, ignoring the hand. "I know what your damn name is. Listen. Did you understand what will happen if you push that button?"

He frowned at her. "I just said I did. It'll destroy that star. Is that what you mean?"

"Yeah. That's what I mean. It will neutralize its gravity, which means—can you guess?"

"Make it explode?" he hazarded.

"Damn straight it will explode," she told him contemptuously. "Like the kind of explosion that will make everybody anywhere near it dead. Like it did Will Barendt when he blew up that moon—you didn't believe Wan was going to let him go free, did you? Like the two of us."

He was puzzled. "But we're dead already, really."

"Idiot. That's just our bodies. Remember, our works are going to be with us, and if this ship gets destroyed, as it will, what do you suppose is going to happen to them?" She nodded somberly. "So then we'll be really,

really dead, Mr. Reverend McClune. So no matter what he says, unless you want to be *permanently* dead, don't push that button!"

He blinked at her. "You mean *dead* dead?"

"That's exactly what I mean. Totally dead. No more alive in any form dead. Meet your Maker dead. Past this mortal coil dead."

He gazed at her in silence for a moment. Then, "Oh," he said. "I see."

17

In Achiever's Ship

The spaceport on Forested Planet hadn't changed in the time—what was it? A month or two, anyway—since Estrella and Stan landed there, but that wasn't true of the spaceship that was waiting for them. It surely had. It was metallic, all right, but neither human silver nor Heechee blue. The front part of it was a shiny raspberry red. The middle was the pale green of a honeydew melon, and the rear—well, that was hard to describe because it kept changing. And the spacecraft was shaped like nothing so much as some weird species of squid, with little finlets up near the nose and tentacle shapes squirming around on the flickering tail. And it was *big*.

Achiever was waiting for them on the landing deck, almost hopping with pleasure. "Welcome!" he cried. "To each of you I say, jointly and severally, welcome! As you see, I fortunately have excellent ship now at my disposal. Very new! Very speedy! Also very agile because, as you see, is interstellar spacecraft but is quite capable of transportation within planetary atmosphere as well. Now come, please, come aboard." He led the way, walking dexterously backward the better to carry on a conversation with them. "Is this not quite excellent?" he asked with pride. "Of course it is a completely new ship entirely, this is going without saying. And—" he gave an explosive little titter—"is entirely mine. Now I ask a question of you: Have you comprehended how it is that spacecraft have become so technologically splendid? It is because Outside of Core, in recent centuries of Outside time, spacecraft of this kind have newly been invented—invented, that is to say, by inventors of my kind, not yours, of course. This particular spacecraft is provided to me for me, copilot and two of you being passengers. Reason for which," he added, "relates to requirement that I am to spend much time in proximity with, or to, persons of your ethnicity. This requirement caused by previous errors in my apprehension, of which you know."

Stan didn't know at all. He was wondering whether he really wanted to be part of this nut case's therapy, and wondering even more urgently why the nut case was allowed out without an armed guard, when Estrella spoke up. "So they gave you this ship just to make you better?" she asked.

Achiever flapped his fingers indecisively. "That reason, yes. Other reason also exists, which is to permit the two of you to inspect other planets as proposed by simulated Earth person Sigfrid von Shrink who have liking for you two, you see."

"Huh," Stan said, a little surprised, a little embarrassed. Estrella asked, "Did he pick out the itinerary, too?"

"Did indeed," Achiever told her. "You wish to know names of planets we visit? I take pleasure in telling you. Are five of same. Number one is Extremely Wet Planet in Binary Yellow-White System, where will visit persons including some of your ethnicity. Number two is Small but Dense Planet of Bright Yellow Star Eighty-Three, where will also visit same-ethnicity persons. Number three—"

But Number three meant no more to Stan than the other two. When Achiever had run through the entire list of five he knew no more than he had before. What he did know was that he had become hungry, and when he told Achiever that Achiever was hospitable. "To be sure! Eat now, all three of us, and can continue conversation over meal as is appropriate behavior."

Estrella hung back. "Shouldn't you be flying the ship?"

"I? Not at all. Some person, for purpose of supervising actual flying, yes, but not at this time. Wait. On way to place where eating is to occur we will pause to peek toward operating carrel where what you call 'flying' occurs. This way. Then this. Now this, and now look," he said, flinging a door open. "'Flying' is now being accomplished by junior copilot given to me for training and for my convenience as needed, so that we in fact are already in orbit."

And when the person perched before the controls looked up, Stan had just time to think she looked rather familiar before Estrella was crying in his ear, "Salt! Is that really you?"

It was Salt. She waved to them, amiably but regretfully, as Achiever hustled them along. She couldn't leave the "operating carrel," Achiever told them, not because it would make any difference to the flying of the ship—which was all but totally automatic—but because he had ordered it so. "Is quite extremely junior to me," he told them with a deprecatory shrug, "with only as you would say two years one month experience, so requiring additional training by spacecraft's commander, who is me."

Estrella had a question. "Did the fact that she's carrying your child have anything to do with this assignment?"

"Not in the least at all! From my own volition that is so, at any rate. This fact you describe entitles no privileges of any kind for her. Now! Here is feeding room! Let us enjoy excellent meal!"

This was easy to decree, hard to fulfill. However shiny-new this ship was, it lacked the personalized food-delivery service Marc Antony had accustomed them to. When Estrella made a remark to that effect, as tactfully as she could, Achiever was amused. "Food here is entirely edible in all respects," he assured them. "So eat!"

They did. They ate as much of the colorful CHON-food jellies, crunchy loaves and gritty pastes as needed to quench their hunger pangs, but it was without enjoyment. Especially as Achiever chattered on through the meal. "But perhaps I exceed preference for conversing," he said at last, thin lips demurely pursed to show that he didn't really mean it.

"Not at all," Stan lied. "But I've been wondering how long we'll be traveling."

"Oh, not of long duration indeed," Achiever assured him. "All five systems are quite proximate, this being reason same were chosen. So you will not have time to grow displeased with my presence," he finished, braying his horrible Heechee-trying-to-be-human laugh.

Neither Stan nor Estrella responded to that, avoiding the necessity of continuing the conversation by claiming fatigue. Achiever showed them to their quarters.

These also were not up to the standards they had grown used to at the Mica Mountains of Forested Planet. The beds were Heechee litter boxes. The lookplates on the walls were displaying a variety of scenes, some of them quite likely to be of interest to Heechee but wholly meaningless to Estrella and Stan. There were no chairs suitable for human buttocks, either, but Achiever glanced around the room with proprietary pride. "Excellently appointed," he informed them. "Even your baggage already delivered here by handling apparatus, including last-minute item next to drencher."

The box he was indicating was hexagonal, blue and wholly unfamiliar to Stan. He shook his head. "Not ours. All we brought is already there on those chests."

"Oh," Achiever said, scowling heavily, "then must be property belonging to Salt. This will mean negative mark on training record, as I can be sure since I will put it there. Perhaps lapse of this sort can be attributed to fact that her primary training occurred not in conventional places but Outside."

Estrella looked at him with interest. "I didn't know Salt had been Outside."

"Has been indeed, for two years one month as aforesaid. Spent nearly whole of one Core night in this way, returning because of approach of pre-fertilization condition." He shook his head. "You see nature of things which happen when trained by others. Now you sleep, for one arrives early at Extremely Wet Planet in Binary Yellow-White system."

"So," said Stan when the door was closed, sitting precariously on the edge of one of the boxes, "what do you think, Strell? Did we make a mistake coming along with him?"

"Too early to say, hon. Anyway, if we're going to visit human colonies they'll probably have human food, don't you think? And maybe we can borrow some chairs and things from them."

"Hey," Stan said, suddenly cheered. "Maybe we can. Well, what about getting a little sleep? Which box shall we use?"

"We'll each use our own," she said firmly. "I don't know if you've noticed, but there's no lock on the door."

Extremely Wet Planet in Binary Yellow-White System was exactly what it was advertised to be. That is, it was definitely wet. At least ninety percent of its surface was ocean, and even the three great land masses of the planet were dotted with large lakes.

There were three separate human colonies on Extremely Wet Planet, all on the largest of the land masses and two of them on the shores of its largest lake, making it easy for the little aircraft that was waiting for them to make the rounds. The aircraft itself had room for a dozen passengers, though only Stan, Estrella and Achiever boarded it. Stan was a little perplexed when he could not find any external sign of either jets or propellers, but, once inside, was pleased to note that nearly half the passenger perches had been ripped out and replaced with seats more congenial to human anatomy. "Is mostly human persons who use this vehicle," Achiever informed him. "They average to have sixteen to twenty-four new residents each day, number which appears to be increasing. Sit now, please. Aircraft is to become airborne."

When the engines started, Stan could hear them, all right. They screamed and yowled. When they were at their loudest the aircraft gave a sort of shudder, and then a leap, and then Stan could see the ground dropping away from them. What he could see was not much like what he would have seen from a plane on Earth: no cultivated fields, no cities. If there were Heechee communities below, as there surely were, they were by Heechee habit mostly underground and thus invisible.

There was plenty of water to see, shining serpents of rivers and tree-shaded, mirror-like ponds. But Stan tired quickly of streams and lakes. He felt his eyes closing, but just as he fell asleep the aircraft twisted and dropped worrisomely, and all at once they were landing by the largest lake yet.

They were met by nearly the total population of this newest human community, amounting to no more than a few hundred people. They were glad to have visitors, if a bit disappointed to learn that they weren't going to stay. The group, they told Stan and Estrella, had recently left Peggys Planet because it was too crowded. At least, that was what Stan understood, with difficulty, from the babble the settlers offered him. They were not easy to talk to. The fact that they were recent arrivals to the Core meant that the Outside they had left behind was not much like the one Stan and Estrella had last seen. The English language had absorbed a great many loan words in the many centuries that had passed Outside, not only of Chinese, Arabic, Polish and other human languages but some that might originally have been Heechee. Or might not.

Achiever was as baffled as they. "This perhaps is language," he admitted, "but cannot personally at all understand. You, Stan? Have spoken this talk with these persons?" When Stan shook his head, Achiever gave the breathy Heechee equivalent of a sigh. "Perhaps best go on to next place," he said moodily. "This does not begin optimally well."

The next group was Greek, and they had been in the Core for nearly twenty days, long enough to be planning to start construction of a church and a school. What they didn't have was many English speakers. The one they called in from the fields, where he had been planting olive saplings, was quite good, though, having got much of his education at MIT. But there hadn't been much need for a civil engineer in the Greek parts of the island of Cyprus, where they had come from. "Because of the Turks," he told them, shaking his head. "All the time having babies and babies and babies. We were being squeezed right out of the island, so we left."

Estrella frowned at that. She whispered to Stan, "But weren't you—?"

"Not really," he whispered back. "But let's get out of here."

The people of the third colony were Asian—mostly Chinese and Korean—and what they had in plenty, courtesy of Marc Antony, was food that Stan and Estrella didn't always recognize but definitely could enjoy. That wasn't all. "Would you stay on for a while?" the woman who greeted them asked, almost imploringly. "No? That is sad. Anyway, would you like some more dim sum?"

They would, would in fact have gladly stayed on for at least two or three more meals, but Achiever announced he had a schedule to meet. "Anyway," he said sunnily, "is good progress. One planet visited, four yet to come. Is not this excellent fun?"

Well, it was more or less fun, even Stan had to admit that. Estrella, not in the least tired or queasy, thought so as well although she would have liked to see more of Salt, if only to compare notes on early pregnancy. That Achiever did not permit. "I ask you question: What are three necessities for becoming excellent pilot like self?" he demanded. "I answer in this fashion: Training. Training. And also training." So he kept Salt's nose to the grindstone, flying the ship when they were in space, remaining aboard it for safekeeping (against what possible imaginary danger he did not say) when they were planetside. "But," he added generously, "am insuring this creates no hardship for yourselves, Estrella and Stan, since you already have adequate companionship for voyage in myself."

Small but Dense Planet of Bright Yellow Star Eighty-Three once more demonstrated the Heechee commitment to truth in advertising. As they landed Estrella complained, "There's something funny about that ocean, Stan!" What was funny was that its horizon was definitely a lot closer than either of them had ever seen before. However the planet's human inhabitants, though few in number, were welcoming—almost pitifully so, Stan thought, because settling on this not particularly pleasant little world offered few incentives to newcomers. All two or three hundred of the immigrants came out to greet them, and immediately offered a meal as well.

Small but Dense Planet began to look a lot better to Stan, but Achiever was restive. "Is dallying quite sufficiently," he said. "Return at this point to spacecraft for immediate departure."

Stan swallowed his mouthful of undifferentiated CHON-food. "What the hell for? We just got here!"

"Nevertheless," Achiever said, unmoved. "Such is my intention."

Estrella was more tactful. "But really, Achiever, this is a whole planet and all we've seen is this one little corner—"

"Remaining corners of no additional interest. I remind you! I am captain commanding spacecraft and thus also of landing parties of all natures. Also desire to determine if junior copilot of spacecraft is appropriately discharging duties as assigned."

Estrella gave him an indignant look. "You mean you want to spy on her?"

Achiever didn't answer. "No further discussion. We return at present time!"

Then, as they entered the ship, Stan began to suspect that Achiever's doubts had been justified.

Salt was not at her post at the controls. No one else was there, either. The operating chamber was empty except that someone had moved that unexplained hexagonal blue box into it. Achiever was fit to be tied. "Not only not present but having littered chamber for operating spacecraft as well! Oh, how very bad will be this blot on junior copilot's record! Now must seek her out for reproving and discussion of faults!"

Estrella held back. "Wait a minute, Achiever. Where are we going?"

He stamped his foot, his belly muscles writhing. "You persons must not delay exercise of authority. Why are you delaying same? We go to sleeping place of junior copilot, which is where she may be when not in operating chamber. Come!"

But he had taken no more than a few steps when he stopped, standing rigid. The tiny hairs at the base of his skull sprung erect and he seemed to be sniffing the air.

"What's the matter?" Stan demanded, suddenly uneasy.

"Be soundless! Wait!" Achiever ordered, moving his head from side to side. "Oh, inexplicable event! Do you not feel it? Spacecraft is presently in takeoff mode! Stand still!" Which he himself did not do, but whipped around and sprang to the controls.

Stan felt nothing, nor it seemed did Estrella, but it was true that the lookplates over the control perch were now showing a pattern of motion. Achiever was muttering distractedly to himself, not in English, as he strove with the controls. His hands strained on the great knurled wheels. The contorted muscles of his arms showed that he was using all his strength, but the wheels would not move.

And then a voice from behind them said politely, "It's no use. We've taken over the spacecraft."

Stan spun around. An elderly man who definitely hadn't been there before was standing at the closed door, shabbily dressed, not recently shaved, a short stick in his hand.

Achiever leaped to his feet, and wordlessly hurled himself at the stranger. He accomplished nothing, though: his body passed straight through the other's and he wound up crashing against the wall.

"Oh, hell," the stranger said plaintively, "didn't I tell you it wasn't any use? You can't touch me because I'm a simulation, can't you see? And you can't do anything with the controls because we've got them locked. Your ship has been requisitioned by Wan, and now I have to ask you to step into another room so you'll be out of the way, okay? We won't hurt you un-less—oh, I wish you wouldn't do that."

Achiever had rebounded to his feet and was heading toward the simulation again. This time he didn't get that far. The stranger lifted the baton and pointed it at him. Nothing came from the rod, but a bright greenish spark flew out of the hexagonal box, and when it hit Achiever, his arms and legs flew wide, he emitted a screech of pain and crashed to the floor. "See," the stranger said patiently, "you don't want to give us any trouble, because if you do we'll just have to hurt you. Hurt you a lot worse than that, I mean. So just step along, please, and anyway I think we might be going to let you out after we rescue up the others because, you know, there won't be anything you can do anyway."

II

The living quarters were all pretty much like Stan and Estrella's own, ex-cept that all the lookplates were off and Salt was waiting at the door. She greeted them with relief and maybe a little satisfaction. "Were in any way harmed? No? Is how they also treated me, except for causing major painfulness. But not you?"

Achiever was busy checking all the doors. Stan answered for them all. "I think Achiever got a dose." He raised his voice. "What about it, Achiever? Did they hurt you?"

Achiever didn't look back. "Extremely yes," he said, then signed for si-lence as he peered around the corner of the doorway. Then, in his captain-in-command voice: "Salt!"

She turned to confront him. "Yes?"

"Are aware all entrances unsealed?"

She said patiently. "Is true, Achiever, as I verified on first being deliv-ered here. However, do not attempt going through, for same greatly painful event occurring at every time, or worse."

He gave her a skeptical look. "You know this because have self tried?

Huh. Nevertheless event is only painfulness, which persons of determination may ignore."

"Not correct, Achiever." She flapped her fingers at him. "In first event,
great pain. Second event, pain much greater still. Third event such pain as
to cause unconsciousness. Have opinion that fourth time become life terminating, but cannot verify experimentally as did not try after third."

Achiever returned into the room, rubbing his chest muscles indecisively. "But same is only conjecture. How can ascertain same is true if is
not attempted?"

"Don't try it," advised an amiable voice from the doorway Achiever
had just left. When Stan turned he saw another of those insubstantial and
uninvited visitors, this one female. She was conspicuously good-looking,
too, and, in a low-cut gown with a diamond-shaped chunk cut out over
her abdomen, not overdressed. "The Heechee lady has it right, hon. My
name's Sindi Gaslakhpard. You can call me just Sindi. I'm machine-stored
like all the rest of us on this tub, so don't get any ideas about jumping us
when we aren't looking. You can't hurt us, and we're always looking."

She advanced into the room, giving Estrella a look of curiosity and
Stan one of some admiration. "Considering you're all natural, hon," she
told him, "you're not so bad. Anyway, I'm here on business. Wan's gonna
be on the screens any minute now, and he sent word he wants you to
watch so you won't do anything stupid. So Horace's activated your screens,
and you better watch. Got it?" She glanced around the four of them like a
kindergarten teacher checking her class for washed faces and combed hair,
stopping at Estrella. The woman regarded her thoughtfully for a moment.
Then, "Hon," she said, "I've been meaning to tell you, you don't have to
look that way. If you went ahead and got yourself machine-stored you
could get your face fixed." And then, pop, she was gone.

The lookplates all went on at once. Achiever hurled himself at them.
If he expected to see the man Sindi had talked about he was disappointed,
for each screen showed a different image. Two were displaying curious-
looking spacecraft of a design Stan didn't recognize. A third and a fourth
displayed individual stars, or different views of the same star, one so
brightly hot that its light was almost bluish, the other a lemony-yellow sun
not unlike old Earth's. The fifth—

But Stan never got a chance to see what was on the fifth lookplate,
because all at once and all together the screens began flashing great gouts
of bright green light and emitting a high-pitched scream. The visual display showed nothing but the exterior of one of those odd-looking spacecraft. The Heechee-language jabbering that went with it meant nothing to
Stan or Estrella. It did to both of the Heechee in the room with them,

though; they were shouting at each other at once. Stan shouted at Salt for attention. "What's happening?"

Salt was actually wringing her long, bony hands. She had to try three times before getting an answer out: "Persons on lookplate speak of happening extremely terrible, possessing danger of terrible devastation. Here! Now! Look at lookplates!"

As she spoke the ship disappeared from all the lookplates. It was replaced by a human face, a face Stan had seen before and almost recognized even before it said its name. "I am Wan Enrique Santos-Smith," it told them—in English! "You people have illegally taken some property which belongs to me. I am talking about the fifty-four kind of human beings, now held in captivity on what you call One Moon Planet of Pale Yellow Star Fourteen."

"Stan?" Estrella whispered. "What's the matter with his picture? Why does it jiggle around like that?" Stan shook his head at her; Wan was still talking.

"I was the one who discovered these people," he said, his tone belligerent. "I want them. So what I'm going to do, I'm dispatching a spaceship to that planet to pick them up. I'm warning you, nobody better try to interfere with my crews, because if these Old Ones aren't immediately boarded onto my ship as soon as it gets there I'm just going to have to punish you. You know what you call Planetless Very Large Very Hot White Star. We've got this weapon that can really mess that star up. I don't mean like a gun or anything. I mean something so powerful that it can make that whole star blow up, and if you don't do what I say it'll do it. If you think I'm bluffing, you just ask your Stored Minds, because they've seen what we did to—What do you call it?" His face disappeared from the lookplate for a moment, then returned. "To the largest moon of Solitary Gas Giant Planet of Small Yellow Star Twenty-Two. If I give the order, the star's going to explode. Then a whole bunch of you are going to die."

And slowly the images faded away.

By then Estrella was clinging to Stan's hand even more tightly than he was holding hers. "Salt?" she implored. "What's going on?"

Salt didn't answer. She was shrieking questions they couldn't understand at Achiever, who didn't answer because he was frantically working to try to restore pictures to the lookplates. When he had failed he stared at them for a moment, then made a harsh moaning noise. "Is a great peril," he said hollowly. "Can be little or no doubt."

Stan squeezed Estrella's hand even harder. "Then you think all this is real?"

"I am indeed so thinking," Achiever said gloomily. "What am I also thinking, you wish to know? I am also thinking that you and I and ship mentioned in threat are all also part of it."

18

The Threat

I

Being chef to thousands, does take time. Some of my special meal orders had been backing up while I was visiting with Thermocline, so my first job was getting out several hundred of them. There was a ceviche of Moreton Bay bugtails for an old lady nostalgic for Australia, some dried cod with leeks and milk for a couple of former Italians, and I hadn't filled Thermocline's order, either. I got busy on them all.

Over the next few seconds or so these orders of my clients kept me busy. I wasn't simply "kept" busy, either, because the demands of the Core's rapidly increasing populations of human immigrants, along with the much smaller but very discerning number of Heechee sophisticates, grew almost exponentially.

That, of course, didn't mean that I had forgotten what Thermocline had told me. I can't pretend that I was actually preparing threat estimates and making contingency plans. I wish I could, but in fact I was giving the consideration of Thermocline's information no more than ten percent of my capacity.

All the same, it was not a total surprise when a queer green flash appeared on all of my screens at once, along with the beginnings of a deep roaring sound.

I knew what that sound was. It was the beginning of what would have been a shrill, high-pitched squeal for the organics, downshifted for machine-stored persons to a basso-profundo rumble. It was, in fact, the Heechee alarm system doing its work.

There is no point in acting before you know what action is required. I went on with my work, but I took the precaution of turning a lot of the new ethnic requests over to my sous-chefs. African, for instance. There had been few Africans on the Wheel, and most of them preferred French cuisine or American hamburgers. Now we were asked for peanut lamb stew and the codfish in pureed tomato they called thu djen, along with the dessert thiaky and ginger root juice as a beverage. I had never made any of those meals before, but naturally the recipes were in my datastore. The subroutines could handle that, and if any of the fish dishes arrived filleted in spite of the fact that Africans preferred their fish on the bone, and if all the rice grains hadn't been properly broken up before cooking, they would simply have to live with it.

The opening siren of the Heechee warning had just descended to the neighborhood of middle C—for the organics, that is; for us now a sub-audible thump-thump-thump—when abruptly all of my screens at once began showing the same picture. It was what I took to be a satellite of some kind—there was a big gas giant in the background. I had just time to wonder why this quite ordinary scene was being displayed when suddenly it changed. The satellite wasn't a satellite anymore. It was a cloud, rapidly expanding. Why or how I could not have said, but it was clearly the total disruption of that chunk of featureless rock.

So I was not surprised when my private communicator called to me in Thermocline's voice. "Please join with me as soon as possible for a conference. Serious events have occurred."

II

Thermocline had changed his surround quite a lot since I had seen it last. Most of the half-dozen or so assorted chairs and perches that now furnished it were already occupied. There was Thermocline himself, looking completely unflustered although the thump-thump was still going on. Next to him was a female Heechee I had never seen before, then a human male (of course, I'm talking about simulations in every case; no organics were present.) I hadn't met the human male, either, but I knew who he was. His name was Sigfrid von Shrink, and he was a subset of the Robinette Broadhead shipmind who was known as Albert Einstein. Next to von Shrink was Gelle-Klara Moynlin's shipmind, Hypatia of Alexandria. Then, as I watched, an older human woman unknown to me popped into existence and took a seat, giving a nod to Hypatia.

She was evidently the last one expected, because then Thermocline said, "I thank you all for coming. I presume that all of you know who Wan Enrique Santos-Smith is, and also that you have all heard the accelerated version of his organic-time communication—" as we certainly had, and in fact were still hearing, at low volume, the organic-time drone as a background sound in Thermocline's surround. "He had transmitted it to the Stored Minds, in electronic-time mode, which is what was forwarded to you."

His lookplates were still cycling their alarm colors while the continuing thud-thud of the organic-time message had dropped still more in frequency. Just then the nearest of the screens erased its alarm colors. As the murky colors on the plate paled, a human face looked out at us.

I had seen Wan only once, long ago, but there was no doubt that the face on the screen was his. Improvements had been made, however. Now that he was no longer organic his skin was less sallow, his hair less wild. But the sneer was the same.

As Wan was finishing his threats, Hypatia was on her feet. "Thermocline! What the hell is he talking about? Do you guys have some kind of weapon you didn't tell us about?"

I will say for Thermocline that he kept his temper. He let Hypatia go on for quite a while, and he just sat there and took it. The thing that struck me as curious, though, was that Hypatia was the only person in the room reacting so violently. I had expected Sigfrid to chime in, but he didn't move and the look on his face was not so much angry as mournful.

Which told me that the news about the weapon hadn't surprised him at all. I tucked that fact away in my datastore, in case I ever needed to be reminded that Sigfrid von Shrink didn't usually put all his cards on the table.

Either Hypatia wore herself out, at last, or some sign from Sigfrid discouraged her from going on. Then Sigfrid was placatory. "Perhaps it would be better if we didn't try to assign blame at this time," he suggested. "But let me clarify a point, Thermocline. Am I correct in believing that you and the Stored Minds regard this as a serious threat?"

Thermocline looked judicious. "We do," he said.

"The word Wan used was 'explode.' He didn't simply mean to fire some sort of bomb at the star, did he?"

"Of course not. What the device does is nullify gravity. With no grav-itational attraction to hold it together, the star will fly apart. . . . Hypatia?"

She was leaning forward, ready to speak again though not, this time, with reproachful invective. "I asked Dr. Ibarruru here just to help us un-derstand things like this; she's an astronomer and astrophysicist. Dr. Ibar-ruru? Can you tell us if such a thing could happen?"

The striking elderly woman did not hesitate. "Given a device such as Thermocline describes, certainly. The star will expand at a major fraction of the speed of light. In a very short time it will become a cloud of gas."

Thermocline looked disgruntled. "This human person may well have studied astronomy, but what can she tell us about matters here in the Core?"

Hypatia gave him a hostile smirk. "Everything, Thermocline. Shortly after coming here she became machine-stored, and has been studying the Core stars ever since. Also—you probably should be informed of this—she is an old friend of Klara's. They worked together in studying a certain supernova, and Klara has complete confidence in her." She nodded as though that settled the matter, and perhaps it did.

Not for Thermocline, though. He seemed faintly put out. "I am sure this human woman is well qualified," he said, not sounding sure at all, "but I also have asked an astronomical expert to join us here. Burnish? Do you concur?"

The other male Heechee flipped his wrists in assent. "I do, Thermo-cline."

"And can you tell us what star Wan was talking about?"

"I think so. It's probably the one called Planetless Very Large White Very Hot Star. It's what Dr. Ibarruru—" he gave a polite nod in her direction "—would call a young type-O star. We only brought one like it into the Core."

"And is it dangerous?"

His expression answered that, but he made it explicit. "My best-case estimate is that the release of gravity on Planetless Very Large White Very Hot Star would cause the loss of between ten and forty-four million lives, with another thirty to two hundred million suffering injury, property loss or severe environmental damage. It could be even worse."

That's when I raised my hand. Hypatia looked at me, one eyebrow lifted inquiringly. "Marcus, do you have a question?"

"I do indeed. This star's name tells us that it has no planets. Why would decohering it harm any other system?"

Hypatia looked at the female human astronomer, who sighed. "There we get into stellar physics. You know, I am sure, that the fusion processes which light a star take place at its center. The energy produced there is in the form of photons, and they are not immediately released to space. A star's interior is quite dense. Each photon is reflected by matter many times on its way to the surface, where it can be radiated into space. The time it takes for this journey is of the order of a million years."

She went on talking, but I had stopped listening because her meaning was clear. A million years' worth of energy, released in a matter of minutes, perhaps seconds.

I stopped her. "Thank you," I said. "There is only one real other question. What we are going to do to prevent it?" I was looking at Thermocline.

He gave a serious nod of his squared-off head. "Nothing," he said.

III

Since I am a reasonable being, I didn't shout at him. I didn't have to; others were already doing so, especially Sigfrid and the astronomers, all of whom were telling him he was making a mistake. Perhaps that is why I was the one he turned to. "Yes, Marc?" he said courteously. "Did you have something you wished to say?"

"Of course I do, Thermocline. It's simple. We have to locate the spacecraft Wan's message came from and destroy it."

He raised his bony hand. "Please, Marc. The Stored Minds have in fact already triangulated the source of his transmission. Unfortunately there is no detectable ship at that point."

That was surprising. "That's impossible. At least there should be ship-wakes—I know sorting them out might be difficult, because they persist for long periods, but they should give some indication."

He was waving those long fingers at me again. "Also done, Marcus. There is no detectable shipwake that could represent a conventional spacecraft at that point."

"Ah," I said. When he used the word "conventional" he gave the answer. "Wan's machine-stored, so he doesn't require a full-sized ship. A messenger torpedo would do."

"Exactly, Marc," he said, all but beaming at me. "Accordingly, let me summarize. We can take no action to protect the protohumans as long as Wan's threat is viable. We can do nothing about Wan as long as we can't locate him, nor do we have any weapons to deal with him if we did—"

It was my turn to interrupt. "We don't need conventional weapons. We could simply ram his torpedo."

He gave me a reproving sigh. "But not without giving him plenty of time to carry out his threat. Which the Stored Minds have determined we cannot afford to do."

Hypatia had been silent for a long time. Now she spoke up. "Then what *are* you going to do, Thermocline?"

This time the reproachful look went to her. "But I have answered that already, Hypatia. The Stored Minds have announced their decision. We will allow Wan to abduct the primitives. After that there is no reason to fear. As the Stored Minds have informed us, no sentient being would commit a violent crime after his demands were met. So we need do nothing."

For most of the company, that ended the matter. Not for me. I said (but only to myself, not aloud), "Dear old friend Thermocline, you still don't know humans very well."

19

Captivity

I

What amazed Stan the most was how fast things happened in Achiever's ship. Only a moment after they heard the ultimatum he felt that little quiver that, so Achiever told him, meant they were spaceborne again. Moments later the simulated female named Sindi Something-or-other popped up right in the middle of the four captives. "Hi," she said. "I thought you'd like to know that we're on our way to—what do you call it?—One Moon Planet of Pale Yellow Star Fourteen. It'll be an hour or so before we get there, so you could take a nap if you wanted to. See you later." She winked out of existence, only to reappear almost immediately. "Forgot to tell you. Until we get everybody on board, you all have to stay right here." And when she was gone this time, she stayed gone.

Stan opened his mouth, but all that came out at first was, "Jesus." Then he recollected himself. "What's she talking about? Where can we get to that fast?"

Achiever gave him a moody look. "Can get most places, Stan. Recall my statement, this spacecraft come from Outside. New. Speedy. What I mean, goes like hell." He stared at the wall for a moment, then added, "Meaning is, nobody can catch us."

Maybe on purpose, maybe just because this coven of hijackers were new and unskilled at their trade, they had left the lookplates alive. Achiever got them going, and they showed the spacecraft landing on the planet. Stan watched in silence, hand in Estrella's hand, until she gasped and pointed. "Look," she commanded. One of the screens was displaying a rabble of ragged-looking bipeds that somewhat, but not very much, resembled human beings. They were being shepherded by some angry-looking humans.

"The Old Ones?" Stan more asked than said.

Achiever confirmed it glumly. "Meaning of this is this Wan has succeeded in purpose."

"Does that mean now he'll let us go?"

"Oh, Stan," Achiever moaned. "How foolishly you speak. This Wan will not ever let us go, for why should he?"

Stan was stubborn. "Maybe it doesn't matter what Wan wants, since he isn't here."

"Ah, additional foolish words! He is. We observed on lookplate while you slept, small message craft rendezvousing with self's ship here. Could only have been boarding of this Wan."

Estrella gave him an angry look. "Why do you make everything sound so bad?" she demanded.

Achiever gave a long, hissy sigh, but didn't answer. He simply pointed. The protohumans were climbing aboard the ship docilely enough—shaggy, bearded elderly ones, shaggy, bearded young adults, even fairly shaggy and beginning to be bearded children. Gender did not seem to make a difference. Most of them were carrying some kind of belonging, sometimes a spare kilt, a floppy rag thing that might have been considered a doll, packets of CHON-food, now and then a stick, a rock or a fistful of limp grasses. Their handlers were all black, and a lot less compliant. Futilely so; Stan saw one man lingering toward the back of the flock and then suddenly whirling to run away. At the first stride he threw up his hands, falling asprawl.

That was when Stan saw that they were not the only ones on the screen. Behind them were three other humans, who looked less angry but more dangerous. One was a woman with two long blonde braids and a whip. Another woman was darker-skinned, also with a whip. Finally there was a man—with a whip—who was shouting angrily at the man on the ground, who struggled feebly, then managed to get up again. He meekly, if dourly, rejoined the others, rubbing his hips and elbows as though they were painful. Stan had no doubt they really were.

Achiever, striving with the lookplates, finally got an interior view on one of them. In the great entry chamber of the ship the new arrivals were milling around, the handlers seeming as puzzled as their charges. One of the black-skinned handlers was a woman who was doing something that Stan and the others couldn't follow, since what she was doing appeared to involve something on the same wall as their camera. Then it explained itself. The woman was picking varicolored packets of CHON-food from the wall and tossing them to the Old Ones. Achiever grunted and turned to their own dispenser. "Is not bad idea, this is not. Do you wish?" he asked, pulling similar packets out of their own dispenser for them.

Stan unwrapped one of them, frowning. "Now what? Are we going to take off for some other planet?"

Achiever made a sound as close to a human tsk-tsk as his nearly lipless face would allow. "Have you no kinesthetic sense to any degree? Have you not felt takeoff already occurring?"

Stan opened his mouth to respond, but Estrella's hand was on his arm. Sulklly he subsided. The impulse to copy Achiever's attitude slowly dwindled . . . and then was forgotten entirely, because one of those annoying simulations popped up again.

This time it was not the same woman. It wasn't a woman at all; it was a stocky, sallow-skinned man, and he took a moment to make sure he had everybody's attention before he spoke. "Hello," he said, his tone more like that of the host at a party than a villainous kidnaper. "My name is Raafat—Raafat Gerges, actually, but you can just call me Raafat. Now that we're on our way Wan says I can tell you that you're now free to move about the ship. You won't get that cattle-prod thing anymore—that is, you won't unless you try to enter the control chamber. That's still off limits. Not that you could do anything even if you were inside, because the controls are locked, but Wan doesn't want you to try. Talk to you later." And he was gone.

"Hey," Estrella said, sounding almost cheerful. "Things are getting a little better. Let's look around."

She was tugging Stan toward the door when he stopped short, sniffing. He wondered if a flock of goats had come aboard, or the ship's waste-disposal system was backing up, or—

Then he didn't have to wonder anymore, because one of the odor generators came ambling through the doorway, bearded, kilted and quite stinky, and for the first time in his life Stan was in the presence of an Old One.

One Old One smelled bad. Fifty-odd of them, in Stan's view, were close to life-threatening. Even their handlers seemed to prefer being in rooms where only a few of the Old Ones were present. Such rooms were hard to find. "We took care of them," one handler—his name was Yussuf something—told Stan, "but we never had to live with them. They stayed mainly outdoors. And they really do stink."

It wasn't just sweat that made the aroma, it was their cavalier disregard of toilet training. The Old Ones knew perfectly well what the Heechee sanitary slots were for. They had no objections to using them when they were quite handy. That is, no more than four or five meters from wherever the need struck one of them. Farther than that the Old Ones found it less troublesome to relieve themselves against any flat vertical surface, or to allow their other wastes simply to fall to the floor. Before the end of the first day, Stan and the others had learned well to watch where they stepped.

They were given the privilege of spending time, though not much time in any individual visit, with the famous Wan himself. It wasn't the humans or the Heechee pair he visited. It was definitely his Old Ones. On the other hand, his simulated presence didn't seem to move them one way or the other. They went right on eating those CHON-food packets, or aimlessly, if amiably, wandering.

They were not entirely on their own. The black people who had seemed to be shepherding the Old Ones were muttering to themselves and pointing to the low Heechee ceilings; the males had to keep their heads bowed to keep from scraping against them, and even the women missed by not much more than a centimeter or two. They nodded to Stan and the others, but their main concern was the Old Ones. They walked among them, patting them, murmuring to them.

And then, without warning, the entire ship abruptly filled with fire-bright motes of light, white, red, yellow, blue.

Stan threw his arm around Estrella to protect her against whatever might be threatening. "What's that?" he demanded, almost angry, mostly apprehensive.

Achiever had not lost his ability to sneer. "What thing could this that possibly be, I am asked. One thing only, I inform you. A disrupter of order has been put into service and we, accordingly, have transited what you call a Schwarzschild. Do you fail still to take my meaning? I put it more simply still. We are Outside. We have now totally departed the Core."

II

As time passed, the smell of the Old Ones got worse. Now and then the handlers would make some attempt to pick up their droppings, but appeared to be too distressed to do a proper job. Achiever didn't even try, though he directed Salt to do so and she did her game best. Stan wouldn't let Estrella do that kind of work—who knew what pathogens the Old Ones might carry, or what those might do to the baby? They attacked the problem from a different angle. Along with the herders they tried to encourage the Old Ones who looked ready for it to use the sanitary slots. Some did. Not enough, though, and with fifty-some Old One metabolisms continually turning food into waste products they were losing the battle.

The head handler was a woman named Grace Nkroma, not at all domitable and pretty thoroughly pissed off. She did her best to keep her helpers busy, but it was a losing game. "You can't blame them," she told Stan and Estrella. "Two weeks ago we were in Kenya, fat and happy and thinking we were going to stay there until retirement. Didn't happen that way. After Wan swiped a bunch of the Old Ones, somebody decided they'd be safer in the Core. They packed all of us up, except for a couple of my handlers that were on leave, and next thing we knew we were on our way to this What-Do-You-Call-It Planet of the What's-It Star, and do you have any idea what that was like? Nothing was ready for us! We had a CHON-food machine, and a kind of off-and-on fountain for drinking water and that was it! No rooms for the staff to live in. Not even tents; we had sleeping bags and that was all there was. No toilets. You can't be too hard on the Old Ones for peeing and pooping all over the place, because that's all they had. Talk about bad planning!" And talk about it she did, and kept on talking about it. Estrella did her best to be a sympathetic listener. Stan only wished she would shut up.

Then there were the simulations. Sometimes it was the pretty girl named Sindi, or the Egyptian, Raafat. Quite often it was Wan himself, chuckling with pleasure as he moved among the Old Ones, cooing at them, singing to them in a horrible tuneless voice, telling them stories about the ways in which the great exterior world of humans and Heechee was set on cheating and destroying them all. Of course, Wan couldn't physically touch the Old Ones, nor they him. Stan couldn't touch Wan either, which he deeply regretted. He would have enjoyed punching out the man who had stolen them from their lives, and showed no sign of letting them go back home.

Estrella, curled up in his arms as they got ready for sleep, turned to face him long enough to ask, "What do you think, hon? Are we ever going to get out of this?"

"Hell, yes," he said stoutly. But even as he said it he was pretty sure it was a lie.

The handlers were openly mourning for the loss of the places and people they might never see again. ("That Nairobi! That's a twenty-four-hour town, all right! All the action you could want—and cheap, too!") They were on terms of easy cameraderie with their charges, calling each of them by name. But the handlers were most interested in Salt and Achiever, who were of a different species. "Oh, sure," the handler named Jared told Stan, "we saw Heechee before, now and then, when they came to look at the Old Ones, and then naturally when we came to the Core we saw plenty. But this is the first time we lived with them."

That kind of attention brought Achiever no joy. He spent almost all his waking hours working the ship's lookplates, dispatching Salt to bring his meals. For nearly two days Stan saw little of him, until one of the Old Ones ambled, or tried to amble, into the control room and was shock-whipped back outside. Achiever popped his head outside to see what all the screaming was about, and caught sight of Stan. "You come on the hell here," he invited. "I possess a thing to show you."

It turned out to be the image of a planet, as blue and white as any other habitable planet anywhere. It was about the size of a grapefruit on the screen and growing perceptibly larger. "Our destination," he declared, flapping his bony fingers at the picture. "I am quite entirely confident that this is to be the case, as no other planetary object has appeared."

"But—" Stan said, "but—" thinking of the endless days and weeks that had taken Estrella and himself to reach the Core in the first place—"but are we there already? So fast? It's only been a couple of days."

"Adequate time for this journey," Achiever declared. "No. No doubt exists. This is quite speedy spacecraft, and we are here. Object in look-plate is to be new home for you, for quite some time almost certainly, perhaps indeed for always."

III

When they arrived on the planet, everybody piled out of the spacecraft at once, humans and Heechee and Old Ones all hurried along by the electronic whips and shouted orders of Wan's invisible crew.

What Stan saw when he caught his balance was a patch of tangled, lush greenery the size of a football field, treed around the edges, with a friendly little lake at the far side. In one direction was a mountainside, rather bleak, bearing a handful of buildings—or rather, Stan corrected himself, all that was left of some ancient buildings that now were in ruins.

A gentle rain was falling. The air was not unpleasantly cool. And—Stan inhaled deeply and with unexpected pleasure—it smelled faintly of trees and grass and more distant vegetable odors, and not at all of the Old Ones.

That was a big plus as far as Stan was concerned, but it was looking a lot like the only one. Moments after the last Old One shambled wincingly out of the ship, bellowing and waving its hands to protect itself from the unseen lash, the ship's ports closed. With only the faintest of shrill whines, it lifted itself off the greenery. It rotated a quarter-turn on its axis, then slid swiftly up and almost out of sight along the mountainside. A moment later it reappeared, setting down on the very peak. And there it stayed, silent and unmoving.

Then everybody began trying to figure out what to do in this place they had not chosen.

The first thing Stan discovered, Grace Nkroma right behind him, was that they did have food. There was a pyramidal structure by the lake that churned out packets of CHON-food from one side and clear, cold water from another. "Good," Grace said, and raised her voice. "Yussuf, get a couple of the others and start passing these out to the Old Ones to keep them quiet." And to Stan, "What are those huts?"

He hadn't seen them before, a dozen of them or so, beehive-shaped and made, as far as he could tell from here, out of clay and pebbles. There was one entrance to each, presumably a door, and nothing at all like a window. "They don't look very comfortable," he said.

"At least you could get Estrella out of the rain," Nkroma pointed out.

That was true enough. Annoyed because he hadn't thought of it himself, Stan took Estrella's arm to help her toward the shelter. She was having none of that. "Oh, Stan," she said, "don't you think I can walk over there by myself? Anyway—Oh!" she said, stopping short.

An elderly man, or a simulation of one, had appeared directly in front of them. He was wearing what looked like something that had been donated to some undemanding charity. The man himself didn't look much better. "Excuse me," he said politely, barring their way. "These places are for the Old Ones, not you."

Stan scowled at him, knowing perfectly well that he could push right through that intangible figure, holding back because of the unknown, but possibly very unpleasant, consequences. "And who the hell are you?" he demanded.

"I'm Horace Packer. Wan's orders were to make our guests, the Old Ones, as comfortable as possible. I don't have any orders like that for you."

20

What Klara Wants

I

When you're Gelle-Klara Moynlin and everybody in the universe knows your name, you have a certain responsibility. You can't, even, go all panicky. Not that I was really about to, of course. When you've lived as long as I have, you can take a death threat now and then without getting all excited about it.

I wasn't excited. What I was was sad, because I couldn't get the vision of the murder of all those innocent people, Heechee and human, out of my mind—yes, and mad, too, because the person threatening to do it was that loathsome toad, Wan.

Why did I loathe him in particular? I hate to admit it, but I had a history with the little turd. For a brief, but not brief enough, time long ago I was his—let me see, what's the word? All right. I was his bought and paid-for whore. Never mind the details. Let's just say that I was in a place I wanted to get out of, and the only way I had to do it was in Wan's private spaceship. The trouble was, the price of passage was high. I worked it off in his bed. Or his bathtub or his dining table or, often enough, his floor, because when Wan wanted what he wanted, he wanted it right then and there.

Enough of that. Let me just say that, sexually, the little wretch was selfish and discourteous, and in his other relations he was worse. I thought he was crazy even then. (Later on, of course, I was sure of it.) I didn't exactly hate him, but I would have been just as pleased to hear he was dead. Especially now that he was willing to murder people by the planetful. Including me, of course, but honestly my own life was pretty nearly used up already. The ones I cared about were all those millions of others at risk, with a lot more to live for than I.

So my mood wasn't great. Hypatia did her best to cheer me up, as much as I would let her. That wasn't much. I didn't feel like girl talk, or actually any other kind of talk either. For a while I let her tell me news bulletins about what was happening with the Wan situation, but there weren't many of them. He had landed on that One Moon Planet of Pale Yellow Star Fourteen where the Old Ones had been taken. He had lashed their keepers with some kind of electronic pain maker until they loaded their charges onto his ship, after which he had pretty much disappeared. After she told me that much, I told her I didn't want to hear any more. Nor did I want to listen to music, or have a bubble bath, or be read to. The only thing I was willing to accept was food. I ate it all, even appreciated the taste of it all, but my mood didn't change. It stayed somber.

Then it got violently bad.

I was picking at one of Hypatia's quiches, and more or less watching some kind of modern-day *Hamlet* that Hypatia had put on the lookplate, when I heard her here-I-am-again cough coming from behind me. As I turned I saw that she wasn't in her usual fifth-century robes. She was sitting bolt upright on a hard bench, wearing a pretty plain kind of private-secretary tailored suit. Her expression was as businesslike as her costume, by all of which I knew she was about to tell me something I wasn't going to like.

I braced myself. "Go ahead. What is it?"

"Sorry to interrupt, boss, but Wan's gone off with all the Old Ones in his ship. They think he's heading right out of the Core."

I shrugged. "Good riddance. Does that mean we don't have to worry about his blowing up that star anymore?"

"I don't know. That isn't what I wanted to tell you about anyway."

That was when I got really certain it wasn't going to be something I was going to want to hear. I could feel all the muscles in my body tensing up. "Damn it, what?"

She said, "Hon, they've identified the spaceship he hijacked. It was the one Achiever was piloting. It looks like Stan and Estrella—and Salt— are all still aboard."

II

Even at that moment I thought that was sort of a funny way for her to say it. But I had more urgent things on my mind.

The thing is, I've never had many friends. I don't mean employees or the kids who lived on my island or bedmates. I mean friends. The kind of friends you hang out with because you just like having them around. Right now, here in the Core, I was even friend-poorer than usual. Not counting Hypatia, I just had three. There was Estrella, there was Stan, and there was Salt; and now all three of them were in mortal danger.

I couldn't help it. I raged at Hypatia. She took it well enough, having had plenty of practice. That wasn't satisfactory, though, since obviously this catastrophe was not her fault. So I ordered her to fetch me some better scapegoats to yell at.

She tried. Or said she did. Neither of the leading candidates showed up, though, when she called them. I suppose Thermocline and Sigfrid probably were pretty busy trying to get a handle on the situation. They weren't really that busy, though. They could have found time if they wanted to. No, there was a different explanation. They were avoiding me.

Likely enough that was smart of them. I wasn't fit to be talked to.

Hypatia kept bringing me bulletins. Nobody had been harmed at One Moon Planet; Wan's whip-bearing simulations had simply scooped up every one of the Old Ones and every one of their keepers unfortunate enough to be on duty just then. Achiever's ship had been one of the ultra-fast ones from Outside, so there wasn't any hope of catching it even if anyone tried. The precise location of the gravity-killing weapon that would blow up Planetless Very Large White Very Hot Star had not been pinned down and maybe never would; best guess was that it was in orbit, some-where near there, but too small to track. And so on. Lots of news, none of it good.

At least it gave me time to cool down. I don't mean I stopped being angry. I was angrier than ever, but it was all aimed at that little weasel, Wan, rather than the ones I had wanted so badly to scream at. I was sad, too. I mean the kind of sadness where you suddenly find your nose run-ning and tears trickling down your face even when you think you're think-ing about something else. The way I had been, after that Kilauea tsunami erased my beautiful little Raiwea.

I sat brooding for a few minutes while Hypatia fluttered around. She was giving me odd looks out of the corner of her eye—watching, I sup-posed, to see if I was going to blow up. When she tried to interest me in food again I shook my head. "Not hungry," I told her. I stewed around for a moment, then I got an idea. Whether it was a good one or not I did not know, but I said, "Get hold of that damn cook, Marc Antony, for me."

I don't know what she told him, but he did show up—not in person, though, but just on my lookplate. "What is it?" he demanded. "I am quite busy."

I wasn't taking anything from him, or from anybody else, either, just then. "God damn it," I said, "they can't do this! You have to do something."

He looked at me coldly. "What?"

"You have to go after them! Get them back. I don't care what it takes, do you hear me?"

"I hear you," he said, and disappeared. There was no good-bye. He just vanished from the plate.

That was what you'd call a mixed reaction. He understood what I wanted him to do, all right. I just didn't know whether or not he would do it, and when I turned around, Hypatia was giving me another of those fishy looks.

I was not feeling patient. "What?" I demanded.

"Hon," she said, sounding even more sympathetic than the situation called for, "I know how you feel."

Usually when Hypatia says things like that she's heading for a real yelling-at. This time, however, I was too upset to do it. I took a deep breath and tried to collect myself. "Pour me a drink," I ordered. When it rolled in I picked it off the server and took a good hit—icy cold vodka, the way I liked it—before I said, "I know you think you know how I feel. What about it?"

Hypatia got up from the couch she'd been lounging on and came over to stand beside me, her expression as sympathetic as the tone of her voice. I think she would have patted my head if she could. "They aren't worth it," she told me. "Men!"

I set the drink down to glare at her. "What the hell about men?"

She backed away a little, but said doggedly, "It's always some man or another, isn't it? Robin, Wan, Bill Tartch, all the others. You just never get over your glands."

It took me aback that even Hypatia would put Wan in the same sentence with Rob Broadhead, or even with Bill, although I understood that, from her point of view, all males were ravening rapists and bullies. . . .

Then I figured out what she was talking about.

"For Christ's sake, Hypatia, have you got it in your head that I'm hot for Stan Avery's body?"

She didn't say yes or no. She just gave me that long-suffering, understanding look and said, "I know. It's something you can't help, as long as you're a prisoner to those ovaries—"

I guess the look on my face stopped her. "Stan is a *child!*" I said—well, more like yelled, probably.

She didn't answer that. She didn't even mention the fact that, compared to me at my age, most of my lovers had been children, too, although it was true. She didn't say anything at all. She just looked at me with more of that patient, understanding expression of hers.

So I did something I rarely do. I tried to explain myself to her.

All right, I know she's just a machine intelligence, but there have been times in the last few forevers when she felt like the only friend I had left. I said, "Hypatia, sweetie, I'll be all right as soon as they're safe. I don't need another man. I don't need to scrape together some genetic material and whip up a baby of my own. I've got a better way to fill out my life now, and all I want is to get it back."

"Yes, hon," she said, bobbing her head, "I understand what you're saying."

What I wanted to do at that point was to yell at her some more. I didn't, though. What would have been the point? It was all outside her programming and experience, not just because she was a machine but because she was the particular machine she was.

Hypatia does, in fact, look and act very much like a human being. Sometimes I forget that she isn't, but then, sooner or later, she does something to remind me.

21

A Season on Arabella

I

In their first week on Arabella a couple of significant things happened. After two or three shivering nights on the bare ground, one morning a weird-looking machine with five spindly legs came rattling down over the rocks to their valley. If it had the power of speech, it didn't use it. All it did was deposit a load of sleeping bags in front of Stan, then back away and climb the hill again.

There were five of the bags. Enough for Stan and Estrella and for Grace Nkroma and her two helpers. There was none for Salt or Achiever. However, Stan and Estrella elected to double up in one bag, so that Salt and Achiever, whether they would have chosen it or not, could do the same with the other.

The other event wasn't as pleasant. Stan was not the only person whose thoughts were on the spacecraft so temptingly perched on the mountaintop, out of reach. After a few days Achiever could resist no longer. He was more than halfway up the mountainside before anyone noticed. He didn't get much farther than that. As he was gingerly picking his way through a belt of jagged rocks approaching the top he suddenly threw up his hands; his body jerked and twisted in improbable ways, and he fell to the ground.

Down below, everybody was shouting at once. It was Nkroma's assistant, Yussuf Pike, who first started up the hill after him. Stan dropped the hand he had been holding, gave Estrella a wild look, took a deep breath and was close behind.

It turned out that heroics were not needed. Suddenly a pair of the five-legged machines appeared from behind the crest of the hill. One loaded the unconscious Achiever onto the cargo flat atop the other, and they carried him back down.

He was unconscious, though writhing in pain. But not dead. Still, for the next couple of days he lay racked on his bedding, every limb and joint excruciatingly reminding him of his mistake.

All in all, by the end of their first month Stan and Estrella had learned more about their place of captivity, though not all of it was useful. They learned, for instance, that Wan would show up many times a day, moving affectionately among his Old Ones, and completely ignoring the humans. They learned that if they needed a bath, which they all quickly did, the little lake was the only place to get one. They learned that trying to get to the ship by climbing some other slope and coming at it from behind didn't work, because everywhere they tried, giant, jagged-edged rockslides made the mountain unclimbable. They learned that trying to subvert Wan's own people was doomed; the humans had nothing to offer that outweighed Wan's considerable capacity for punishment.

And yet, when Wan was with his Old Ones, he didn't seem so bad. He crooned to them. Whether the Old Ones enjoyed it very much was unclear. They were certainly aware of his presence, though not apparently much interested. Sometimes they would grunt back in response to his endearments. Mostly, though, they just ignored him.

"I bet he wishes he could scratch their tummies," Estrella observed, watching Wan's simulation murmur fondly to a couple of the Old Ones as they idly munched CHON-food in the shade of a giant tree.

Estrella pointed out, "At least this way he doesn't have to smell them." And suddenly sat erect, looking worriedly around, as a voice from nowhere asked, "Do they really smell bad? Smell like what?"

"Well," Stan began, a little startled but game, "it's kind of like—"

Estrella cut him off. "We don't like to talk to people we can't see," she said loftily. "Why don't you show yourself?"

A long pause. Then, hesitantly, "I better not. He's still here."

"What he?" Estrella demanded. "Are you talking about Wan?"

"Of course I'm talking about Wan. I don't know if he'd like the idea of me showing myself."

Stan was about to speak, but Estrella laid a hand on his arm. "All right, if you're afraid to be seen, at least tell us your name."

A pause longer still. Then, "Oh, all right. I'm Raafat Gerges. You can just call me Raafat. I'm the one who got you the sleeping bags. I would have thought"—the voice now sounding injured—"that you'd've been grateful."

"Oh, we are," Estrella assured him. "That was kind of you, even if you didn't give us enough to go around."

Another of those pauses. Then, the voice now sounding puzzled, "I saw what you did for those Heechee, but I don't know why."

"They're our friends," she explained.

That brought about the longest pause of all, as though Raafat Gerges was trying to digest that concept, but Estrella didn't wait him out. She stood up, looking around all the parts of the compound. "Raafat? See for yourself, Wan isn't there now. Why don't you let us see you?"

That took some thinking over, too, but then he said, "Okay," and appeared before them at the same moment.

Raafat Gerges was a sight worth waiting for. Not physically. He had black hair and a sallow complexion, not a spectacle to turn anyone's head. What he wore, on the other hand, was undeniably impressive: a snow-white tunic, jeweled bracelets, sandals studded with what looked like more jewels, and a headgear—you couldn't call it a hat—that looked something like a brimless stovepipe, though made of some sort of colorful fabric and studded with the most jewels yet.

He knew what a spectacle he was, too. He preened himself some more, explaining, "I'm Egyptian, you know. But I didn't want to look like just any old Egyptian, so Wan let me dress myself up a little." He struck an attitude. "I think it works well, don't you?"

Raafat Gerges was the first of their bashful visitors to show himself, but not the last. While they talked, one by one, others appeared—two women and a pair of remarkably muscled men. "When you get a chance to simulate a body for yourself," said one of them—he was velvety black and very tall—"you might as well do one that looks good. I'm DeVon Washington," he added, and the others in turn introduced themselves: a man with a shaved head and black, closely cropped beard, Khoa Yukman; a woman with almond skin, delicate little nose and masses of wavy blonde hair, Sindi Gaslakhpard; and another woman, also blonde, though a lot less sexy, with the name of Phrygia Todd.

The simulations gazed at the captives silently, seeming wary, until Estrella remembered her manners. "I'm Estrella Pancorbo," she said. "This is Stan—"

DeVon raised a hand. "We know your names," he told her. "You people also," he added to Grace Nkroma and some of the others as they began to gather around.

"Oh," Estrella said, and then ventured small talk. "Raafat's been very kind to us," she told them. "He got us sleeping bags—"

"We know," the blonde named Sindi said.

"Ah," Estrella said. She tried again. "We had some excitement when Achiever tried to get into—"

"—the spaceship," the blonde named Phrygia finished for her. "We saw it. Can we ask you something? What's the matter with your face?"

Years of getting used to the question hadn't made Estrella like it. "Accident," she said shortly, and changed the subject back. "It seems you guys spend a lot of time watching us. How come?"

DeVon Washington grinned, more rueful than amused. "We've got a lot of time."

He stopped there, looking over Stan's shoulder. "Oh, hell! So long," he said, and all four of them disappeared at once.

When Stan turned he saw that Wan was back again, now murmuring to a pair of Old Ones by the shore of the lake. Grace was looking at him, too.

"You know," she said, "I think they're more afraid of him than we are."

Behind her Achiever made the sound that he intended for a chuckle. "Of course this is so. You ask why? I answer this for you: it simply is because of their knowing him better than we."

II

The second month wasn't any better than the first, and the third was worse than that. There was the boredom. There was the unacceptable food. There was the boredom. ("If we had Stork at least we could look at the baby." "Please, Stan. It wasn't my fault, the way they hustled us out of the ship." Every morning at sunrise Stan lifted his eyes to the hilltop where the spacecraft was perched. He wasn't just looking. He was yearning, not just for the hope of escape, not just for the Stork bracelet that was still in it. He knew, of course, that he was yearning for the unattainable, as Achiever had demonstrated. Was still demonstrating sometimes, going to sleep, when his eyes were closed but every muscle in his torso was rippling wildly.

When Estrella and the others challenged him, he insisted he was all right. "Sleep badly for reason of having no good sleeping grasses, merely.

In regard to sleeping bag, what I declare is, ptui. Better than nothing? Perhaps. Arguable. However, assuredly less good than nearly any other possible thing." To show that that subject was finished he turned his narrow head and stared up at the ship. "In any event," he said, "on next attempt will surely achieve purpose, as person named Achiever would properly achieve." He gave them a thin-lipped grin to show that he had just made a joke.

Salt was not in a joking mood. "This cannot occur," she declared. "You don't remember? Ship was made obedient to machine commands by means of servomodule, not persons. You could not operate same."

He gave her a superior look. "Not correct. Have spoken of this with Raafat Gerges. Wan has since nullified machine override. Reason due no doubt to keep Raafat or other such person from flying it away."

Stan straightened up. "So if you could get into the ship you could fly it?"

"Mean exactly this, yes."

But Salt was flapping her bony fingers at him. "Nevertheless," she said sharply. "Never-the-*damn*-less. May not survive a second punishment. No. If person is to make additional attempt I am to be that person."

"Are not!" Achiever roared. "Are carrying child of mine, which cannot be risked! I firmly and irrevocably order this to you!"

"But it can't be you, either," Estrella put in. "You tried it once, and the second time could kill you. Right?" She was looking for confirmation at Stan and a couple of the Old Ones' handlers, who had been drawn to the discussion.

Most of them were nodding, but not Stan. He took a deep breath. "I'll do it," he said.

Estrella gave him a horrified look, but again it was Achiever who demurred. "How foolish you are," he said, flapping his bony fingers at Stan. "What is point of entering ship? To bring same down here so we can enter and depart this planet. Who can do this? Trained pilot can do this. No other person can. Are you trained pilot? You are not, apart from childish task of sitting in spacecraft others have programmed when coming to Core. Especially have you piloted spacecraft of this new and quite fast model? No. Have not. Therefore have no hope of achieving."

While Achiever was laying down his logical proofs, one of the Old Ones' handlers, Geoffrey, was listening intently. "I'm a pilot," he said.

Achiever gave him an unbelieving look. "You? Pilot of spacecraft?"

"Well, no, I never actually piloted any spacecraft," Geoffrey conceded. "I flew our ultralight back in the Maasai Mara, though." ("Hah," Achiever sneered.) "Well, that's not all. When I was a kid I was going to go to Gateway, only this job came along and I didn't. But I studied for it."

"Studied operation of spacecraft?" Achiever asked skeptically.

"Sure. Well, sort of. There was a vid game about Gateway, you know—you got in the ship, and you took off, and flew to some planet. They said it was really realistic. I played it a lot."

Achiever said, "Hah!" again, but this time with less force. He studied Geoffrey's face for some moments before, at last, saying, "Tell of this game. Describe for me layout and purpose of controlling implements. And do so quickly and in detail."

For the next four days Achiever was constantly drilling Geoffrey in how to use the ship's controls in the unlikely event that he ever did get his hands on them. Stan eavesdropped on as much of it as he could, trying to relate what Achiever was talking about to his memory of their old Five. More complicated, sure, he thought. But not hopelessly so.

Then, on the fourth day, Geoffrey began the climb.

Every person in the compound—human, Heechee, Old One—was watching. As Geoffrey at last stood up and began that final run across the rocks at the top of the mountain, Stan, for one moment, allowed himself a dizzying feeling of hope. . . .

Blighted, of course. As with Achiever, Geoffrey's arms suddenly flew wildly about. He dropped to the ground and did not move.

The handling machines had him halfway down the slope before Stan and Grace Nkroma and the others could reach him. It was too late. "He's dead," Grace said, straightening up. "That does it."

Achiever bobbed his head. "All greatly unfortunate," he said, "but next time—"

Grace gave him a look between sorrow and rage. "There won't be a next time! Not ever!" she snapped. "That's over!"

III

Then, for a time, things began to look a little better for the castaways. Not actually good, no. But not quite as bad.

The first sign came after Wan's visits to his Old Ones had dwindled almost to nothing. Perhaps that was what made the simulations a little braver. When one of the handling machines appeared with something on its back the captives found it was a gift for them.

What kind of a gift was another question. "Is that a school desk?" Grace asked.

"I think it's the kind the Heechee use sometimes. It's got one of those flowerpot things on the back."

"So what does it do?"

Though Stan and the other humans puzzled over the desk, its secrets remained unlearned until Achiever turned up. "Oh, how fractionally witted you all are," he remarked, and Stan was reminded that, although Heechee didn't smile very well, their sneer was nearly perfect. "Simply step back. Farther. Now, you see." When he twiddled with something under the ledge of the desk there was a faint click and a nearly silent hiss as three racks of prayer fans rolled themselves out from storage. Achiever glanced at them and saw no reason to alter his look of disdain. "How outmoded! Simply resembling those of my childhood or somewhat more recent, before adoption of faster, smaller, more capacious recording systems invented Outside. However, may be of use. You are familiar with method for same?"

They were. Grace especially; before Achiever had finished speaking she had already picked a fan at random and slipped it into the receptacle. An image at once sprang into light. Image of what, though?—poster, advertising sign, title page of a book? They all crowed around to study it, and Estrella was the first to speak. "It's printing," she said.

"But not English printing," Stan added, his mouth ajar in concentration. "I think—yeah, maybe it's Russian. There was this Russian embassy kid in school with me and he had magazines that looked like this. He tried to teach me the alphabet. . . ." He was tracing some of the letters with a finger. "I think that's a T . . . and an O . . . that next thing is an L . . . the C is an S . . . another T and an O—Oh, cripes," he said, suddenly grinning. "You know what we've got here? I think it's probably the Russian-language works of Leo Tolstoy."

Estrella wrinkled her nose. "And how are we going to read them, would you say?"

Stan would not be discouraged. "There are lots of other fans. Let's look!"

There were indeed lots of others, twenty-two by count. Fifteen unfortunately were in the same undecipherable Russian, but seven were more useful.

Whichever of Wan's long-ago organic servitors had assembled them, she—it had to have been a she—had obviously been young, lonely and foreign-born. The Russian-language fans were—well, Russian. Stan concluded, by his best attempt at phonetic reconstruction, that a wide spectrum of Russian literature was represented, though the only other author he was reasonably sure of identifying was Solzhenitsyn. Some were even poetry, or looked that way in the manner they were set on their pages. Some were not books at all: they were ballet performances (beautiful), or plays (as incomprehensible as the texts), or musical numbers (splendid, at least where nobody was singing in Russian).

The whole camp, a few of the Old Ones included, was watching some sort of incomprehensible musical thing when DeVon Washington popped up, smiling, pleased with himself for having thought of such a clever gift. No, he admitted, the fans weren't actually his—weren't anybody's, really, because they had been left behind by one of Wan's long-ago organic concubines.

Which made Grace Nkroma look up. "What else did she leave?" she demanded.

Washington held up a finger, flicked out of existence for a moment and returned. "This is what we've got," he said, and began to recite a catalogue of available leftover goods. There wasn't anything really useful. No food or clothing; everything of that sort had long since rotted away. Most ceramics had survived pretty well, though, and so of course had everything made of the nearly indestructible Heechee metal. So when Washington's next load of gifts arrived, Estrella had a mirror that not only reflected well but radiated a faint blue glow, and everyone in the compound had teacups to drink their water out of, though of course no tea.

IV

There were many things Stan missed, in this dismal corner of the universe, but none much more than Stork. He missed his daily viewing of his child. He saw that Estrella's belly was getting a little rounder every day, and he listened to her tell about all the little kicks and twitches she felt— but, even when he put his hand on her, he couldn't feel them. He supposed that by now the tiny thing might have changed in wonderful ways, actual features, usable limbs, all sorts of things he could have seen for himself.

But then, while they were having their before-bed dip in the lake he saw something that even Stork wouldn't have shown him. He was staring at her gently rounded midsection. "Hey! What happened to your belly button?"

She laughed at him. "You just noticed? Right, I used to be an insy and now I'm an outsy. That's what happens when you're pregnant. The baby's growing. Like babies do." She tossed the last of her laundered garments on the narrow beach to dry. "But don't worry," she told him. "I'm still pretty spry for an almost mom. Let's race back to the bedroll to warm up."

They did warm up, actually very enjoyably, but then Stan lay next to the sleeping Estrella, wide awake, staring up at Arabella's unfamiliar stars, thinking about the morrow. It was not a happy thought because after tomorrow there would be another tomorrow, and another. And some time, after all those tomorrows had passed, would come an inescapable today, the today when Estrella would come to term, and the only person around to help her through childbirth would be the veterinarian, Grace Nkroma.

The next morning, the first minute he could get away from Estrella herself, Stan sought out Grace Nkroma. When he began to tell her his worries she didn't provide much comforting. "For God's sake, buck up!" she ordered. "She'll be all right. I know what I'm doing."

Stan gave her a ferocious look. "You? What makes you think you can handle Estrella having a baby?"

"Well, let's see. I got my Doctor of Veterinary Medicine in Johannesburg and then I had two years with the Bureau of Game in Nairobi, mostly on breeding programs, before this job with the Old Ones came along."

"Game! You're talking about *animals*!"

Grace's expression froze. "The Old Ones are animals, all right. Just like you and I are animals. The kind of animals they are is called primates. Same as you and me. How much difference do you think there is between one primate and another?"

"Yeah, but have you ever actually done a childbirth?"

Grace sounded exasperated. "Sure. Shelly had twins right after I got there. You've seen them running around, haven't you? There was no problem."

"And how did you prepare her for the birth?"

Grace regarded him with annoyance, then with the kind of look that conceded a point made by the other debater. "I loaded Shelly into the ultralight and flew her into Nairobi for ultrasounds, is all. Okay, we don't have any of that stuff. I'll just have to get along without it." She turned away, then back. Her voice softened. "Listen, there's every chance she'll be all right."

"And if something goes wrong?" A shrug. "You know what I wish? I wish I had one of those what-to-do books."

"And what kind of books are those?"

Stan turned defensive. "I saw one once. One of the, ah, girls who lived near us in Istanbul had it. It was in Turkish, actually, but that didn't matter. When Tan and I sneaked it once all we were looking for was dirty pictures. There weren't any, though."

Frederik Pohl

"Oh, for Christ's sake," Grace said, her annoyance no longer faint. "Take a good look around. I don't have one of those books. I don't have any equipment, either. All I have is what I know, and if that isn't good enough—If that isn't good enough—" Her voice trailed off. She was silent for a moment. Then in a different tone, "Never mind that, Stan. She's healthy. I don't anticipate any big problem. Just make sure she gets food and rest and you don't aggravate her too much. I think we'll be fine."

Grace's reassurances didn't reassure Stan. He couldn't get the worry out of his mind, and couldn't help talking to everyone who would listen about the problem—when Estrella wasn't nearby, that is. It didn't take long for them to get tired of the subject, though. He began on Wan's people.

DeVon Washington showed some tolerance for the discussion. His patience wasn't endless, though, and when Washington began to look as though he might flicker away at any moment Stan changed his tack. "Okay, DeVon, then tell me something else. What do you think are the chances that somebody will come to rescue us in the next month or so?"

Washington was amused but patient. "Who would that somebody be?"

"God, I don't know. There must be some inhabited planets somewhere near here, mustn't there?"

Washington considered the question, shook his head. "Um . . . no. I don't know much about it, but I don't think so. The way I heard it there are only a few inhabited planets left in the outside galaxy. Maybe a dozen, and most of them pretty nearly empty anyway—you know, religious cults that don't believe in machine storage and so on. I heard Wan say once that there was less than a billion flesh-and-blood people left out here."

Stan was taken aback. "I had no idea. What about machine-stored?"

"Oh, sure, there's plenty of them out there, but they wouldn't help you. They don't care a bit for anyone but themselves. Can you blame them? You know what it's like to be machine-stored? When you own your own works, I mean, so you can do anything you like, with anybody you like, as long as you like? Hell, I can't wait for Wan to turn me loose."

Stan said stoutly, "Then somebody will come after us from the Core."

Washington gave him a look of wide-eyed surprise. "From the Core? How could they?—oh, maybe you didn't know!"

"Know what?" Stan said, afraid to ask the question because he wasn't sure he wanted to hear what the answer would be.

It was as bad as he feared. Worse. "That star," Washington said. "It's going to explode. Honest. Never mind what Wan said. Letting people he hates get away with anything isn't his way. He left orders. Give us enough time to get clear out into the galaxy, he said. Then blow the sucker up.' "

The first thing any one of the captives did when they heard Stan's news was to deny it. "Jesus, Stan, can't you see that's just some of Wan's crap to make us suffer more?" Or just, "You're crazy." But then they began third-degreeing each of the simulations from Wan's retinue, every chance they got. And then, when it finally sank in, they just stopped talking about it at all. Because what was the use?

They didn't stop thinking about it, though. Long after Estrella had gone to sleep, Stan lay awake, thinking, until he heard the sound of one of the handling machines coming, then going away again, heard no sound of anyone else getting up to see what the machine had left, and dismissed it from his mind until he had to get up to pee.

It was, he thought, pretty nearly time to fill in this slit trench and start a new one. Wondering if some of the Old Ones could be taught to dig a latrine, he was strolling back under the stars when he caught sight of what the machines had left. It was a simple record fan, set down next to the desk, on top of a sheet of blue-glowing Heechee metal so that it was conspicuous in the dark.

Estrella was still sound asleep, her cheek on her two joined hands and very faintly snoring. He debated waking her up to see. Curiosity won out. He juggled the fan into the flower-holder receptacle as he had been taught, and at once a picture sprang up.

What he had there, he discovered, was an actual book. A book that was in the English language, perhaps once the property of one of Wan's organic lovers, back when they were all still organic. And its title was *From Zero to Thirty-nine: The Weeks of a Pregnancy*.

It was the work he had longed for, the gift of one of Wan's people. Which one Stan could not guess, but whoever it was had earned a deep gratitude. He couldn't wait until morning to dip into it.

His intention was to read it from the beginning, but as he scrolled through the pages it became evident that the beginning dealt with things that had already happened. Trying to read about them made his own eyelids droop. He promised himself that one day quite soon he would read every word, but meanwhile he sped through the chapters. There was one for each week, and each chapter had a drawing of what the unborn child should look like at that point. The book was no Stork, of course. But it was a lot better than anything he had had before. He scrolled right through to the end of that part with pleasure.

Then he turned to another page and the pleasure rapidly diminished. The next chapter was on the possibility of miscarriages.

Stan was astonished to find how many things could cause a woman to lose her baby, from lupus (whatever that was) to congenital heart disease. As well as bacterial vaginosis (whatever that was), and even things like high fever and smoking (whatever *that* was.) Furthermore, the immune systems of some women might mistake the embryo for an invading microorganism, and do their best to destroy it. Some women might have a malformed uterus, or some sort of growth there, and that might be just as deadly.

How could he tell if Estrella had any of those things? He couldn't. Sigfrid might have been able to tell, or Dr. Kusmeroglu, but neither of them was present.

He turned the book off and stared up at the unfamiliar stars in the night sky of Arabella. He was no longer at all sleepy. He was worried. It occurred to him that there was more to the book, possibly even some healing thing for it to say. He scrolled through the book again, looking for cheer.

It wasn't there.

What he found was even worse than the chapter on miscarriages. It wasn't just that a baby might be lost. It was more horrible by far. The baby might be born, but born as a monster. Born with two heads! Or born as a Cyclops, with a single great central eye. Or as a kind of preparation for a student course in anatomy, with the internal organs on the outside of the body; or with a tiny head that held no brain at all; or—

Oh, there was no limit to the things that could go wrong! For instance, what about twins? They did not always turn out to be a lovably cute pair. Sometimes what you got was two babies joined together at skull or spine. Or one twin so ravaged by the other's hunger that it was born no bigger than a finger, sometimes as a tiny, hideous animalcule still attached to the larger twin.

And even if none of those terrible disasters happened, what could occur if the baby simply took a little longer to be born? With no more than an extra week or two in the womb it could arrive with skin cracked or peeling, or thin and wrinkled, likely enough having moved its little bowels while still unborn, so that it was stained green with meconium, which it might well have inhaled . . . likely gasping for breath . . . likely born with a more difficult labor, and thus with the greater chance of the baby twisting itself into strangulation inside the coils of the umbilical cord.

Stan raised his horrified eyes from the book because, two meters away, Estrella was stirring. He quickly turned the book off again, debated destroying it, but was too late. "Hon?" she said drowsily. "What are you doing?"

"I had to pee," he told her, desperately looking for a hiding place for the book.

"Well, come back to bed," she ordered.

"In a minute." The only place to put the book was in one of those little closets at the base of the desk. He shoved it in, hoping to find a better place in the morning, and slid into the sleeping bag next to her warm, soft body.

It was becoming a tight fit, but she commanded, "Put your arms around me," and he did, the two of them spooned together under the bright stars of no constellations Stan had ever seen before. Over the top of the mountain the sky was paling, the sun—whatever nameless sun that was— almost ready to rise.

Estrella was asleep again already. Not Stan. Stan had lost any desire to sleep at all, his mind filled with thoughts about the woman next to him, and the growing organism in her belly, and how he was going to deal with such matters as the kind of pregnancy disorders he had been reading about, or indeed with simple childbirth and infant care, in this place where no baby had been born for thousands of years.

There was no good answer to that. And half an hour later, leaving Estrella sleeping behind him, Stan began the long climb up the mountain.

Climbing the slope was harder than he had expected. Forty-five minutes later he was covered with dirt and blood from the dozen slips and slides that had come when he lost footing on a rock, or tripped over some of the tangled undergrowth. Most of the scratches were still bleeding.

But now in the dawnlight the ship, bright red and icy blue, gleamed clearer than he had ever seen it before. Panting, he paused for a moment before his last push. Between him and the ship was that outcrop of tumbled rocks, edges ominously jagged. There was an excellent chance of slipping and falling as he tried to cross it. More than that, he was right about where Wan's punishing nerve weapon felled the others who had tried the climb.

He had not forgotten that the punishment could be death.

He stopped cold. It had just penetrated his mind that the word "death," so easily spoken by those who had no immediate fear of it, might have a quite literal meaning for him. He might not be alive when the sun rose at the end of this night. Nor was there any Here After down the hill, nor was it likely that any of Wan's people would risk displeasure by attempting to machine-store him.

No. What dead meant to him in this place was never being alive in any form ever again. It meant never touching his living daughter, never finishing his lessons with Socrates—never doing anything at all that took an act on his part, nothing but lying forever in Arabella's unfriendly soil until all the parts of him had decayed away.

He swallowed, and then he found another fear.

Even if he did gain entrance to the spacecraft, what would happen then? The little bit he remembered of the Gateway ships and of Achiever's instructions to Geoffrey no longer seemed even remotely adequate. He might inadvertently fly the ship a thousand kilometers away and be unable to get back. Or crash it into the mountain. Or, most likely of all, never get it off the ground in the first place. Every one of those modes of failure seemed more likely than that he would somehow succeed in flying it, landing it and boarding all the captives—or at least boarding Estrella, with either Salt or Achiever to fly the thing home. He considered all those chances, then sighed and got back in crawling position—

But didn't crawl anywhere, because an unfamiliar voice in his ear was speaking to him. "You are Stan Avery, aren't you? Don't go any farther. We need to talk."

Stan looked around, saw no one, hazarded a guess. "Is that you, Raafat?"

"No. Who is Raafat? In any case I am not he. I am Marc Antony, formerly your chef and now"—there was a hint of humor in the voice—"perhaps your rescuer. That is, with some assistance from yourself."

V

Then everything went quickly. The last bit of the climb was the hardest. It was also the shortest, though, and if the climber didn't worry about more scratches and scrapes—and now had no fear of the weapon that had killed Geoffrey; Marc Antony had disabled it—it could go quickly. By the time he reached the door Marc Antony had opened it. "Sit down by those knurled wheels," he commanded. "Sorry about the perch, but you won't have to be there long. Now, the first thing you have to do . . ."

And Stan did as ordered, setting the smaller knobs on the right side just so, then the ones on the left side moved just a smidgen, then this, then that, then quickly this other—

It all worked out just as Marc decreed. The spacecraft lifted. It slid gracefully through the air to the encampment, touched lightly down on the greensward, and there they were.

The first captive to see the ship coming down for them shouted so loudly that everyone was awake and yelling with excitement by the time it touched down, a few meters from the lake shore. Then it was simple. Everyone began boarding at once. There was nothing to pack, nothing that anyone wanted to take away from the planet of Arabella.

Achiever was the first aboard, twitching with excitement as he saw his ship's controls again. Salt was next, but not by herself. She was shepherding Grace and the brightest of the Old Ones, the youth named Pony, as between the two of them they were helping Estrella aboard.

Stan spent the next few minutes hugging and being hugged. When the last of the Old Ones, grumbling and belching, came aboard the ship Achiever—already perched at the pilot's seat, his hands already on the controls—called impatiently to Marc Antony, "Is proper time for departure, I expect?"

"One moment," Marc Antony commanded. He indicated one of Wan's handling machines, stilting down the slope. It bore eight or ten storage fans. "Bring them aboard," he ordered. "Then we can leave."

Stan had been waiting for that moment. "Where to? Do you know where the nearest civilized planet is? I mean really civilized, with a good hospital and everything?"

"I do not think the matter is that urgent, Stan. Estrella looks reasonably well to me. I prefer to return to the Core."

Stan looked baffled. "But—Oh, I see! It hadn't gone off before you left, so you don't know. Look, Marc. I wouldn't guarantee there's anything left of the Core. Wan left orders to blow up the star anyway."

That got Marc Antony's full attention. "Explain that," he ordered.

"What's to explain? Before Wan left the Core he ordered one of his people—Orbis? Some name like that—to give them enough time to get away, and then fire it off. This Orbis sounded like a real nut. He wanted—"

"How long a time?" Marc demanded.

"Oh, I don't know. Not long."

Grace cut in. "It was twenty-four hours. DeVon Washington told me."

Surprisingly, Stan saw the first smile he had ever seen on Marc Antony's face. "Twenty-four hours," he said. "Core time, you mean. That is twenty-four hours multiplied by the 40,000-to-1 differential. No, we're in no hurry, Stan Avery. No hurry at all."

22

The Rescue

I

I was not umoved by Gelle-Klara Moynlin's passionate entreaties. I shared her impatience with the pusillanimous behavior of the Heechee. There is such a thing as being too unremittingly logical, and besides the Stored Minds had had no right to make decisions for human beings.

However, it was true that the danger to Planetless Very Large White Very Hot Star overrode any personal considerations. My primary efforts, therefore, had to be directed to neutralizing that menace.

It is embarrassing to me to admit my efforts did not succeed.

The difficulty was in locating the torpedo that carried the starbursting device. To do so required sorting through every spacecraft trail that had ever approached that star, identifying the approaches and departures for every one of them until the one which approached the star but did not depart again was found. That, of course, would be the one we sought. In principle it was quite a simple task, though arduous. When I displayed the trails for my analysis there were a much larger number of them than I had anticipated.

While I was considering that matter, Klara's shipmind called.

I heard them out but made no promises. Then, when I returned to my own surround, I came to a decision. I summoned one of the high-speed torpedoes, and while waiting for its arrival gave my sous-chefs new instructions. No one of them was anywhere near as able as myself, to be sure. But there were 293 of them and, collectively, they possessed great analytical power.

Diverting them away from their usual tasks meant that many clients would be getting a restricted menu for a time, but I saw no choice.

Then I took off.

It was a tedious fllght, but not a challenging one. I had had no difficulty in tracking Wan's ship-traces to his hideout. Its identity was not a surprise to me. There is a saying I have heard, though I was never given the source—most likely Plato, or George Washington, or some other ancient political person: "The dog returns to his vomit." Wan had. Its name was Arabella.

Truthfully, I had rather expected that would be the case. Even for an organic, Wan was not particularly inventive.

After I had left my vessel in a forced orbit I sought for and quickly found Achiever's ship. It sat on top of a smallish mountain, below which lay the little valley where the captives were held.

It was a nuisance that Wan had removed the servomodule, thus deprogramming the ship so that no nonmaterial person could fly it anymore. I suppose he did that because he was afraid that, given a chance, some of his nonmaterial people would get bored with life on Arabella and fly off with it. But with the help of one of the organics—it was that young Turkish boy that Klara had been concerned about, Stan Avery, the one who had excluded me from his residence for a time—I flew the ship to the valley. The captives seemed to be in good shape, or as good shape as organics ever are in, so I opened the ship's doors to them. While they were boarding everyone my presence was not required, so I attended to the more important business.

Dealing with Wan presented no real difficulties. I easily identified the collection of rabbit warrens tunneled into the mountain that Wan and his servants had occupied. It had not changed much since my last visit, except, of course, that everything that could decay had done so. (Not a surprise. By Outside standards, that had been a seriously long time ago.) Most of the tunnels were no longer in physical use, since there were no longer any organics with his company. But Wan did have to have a physical place to store their data fans, and that too was easy to locate.

Wan's people were all there, waiting for me as I entered the storage chamber—rather unimaginatively protected with bars and locks, but with nothing that could keep out even the feeblest AI. And his entire company of machine-stored servants were deployed around the rack of storage fans that held their—well, I've heard organics call them their "souls." Most of them stood silently, looking as though they wished they were somewere else. One, however, seemed pugnacious.

I recognized Wan immediately. Since becoming machine-stored he had elected to make himself a good deal less unattractive, but he was the most belligerent-looking of all. "Who the hell are you?" he demanded. "What the hell are you doing here? Anyway, you're not leaving. Robin! De-Von! Take this man prisoner."

He was quite amusing, really. I didn't bother to answer. I merely wrapped myself around him, as I had done to his servant long before, and began to squeeze.

None of his present servants interfered. I hadn't expected them to. It would have made no difference if they had, of course, nor did Wan's own struggles. In less than ten milliseconds I had him cooped up in his data fan; I turned it off and ordered the others: "Have this delivered to the spacecraft in the valley."

They didn't look eager to carry out my instructions. They didn't look as though they objected much, either. After a moment one of them spoke. She was human and female, and she apparently had given much thought to her appearance. "Take us with you, please?" she asked.

That had not been among my priorities, but I could see no objection. "You are not to waken Wan," I told them, "or you will deeply regret it. However, you may include your data fans with his on the ship." They had started a handling machine loading their fans for the trip down into the valley and I returned there as well. After that it was only a matter of completing the boarding and flying back home.

23

In Orbis's Ship

I

That hotshot AI that calls himself Marc Antony never asked, but I have a name. It's Phrygia Lorena Todd. If he blamed me for working for that freak, Wan, that's his problem. It wasn't my idea. I certainly didn't want to get involved in the Planetless Very White Very Hot Star thing at all, but Wan didn't give me any choice. He claimed he had the right to do anything he wanted with me, since, after those damn buildings collapsed into the subway station in Kuala Lumpur, where I was unlucky enough to be driving one of the cars, he claimed he owned me.

Wan wasn't the first man who thought that. He was the first one who had the law on his side, though. So when he told me I had to pilot Orbis McClune to where he could blow up that star, I didn't see any way of getting out of it.

Anyway, the way he put it to me, the blowing up wasn't necessarily going to happen. I listened to the broadcast when he made it and, sure enough, he said if they'd give him his damn cavemen he'd call it off.

All right, I shouldn't have believed a scum like him. But I wasn't in any position to argue, was I? If you think you could have handled the whole thing better, well, maybe you could, and I hope next time you're the one who's stuck with the problem, not me.

Still, the way it worked out, it was a damn good thing for everybody that I was there.

Maybe I shouldn't have taken so seriously the way Marc Antony treated me like dirt all the way back to the Core. He treated everybody else like dirt, too. All the same, I couldn't help snickering when he got his comeuppance.

See, the minute we passed through the Schwarzschild he got on his communicator, talking to whoever it was he'd left in charge of things when he took off for Arabella, and I could tell he wasn't liking what he was hearing. Most AIs won't lose their temper, but Marc Antony sure lost his. "You have not located the vessel with the nullifier?" he was snarling—it wasn't a statement, it was a question, and a rhetorical one at that. "That is unacceptable! It is also unacceptable that you cannot undertake to complete the task of locating it in less than two hundred million additional milliseconds! That much time is not available!"

When Marc Antony cut the connection he was looking—well, not worried, I'd say, because I don't think AIs worry much, but certainly kind of concerned. I asked him, "What's the problem?"—not really caring what the answer was.

I thought at first that he wasn't going to answer, but he did. "I do not think you would understand," he told me, "but it is a very serious matter. I left my subsets a task to do in my absence. It was a long and tedious job, to be sure but not a particularly demanding one. However, they have failed. Now I have no way of reaching the vessel in time to prevent the explosion."

"Huh," I said. "I do, though."

That got his attention. "Do not make jokes with me," he said, sounding dangerous.

"No joke. I was the one who set it in its orbit. I can take you right to it."

Antony probably didn't believe me right off, but he didn't have any better choices. When we got there and I showed him Orbis's torpedo on the lookplate I thought he might have said something a little bit apologetic to me. He didn't. "You, pilot," he said, looking straight at me. "Now you will do something else for me." Then he told me what the something else was.

I wasn't thrilled about taking orders from a bad-tempered AI in an apron and white cap, especially when he was ordering me to do something I'd never done before. "Let me get this straight," I said. "You want me to, what, project myself to Orbis's ship? How do I know it will work?"

He gave me an impatient nod. "It works. I've done it myself."

"Okay," I said, not entirely convinced but going along with it. "Then why don't you do it this time?"

"Because he knows you. I'll be there with you, but I won't show myself. I don't want to frighten him."

I didn't say what I thought the chances of Orbis McClune being frightened by a man in a chef's hat might be. I just said, "I'm not easy in my mind about this."

Then he just said, "Do it, pilot," and the tone he said it in didn't encourage any more argument. And it didn't actually sound so hard, you know. I figured about all I had to do was convince Orbis that, if he pushed the button, he'd die too. So I did what Marc Antony said.

II

Altogether I think I was talking to Orbis for something like thirty-one or thirty-two minutes, organic time. That may sound like a fair amount to you, but you don't know the half of it. That's thirty-one minutes times sixty seconds in every minute and a thousand milliseconds in every second—what I mean, it was a lot of time. I can't say I talked myself hoarse. Machine-stored people don't get hoarse. What I did do to myself, or really what that SOB Orbis did to me, was to pretty near drive myself as batty as he was.

When I looked around Orbis's tiny ship it appeared he wasn't expecting much of a career in it. He hadn't even made a surround for himself. The place looked like a garbage dump. There were odds and ends of all sorts of things sliding around on the floor—physically real things sliding on the physically real floor, I mean.

See, the thing was that Orbis wasn't giving me any chance to interfere with him. He was already holding the triggering thing—well, the simulated but nevertheless quite functional triggering thing—in his hand. I don't know why he was doing that. Maybe because he thought I was a more violent person than I really was. I thought it might have been because he'd been sort of toying with the idea of pushing the button right there and then. You know, like a nut with a razor might be laying the flat end of it against his wrist a couple of times while he made up his mind whether or not he was going to start slicing.

Then the argument started. "If you're in such a hurry to die," I'd say to him "—I mean really die, so you aren't even machine-stored anymore—why don't you just get a gun and blow your brains out? Or something; you know what I mean." "Can't do that," he'd say. "Suicide's a sin." "Then it's a sin to push that button, isn't it? Cause you'll be killing yourself too?" Then he'd give me a big smile. "That's the part I haven't figured out yet," he'd say. "After all, Wan didn't say I'd be killing myself. I only have your word that that's true. And there are other considerations." But he wouldn't say what the considerations were, and so when we'd get to that point I'd start screaming things like, "Are you crazy? Killing yourself's a sin, but killing Christ knows how many goddam people that are going to die when the goddam star blows is, like, just a misdemeanor or something?" And then he'd give me another smile—he was the smiliest SOB I ever knew—and say he was studying it over and he'd let me know if he figured it out. God almighty! I could've killed the bastard. Would've been glad to, too, if only I'd had some way of doing it.

I gave up—I mean, I gave up about a thousand times, but each time then I'd shut up for a while, trying to calm myself down by thinking about something else—as if there was anything else I could think about!—and wondering if Marc Antony was really out there somewhere, and if so why he didn't show himself, because I was running on empty. And then I'd think, well, if he did, what could he do anyway? And then the whole thing would boil up in my mind again, and I just couldn't not go at it again with him.

It wasn't just my own life I was worrying about. Not entirely, anyway. Honest, those millions and billions who were going to die if I couldn't talk him out of it were on my mind, too. Maybe not as much. But there, all right.

A lot of what we said was just, me, "Please, Orbis!" and, him, "Screw you, Phrygia" in one variation or another. I tried all sorts of other things, too. I tried just working up a friendly conversation with him, just us two people that were stuck together and might as well be sociable. I tried asking him what did he miss most about not being organic anymore? (Not having a congregation to preach to, he said.) Another time we got to talking about how Wan came to own us. I told him about that damn Indochina-Malaysia war, and how when they bombed K.L. and the towers collapsed there were so many people getting killed that the Here After people weren't checking anybody's credit, just getting us all machine-stored as fast as they could. (Only when they did check credit I didn't have any, so Wan could buy me.) Orbis was much the same, only what did him in wasn't a war but an earthquake that dropped a big stone statue on his head. (Funny thing. It looked like what bothered him most, being a Protestant himself, was that the statue was of some Catholic priest.)

And so on, and on.

———

So, having done everything I could think of to get Orbis to change his mind, I more or less did it all over again. I was telling Orbis how I came to go from Homecoming Queen at Eastern New Mexico University to black-jack dealer in one of the big Los Angeles casinos to my last job, driving a subway train in Kuala Lumpur. (What a laugh that is. When Wan found out I'd driven a subway, he decided I was their best bet to learn how to pi-lot a spaceship. Go figure.)

Then I noticed that Orbis wasn't looking at me. He was staring at the lookplate, so I did too. (All right, no, I didn't exactly see anything on the lookplate. We didn't have a lookplate. Didn't need it, any more than we needed to display simulations of ourselves to each other. We skipped the middleman and went right to observing the inputs.)

What the inputs were showing us was the star itself.

Most stars look ordinary enough. This one wasn't ordinary. It looked to be eye-hurtingly white and scarily hot, and I could just imagine what it would be like if it did, in fact, blow itself to smithereens. I gave up. "Marc Antony," I said, "I give up. Show yourself. It's time for you to take over."

He didn't do that. He didn't show himself. He just whispered in my ear—all right, he "whispered" in my "ear"—and what he said, the son of a bitch, was, "No need. You're doing reasonably well."

I wasn't. I knew I wasn't. *He* knew I wasn't. I sighed and went back to what he said I was doing reasonably well at. I said, "Well, shit, Orbis—oh, sorry."

He said mildly, "There's nothing in the Commandments against hav-ing a dirty mouth. Say what you want to say, Phrygia."

"I was going to say I don't know what your problem is. If I wanted to die, I'd do it."

He said reprovingly, "Suicide is sinful. I don't want to add to my bur-den of sins when I face my Judge."

"But blowing up a star and killing millions of people—"

"Not millions of *people*. They're mostly Heechee."

"Again shit. So, murdering even one single human being, are you say-ing that's not a sin?"

"Haven't I answered that already?" His voice sounded absent-minded. He was. He wasn't giving me much attention, because his look was on the piloting plate.

What I noticed was that, in his concentration on the image of that nasty-looking star on the lookplate, he had set his end of the triggering servomodule down. That appeared to be my best chance yet. I sidled over toward it, as inconspicuously as I could. . . .

Not inconspicuously enough. He looked up and gave me one of those bullshit smiles. "Do you want the trigger? Help yourself. It might work if you push the button. It doesn't matter if it does."

I glowered at him. "What are you talking about?"

He sighed. "Oh, Phrygia, haven't you figured it out? Wan knows how I feel about suicide. He wouldn't trust me to do the job. He put it on a timer. I don't have to pull the button, it's going to blow anyway. I don't have to do anything at all. I can just let it happen. And do you know what that means?"

I didn't. He could see that was so, so he explained. "It means that if I die, no matter how many people die with me, it will not be due to an act of sin. You see," he said, sounding more like a lawyer than some godly person talking about his own death, "I've given this a lot of thought. If I take any action at all to change things it means that when I die an act of volition is included. That makes it suicide, and I don't want that on my soul. Do you understand me so far?"

I didn't, and I said so, but he went right on anyway. "But there may be a way out of that. At least, I hope so."

Then he put his hand on the ship's piloting controls—yeah, yeah, I mean he put his "hand" on the "controls"—and the little bits of actual physical trash on the ship's floor suddenly raised themselves up and floated in the air. "What the hell are you doing?" I yelled.

He didn't answer that directly. "You might prefer to leave now," he told me. "Your friend who's hiding, too." Pop! Marc Antony at once displayed himself, standing right beside me and, for the first time in my experience, looking almost baffled.

He didn't let it interfere with business, though. "You're flying the ship right into that star, Mr. McClune," he said. "Why are you doing that?"

"Actually," Orbis corrected him, "I've already done so. I believe we are now in what is called the star's photosphere."

We were certainly in some inhospitable place. Everything around me began to warp and twist and turn fuzzy—whether because the ship was physically stressed or because the star's radiation was interfering with our simulations I did not know.

"We don't want to leave this bomb thing around where the same thing might happen all over again, do we?" Orbis was saying. "Better turn it into plasma and get it over with." Then he looked up, all twisted out of shape and blurry around the edges, but with the biggest, warmest smile I'd seen from him yet. The last thing I heard from him was, "There is no doubt that suicide's a sin, but I'm pretty sure that a man can unsinfully give his own life if it's in order to save others—"

And then I didn't hear any more from him.

24

On the Way to Forever

I

Stan and Estrella's trip back to Forested Planet of Warm Old Star Fourteen took them no longer than the trip out. When the ship's port began to open they heard a puzzling noise, something like the patter of a drenching rain, something like the buzzing of many bees, that came from outside the ship. Then they saw what was making it. At least a thousand Heechee, maybe more than that, filled every open space around the landing area to welcome them back, doing their best to applaud them with stringy Heechee hands that had never been designed for such work.

The crowd wasn't entirely Heechee. In the forefront of the crowd were the twenty or thirty human beings that were Forested Planet's human population, and in the forefront of the forefront was Gelle-Klara Moynlin, actually having come out of her home for the purpose of greeting them, arms already outspread to hug Estrella.

The crowd was not unruly—unsurprising, since they were mainly Heechee. They didn't press around the returning heroes for pats or handshakes or to snatch the odd button off their clothing. They contented themselves with continuing to clap. That is, everyone but Klara did. She would not be denied. She swept past everyone else to give Estrella that hug—as copiously as she could, considering that Estrella's belly was the size it had become—and even took time for a briefer hug for Stan. Then she was tugging them to a waiting car, the crowd parting decorously to let them through.

The car wasn't the usual Heechee tricycle. It wasn't Heechee at all. It was four-wheeled and human-made—imported-from-Earth human-made—though not very like the vehicles Stan used to dodge on the streets of Istanbul. It was more comfortable than those and a lot quieter and, Stan was certain, a very great deal more expensive than any vehicle he had ever been in before, even if you didn't count what Klara had to have paid to bring it in from Outside.

There wasn't anybody at the steering wheel until Klara saw Stan staring at the empty seat. She called to the air, "Quit clowning around, Hypatia. Let Stan get a look at you." And, when her shipmind instantly appeared, "Thanks. Was that so hard?"

Hypatia's simulation didn't turn around. "I just thought you might like a little privacy."

Klara gave her a grunt. "As if you were going to give us any. Now shut up so Estrella and Stan can tell us about their adventures."

Stan was willing. He began at the beginning and, by the time they were climbing the spiral way to their apartment, had reached the point where Marc and the female pilot had brought them to the point in space where the anonymous but definitely bomb-bearing ship was slowly circling Planetless Very Large Very Hot White Star. "And then," he told her, "the two of them sort of projected themselves onto the bomb ship. That was all we could see. Anyway until it turned around. Broke out of orbit and began to nosedive, picking up speed all the way, right down into the big old star's something-or-other sphere. The star didn't even hiccough. Marc said the little ship was vaporized right away, the bomb thing and all, so that not only isn't it dangerous anymore, it doesn't even exist. I don't know. Marc sees the inputs directly, doesn't have to display them on a lookplate, so he can see better than I. All I saw was bright light."

"And that's the only one they had?"

"I don't know. Maybe not. He had to have had some others to blow up those other things, but if he did they're still somewhere on Arabella and Marc'll find them."

There was a moment of silence, and then Hypatia piped up from the front seat: "His name was Orbis McClune."

Stan looked puzzled. "Whose name?"

"The one who dove the ship into the star. Some of Marc's people located a woman who used to be married to him. He was a minister, before he got killed."

"Huh," Stan said, faintly disgruntled. "Marc didn't tell me."

"He didn't know until he got back here, Stan," Klara said as the car stopped before a familiar door. "Anyway here's where you get off."

Stan jumped out, tenderly helping Estrella get out of her seat. Puffing, she turned and asked politely, "Do you want to come in for a minute?"

Klara shook her head. "Hell, no. I mean, my God, the last thing you need right now is company. Only. . . ."

Halfway out of the car, Estrella turned to look at her. "Only what?"

"Well," Klara said, "while you kids were gone, I did a lot of thinking about you. About babies. About your baby in particular."

Stan was holding Estella's hand and begining to get a bit impatient. "So did we. Is that what you wanted to tell us?"

"Well, no." She took a deep breath. "What I wanted was to ask you if I could be your mother-in-law."

That came from about as far out of left field as anything in Stan's experience. He almost let go of Estrella's hand, caught it just in time and asked, "Whose? Mine? Or Estrella's?"

"Actually," Klara said, "both of yours." She looked suddenly in a way Klara never looked, which was embarrassed. She shook her head. "Hey, this is the wrong time to be talking about this kind of thing. You kids go on in, I'll talk to you later." And, as the car door began to close, "And, listen, it's good to have you back."

It was good to be home, too. They jumped in the drencher, thrilled to be bathing in *hot* water again. But while they were still in the chamber, Estrella paused in the middle of drying herself. "Hon?" she said. "Do you know what that was all about?"

He didn't, though, and he gave it no more than a few moments' thought. "Who knows?" he said. "Listen, let's take a look at Stork."

And they did, hungry for the sight of what the baby was doing. (Which turned out to be pretty much what it had been doing all along, namely getting bigger. In fact now quite a lot bigger.) And then, while they, rather inadequately dressed, were ordering a decent meal—actually two decent meals, one right after the other, to make up for all those months of unimproved CHON-food—the door let them know that someone was there.

It was Dr. Kusmeroglu. "How'd you get here so fast?" Estrella asked, half dressed and still chewing, as she let the doctor in.

"It was that Marc person," said Dr. Kusmeroglu, bright and eager. "You know, the cook? Is he here?" She looked around and found the answer to her own question. "Well. Anyway, he signaled Dr. von Shrink and Dr. von Shrink signaled me, so I came right over. First time I was ever in one of those new ultrafast ships. Were either of you ever—Oh, sure, of course you were. I just can't wait to hear about all you've gone through!" And then, when Stan opened his mouth to begin to tell her, she gave him a shake of her head. "But that'll have to wait, because right now Estrella and I have work to do. If you'll just go sit on the balcony for a little while, Stan. . . ."

What she was there for was a childbirth thing, at which, Stan understood, male persons were unwelcome. Stan grabbed some clean clothes of his own and followed orders.

He wasn't cut totally out of the loop. As he dressed, he could see through the balcony door that the first thing the two women were doing was just what he had immediately done, namely to study Stork's display of the fetus. Then they disappeared from his sight, leaving him to, alternately, take in the warm breezes from the Mica Mountain and bite his lip in worriment over what the doctor might find. For months now Estrella hadn't had a proper diet, hadn't had a real doctor to look at her, hadn't had a decent bath or a haircut or a toothbrush or, for God's sake, toilet paper or—well, or anything at all that civilized people always had. And if that had had any bad effect on the baby—had, for instance, brought about any of those terrifying conditions that that damned book had told him about—

He tried to put that thought out of his head.

Fortunately none of it had. When they came out of the bedroom Estrella, too, was now fully dressed and the doctor began to talk. What Dr. Kusmeroglu had to say amounted to a lot of information about the baby's having nearly completed brain growth and why the baby had stopped kicking. (It had no choice. It had grown so large that there no longer was enough room in the uterus to kick.) "But she's all right?" Stan demanded after the first five minutes of increasingly obscure medical details.

Cut off in midstream, the doctor blinked at him. "Well, sure she's all right. Barring that she needs more rest and better food, anyway—and, if you can possibly arrange it, Stan, as little aggravation as possible. Those contractions she's been having—"

Stan instantly turned his attention to Estrella. "What contractions?"

She shrugged. "Well, they weren't very strong and I didn't want to worry you."

"But—" he began, but the doctor overrode him.

"She was fine, Stan. They were just the Braxton-Hicks contractions that are perfectly normal at this time. Think of it as the uterus practicing up for when the labor starts, all right?" She glanced at her wrist screen, moving her lips silently as she checked over her notes and finally said, "I guess that's about it. I'm going to make some dietary recommendations, but outside of that—What?"

Stan was demanding attention. "The baby. When is it going to get born, can you say?"

The doctor pursed her lips. "Ah. Good question. It's a little tricky to calculate, because I don't know exactly how long you were Outside," she said, "but probably somewhere around two to four weeks from now. Maybe six. Stork will keep an eye on things and let us know how they're progressing."

She looked up as the door announced another visitor. "I'll get it," Estrella said, rising with some difficulty from the deep armchair she had been sitting in. With mixed emotions Stan watched her—what was the word?—yes, *waddle* toward the door. Pregnancy was not just a dangerous event that at some point involved a lot of misery, it was an event which, every day, was a stiff pain in—well, in everything there was to have a pain in.

The person standing outside was again Klara's shipmind, Hypatia of Alexandria. She acknowledged Estrella's introduction to Dr. Kusmeroglu civilly enough, but then turned her back on the doctor to address Stan and Estrella.

"Klara has a suggestion. Everyone you ever met has been calling her, wondering when they can see you. She thought you might like to do them all at once and get it over with. A little gathering at her home, for instance."

Stan was suspicious, but Estrella wasn't. "That's a wonderful idea," she said. "Stan? When would you like to do it?"

"Well," he began, "I'm kind of tired—"

She made a face. "Let's not put it off. Hypatia, we could do it right now, if that's all right."

"Well," Hypatia began, and then stood glassy-eyed for a couple of moments, letting the rest of the sentence hang there, until she finished. "Yes, that would be fine." Then she turned to Dr. Kusmeroglu, who was looking as though she wanted to say something. "Yes?"

"I've never actually met Dr. Moynlin," the doctor said, sounding wistful. "I don't suppose—I guess it wouldn't be a good idea at this time—"

"You are quite right," Hypatia told her. "It wouldn't." Then she dismissed the doctor from her attention. "I've ordered a car. Shall we go?"

I I

This time it was a Heechee car, driver and all, open to the world. As soon as she saw it, Estrella insisted they go straight across the valley instead of on the usual underground roadways.

Stan had to agree that she'd made a good decision. After their captivity on Arabella, their valley was like a brief cruise through Heaven. The whitenut trees smelled as sweet as ever, the flying tree snakes were as hungry, the open air was filled with a cinnamonly tang. "You know," he told Estrella when they were not much more than halfway across, "this isn't such a bad place."

She didn't answer him directly, just sat up straighter and tried to see something that was going on at the entrance to the institute. "What in the world is that?" she asked.

Stan couldn't answer. Their Heechee driver did. "Persons there are recent fellow shipmates of both you, names of those being Salt and Achiever, plus certain others desirous to make welcoming home for you. You wish to stop for conversing? No? All right, those two to join you later and anyway are almost at destination. Are already here," she corrected herself as the little car reached Klara's entry porte.

Klara herself opened the door. Herself. Manually. "Come on in," she said. Stan half expected that she would say something about that baffling mothers-in-law thing. She didn't. She gave them each a hug. "We're ready for you," she said fondly. "My dears." They were clearly still getting the return-of-the-heroes treatment. Not only from Klara, either. The second thing Stan noticed—the first having been the beaming, welcoming presence of Sigfrid von Shrink, who obviously was failing to hug them both only because he physically couldn't—was the trays, bowls and platters of good things to eat that filled every flat surface in the room. "From Marc," Klara explained. "You know, the chef? Or general, or whatever he is right now. I think it's his way of saying thanks. Maybe he'll do it in person—I expect he'll drop in a little later—but don't count on it."

"Oh," Sigfrid put in, "I think you can count on it, Stan. Marc doesn't make friends easily, but he thinks quite highly of you." Stan started to assume his aw-shucks look, but Sigfrid paid no attention. "I believe Hypatia told you that Klara was expecting some guests, but I don't think she told you who they were. One of them's a woman you may have heard of. She's stored, and—what? Oh, of course," he said remorsefully. "Estrella, Klara would like you to go with her into another room. Bring your Stork thing. I suppose she wants some of what is called 'girl talk.' Go ahead, dear. Dears. Stan and I will be fine out here." He smiled benevolently at the

sight of Estrella giving Stan a kiss on the cheek before letting Klara lead
her away.

Stan was already returning to Marc Antony's spread. Chewing, he
said, "You were talking about some woman."

"Yes. She's quite an unusual person. Her name is Rowena McClune."
He paused long enough for Stan to make the connection, then nodded.
"Yes. Orbis McClune's—well—is 'widow' the right term? At any rate, they
were once married. She's been in machine storage since McClune himself was organic—quite a bit longer than he, in fact. She hasn't wasted her
time, either. Unlike those organics who seem to think that machine storage is just a license to do nothing but play and have fun for eternity. I'm
sure you know what I mean."

Stan, who didn't, said absently, "Of course," while prospecting among
some tiny meat tarts.

Sigfrid went on, sounding oddly proud. "Marc had located her out of
his client list here in the Core—she's been here for a couple weeks, it
seems—and, actually, it turned out I'd known her long ago, because she
was one of my students."

That explained the pride, Stan decided. Making conversation while
sampling some of Marc's exotic dips, he asked, "And she's coming
here?"

"Indeed she is. In fact, I expect she's here already. Just a minute—yes.
Stan, this is Reverend Doctor Rowena McClune."

Stan looked up. Sigfrid was now accompanied by an attractive woman. Though no longer young, she was quite beautiful, with her blonde hair
done up in a swirl that Estrella later identified as a French twist. ("A real
old lady hairdo," she called it, but added, "All the same, she looked pretty
good.")

"I've been hoping to meet you and your wife," the woman said. "I don't
know whether you know it or not, but she's even more famous than you
are in some ways. Because of the baby."

"That's nice," Stan said, wondering whether it was worth it to correct
that word "wife." He didn't get the chance. On his right side Yellow Jade
appeared, with only one of his senile sons. ("Warm now with Stored
Minds," he reported. "I and Ionic Solvent very happy.") And at his left
Sigfrid showed up, shepherding a couple of other Heechee. "This is my
dear Stored Mind friend, Twin Hearts—I don't think you've met him before—" And when Stan looked around Rowena McClune was heading toward a quite different group at the far end of the room.

———

A party it was, too. Twin Hearts was described as one who had special knowledge of such non-Heechee matters as "currency" and "debt" and even "profit," and, not only that, had somewhere acquired a very considerable repertory of human round-the-campfire songs (though not really the right voice to sing them with). Stan and Estrella weren't the only organic guests, either. Achiever, turning his nose up at most of the food, looked puzzled when Estrella asked a question. "Salt? Consult memory, please. Have not just in short recency joined Salt in welcoming you and inseminator. For what other purpose would I have felt need to invite companionship of Salt? Already have established fetus is doing quite healthily, have no other concerns with same. This statement represents actuality of fact, unregarding any other statement perhaps emanating from Salt." Then, with a firm head-bob, a different tone: "Ah, apples! Can forgive human nastiness of diet for many things for having provided apples!"

A moment later Marc Antony appeared. He wasn't wearing his chef's hat. He wore what Stan was pretty sure was an army uniform from some war or other—white pants, flashes of scarlet on the blouse, cocked hat—but from what war it was Stan couldn't say.

"Sorry if I am late," Marc said. "The specialists needed to talk to Wan. I had to wait until they were finished, to make sure he was properly deactivated again before I left." He paused to look aroung at the tables of food. "Is everything all right? Is there anything anyone would like?"

Stan had his hand up. "What specialists are you talking about?"

"I believe most of the party was lawyers and accountants," he said, with approximately the same intonation he would have used if he had been saying "whores" and "lepers."

"Indeed they would have been," Sigfrid explained, taking over. "It isn't just Wan himself that we wanted, you know. It's his money. We're going to fine him for all the trouble he caused. That'll probably come to just about everything he owns, and naturally, after all these years Outside, it isn't going to be easy to identify all of Wan's assets." The smile broadened. "But then, taking it along with Klara's earlier generous contribution, that should be quite enough to pay for all the monetary expenses of immigrating, housing, feeding and settling in all our new citizens from Outside." He paused and changed the subject. "We'll talk about all that at another time. Marc? Can't you provide us with some wine?"

Marc could and did, both material and simulated kinds. He hadn't stopped with wine, either; he had provided little glassy bowls of the fungus that Stan recognized as the Heechee social drug of choice. Klara herself gave

Estrella a glass of physically real wine, Sigfrid hovering at her shoulder to assure Stan that one glass would do her no harm at all. Apparently it didn't. Didn't harm Stan, either, so he had a second, and then a third.

He wasn't the only one. When he wasn't looking a dozen or so other guests had appeared, a couple organics of both species but a number of Heechee, mostly Stored Minds. The fact that both they themselves and the fungus they were helping themselves to were simulations didn't seem to hamper their pleasure. Didn't seem to diminish their animated conversations, either, most of them being with at least one organic person included and thus conducted in organic time. Stan had no idea what the conversations were about, though, and he was beginning to feel a bit warm. It occurred to him that it would be a good idea to sit down. There was a vacant space on one of Klara's couches. He collected some more wine and, as he was sitting down, saw that the other side of the couch was occupied by Rowena McClune, sitting by herself. Although she was holding a glass, three-quarters of the wine was still in it. When she saw that Stan had drifted toward her she gave him a polite smile. "I've just been sitting here envying you and your wife," she said, glancing in Estrella's direction. "To have a child! I don't think there's a more joyous occasion in the universe."

"Thanks," Stan, who wouldn't have put it that way but was willing to go along, said. He noted that Achiever, munching a large clump of the party fungus, was standing behind them, listening attentively. Ignoring him, he addressed the McClune woman. "That word 'wife' wasn't quite right. We've never married." And then, to keep her from pursuing the subject, "I see you aren't a big drinker."

"Well," she said, "it wouldn't make any difference if I were, would it? Simulated alcohol doesn't make you drunk. Unless you want it to, that is, and it's been a long time since I wanted anything like that." His expression, balancing curiosity against manners, made her smile again. "When I was first machine-stored, I confess I tried that sort of thing. Many different sorts of things, really. You wouldn't believe some of the surrounds I made for myself, and I'm definitely not going to tell you about them. But I got tired of that. I began looking for something useful to do with my new life."

"That's very interesting," Stan said, glancing at Achiever, who at least didn't seem eager to tell his life story.

Rowena McClune wasn't finished. "Why not?" she asked.

He blinked at her more seriously. "Why not what?"

"Why aren't you and Ms. Pancorbo married?"

It was one of the harder questions Stan had been asked. He considered several different answers: It wasn't a custom here in Heechee land. They didn't have anyone to perform the ceremony. They never thought of it. They hadn't, after all, known each other very long. None of those seemed good enough, so he settled for, "We're all right the way we are."

Achiever gave his braying laugh. "Good response just said by you, Stan," he told them both. "Above-mentioned marrying custom is foolish ancient tribal affair of your tribe, unnecessary in civilized world. My people have done such thing never."

Surprisingly, there was a rumble from behind Stan. When he turned, it was Thermocline. Stan considered asking him why everybody was sneaking up on him, but Thermocline was speaking. "That is not entirely correct, Achiever," he said, polite but positive. "Many of our people on the Wheel found the human custom of 'family' attractive, and formed such groups: mother, father and one or more offspring all living together and forming a family unit."

"Huh," Achiever said, temporarily derailed. He recovered himself well enough to produce a sneer. "Such persons were living among human persons much too length of time, Thermocline. Such situation can cause serious problems of decreased concinnity, as has been demonstrated in unfortunate case of myself."

He turned a challenging look at Stan. Since he had supported Stan's position, clearly he now felt it was Stan's turn to support his. Stan might have done so. What prevented him was that he was having a hard time following the discussion. "I guess," he said vaguely, and then, "Excuse me."

It occurred to him that another glass of wine might clear his head. But as he turned to go in search of one he almost tripped over a short, dark organic human woman standing just behind him. He stared at her with astonishment. "You look just like that baby doctor, Kusmeroglu. Can't be, though. Hypatia told you not to come."

The woman looked pleased with herself. "Hypatia changed her mind. She caught me at the spacecraft terminal, told me Klara wanted me to stay so I could keep an eye on Estrella. And here I am. So you see, I did get to meet Klara after all."

"But—" Stan said reasonably. "But—" He stopped there. He was clear in his mind that the woman must have made some egregious mistake, but he was having difficulty in framing the sentences that would straighten her out. "I think I need to sit down," he said, and looked around for the nearest chair, and did.

Dr. Kusmeroglu bent swiftly to sniff his lips. "Oh, I see," she sighed. "Listen, Stan. Let me collect Estrella. I think we need to get you home."

III

When Stan woke up, he immediately wished he hadn't. He had little previous experience of hangovers, but he recognized the symptoms at once. When his eyes were open enough, he identified Estrella standing over him, but much too close, and holding something out to him, but he could not tell what. He checked his memory, found it empty and muttered weakly, "Hon, I'm sorry."

Or thought he had. Estrella didn't seem to have heard. She not only was not appropriately sympathetic, she seemed somehow pleased about something. "Come on," she said, hardly comfortingly at all, "drink this. I want to tell you something."

The sense of what she was saying penetrated to Stan's brain. It didn't elevate his mood. In Stan's experience, when someone said she wanted to tell him something it was unlikely to be something he wanted to hear. Puzzlingly, though, Estrella didn't seem to be angry or offended or any of the other things Stan associated with that sort of remark. She was grinning. Her eyes were—yes—dancing. "Oh, for God's sake," she was saying. "Are you going to drink this or not?"

It appeared to be a cup of coffee. Not the good, thick Turkish kind, but the only marginally less good kind that Americans liked to drink at breakfast. He swallowed it as rapidly as he could, but Estrella was already tapping her fingers before he got it all down. "Well?" she demanded. "Sigfrid said he'd get Marc to put something in it."

Stan moved his head experimentally. Apparently the chef had. The blinding pain was gone without a trace. The inside of his mouth still tasted of ancient cigar ends, and he had a sudden overpowering thirst—

For which Estrella was ready. She was handing him a cup of something that fizzed. "Sigfrid said this would help, okay?" Sipping, he nodded. "So guess what? I had a long talk with Hypatia while Klara was busy with her guests. Did you know Klara had practically a nervous breakdown after the tsunami ruined her island?" Stan shook his head, which happily did not fall off. "That's why she's on this planet. Sigfrid suggested she come here. At first he thought she might want to set up something like her island—for orphans, you know?"

Stan experimentally stretched his muscles. Everything seemed to be working all right. He said, "Strell, hon, is this going to be a long story? Because I'm kind of hungry."

"Almost done. Klara said no. Said she couldn't face being a mommy.

"Then she met us."

Stan hadn't exactly stopped paying attention, but it was true that his mind was filling with visions of ham with red eye gravy and stacks of fries. When he realized Estrella had stopped talking and was regarding him he blinked. "Oh. Right. She took an interest in you."

"In the baby, mostly. So do you know what the mother-in-law stuff was about?"

"The baby?" he hazarded

"Sort of. If Klara was your mother-in-law or my mother-in-law—or both our mothers-in-law—what would that make her to the baby?"

The scales fell from his eyes. "Oh, my God," he said wonderingly. "She wants to be the baby's grandma."

Estrella was nodding vigorously. "Exactly. What do you think about that?"

Stan didn't hesitate. "Oh, absolutely sure," he said. "She'll be good at it. Now can we get some breakfast?"

IV

Estrella and Stan no longer lacked for company. People kept calling and dropping in. Stan didn't care for it, but Estrella seemed pleased. She told Stan, "You know, this is kind of nice. Back home people were visiting all the time—for a cup of maté, or to bring back something they borrowed, or just to sit and gossip for a few minutes. I miss that. Don't you?" Since Stan had never had any experience of that sort of neighborliness he had no good answer except to smile, and pat her on the shoulder, and ask brightly if it wasn't getting close to time for lunch.

Then, when Stan was in the drencher, he came out and Estrella was waiting. "Hon? Rowena McClune called."

He stopped drying himself. "What about?"

"Well, she was real interested in the baby, and I invited her to come over. So she wants to do it now."

Stan groaned. "Strell, don't we have enough—"

"So I told her to come away. I liked her, Stan. You'd better put some clothes on."

While he was doing it he heard the door. When he came out, there she was, sitting in the overstuffed chair (but, he noticed, revealing her immaterial status because she put no dent in it). When they turned Stork on she seemed really fascinated, not only by the chubby little image with the Buddha smile that floated before, but in Stan's account of all the changes it had gone through. She was a good listener. Good talker, too; she was perfectly willing to answer every one of Estrella's questions about her other life. "Well," she said, "the first part, right after I died, wasn't too interesting. I just fooled around, like everybody else. Then I got tired of just having fun, the way most of the other machine-stored were doing, and I found out there weren't too many other kinds of things for a woman without much education to do. That could be dealt with, though. There were enough people in storage by then, some of them serious-minded, to have started some kind of correspondence-school things. I took courses. I don't know if organic Harvard would have let me into graduate school, with what I had in the way of a baccalaureate, but the machine-stored Harvard did, and before you knew it I had a Ph.D. Three of them, in fact, because I kept getting interested in different things."

Stan cut in. "That's all you did? Study?"

"I thought it was quite a lot, Stan. Wouldn't hurt you to try it, either."

Caught by surprise, Stan could only think of saying, "But, Rowena, I'm just about going to be a father."

"And you're barely eighteen years old," she reminded him. Then smiled. "We can talk about that another time. And, yes, I did do some other things. I simulated myself, and went back to see how Orbis was doing, with a face that wasn't my own. He was in mourning. Real mourning. I could see that my organic death had hit him hard. And he wasn't doing very well. His congregation was drifting away.

"But he was doing his best, because he thought they needed him.

"So my conscience began to hurt a little and I went back to school. Divinity school, this time. I became a fully credentialed minister of God. Did that for a while, then I realized I wasn't making much progress converting the unsaved—even tried it with Heechee, you know. With no luck at all.

"So I got Sigfrid to teach me something about psychology. To help me reason with the doubters, you know. And to help me with a few other things." She gazed benignly at Estrella and Stan. They were sitting together, rapt, holding hands. "Like, for instance, I can perform weddings. I can conduct a burial service if anybody wants one—in fact, I was doing it while we were talking at the party. It was for a man from old Earth who didn't like the Heechee way of disposing of the dead."

Stan looked doubtful. "I guess I don't know what that is."

She gave him a wry look. "Maybe you don't want to know. Actually, they put the body in one of those fish ponds—you've seen them? With those toothy fish? So the fish eat the corpse, and then—this is the sticky part—after a while the mourners eat one of the fish."

She sat silent for a moment while Stan and Estrella digested that news. It didn't seem to agree with them. Then she flashed them another smile. "Did I mention that I can also perform weddings?"

Stan swallowed. "Dr. McClune, neither of us is very religious," he offered.

"I didn't think you were, Stan. I just thought that the two of you really loved each other, and that you might want to make it on the record."

"Well," Stan said, looking at Estrella, "when you put it like that, I guess—"

"No," Estrella said firmly. "We don't guess. We definitely know that, yes, we positively do want to get married. So will you do it for us, please? And as soon as possible?"

V

Well, it wasn't quite that quick. Wasn't really simple, either, because Gelle-Klara Moynlin wouldn't allow that. ("Being mother-in-law of the groom makes me mother of the bride, hon. Just put yourself in my hands and let me do my job.") She did it, too. She told them they had to have, at least, music. And flowers. And a nice dress for Estrella to wear; and a few friends to wish them well; and when you put them all together not only was their own apartment too small but so was Klara's. The only suitably large space anywhere nearby was the institute's main hall, and the institute was glad enough, indeed delighted, to grant any request at all from the person who had, more or less, helped save the Core.

When Stan and Estrella arrived for the ceremony, they were delighted too. "Roses!" Estrella exclaimed, wonderingly. "And, look, calla lilies too! I wonder where they got them. Do you suppose Marc Antony could've made them out of a Food Factory?"

Stan would have agreed, because he was pretty sure there was no limit to what Marc Antony could make out of CHON and a sprinkling of other elements, but he had a wonder of his own. "And where the hell did they get that band?" Half a dozen Heechee were established on a platform at one end of the room, tootling away on a variety of instruments—not only drums, a piano and a pair of banjos but a horn and a clarinet, just as though those were anatomically feasible for them. He even recognized the tune they were playing. It was "Embraceable You," played just as it had been on the vid disks Klara had imported for him—

"Oh, hell," he said, surprised into a grin. It wasn't *like* Dizzy Gillespie doing the set. It really *was* Dizzy Gillespie. The Heechee were only miming the instruments in their hands; the actual music was coming from speakers all around the room.

And when he looked around, Estrella was gone.

He peered around the room, and was just in time to see Estrella,

tugged along by Klara, Salt and a couple of female Heechee he didn't recognize, disappearing down one of the institute's interior hallways. He
didn't have time to look after her very long, because he was immediately
surrounded by well-wishers, Sigfrid and Achiever, Dr. Kusmeroglu, Klara's
shipmind, Hypatia, a dozen or more persons whom he recognized only
with difficulty or didn't recognize at all. They all seemed glad to see him.
When organic, they slapped him on the back (if male) or gave him warm
hugs and chaste kisses (if female). The simulated ones had their own
modes of expression, from blown kisses to casual waves, but, however expressed, they were uniformly affectionate. In the middle of having not
only his back slapped but his hand wrung simultaneously by two of the
Old Ones' keepers from One Moon Planet of Pale Yellow Star Fourteen
Stan was struck by a belated thought. "Damn it," he said to the room in
general, and looked wildly around until he caught sight of Sigfrid von
Shrink. Who came over in response to Stan's wave, politely asking, "Yes,
Stan?"

"I didn't think! I need a best man. Will you—?"

Sigfrid would. Was honored to be asked, he said, and went away for a
moment. When he returned he had changed his clothing entirely. He now
wore striped trousers, a morning coat, a handsome cravat and an expression of dignified delight.

Not that Stan had much time to admire his new best man. Everyone
in the room was surrounding him at once, most of the organic ones trying
to press glasses of wine on him (uniformly refused; Stan was capable of
learning from experience). Most of the males had little jokes to whisper in
his ear—seldom understood by Stan—and most of the females were
telling him how lucky he was to be about to have a child.

And, having said it all, they generally went on to say it all over again.

Before Stan could get really annoyed with all the attention, though
not much before, he became aware that the press of well-wishers was
thinning. One by one, they were leaving his side to seat themselves in
decorous rows of chairs and perches, opening up an aisle that led to
where, he discovered, Rowena McClune stood waiting, sumptuously
robed in what looked like pure white silk. If Marc Antony had made that,
too, out of the ingredients for CHON-food, Stan was willing to consider
him a master couturier.

And Rowena gave Stan a small beckoning wave and a smile.

Stan took the hint. By the time she had positioned him next to her
side the band stopped in the middle of a Fats Waller "Tea for Two" and
all of the Heechee mimes stood silent and unmoving. A different kind of
music began from the speakers. It was Mendelssohn's wedding march,

played by some unidentified symphony orchestra. And out of the corridor Gelle-Klara Moynlin appeared, bearing a bouquet of lilies as she decorously walked in slow time up the aisle. A moment later Estrella followed. She wore a gown of whitest silk and most delicate lace, acquired from where Stan could not imagine. Her belly was big enough to hold a watermelon. Her eyes were still misaligned. The rest of her features had never been particularly remarkable . . . but as far as Stan was concerned, he realized, why, yes, she really was one beautiful woman.

He held her hand tightly as they turned to face Rowena McClune. Who gave them a fond smile as she began, "Dearly beloved, we are gathered here this day. . . ."

There was food for everyone, also drink, also another set of Stan's favorite old jazz numbers, "Paper Doll" and "St. Louis Blues" and "St. James Infirmary Blues" and half a dozen other blues numbers, again simulated by the Heechee sextet. There was even dancing. First there was the one obligatory turn around the cramped floor by the newlyweds, then some odd impressions of ballroom steps by humans and Heechee alike.

Back in their seats of honor, neither Stan nor Estrella had much use for the drink, but they couldn't escape the food. Didn't want to, when you came right down to it. Marc Antony had outdone himself. Fresh, chilled raw oysters. Delicate little sausages in the lightest of tiny rolls. Bowls of fresh pineapple and blueberries, cherries and kiwis, suitably chilled and still bearing their fresh (however manufactured by Marc) drops of dew. Stan ate a great deal. Probably to be polite Estrella did too, and Stan was not surprised when she excused herself to visit the sanitary slot. He did notice that when she came back she seemed a bit subdued. He was considering following her example when Hypatia of Alexandria popped into existence between them. "Estrella! Stork indicates that something's going on with the baby! How do you feel?"

Estrella gave her a game smile. "Oh, I guess I've had too much rich food, too fast—"

Hypatia was wagging her bejeweled head. "That's not what Stork's indicating. I think we'd better get you to the birthing room. I'll call Dr. Kusmeroglu. Let's get moving. I mean now!"

VI

Once again Stan had crash-dived from being the center of attention, or at least 50 percent of the center, to the status of largely overlooked onlooker.

It didn't take long, either. At one moment he and Estrella were receiving congratulations and badinage. At the next Estrella was gone, escorted by about a dozen of the female guests, Dr. Kusmeroglu in the lead. Oh, there were plenty of people left in the room. But they were all in small knots, animatedly talking over this new development, and Stan was left, almost alone, to gaze after his departing bride.

Achiever was the one who took pity on him. "One exhibits feelings of sympathy," he announced, taking Stan's hand in his own skeletal one. "Come."

He didn't say where. Didn't need to, really. He was pretty strong, and Stan didn't resist.

It was the first time Stan had been in a nonpublic part of the institute. It was interesting, too, or at least tantalizing. Through doorways they passed Stan caught glimpses of odd-looking machines (?), or furniture (?), or, perhaps, art objects (???) In spite of the circumstances, and of the fact that he kept bumping his head on the low Heechee ceilings, he thought wistfully that it would have been nice to have had a better look at them. He had no such look. Achiever had a goal in mind. It wasn't until they had almost reached it that he stopped and stood for a moment gazing at Stan. "Have a thing to mention, in some degree not unrelevant to variety of custom you with Estrella have just observed," he announced.

Stan had too much on his mind to be tolerant of Heechee ditherings. "So mention the hell away," he snapped.

The Heechee's belly muscles were rippling wildly under his tunic. "Is not really a matter of any large significance entirely," he said. "Happens self with female Salt recently did significant discussing of future planning. That is, joint future is meant here."

That got Stan's attention. "What do you mean, 'joint'? I thought you said marriage was a—"

"Was foolish ancient custom your people, yes. What is purpose to mention this word 'marriage.' You have not heard me say word 'marriage.' Is quite not in contemplation at all."

"What then?" Stan demanded

Achiever spread his bony fingers. "Other thing entirely. Propose repeated alternation of dwellings occupied by I and she, this time both in one, that time both in other. Will now be one-on-one cohabitation."

"And the difference is?"

"Very large difference indeed! Joint habitation purely as temporary convenience. To continue no longer than, let us say, time necessary for child to grow and become adult. You have understanding of aforesaid statements?"

"I guess so. It'll be temporary, just for twenty years or so."

"Exactly correct. Now here is place for you."

The place was quite nice—lush balcony with its scented ferns and flowering mosses—and someone was waiting for him at one of the little tables. "I thought I'd keep you company, Stan," Sigfrid von Shrink said. "I know what it's like."

Stan forebore to ask the AI how he would know that, his mind still trying to get used to the fact that Salt and Achiever were actually setting up housekeeping. He abandoned both questions and said just, "Thanks," as he sank into one of the physically real chairs.

Sigfrid said, "You're welcome," and stopped himself there, regarding Stan.

That was new. It was not possible that Sigfrid was having trouble, in real time, in deciding what to do, so, Stan decided, it had to be something he was waiting for Stan to do. He took a stab at, "Was there something you wanted to talk to me about?"

Sigfrid still seemed hesitant. "I understand Rowena McClune spoke to you," he offered.

Stan was tempted to grin. "You bet she did. Look what came of it."

"Anything else?"

"Oh," Stan said, relieved. "Sure. She thinks I ought to go back to school."

Sigfrid nodded. "And what do you think about that, Stan?"

That had not been one of the questions uppermost in Stan's mind. He shrugged without much interest. "I guess, maybe. I mean sure I should sometime or other. But right now I've got other things on my mind, and anyway I wouldn't know what to study."

"I see," Sigfrid said, stroking his chin as though considering the matter—more of his theatrics, Stan knew. "Well, you might just study everything, Stan. Everything you need to be a well-informed human being. History. Political science—well, that's kind of a misnomer, because there isn't much that's scientific about it. Like economics and social studies and all those, it's basically about how human beings behave, so, really, they're all branches of psychology. . . . Oh, sorry," he said, noting Stan's expression. "I didn't mean to make it so, well, forbidding. You look like you have a question."

"I certainly do. The question is, 'why?' "

Sigfrid looked pained. "I'm not sure which 'why' you're asking about, Stan. If it's why learn, the answer is because you can. You've got a good mind, but there's not a whole lot of knowledge in it to prepare you for the kind of life you should think of living. If the question is why I mention these particular subjects"—the look on his face had suddenly become grave—"it's because they all bear on the art, I won't say the science, of governance."

Stan was beginning to feel alarmed. "You mean so I'll know, like, how to vote? If we ever have anything like elections, I mean?"

"Or be voted for, Stan," Sigfrid said gently. He raised a hand to forestall Stan's objections. "If not you, who else? It has to be somebody. The millions of human beings in the Core need some kind of government."

Stan looked dubious, and was. "Isn't that what the Stored Minds do?"

"They do that for the Heechee, yes. They are of course wise and just and all those things. They aren't human, though. They don't think the same way we do. The Stored Minds are well aware of that; I'm confident that they would refuse to govern humans, even if asked."

Stan thought it over for a moment, then brightened. "But we already have a government we can get to help us, don't we? All those other planets in the outside galaxy have to have some sort of governing body—"

Sigfrid was shaking his head. "They don't, Stan. They never did, really; there were always disputes that no one could settle and, anyway, what little they did have has long since vanished. Do you know that there are more organic human beings in the Core than in the whole outside galaxy?"

Stan didn't answer. Didn't have to; the expression on his face was answer enough. "It's because of machine storage, Stan," Sigfrid told him. "It began with the Here After facilities. First people were stored when they died. Then, when people began to realize what machine-stored existence could be like, they stopped waiting for death. They got stored whenever they chose to do it, and then they could have anything they wanted. Could create any surround. Could invent other people for themselves, or interact with those other stored ones. And then—"

He paused, shaking his head. "You remember all those discoveries and inventions that were coming from Outside? Have you noticed that they've pretty much dried up? Machine-stored people don't do much inventing. They don't do research, either. Why would they, when there isn't any need for them to do anything that requires work, or anything at all but enjoy all the pleasures they can imagine? They're the lotus-eaters, Stan. The people who need nothing, and thus do nothing useful at all!"

He gazed for a long moment at Stan, who had no idea what lotus-eaters were. He decided to nod wisely. Sigfrid returned the nod. "So we can't rely on anybody else, you see. There has to be something to deal with problems—call it a government—something like a Core-wide congress. The members will be elected, as soon as somebody can figure out how to go about it. I think you should run."

It took Stan a moment to get his breath. "Wha—What about my getting an education?"

"The two things aren't mutually exclusive, Stan. Anyway, that's what I wanted to talk to you about. You don't have to say anything now. Think it over. Talk to Estrella." And then, smiling, "Whom I'm told you can see now, along with your new daughter."

VII

It had been a long time since Stan had seen a human baby, not since one of the girls in Mr. Ozden's brothel had got herself pregnant. That sort of thing was an economic hardship for Mr. Ozden when it happened. To deal with the problem he kept a neighborhood abortionist on permanent retainer. Not this time, though. The baby's father, or at least the customer considered to have been the likeliest to be the baby's father, was a man high up in Istanbul's city government. When the father indicated he would prefer it, the girl had been allowed to keep the child, and even to show it off to such neighbors as young Stan.

As far as Stan could remember, this baby looked pretty much the same as that long-ago one: eyes screwed tightly shut, mouth closed except for the occasional little whimpering cry, scalp bald, fingers made into tiny fists.

He sat down on the edge of the narrow cot, and looked down at Estrella. She looked tired (naturally enough, because she had just been trying to push a bowling ball through her private parts), and happy (well, of course she would be happy: it was over) and—yes—proud.

"Strell?" he said, pondering on how best to bring up the subject of the proposition that had been made to him. "There's something we need to talk about."

"Sure," she said. "Just a minute. Here."

And when she handed him the baby he felt the warm, solid weight of it. He looked down at the guileless face. The lips puckered for a moment. The eyelids flickered. The fingers wriggled. The eyes opened—

And something grabbed at Stan's heart.

When he looked up he saw Estrella's questioning eyes on him. "Was there something you wanted to say?"

He took a deep breath. "Yes, there is, Strell. I was talking to Sigfrid. He thinks I've been screwing around long enough. I should try to make something of myself."

Estrella, closely supervising the way he was holding the baby, said, "Is that what he said?"

"It's what he meant, and he's right. Someday there's going to be a human congress in the Core. When it comes along I'm going to try to get elected to it. And I want to be ready for the job if I get it, so I'm going to get an education first."

Estrella reclaimed the baby. "That," she said, lowering one flap of her gown to see if the baby would take it yet, "sounds like the best idea yet. I'll help all I can."

That's what they did, with the help of the greatest of grandmas to make sure everything was under control when they were studying. They got the best education that the resources of Socrates, Marc Antony and Sigfrid von Shrink could provide for them, and when the first planet-wide election was held, Stan Avery was indeed a candidate. He didn't win, though. He lost narrowly to the only other candidate in the race.

All the same, Stan was not gravely disappointed. He shook the hand of his victorious opponent with a glad heart. His consolation was that by then he was deeply immersed in his continuing studies. Anyway it meant he had more time to spend on caring for, playing with and generally adoring his daughter when congressional duties took away from home the person who had won the election, Estrella Pancorbo-Avery.

Author's Note

On the Mutability of Science

Technically speaking, science fiction need not have any real science in it at all, and quite a bit of it does not. I do feel, however, that some of the best kinds of science fiction rest on exploring the wonders of actual scientific theories or observations, especially when they are first advanced and not yet dogmatic. I use things of that sort often. When I do I try to get them right.

Unfortunately, what is "right" at one point in time isn't necessarily still right a couple of decades, or even a couple of years later.

For example, black holes.

When I wrote *Gateway*, the first of the Heechee books, in 1978, black holes were quite a novelty. Most scientists were willing to believe that such objects did exist. However, not one of the things had ever been unambiguously detected, and speculations about their precise nature were both plentiful and diverse. For the novel, I placed my bets on a couple of the most interesting of the scientists' speculations. One, that there was a great black hole at the center of our galaxy. And, two, that whenever a sufficiently densely packed amount of matter or energy existed anywhere a black hole would automatically form around it. Therefore within such a black hole a number of stars and planets might exist.

For the record, I got it half right. No reputable scientist known to me still thinks organized matter of any kind can exist inside a black hole, so that is a definite miss. On the other hand, it turns out that there really is at our galaxy's core an object known as Sgr A*, pronounced "Sagittarius (or, for short, simply Sajj) A Star." And it is pretty definitely an authentic black hole.

However, when we look at the fine print we find that Sgr A* isn't much like the black hole I was describing. I never specifically identified the mass of the Heechee's Core, but it would have had to have been some thousands of solar masses. It seemed to me that this would be massive enough for any normal purpose. I was wrong, though. Actually Sgr A* weighs in at some 3.7 *million* solar masses, which, as you can see, is a very great deal bigger.

What's more, a couple of other variorum kinds of black holes, including the kugelblitz that the Foe lived in, are also pretty much out of favor these days. Still, I did not feel that I could omit them where indicated, and so they are still part of the background referred to in the present novel.

I should add, however, that I am unregenerate enough so that I won't let any of this keep me from continuing to try to pick up some of the hairiest of scientists' speculations and do my best to work them into science-fiction stories. So you are warned.

FREDERIK POHL
Palatine, Illinois
2004

ABOUT THE AUTHOR

A multiple Hugo and Nebula Award–winning author, FREDERIK POHL has done just about everything one can do in the science fiction field. His novel *Gateway* won the Hugo, Nebula, and John W. Campbell Memorial awards for Best SF novel. *Man Plus* won the Nebula Award. In addition to his solo fiction, Pohl has collaborated with other writers, including C. M. Kornbluth and Jack Williamson. The Pohl/Kornbluth collaboration, *The Space Merchants,* is a classic of satiric science fiction. *The Starchild Trilogy* with Williamson is one of the more notable collaborations in the field. Pohl became a magazine editor when still a teenager. In the 1960s he piloted *Worlds of If* to three successive Hugos for Best Magazine. He also has edited original-story anthologies, including the notable *Star* series of the early 1950s. He has been a literary agent, has edited lines of science fiction books, and has been president of the Science Fiction Writers of America. He and his wife, Dr. Elizabeth Anne Hull, a prominent academic active in the Science Fiction Research Association, live outside Chicago, Illinois.